MW00928045

THE

CALL

OF

THE

WYLDES

STEPHEN M. RATHKOPF

 FriesenPress

Suite 300 - 990 Fort St
Victoria, BC, V8V 3K2
Canada

www.friesenpress.com

Copyright © 2020 by Stephen M. Rathkopf
First Edition — 2020

All rights reserved.

No part of this publication may be reproduced in any form, or by any means, electronic or mechanical, including photocopying, recording, or any information browsing, storage, or retrieval system, without permission in writing from FriesenPress.

ISBN
978-1-5255-8007-9 (Hardcover)
978-1-5255-8008-6 (Paperback)
978-1-5255-8009-3 (eBook)

1. FICTION, MYSTERY & DETECTIVE, TRADITIONAL BRITISH

Distributed to the trade by The Ingram Book Company

THE CALL OF THE WYLDES

PRE-PUBLICATION REVIEWS

KIRKUS REVIEWS

In Rathkopf's debut mystery, the wife of a wealthy New York City businessman is dead, a pill bottle beside the bed — but there's more to the death than meets the eye....[T]his is an ambitious effort by Rathkopf with [an] entertaining plot and some neat twists. Despite the fact that it's narrated, in part, by Simon Crandell, an aspiring crime writer with a taste for hard-boiled classics, the old school mystery plot feels more indebted to Agatha Christie's works than Raymond Chandler's, and more melodramatic than either. The author is clearly capable of putting together a solid, engaging story....[F]uture mysteries from this author look promising.

PUBLISHER REVIEW

A really interesting premise and a cool main character in Simon Crandall...[T]here is an audience for this style of story telling...[A] lot of humor and style, [it will do] very well with mystery readers.

DEDICATION

As always, to my loved and loving wife, the one with the real talent.

PROLOGUE

Charlotte Wylde was murdered. She was found in her bedroom in the late morning, fully clothed, lying atop her $1,500 Yves Delorme duvet that covered her 1890s signed, English four-poster bed. She was still elegant and stylish in her demise, finger nails subtly polished, toes artfully pedicured, copper-colored hair flatteringly styled, body well-toned and attired in an outfit that would have made Anna Wintour proud. A perfect picture of wealth and entitlement but for the fact that she was now just a still life, all vibrance gone.

On top of the night table was the murder weapon, a prescription pill bottle, the contents the proximate cause of her death. No note nor sign of struggle, so it was determined after investigation to be the result of an accidental drug overdose, neither suicide nor homicide. There was no reason to believe otherwise, at least none uncovered by the police in their initial round of interviews. No person or persons of interest to be further interrogated. A murder plan perfectly executed, providing the killer an even easier than anticipated escape from detection. To the victor would go the spoils. Who says justice is blind?

CHAPTER I

You can never be killed in your dreams. No matter how horrible the dream, you always survive whatever has threatened you. Real life, well that's different. There are myriad ways you can die, some caused by your own actions, others by the actions of someone else and still others by no action by anyone, just bad, dumb luck.

I am a mystery writer. In my case, that has a double-edged meaning: I write mystery books or I write books that few people read and so I remain a "mystery" to all but my family, friends and small coterie of readers.

In any event, I have become expert (thank you Google) in the many ways people can die. I kill them off frequently in my line of work. Not for real, of course. But no matter. If it's not you or a loved one, death today is quite impersonal. It all seems like fiction because it bombards you from all directions, hour by hour, in a torrent of streaming internet and social media headlines. My name is Simon Crandell. I'm discussing this with my long-time best friend, Jeffrey Muss. We are sitting in the kitchen in his parents' house in Brooklyn while his mother, Barbara, a surrogate mother to me, is making us sandwiches to eat (as if we're still the little and then big children she once hovered over). Jeff is her only child and, in every good sense of the word, she is the prototype of the helicopter mom. She has three full-time jobs — wife, mother and social worker in the NYC Administration for Children's Services

— and, as far as I can tell, performs them all to perfection. Wish she were my real mom, but it is what it is.

It's not unusual for Jeff and me to meet here, although more often, when we see each other, it's in my house, his apartment or a bar or restaurant somewhere. Tonight Jeff is visiting his parents before we're to meet up with his girlfriend, Kristina, so we're back where we both spent many a happy day, in the warm embrace of his boyhood home.

We are discussing my books and I've been explaining to Jeff how hard it is to come up with different ways to kill off my victims. And to keep it interesting, since just about every means possible has already been written by others. "Fetanyl," I say to Jeff, in the manner that "plastics" was suggested to Dustin Hoffman in "The Graduate," "that will be my next method of murder."

"I keep hearing about the opioid crisis and fentanyl. What the hell is fentanyl?" Jeff asks.

"I've researched it," I respond. "It's a synthetic drug 100 times stronger than morphine and way stronger than heroin. Even a dose the size of the head of a pin can kill you."

"So who prescribes this shit, what type of crazy doctors?"

"The stuff killing people is not obtained through prescriptions but online from China or through cartel-related drug dealers. The ingredients to make it are readily available overseas and the fentanyl comes in many forms, mostly powder, patches or pills."

"Enough," interjects Barbara, as she places triple-tiered cold cut sandwiches in front of us. "You boys are about to eat. And I'm joining you. Let's not spoil the food by continuing this morbid dissertation."

"I don't 'dissertate.' Just maybe pontificate," I jokingly reply, smart-aleck that I am. "But I enthusiastically endorse the recommendation that we defer to the food."

As we gobble down our sandwiches, chattering in between swallows, Jeff is "pinged." Seems to me, we used to take great joy in fucking as much as possible. Now, we seem to take even greater pleasure in being constantly "pinged." In fucking, most of us tend to be monogamous, or at least serially monogamous. But in "pinging," we can be "pinged" by multiple people repeatedly with no sense of guilt. It's amazing that the joy of fucking, a "hands on" interaction so to speak, is being superseded by "pinging," an interaction that actually is insular in nature. But I digress.

"It's Kristina. Time to go," Jeff says to me as he abruptly rises from his chair at the kitchen table, still chomping on his last mouthful of food. He hugs his mom and hastily makes his exit. "Say goodbye to dad for me. I don't have time. Kristina is waiting for us."

And, on that note, we depart.

CHAPTER II

As Jeff and I leave to meet Kristina, I think about how long Jeff and I have been friends. I can't remember when I first met Jeff. We grew up together on the same block in small brownstones in Cobble Hill, Brooklyn. So the short answer is: 29 years, since that's how old we both are.

As young children, we often did things together. Barbara's job in those formative years was that of a full-time mother. In nice weather, she would take us to the playground or the beach; in bad weather, to movies or museums, clothes shopping or to eat at some kid-friendly restaurant (Chuck E. Cheese, anyone?). My mother, on other hand, was anything but a full-time mother when I was young. She seldom stepped in to take Jeff and me anywhere or even do anything with me alone. She was almost always too busy shopping for food, cleaning the house or cooking for my father. In truth, she was a full-time maid and only on rare occasion, a mother.

I have a sister, ten years younger than I. Her name is Felicity. I call her "Accident." Shortly after Accident was born, my mother abandoned her job of full-time maid to play the role of mother. That worked out pretty well for my sister, but was way too late for me. I was long gone to the tender care of another, Jeff's mom, Barbara.

I don't want you to think my childhood was unpleasant. Quite the contrary. I learned early on to rely on myself to a greater degree than Jeff and my other friends did. And my father always made time for me.

He worked six days a week and late hours as a middle management executive at a mid-sized cargo company but, when he was home from work, he'd watch TV with me and sometimes we'd play a game. I loved the old movies we'd watch on TV. Since my mother was doing all the household chores, I guess he had time to spare.

From my description of the dynamics of my family, you can surmise that the women's rights movements of today, and even of 30 years ago, were not in the forefront of my parents' thinking. Quite different that they were, my parents were not friends with Jeff's parents. They did not go out together socially and the only interaction they had with each other centered around what Barbara might be doing with Jeff and me.

So it was that Jeff and I monkey-barred together, went to kiddie gym, watched Sesame Street at his house and went to pre-school together. I have vague memories of all this, but a strong impression of Barbara's crucial role in my early years.

When it came time to go to regular school, we both attended the public school in our Cobble Hill district and sat next to each other in most classes. We lived in a racially mixed neighborhood and neither Jeff nor I had any problems playing and being friends with the black and Hispanic kids in our school and neighborhood, and to our parents' credit, neither did they.

When we weren't in school, we either engaged in sports or watched old movies together. As I mentioned, I loved the old movies and the old movie stars: Cary Grant, Marilyn Monroe, Kirk Douglas, Elizabeth Taylor, Tony Curtis, Paul Newman, Sidney Poitier, Marlon Brando. I could go on and on.

I was always a good student, all the way to and through college. It came easily to me. I was brought up in the belief that brains and effort were all you needed to succeed. Unfortunately (I guess), I had enough smarts that I never had to make that much of an effort to get good grades and then attend and graduate summa cum laude from the University of Wisconsin.

I went to the University of Wisconsin for a few reasons — it had the reputation of being a party school, it was far away from home and, most importantly, Jeff had managed to get accepted there.

Jeff was not much of a student — a lot of effort to get a barely passable result. But he was a terrific athlete, something I was not. They say opposites attract — so to the extent of my scholastic abilities and his athletic prowess, I guess that's true.

Jeff ran track and field and played basketball for our high school teams. In his senior year, he made all city PSAL as a six-foot shooting guard and was good enough to obtain a full athletic scholarship to the University of Wisconsin. I received a full academic scholarship and so off we went, certain that this would be an incredible shared life experience.

But, as is most often the case, things did not happen the way we anticipated. In the second game of his college career, his basketball life ended with a torn ACL and shredded meniscus. So did his desire to continue at college. But he sucked it up and did the best he could — he joined ROTC, graduated and served four years in the Army, the latter part overseas, returning home at age 25.

Despite Jeff's extreme disappointment over the abrupt end of his ball-playing days, he never fell into the vegetative state you might expect. I attribute a good part of his emotional recovery to the nurturing efforts Barbara undertook to help him overcome this life-changing event. It also helped that Wisconsin was, indeed, a party school and that we managed to get drunk and get laid with a great deal of frequency over the course of our college careers.

I was good at everything, exceptional at nothing and interested in very little. So I majored in English and decided creative literature would be my raison d'etre, the path of least resistance.

Jeff majored in ROTC, one might say. His athletic ability and physical prowess well-suited him to being a soldier. He was not drawn to it by any overwhelming desire to hurt anyone, that wasn't his nature (it couldn't be, not with the mother that Barbara was to him — to both of us). If it were, we never could have become such close friends, brothers if you will. But he did have a sense of discipline and duty that his father, Dan, a straight arrow, instilled in him, despite their not having a very good relationship. Dan had himself served in the military, but with a nasty streak at his core, which he exhibited when his temper got the better of him (which was all too often). He and Barbara were another case of opposites attract, as far as I could see.

When we graduated college, our paths diverged but our friendship didn't. We stayed in constant communication via email and mobile phone and saw each other as frequently as his postings would allow. Luckily, most of his overseas time was NATO related, and he spent a good amount of time based in Germany with ample leave to visit family and friends back home.

When I graduated college, I didn't have the military to direct my course and I was adrift. It was during this time that my parents (and I) hit the proverbial jackpot. Some distant aunt of my mother's died without a will and no apparent living family members. After an investigation required by the laws of the State of Oregon, where she lived, it was discovered that my mother was her closest living relative and my mother inherited $2.3 million dollars which she never knew might ever be her good fortune.

With the news of her serendipity, my parents decided to immediately pack up and move with Felicity to Florida in an effort to establish a Florida residency and avoid the corrosive effect New York taxes would have on their nest egg. This ill-conceived plan nevertheless left them very well-situated (even after taxes) and me with ownership of our Cobble Hill brownstone, a gift they gave me out of a sense of "take the money and run" guilt.

So I had a mortgage-free home to live in (after 25-30 years, even the working class can pay off a mortgage) and enough of a base, with the aid of odd jobs, to pursue a writing career. Then came Airbnb. Over the past few years, the money from rentals of portions of my house, coupled with my relatively small, but slowly increasing, book sale royalties, has enabled me to continue to stay financially afloat while I strive for the elusive Edgar Award that I see in my future.

When Jeff got back from overseas, he had to find a job. He had determined that the Army wasn't for him as a long-term life choice, that his required four years of service (even though pleasurable for the most part) was quite enough. Jeff was now six foot two, broad-shouldered and well-muscled (that's the Army for you), and quite handsome, with dark hair, an angular face and a cleft chin. He was and is very natural and outgoing to boot. With all that going for him, what else? — he became a car salesman.

He and I laughed about it frequently, but he made good money from the commissions he received as (almost immediately) one of the best car salesmen at the Bay Ridge Brooklyn Lexus dealership. So who was I to criticize his choice — a mystery writer in large part still living off his boyhood home.

Things continued relatively smoothly for us over the next few years. Jeff moved into an apartment near the Greenwood Cemetery in Brooklyn (not as trendy as Williamsburg and other areas, but more affordable) and we saw each other frequently. Together, we dated, partied, went to sport events, played in a monthly poker game, and often had Sunday night dinners at his parents' house. Over time, largely attributable to his salesperson's job and army experiences, he became quite adept at using his looks and people skills to his ever-increasing advantage, developing an opportunistic edge to his personality that previously had been lacking but suited him well.

Although Barbara was by now working full-time as a social worker in New York City's child protective services agency, she and Jeff spoke almost daily and she always found time to cook a lavish dinner for us those Sunday nights. And when I had a problem I wanted to discuss with someone other than Jeff, it was Barbara I thought to call (and often did).

Then one day Jeff met the stunning and wonderful Kristina Nolan, brought up in the wilds of Oklahoma City, and things, for Jeff, got even better.

CHAPTER III

I first met Kristina several weeks after Jeff and she started dating. This was a little less than a year ago, shortly after Jeff's twenty-eighth birthday. I guess you could consider her a belated birthday present.

They met when Jeff was shopping at Saks Fifth Avenue for a present for a girl he was dating. The girl, Penelope, came from a very wealthy family and Jeff felt the need to impress her. Jeff was starting to tire (no pun intended) of being a car salesman, even though the money was pretty decent. I think he saw Penelope (and her parents, presumably) as a possible way out.

Kristina was a salesperson working behind the cosmetics counter and, more often, in front — offering to spritz the latest fashionable perfumes on customers as they passed by. Vanity perfumes sponsored by various celebrities lined the countertop in dazzlingly designed, ornate bottles, with prices to match. The "sweet smell of success" was the lure that was expected to entice a perfume purchase (who wouldn't want to smell like Paris Hilton, or at least take a sniff of her?). So it was that Jeff first met Kristina. Sprayed (nay, slayed) at first sight. It must have been a love potion.

Kristina was relatively new to New York. She had a degree in philosophy from the University of Oklahoma but once she graduated and started to look for work, quickly came to realize that deep thinking doesn't often provide a livable income. Since she was not suited by inclination or physique to toil in the oil fields surrounding Oklahoma City, she decided to seek her future elsewhere.

Lest you think her decision to venture forth exceptionally courageous, her nascent modeling career virtually compelled it. Being five foot seven, with reddish brown hair, naturally long eyelashes that curl upwards from large green-tinged eyes, high cheekbones, heart-shaped lips, and shapely breasts, not large but not pearl-sized, enabled her to get occasional modeling gigs until, eventually, she signed with a New York City-based modeling agency and relocated here.

The Nostradamus Agency should have been called "Girls, 1,000, Girls", because that's how many female models the agency seemed to have under exclusive contract and with whom Kristina had to compete to get even a single, well-paying modeling job. Sharing an apartment with two other aspiring Nostradamus models and having her best meals (sometimes her only meal of the day) paid for by some guy trying to bed her was not optional. Worse, as one year became two, far too often she found herself shoplifting or even having to make ends meet by accepting expensive gifts from guys with whom she then felt compelled to sleep. Not liking what she had become, she concluded that modeling was no longer for her and that she needed to seek less hazardous employment. In short order, she found herself selling cosmetics at Saks and contemplating what the next step in her life might be.

Once she and Jeff met, it was fireworks exploding, instant mutual attraction, just like in the story books. When Jeff came up for air, several weeks after their initial encounter, he couldn't wait for me to meet Kristina. Since then, I have been with them many times, occasionally with a date I brought along because I didn't want to feel like the "odd man out" that I actually am. On this weeknight get-together after sandwiches at Jeff's house, I'm without a date. It doesn't make much of a difference. In fact, I find it easier and more fun in some strange way.

CHAPTER IV

William and Charlotte Wylde were a happy couple. Once. Now, not so much. Indeed, truth be told, not at all. A couple by marriage certificate only.

"What time will you be home tonight, William?", Charlotte petulantly asks.

"I won't be. I'm working late in the City and will be staying at the apartment," William rotely responds while stifling a yawn.

"You're never home. Why do we have a cook?"

"Because you don't," he curtly says, as he heads for the door, briefcase in hand.

William and Charlotte live in the tony village of Sands Point, Long Island, in a majestic waterview home with 23 rooms, nine bedrooms, 8-1/2 baths, three kitchens, indoor/outdoor pools and a private path to the beach. They have a full-time cook, maid and two chauffeurs (his and hers). They also have a pied-a-terre in Manhattan, a lavish apartment in London and a vacation estate in Carmel, California, where, in the better days of their marriage, they summered with their children.

Their marriage, once passionate, alive and resilient, has eroded, slowly at first but then quite rapidly, bottoming out several years ago to a cold war marked mostly by a resigned silence at best and Charlotte's needy complaints at worst. Over the years, Charlotte has pretty much given up on doing anything by or for herself, and, like Blanche in "A Streetcar Named Desire," she has come to rely on the kindness of strangers (or, in her case, hired help), and William has pretty much given up on her in every way possible except financial support, and there, absent a pre-nup, he has little real choice. In short, their marriage has long since passed the point of no return, the tipping point, and now William only wants to be rid of Charlotte, one way or another. Quoth the Raven, "Nevermore."

Charlotte grew up living a life of great wealth and privilege, with parents eager to appease her every whim. Her mother was an economics professor at Harvard University when she married Charlotte's father, Gordon Houghton, who at the time of their May-December marriage, was the head of a prominent merchant bank, advisor to and financier for many Fortune 500 companies. Harvard's Houghton Residence Hall is a result of his generous gift to the University the year after Charlotte was born.

Charlotte and her two-year younger sister, Donna, grew up in a chateau-like 20,000 square foot home in Kings Point, a house even bigger and more luxurious than the Sands Point home in which Charlotte now resides. Always quite beautiful, both as a girl and then a young woman, Charlotte, just past 50, still turns heads.

Her physical features readily attract both sexes — full lips, high forehead, small nose, narrow jaw, prominent cheekbones, wide-set blue eyes, and copper-colored hair, all set off by an almost hour-glass figure. Charlotte's natural beauty has been maintained in her later years by the tattoo of manicures, pedicures, massages, pilates and cycling workouts, hair stylist visits, and nutritionist-directed meals which mark her daily life.

Not so appealing is the barely-hidden rot that lies beneath her polished veneer: her narcissism, her sense of entitlement, her reliance on others to do things for her, and her lack of the desire to achieve (needed to give purpose to one's life). Her weekly psychotherapy sessions have done little to smooth these out.

Even though marginally successful in her class work at Harvard, she never thought much about what she might do once she exited academia. She was emotionally suited only for what eventually she did — marry well, indulge herself and have children — and even there, not surprisingly, she failed in the job of being a nurturing mother to her three children, although, to her credit, she tried. She spent many an hour with each of her children, playing games with them, taking them on fun shopping sprees, helping them with their homework, accompanying them to their weekend activities (soccer games, karate lessons, little league and the like). But despite her best efforts, her interest in doing all this was too weak, her narcissism too strong and nannies, tutors and chauffeurs too easily available for her to substitute in her place. Love and concern for her children she had, but her needs, not theirs, were her priority and increasingly she deferred to others to do what would have been better to have been done by her.

In college, Charlotte was the belle of the ball. Lead cheerleader on the Harvard cheerleading squad and its spokesperson, she had a series of lovers, mostly of the opposite sex, and fluttered around as if she were Heide Klum on a fashion runway. That was the Charlotte that caught William's eye and he was so blinded and besotted by her physical beauty that he never probed, nor cared much, about anything else.

What William has ended up with is a life partner who's so needy, so dependent, so cloying, so insecure, so unhappy and so unfulfilled, that she tries to blunt her pain with an ebbing stream of medications, Percocet for her frequent migraine headaches and Xanax and Oxycontin for everything else. William can barely tolerate spending time with Charlotte, no less being married to her. He thinks that he might do anything to be done with her, except the one thing he actually can do: divorce her.

William first met Charlotte when, four years after he'd graduated from Harvard, he returned for an alumni gathering where he was among those recent graduates being honored for their donations to

Harvard's endowment funds. William at age 25 was already well on his way to becoming a very wealthy man, one of the leading traders at Natboner Capital, a $10 billion hedge fund. Using his mathematics and economics expertise, he had developed an algorithm for arbitrage trades that helped enable Natboner Capital to return a 35% year-over-year profit to its select group of institutional investors. And his career had only just begun.

Today, at age 55, with his distinguished (almost patrician) looks, a take-no-prisoners personality and a deep baritone voice, he has risen to prominence. A frequent pundit for the media talking heads, a voice of reason and calm in their daily (if not hourly) discussions about the problems confronting the United States in the ever-changing global economy, it is rumored that he might be the next Secretary of the Treasury.

Unlike Charlotte, William did not grow up wealthy. In fact, quite the contrary. He came from a middle-class family in Queens, where both parents had to work to make ends meet. There was always food on the table, but not much else. From an early age, William was self-reliant, confident and ambitious. He started his working life at age 13, Saturdays and after school at a local supermarket.

William's defining feature has never been his looks (although they are quite acceptable), but his razor-sharp mind — he is exceptionally smart. By the sixth grade, he was doing the New York Times crossword puzzle in pen during class recess and by age 15 was earning money tutoring his schoolmates and helping the older ones prepare for college admission exams. He not only has a brilliant mind, but street smarts too, a combination that has stood him well to the present day.

No surprise that William graduated public high school as a national Phi Beta Kappa honoree, number one in his class of 850 students, nor that he attended Harvard on a full scholarship, obtaining a dual degree in mathematics and economics. And no surprise that he's applied his skills to make himself a very wealthy man. But it is a surprise that his common sense didn't warn him that even though Charlotte had come from great wealth, he would be well advised to have a prenuptial agreement in place before they married, because there might come a day that the marriage would end and he'd want to protect as much of his self-earned prosperity as he possibly could. Unfortunately, his little head governed his big head, and he's now faced with a price that he's unwilling to pay.

Quite apart from any division of assets (nearly impossible, given their illiquidity, complexity and the taxes that would ensue), a divorce from Charlotte will be messy, not amicable, because she's not prepared to let him go under any circumstances and no matter what the reason. He's well aware that, over the years, she has had a series of one-night stands and affairs and knows that she's aware of his many peccadilloes as well (although not that he is involved in what has become a serious relationship with his current mistress). He believes that his reputation, his possible cabinet appointment, and his future earnings (institutional investors are very sensitive to scandal) will be severely damaged, if not completely torpedoed, by the publicity that will follow if he were to seek a contested divorce from Charlotte. What galls him most is that he will no longer sit on an iron throne, admired by his legions. With his family's dirty laundry hanging on the line for all to see (and his children have some to hang as well), he will be exposed to the type of scrutiny that engenders scorn and even pity among the masses. This prospect he finds intolerable; he has worked long and hard to become a "Very Important Person" and intends to remain one, at all costs.

CHAPTER V

Charlotte's sister, Donna, awakes with a start, popping up from her sleep like a jack in the box when the lid is lifted. She'd been on a date last night but has no clear memory of it. In its place, is the very bad dream from which she has just awoken. The dream, she believes, must be connected to last evening, but she can't imagine how. It's so grotesque.

In the dream, a man and woman hold hands as they walk home from a movie. Not a typical date movie, but horror movies are back in vogue and the man has chosen it because it's an appropriate touch for the evening he has in mind for the person he's with. He's thinking how free and liberated he feels, as his fingers touch the handle of the gravity knife in his pants pocket. As the couple strolls hand-in-hand along a side street, his grip tightens on the knife as he starts to slide it from his pocket. It's waiting to be used and he's eager to accommodate it.

Just then, a voice calls out from the shadows. The man jerks involuntarily, staring at the figure six feet away stepping towards them. "Do you have money for some food?" the disheveled stranger asks as he approaches, a beggar's hand turned palm upward. "I lost my job and am living on the streets. Anything you can spare to help tide me over is appreciated."

An inadvertent, growling sound catches in the man's throat. His moment has been interrupted, his opportunity not seized. He quickens his pace as he walks away from the homeless person without responding. His date can barely keep up.

"Slow down. There's no danger," his date says. He does not respond. He's too angry, too frustrated, he has to get control of himself. He's come too close to revealing himself without result. He takes a deep breath and slows down, smoothing his hair as he forces a smile to his lips, "You're right. I don't know why I got so upset. There's no reason to spoil our evening." He has caged himself for the moment, but the lock no longer needs a key and he can come and go as he pleases. He can wait for tomorrow to come.

Donna is unsettled. Yes, by the dream, which lingers in her mind, leaving her off balance, feeling both threatened and protected at the same time. For some reason, she identifies with the man in her dream, almost thinks he's supposed to be her. But how can that be? It makes no sense.

Even more troubling is that last night is almost completely blacked out from her memory. She remembers who she went out with, of course, and a movie, but that's all. Did she drink too much or do drugs? For a variety of reasons, she isn't about to call her boyfriend to ask what they did.

She doesn't even know why she went out with him again. Their relationship has deteriorated beyond any possibility of salvage. He's become increasingly abusive, verbally and physically, as his alcohol consumption has gone out of control, swelling his gut and clouding his judgment. She had vowed to end things, to not see him anymore. So why did she agree to go out with him again last night? Is she that needy? It's a six-month relationship whose time is up. # Time's Up Donna.

For reasons known only to the gods (or God, depending on one's beliefs), Donna is the polar opposite of Charlotte. She's not beautiful, far from it: she has a horse-shaped face with a prominent nose, narrow lips, close-set eyes and a noticeable chin. Her figure is pear-shaped, somewhat large at the hips and small in the chest. Donna is bookish, shy, kind and caring. All her life, Charlotte's beauty has cast a dark shadow over Donna, causing her to be barely seen by her parents and those around her.

The Houghton family wealth has had a different effect on Donna than it has had on Charlotte. Not wanting for anything money can buy, instead of a series of boyfriends, Donna has had a series of causes: protect the environment, end all wars, feed the homeless, educate the poor. After graduating Harvard with honors, she became and is a teacher in a public school in the Bronx (although living in a three-bedroom, mortgage-free upper west side condo).

Like Charlotte, Donna goes to a therapist, but only recently and for a different reason. She blacks out from time to time and wakes up with only partial recollection of an evening or a day. These blackouts have increased in frequency and a spate of medical tests have found nothing that is physically wrong. In desperation, Donna has even undergone hypnosis, the result of which is the possibility that someone might have physically abused her when she was very young. Much more probing (medical and psychological) needs to be done before the cause of Donna's blackouts can be identified with certainty and the problem can begin to be resolved.

Donna has always been resentful of the attention heaped on Charlotte and that resentment, coupled with Charlotte's narcissism and sense of entitlement, has prevented Donna and Charlotte from establishing a close relationship. As kind and caring as Donna is, those qualities do not extend towards her dealings with Charlotte, who, meaning to or not, has always made Donna feel inferior and unloved.

Her present course of psychotherapy doesn't seem to be helping eliminate, or even abate, her memory lapses. She's frightened. But para-doxically, at the same time, she has an inner sense that her blackouts are not all bad, that something is happening during that time that might actually be beneficial for her, if she could only come to understand what that is and why she's losing memory. And why she so strongly identifies with the man in her dream, shares his feelings, not just empathetically, but as if she were he, shares his urge to kill someone, not just anyone, but someone close to him. There's something tenaciously gnawing inside her unconscious that she senses has made its way close to the surface. She's confident that when whatever it is bursts free, into her consciousness, she will be the better for it, and that that will be very soon. One thing Donna does understand: if she were the type of person who could kill someone, it would be Charlotte.

CHAPTER VI

It is a clear, sunny March day, blue skies, almost as perfect a sky as on 9/11 before all the destruction and devastation occurred. So, naturally, Charlotte has chosen this day to have her chauffeur drive her to Saks Fifth Avenue to attend a day-long designer fashion event. Charlotte arrives early and is killing time browsing through the cosmetics counters when Kristina approaches her.

"May I help you? Are you looking for anything in particular?" Kristina politely inquires.

"No. Nothing in particular," Charlotte distractedly responds.

"Might I suggest a new perfume that we just received? It's called 'Fulfilled' and smells quite lovely. It's a limited production from the House of Pepi Pierre in Paris that took years for its fragrance makers to create. May I spray a drop on your wrist?"

Charlotte acquieses and, after delicately sniffing her wrist, turns to Kristina and delightedly declares: "What a wonderful fragrance. Thank you for the recommendation. I'll take a bottle."

Kristina smiles at Charlotte and, as Kristina heads behind the perfume counter to get "Fulfilled," Charlotte calls out, "Is there anything else that you might recommend?"

Looking back over her shoulder, Kristina turns around, walks towards Charlotte, looks at her face for a brief moment and then says: "I'm not sure what you might be interested in, but how about some eye shadow highlights that I think would look great on you when you go out for an evening?"

Charlotte nods her consent, so Kristina takes her to another counter and shows her various eye shadow highlights. One thing leads to another, and soon an hour has passed with Kristina having made several make-up suggestions that she thinks appropriate for Charlotte. Charlotte purchases almost everything that Kristina has recommended.

Charlotte thanks Kristina and, as she leaves the cosmetics section to attend the fashion show, asks Kristina for her card, which Kristina gives her, saying: "Please come again. It's been a pleasure to meet you and I'm glad I could be of service."

A few days later, Charlotte is out shopping in Manhattan again, this time looking for just the right dress to wear to a charity ball that one of her Sands Point friends is sponsoring. After visiting two designer stores but finding nothing that pleases her, she ends up back at Saks looking at several dresses, but can't make up her mind which to buy. She considers purchasing all of them, but then she still would have to decide which to wear. William could care less and, as usual where Charlotte is concerned, probably have no opinion at all, deeming Charlotte's selection of a dress a matter too frivolous for him to be bothered with.

On a whim, Charlotte goes downstairs looking for Kristina. She finds her, approaches and says: "Hello again. It's me, Charlotte Wylde. I've a favor to ask."

"Sure. How can I help you, Ms. Wylde?"

"I can't decide on which dress to purchase for an important event that I need to attend. I wonder if you could come upstairs with me and help me decide. You were very helpful a few days ago."

Kristina agrees and, after getting permission to leave the cosmetics section to assist a customer, goes upstairs with Charlotte. Charlotte tries on five dresses and, with Kristina's help, selects two to buy. A grateful and quite relieved Charlotte says: "Thank you, Kristina. I very much appreciate your help. You seem to have an eye for what works best for me in make-up and now cocktail dresses. Do you have an education in fashion?"

Laughing lightly, Kristina responds: "Unless you count some modeling assignments, no. My college major was philosophy."

"Philosophy. How wonderful. And modeling. You're quite an engaging young woman." With that having been said, Charlotte invites Kristina to a late afternoon tea with her at Laudrée in Soho, with a stop on the way to look at jewelry at Boxer's Box Up Gallery. Kristina's shift is over and, curious to learn more about Charlotte, she accepts the offer.

After Charlotte purchases some dangling, hand-crafted sterling silver earrings with necklace to match that Kristina has pointed out to her, they go for tea. Kristina has never before been chauffeured around Manhattan and is having difficulty taking it all in. She's in awe of this lifestyle, where in a single day Charlotte has spent more than Kristina earns in half a year.

As they drink their decaffeinated raspberry-flavored blend tea and eat from the plate of different flavored Laudrée macarons that has been placed between them, they chat. Mostly, Charlotte asks Kristina some questions about Kristina's life. Kristina tells her about her background, about her boyfriend, Jeff, and an edited version of how she came to work at Saks. After telling Kristina a little about her family and where she lives, Charlotte implusively, excitedly but tentatively, asks: "Would you consider coming to work for me full time? I know we've only recently met, but I've decided that I need a personal assistant. Someone to keep my calendar and accompany me to some of the places I go, certainly shopping, and doctor visits, and maybe some other things I do. You'd enjoy going to my exercise classes with me, I'm sure. What do you think?"

Kristina is taken aback and slow to respond. A suddenly decisive Charlotte throws in: "Just so you know, I'll pay you one and a half times whatever you are making at Saks, plus pay your travel expenses on days I need you to come to me in Long Island."

After a much shorter pause, Kristina looks at Charlotte and says: "That's a very generous offer and the job sounds like something I might like. Can I get back to you in a day or two? I want to think some more about it."

"Certainly. I understand. It's a big decision for you. It is for both of us. Please think it over carefully, maybe speak to your boyfriend, and then let me know. I hope you accept my offer. I need someone like you, someone on whom I can rely to help me take care of all the things that I need to do each day."

After Charlotte texts Kristina her contact information, she pays the bill and says goodbye, waving her hand in the air with a queenly flourish as she walks towards the door. She thinks to herself, if necessary, I will offer to pay her double her salary. Look what a help she's been to me already. She's delightful. I'm entitled to someone like her in my life. I should have done this a long time ago.

CHAPTER VII

Kristina rushes home excited, but at the same time trepidatious, about this new, unexpected possibility in her life. It's a very big step to take. After a hot shower and a relaxing glass of chardonnay, she thinks about it more calmly, weighing the pluses and minuses in a relatively dispassionate manner.

Although she still wants to talk about it with Jeff, she pretty much has made her decision. It's more money, Charlotte seems nice, even if perpetually flustered when it comes to making decisions, and Kristina can always quit if she doesn't like the job. She's not giving up anything of very much value; working at Saks was stop gap, never going to be her permanent vocation. And being a personal assistant to a rich woman eventually could open many other doors for Kristina.

Kristina and Jeff are meeting for dinner tonight at Spaghetti Mountain in Williamsburg, so she can talk to him about all this there. They've become very close and each believe they have met someone with whom they want to spend the rest of their life. Jeff's opinion will be very important to her and might even change her mind.

Over drinks, they scrutinize the day's unexpected events and what Kristina has tentatively decided. Jeff tells her that he agrees with her decision, but that she should ask for some type of employment agreement, including the promise of a few weeks' notice if she's ever fired. She responds: "That's sensible, but I don't feel comfortable asking for that. Maybe just a letter saying what my weekly pay will be. Ms. Wylde is taking a bigger chance on me than I am on her."

With that major decision having been made, their evening continues with some of the small talk in which people in love engage. Jeff comments: "You know, we live in a bizzaro world. When I was in my teens, you got a date by meeting someone somewhere and asking her out. Like you and I first met. Recently, most of my friends tell me about whom they 'met' on Tinder, OKCupid or some other dating service. They look at pictures, which have probably been photo-shopped or airbrushed, and the person's profile, most likely exaggerated or a total work of fiction, and tell me about the wonderful person they are going to have a drink with. Jeez, thank God I met you."

"I feel lucky to have met you, too, babe" Kristina lovingly replies. "But I do admit that I have often considered signing onto SugarDaddy. com," she jokes. (Half jokes, since in the waning moments of her modeling days she once came close to actually doing it.)

"Hey, funny story. Did you read about the African grey parrot and Alexa?" Jeff asks.

"No. Is this going to be a joke?"

"No joke. Not the way you mean. A true story, apparently. But hilarious. I read about it on Yahoo news. This guy gets a delivery of food to his house from a delivery service, some strawberries and ice cream, and from Amazon.com, a cd of romantic music. But he didn't order any of this. It turns out that he has a pet African grey parrot and the parrot ordered all of this through the guy's Alexa device, which he kept in the kitchen near the parrot cage."

"That's funny, very funny," Kristina giggles. "Oh my God!" she bursts out.

After her giggling subsides, she says: "I have a story for you. Not so funny. I read about it the other day. Do you remember that we talked about how wonderful it was that this homeless war veteran who was huddled in a blanket outside a bar on a snowy, below-freezing day, without shoes, was given a pair of boots by a married couple who took pity on him and then raised a lot of money for him in a GoFundMe campaign that they initiated?"

"Yeah, I do. But it turned out that they stole most of the money they raised for him. I read about that too."

"No worse. It was all a scam. It came to light because they didn't give him his fair share of the money. He wasn't even a homeless person and the three of them concocted the whole thing."

"Ugh. That sucks. The internet certainly has changed the way we live, that's for sure," Jeff says, and then continues: "When my parents were young, they played board games. Monopoly, Risk, Sorry, Life. I even played these with them sometimes, mostly with my mom and Simon. She called it a 'shared experience' for her and us. But today, who wants to move pieces around a board when you can play a video game online, browse the internet or play fantasy sports? Those board games of old have become boring games, except for the old."

"Wow. You sound like the philosophy major instead of me. Where did that come from?"

"I don't know. I've been thinking about a lot of things lately. Mostly, my job and my prospects for the future. Jobs that I thought about as a kid seem absurd today. Many don't even exist anymore or, if they do, are not all that desirable. Airbnb, the largest hotel company, doesn't own any property. Uber, the largest taxi cab company, doesn't own a single car. I can buy pretty much anything I want without leaving my house — just go to Amazon, Ebay, Etsy, Fresh Direct or Seamless. And the internet and social media are making people rich who don't even have a job, certainly not one in any sense that I could imagine as a teenager."

"Okay. I see all that, but so what? Why do you sound so down about it?"

"The 'what' is that I make good money selling cars. But for how long? Someday soon, most cars probably will be driverless and I will be out of a job. And while I don't look into other people's pockets, a nine year old kid earns $20 million a year because of You Tube, where he's seen playing with toys and ends up having a line of toys being sold in his name at chain stores all over the country. And all these bloggers, instagramers, twitterers and facebookers who develop a following from some silly internet meme and then earn humongous amounts of money from product endorsements they do while sitting on their ass clicking away on their website. I'm not 'down' about all this. It's just that I've begun to realize that I need to adjust my goals and look to what I should be doing in the future." After a slight pause, Jeff leans towards Kristina, takes her hand in his and adds: "A future I hope to share with you."

Kristina warmly responds: "That almost sounds like a proposal. I love you too. Very, very much."

The evening ends with the passion one might imagine from two people in love and the encouraging prospect of a probable permanent life together. Kristina's going to call Charlotte in the morning and accept the offer to be Charlotte's personal assistant, and Jeff is going to think about what type of other opportunities might be available to a person like him that he might want to pursue. He is, at worst, an excellent salesperson, with the looks and a personality ready-made for the internet and social media.

CHAPTER VIII

It is just after 7:00 a.m., the gym has only opened a half-hour earlier, yet the treadmills are all in use. On one, a young man in his early twenties running next to a look-alike, middle-aged woman, apparently his mother. On another, a man in his 70's in plaid Bermuda shorts, knee-high white socks, walking shoes and a collared shirt. From the way he's laboring, it isn't clear who will run out of time first — man or machine. The prize of the group by far is a blond with not an ounce of loose flesh and a spandex outfit to demonstrate it.

I push my walking speed up to 5.0 and start to jog, in futile competition with a muscular 25-year old with black hair tied in a ponytail and chest and arm muscles protruding from his tank top.

I'm manly looking but slightly out of shape. I still have most of my curly brown hair, most of my physique and all of my strange sense of humor. My approach to my social life, at least until recently, is not much different than it was when I was in college — no need for any serious foreign entanglements. In and out (so to speak) skirmishes only, so no risk of substantial damage to vital organs (particularly, my heart).

This has changed, however, with the introduction of Kristina into Jeff's life. He's crazy in love, and I am, for the first time, both envious and resentful of my best friend. She's fabulous and I wish it were me. I think I need to start to make an effort to find my Kristina.

The blond strides off her treadmill and six sets of eyes follow as she enters an aerobics room. To the right of my treadmill, through a large glass window, I can still see her, as she bounces in silent rhythm with women of all ages and sizes, to the gestures and cadence of the instructor. In her own way, she's Ginger Rogers to my Fred Astaire (yes, I loved watching their old movies too) and we are "dancing cheek to cheek." But then my eyes divert and I find myself staring vacantly at big bottoms, round bottoms, tiny bottoms, sexy bottoms, not so sexy bottoms, here, there and everywhere, bobbing up, down, left cheek, right cheek, both cheeks, a sea of cheeks and bottoms, mesmerizing me as I continue to jog, oblivious to all except this mass of bouncing bottoms. But all good things must come to an end (pun intended) and so this does.

I finish my workout, shower and get dressed. It's 8:30 a.m. and I have a 9:30 a.m. meeting with a Brooklyn bookstore owner whom I am trying to finagle into arranging a book signing event for me at his store. As I head towards the subway, past the corner Starbucks, my eye catches a glimpse of the blond from the gym inside. Opportunity knocks, so I pivot sharply and enter the coffee shop. Ordering the flavor of the day, casually (I hope) I saunter over to the blond, my intended flavor of the month.

"Hi. I saw you in the gym. Are you new to the neighborhood?" Not exactly my wittiest opening, but it will have to suffice.

Apparently not put off by my less than artful approach, she responds: "No. My boyfriend and I moved in about six months ago and we used to work out together nights after work. Now that I sent him packing, I prefer the gym in the early morning, before work." She volunteers, "I'm Patricia."

"What do you do?" I ask, trying my best to refrain from staring at her more than ample, jutting breasts.

"I'm an associate in the private wealth management group at Citibank. How about you?" she says, puckering her lips (oh God, she's my Marilyn Monroe) and blowing on her coffee to cool it down.

Trying to sound nonchalant, yet impart a sense of importance, I reply: "I write books. I'm an author."

"Are you famous?" Have I read any of your books?" she inquires flirtingly.

"Perhaps one of my poems. 'The Road Not Taken', 'Splendor in the Grass', 'Ode to a Woodchuck,'" I banter.

She laughs, "I'm afraid not."

Having scored on my opening shot, I'm encouraged to shoot again: "I'm late for a meeting. How about we continue this tonight, over a drink somewhere?"

"I believe in first things first. Such as telling me your name."

"Simon. Simon Crandell."

"Well, Simon, Simon Crandell, I'm a pretty traditional person. I prefer a little slower track than the one you seem to be running on this morning."

She reaches into her pocketbook and takes out her cell phone. "Tell me your number and I will text you mine." So I do and she does and off we each go, in my mind certain that we will very soon converge.

But as I leave the coffee shop, flush with victory, I stop in mid-step. I've been flippantly charming (I hope), certainly enough to exchange numbers. But I need to be less of the superficial and more of the real me if I want to seize the brass ring and get off the merry-go-round. I'll have to think more about this. I hope Jeff and Kristina's relationship continues to be my new bellwether.

CHAPTER IX

William Wylde has lived his life guided by certain adages, one of which is that random acts are to be feared but strategies are to be embraced. Charlotte has just told William (always "William" to Charlotte, but "Wild Bill" to his colleagues and competitors) of her random (in this case, impulsive) act in hiring Kristina, who called Charlotte earlier this morning and, after agreeing on the salary, accepted the job she'd been offered. But, for William, this hiring triggers a glimmer of a strategy that he might employ to his advantage.

If this person to whom Charlotte apparently has taken a liking works out, if she can survive the demanding servitude, both physical and emotional, that Charlotte will no doubt impose, then William can widen even further the separation of his life from Charlotte's. This personal assistant whom Charlotte says she needs (to do what, William cannot fathom) should reduce the number of calls and texts that Charlotte makes asking William for his opinion on one mundane issue or another, or asking him when he is coming home or where he is going, or telling him where she would like him to be. And maybe, if she's the right type of person, this assistant can become a true companion for Charlotte, someone to be first responder to Charlotte's myriad needs, a person to take the spotlight off William's unwillingness to play that role in Charlotte's life at this late stage of their failed marriage. William thinks to himself that he needs to meet Kristina very soon, so he can gauge her suitability for what he has in mind.

With these thoughts, William puts a smile on his face and tells Charlotte: "I think it's a terrific idea for you to hire a personal assistant. She'll be a big help, no doubt. I look forward to meeting her."

"Oh good. I'm glad. I thought you might think it foolish and unnecessary. But I've really needed a personal assistant for a long time and only realized that recently."

"When will she start?"

"In two weeks. She wants to give the traditional amount of notice to her employer before she starts working for me."

"You'll need to have some type of written agreement spelling out the details of her employment. I'll have our lawyer contact you."

"All she's asked for is a letter spelling out her compensation. I don't want to scare her off with a wordy agreement from some lawyer. She's from Oklahoma and young. Can't you write something up for me?"

"No problem. I'll do that today and e-mail it to you."

"Thanks," Charlotte says as she rises from the kitchen table and brushes William a brisk kiss on the cheek.

William has had a cup of coffee but hasn't eaten anything this morning. It's Saturday, and usually he eats a full breakfast on weekend mornings and he will do so today. Just not with Charlotte. He has promised to have breakfast this morning in the City with Vanessa Washington, his mistress, a promise he's most anxious to keep.

As Charlotte is leaving the kitchen, William calls out: "Charlotte. I forgot to tell you. I've a meeting this morning in Manhattan starting at 10:00 a.m. with a client who's here from overseas. It will run most of the day."

"I wish you had told me earlier," she dejectedly responds. "I thought we might do something together today, maybe go to the new exhibit at MOMA. I could meet you there this afternoon, after your meeting."

"No can do. Sorry. My meeting will run into the late afternoon."

"You never have time for me anymore," she pouts. "You're the head of the company. Why do you have to work so hard all the time? You have lots of younger partners. Let them work on the weekends. Not you. It's bad enough that you have to stay in the City all week because of work."

"Look around you. Look at our house, our staff, our life," William responds with some anger. "This all stems from me, not my partners. I have to stay on top of my business or it will run aground. My partners can't do it. At least not yet. The company is called 'Wylde Capital' for good reason. And let me remind you virtually all the money you inherited from your parents and the $2 billion I've earned are invested in the funds that Wylde Capital manages."

"It seems to me that you could reduce your time at work if you really wanted to," she says, her face crinkled, still petulant and disappointed. "Instead, each year we spend less and less time together. I need more, not less, of your time. This was never a problem when we were younger."

"Things change. No matter what you think, this is my career, my life's work, and it's what's required of me. I didn't grow up in the lap of luxury the way you and your sister, the Houghton girls, did, with a silver spoon in my mouth. I had to earn my affluent life and I intend to keep doing it."

"Well, you need to keep at your marriage too. I'm entitled to a fair share of your time and attention and haven't been getting it for too many years now," Charlotte angrily replies. "And that goes for the bedroom too!" she exclaims.

William starts to further engage with Charlotte but pulls back at the last moment. This conversation has deteriorated rapidly, too rapidly, to a danger point, and he does not want it to plunge any further. But it does highlight for him the need to figure out how to better handle Charlotte going forward, short of the divorce he knows she won't give him. This is a delicate time for William, what with the prospect of a cabinet post nomination in the air, and he doesn't want to do anything that might blow that away.

William gets up to make his escape, saying: "I have no time to continue this. I have to go. I can't be late for my meeting." "I guess you're just not hearing me." As usual," Charlotte dispiritedly responds, as she sighs in resignation as William leaves. Once out the door and in the car, William's spirits lift. He has always had the ability to compartmentalize things, both in business and in his personal life. So he tucks away the unpleasantness with Charlotte and eagerly heads to his liaison with Vanessa.

Breakfast starts off well enough, as Vanessa serves him his eggs while dressed only in a revealing negligee in the breakfast nook of the small but comfortable apartment he has rented for her. William has been beguiled with, and bedeviled by, Vanessa for approximately eight months now, the longest he has ever been with a woman other than Charlotte. He feels as passionate towards Vanessa as he did when he first met Charlotte. Vanessa is 18 years younger than Charlotte and, while nowhere near as classically beautiful as Charlotte was at Vanessa's age, she's just incredibly sexy and alluring. That Vanessa is black is of no moment to William. If anything, it enhances her appeal. She's something exotic and intoxicating to him, his very own Rihanna or Zoe Saldana.

Vanessa was raised by loving Southern Baptist parents, who believe that God's purpose in creating men and women was for them to fall in love, pledge themselves to each other and have children together; only as a family, can the wonders that the world has to offer be fully embraced and appreciated. At age 33, Vanessa is feeling the pressure of her upbringing, more so with every passing conversation with her parents. She's found someone she loves and who loves her, but she is no closer to being married and having children than she was ten years ago. Time is starting to rush by and Vanessa is intent on not being left behind.

As they finish breakfast, and William helps clear the table, Vanessa blurts out: "I've been offered a job in Washington, D.C. In public relations for Resnik, Tanenhaus. It's an up and coming agency that does damage control and crisis management for several major companies and the salary offered me is quite substantial."

"Apparently young, black, beautiful women are in very high demand these days," William reacts without really thinking.

"I don't know whether to take that as a compliment or an insult," Vanessa replies questioningly as she looks into William's eyes.

Ignoring her comment, he continues: "I assume you're going to turn it down."

This statement, his proclamation if you will, adds some fuel to a growing fire, as Vanessa takes umbrage, and squaring her shoulders (which only promotes the prominence of her breasts and their proximity to William) angrily replies: "I don't like being taken for granted. I love you very much. I know you love me too. But you've made me no firm commitment. So where's this heading? I don't intend to be just your kept mistress."

"You aren't. And I don't want that either. But you have a good enough job in public relations right here in New York. And if money is an issue, I'll give you more, whatever you need."

"I don't need money. What I need is you fully committed to me and to us having a life together, some day a family. I need you to get free from Charlotte, a wife you no longer love and can barely tolerate."

"I'm as fully committed to you as I can be at present. I've explained this all to you before. I love you. Just be patient. Things will have a way of sorting themselves out. I'm working on it, on a life for us."

Somewhat placated, Vanessa hugs him, but with her head on his shoulder, looks up and says: "I'm not going anywhere for now. I just want to be with you. But please, try harder, find a way for us to be truly together."

William has lost some of his appetite for the bedroom, weighted down by the not so veiled threat that lurks beneath Vanessa's plea. But once again in his life the little head takes control of William and he is, at least momentarily, all the happier for it to have occurred.

CHAPTER X

In the course of his success, William has made enemies, many of them, some in the financial world, some in the political world and some in his personal life. The recent rumors of his possible nomination to be Secretary of the Treasury have caused the long knives to be drawn. Bearing the largest sword is Franklin Demarcus, a prideful man, a former dalliance of Charlotte's whom she casually cast aside after several weeks despite his declaration of deep affection for her. He has neither forgotten nor forgiven. His lingering bitterness was inflamed when, a year ago, William crushed him in a hotly contested fight over the valuation of a struggling home furnishings company. Wild Bill shorted the company at a time that Franklin owned a controlling interest in it, and eventually, under the weight of a spate of unfair adverse publicity generated by Wild Bill and his investor allies, At Home In Your Home collapsed into bankruptcy. William and his allies made in excess of $150 million on his bet against the company and Franklin lost his entire investment, twice that amount, not to mention his public humiliation at having been bested by his competitor in such a high-profile matter.

Franklin is not only prideful, but violent and a man who holds a grudge, one who believes in evening a score. Having grown up as a foster child who from time to time lived on the streets, he was no stranger to violence, whether inflicted by or on him, nor unaware of the benefits of his being a member of a gang. To this day, he's not shied away from resorting to acts of violence to accomplish his goals. He escaped the rat hole of his childhood after he was befriended by one of his high school teachers, the son of a very successful business man, who, seeing a spark in Franklin that even Franklin did not know was there, convinced his father to pay for Franklin's college education. Franklin went on to great success as first the mentee of Asher Rawlings, his teacher's father, and then his successor as the head of Rawlings & Demarcus, a competitor of Wylde Capital in investing in and restructuring various businesses.

With rumors of William's possible cabinet nomination having been floated, Franklin has decided that he must sink that ship before it sails and has begun to examine how best to accomplish that. Scandal would scuttle Wylde's chance at the post. And a scandal involving Charlotte would be double sweet revenge. As a first step, Franklin will hire Shirley Duzz from Duzz Investigations to see what she can come up with.

Franklin wants nothing more than to inflict maximum pain on William. He's been thinking of how to do this for a while, even before he heard the rumor that Wild Bill might be the next Treasury Secretary. Hiring someone to kill William is, of course, one possibility, but while the immorality of it is no bar for Franklin, the risk of discovery is too great and the reward far from satisfying; Franklin wants William to suffer, not simply cease to exist.

At a charity event a few weeks ago, at which Franklin spoke first with William and then Charlotte in what he disguised to be polite conversation, Charlotte appeared to be high on something: the pupils of her eyes were small, her speech was slurred and her attention unfocused. His encounter with her has sparked a thought. If his investigator discovers that Charlotte is abusing drugs, a distinct possibility based on what Franklin observed, then her death from an overdose should be just the type of scandal to deprive Wild Bill of the nomination. Charlotte overdosing is something Franklin is confident he can arrange with minimal risk of discovery. Since William thrived in the media, he would die in the media and his pain would be palpable and enduring, Charlotte's demise the cherry on top. On second thought and better still, let the nomination happen, let William get even closer to his prize, then take it away. That's the ticket.

CHAPTER XI

"I'm a shamus. A private dick. Kent Marlboro's the name. Some people, referring to my softer side, just call me Dick. I work out of a dump above a Chelsea dive bar, but it suits my clientele. They're not the type that get great ideas while playing ping pong at their WeWork office."

"So this narrow-waisted doll in a pencil skirt, with a low-cut top and a pushup bra that squeezed her bosoms so high they almost hit her chin, sashays into my office one day, and pleads: 'Mr. Marlboro. I need your help. Very badly.'"

"'What's up, miss? And how did you find me?'"

"'You helped my friend once. Twatty O'Toole.'"

"'The stripper? Yeah, I remember. Tough case. Do you strip too?'"

"She bats her baby blues at me and coyly responds: 'Sometimes. But not at a strip club.'"

"This gal's my type. Now, if she can pay me, I'm the guy for this job. 'So what's your beef?', I ask."

"She says: 'My ex-boyfriend. He made a video of me and him that I didn't know about. And I did some stuff that's pretty out there. Now I have a chance at hooking a decent guy, but not if he sees this video. I'm being threatened by my ex. He'll expose me if I don't do what he wants.'"

"'You're pretty exposed already,' I respond. 'Maybe if he posts it on the internet you'll become an honorary member of the Khardasian clan or at least a Redtube premium view.'"

"'You're making fun of me,'" she scowls. "'This isn't funny. I need him to stop and to have the video — or him — erased.'"

"Don't pout. It wrinkles your lovely face. I get $500 a day plus expenses. Three-day minimum. That's the cost for you to sleep better at night."

"So what do you think of this possible start to my next book?," I ask Jeff. "This is something new I might try. An old fashioned, hard-boiled noir detective story."

"Seriously? Or are you joking around, as usual?" he responds. "If this is for real, you won't have much of an audience. Maybe people in senior living and nursing homes. But that's about it."

"Hey, everything old is new again. In Hollywood, they remake things all the time. Take the movie 'The Shop Around the Corner,' with Jimmy Stewart and Margaret Sullavan. Remember it? We saw it together with your mom when we were kids. On Turner Classic Movies. Two co-workers who dislike each other and don't know that they are the pen pals that each of them is falling in love with through the letters they write to each other. This gets re-made in 1949, just nine years later, to a musical, 'The Good Old Summertime' with Judy Garland and Van Johnson — which we also saw— and then in 1998 it becomes a big hit once again as 'You've Got Mail' with Tom Hanks and Meg Ryan."

"Okay," Jeff says. "I know they've done that with lots of movies."

"Yeah," I continue. "Wash, rinse and repeat. So why shouldn't I test the waters?"

"I can't tell if you're just playing around with me. In the off chance you're not, pulp fiction is long dead and buried. Don't waste your time. Dashiell Hammett, Raymond Chandler and Mickey Spillane would not have much of an audience today."

"Oh yeah. Walter Mosley and James Ellroy have done pretty well. You'd have 'The Thin Man' novel be written in a modern, politically correct style and be called 'The Narrow Person' — gender non-specific and no body shaming."

"Enough," Jeff exclaims, as he throws his arms half-way up in the air in a sign of surrender, both of us laughing. Then I say: "Hey. I've got another great book idea."

"Can't wait."

"Have you read about the scientist who supposedly has created a genetically-edited baby by altering a gene in the embryo before implanting it in the mother's womb?"

"Yeah, right," Jeff says incredulously, as he scrunches his face into a disbelieving frown.

"No. For real," I respond. "Things are getting crazy. Another scientist just recently claimed to have used a 3D printer to create a mouse-sized heart, with a view to artificially printing human organs for transplant."

"O...kay," Jeff slowly drawls, exhibiting his skepticism. "So, thanks for the latest scientific updates. Is your other great book idea for you to write a science manual?"

"No, much better. I'm going to write a novel where neo-nazis attempt to clone Hitler from his altered genetic DNA. Their plan is then to 3-D print an army of Hitlers to spread around the world, where they will rise to power and seize control of various countries and eventually rule the world."

We share a good laugh, although I'm not sure I've actually been joking around with either of the ideas that I've floated to Jeff. In particular, I kind of liked what I wrote for the Kent Marlboro character. Switching gears, I ask Jeff: "So, what's new with you? I haven't given you much of a chance to talk."

"Plenty," he says. "I waited until I could see you face-to-face, to tell you. I plan to ask Kristina to marry me."

"Wow," I gush as I walk over to give Jeff a bro hug. Then clapping him on his shoulder and shaking his hand, I say: "Congrats. She's definitely a keeper. Good for you!"

"Thanks, pal," Jeff says with a big smile lighting his face. He seems beyond happy and I can't say that I blame him. I'm very happy for him, for my de facto brother, my best friend. But as happy as I am for him, I'm also sad. This marks a definite turning point in our relationship. I knew this was coming. But this makes it for certain. And a voice inside me is saying that I have to up my game if Jeff and I are to remain anywhere near as close as we've been until now. I need to find a person who can be my life partner. Otherwise, Jeff and I are going to grow in different directions, still brothers, but probably more distant a relationship, as if we lived on opposite coasts. I don't want that to happen.

After some congratulatory small talk, Jeff tells me about Kristina having just started a new job, working as an assistant to some rich Long Island woman. He says Kristina is not 100% sure as to what she'll be required to do, but that Kristina says the woman seems very nice and it may be a valuable working experience that could open other doors for Kristina.

A few beers, a shared joint and some sentimental reminiscing later, Jeff heads out to meet Kristina for dinner. He invites me to join them if I don't have other plans, but I do and, even if I didn't, tonight is not a night that I feel like tagging along. I need to first come to better grips with my ambivalent feelings, both wishing them all the happiness they deserve but, at the same time, a dark desire that Jeff had not met Kristina so that things between us could remain the same. I know this is unfair and selfish, but that's the still infantile part of me. I definitely need to grow up and sooner rather than later.

CHAPTER XII

It is Kristina's first week working for Charlotte. She's been given a letter of employment specifying a very generous salary, as Charlotte had promised when she first asked Kristina to become her assistant. Kristina is excited to embark on what she hopes will be an interesting and rewarding new adventure. And, if not, she has a wonderful safety net to fall back on — Jeff, whom she so dearly loves and with whom she expects she will be sharing her life forever. They've been talking about finding an apartment to move into together and he's been hinting that he soon intends to propose. Either way, with or without a proposal, she's ready for this next step in their relationship.

Kristina meets Charlotte at 10:30 a.m. Monday morning in front of Tourneau Time Machine in Manhattan to help her pick out a watch for her eldest son Wharton's birthday. "Hello, dear," Charlotte warmly says as she walks towards Kristina after having stepped out from the back seat of her chauffeur-driven car. Charlotte is dressed in a low-cut, floppy-sleeved solid yellow blouse on top of a floral-designed, high-waisted, tight mini-skirt. She looks closer to 30 years old than 50. As they walk into the store, Charlotte says: "Let's get some sales help to look at the watches. There are way too many counters to browse through. We'll waste the entire day."

"Do you have any particular type of watch in mind?" Kristina asks.

"No. Just not a Rolex. They seem so pedestrian to me — everyone walks around showing off one type of Rolex or another. Sure, they're expensive, I guess. But just too everyday for my tastes and especially for Wharton's. He likes things that are out of the ordinary."

Kristina approaches a salesman and asks him to please help Ms. Wylde select a watch for her son. The salesman and Kristina walk over to Charlotte and he asks: "May I be of service? What type of watch are you interested in?"

"I really don't know. What do you suggest that isn't a Rolex?"

"Do you have a price range in mind?"

"Not really, but I want something nice. A watch that a young man in his late twenties would be proud to wear. Something showy, yet stylish. Price is not an issue."

"Let me show you our selection of Patek Philippe and Audemars Piguet watches. I think you'll find what you're looking for there."

Charlotte and Kristina spend a half-hour browsing through a dizzying array of watches, each presented with an exaggerated gesture and pompous description by a salesman eager to earn a commission, whose annual compensation is not much more than the cost of any of the watches he's so grandly recommending. Kristina likes almost all of them and, although she knows nothing about him, thinks that Wharton would as well. There can be no bad decision here, but Charlotte cannot decide, so Kristina does.

A very pleased Charlotte ends up with a two-tone blue Patek Philippe Nautilus. Kristina gasps at the $65,000 ticket price, only to discover that the two other watches that she had been considering each cost far more. Kristina is now first truly realizing that she's entered a twilight zone of great wealth and privilege, in a galaxy far distant from the one in which she dwells.

Leaving the store, Charlotte tells Kristina: "Next stop, Freds at Barneys for lunch. It's nearby. I skipped breakfast this morning and I'm famished. We'll celebrate your first week on the job."

"Do we have a reservation or should I call and try to make one?" Kristina asks.

"Don't worry. They know me. We'll be seated right away."

They walk the few blocks from Tourneau to the restaurant and, as Charlotte predicted, are immediately seated upon arrival, with an effusive welcome from the maître d' to whom Charlotte introduces Kristina as her personal assistant. Kowtowing to Charlotte, he says to Kristina: "What a pleasure it must be for you to work with Ms. Wylde, one of our favorite customers."

After two glasses of white wine and a meal consisting of roasted shrimp with lime and ginger for appetizers and lobster salad main courses, Kristina feels sated, sluggish and sleepy. Fortunately, Charlotte feels the same and says: "I'm heading home. You can go home now, too. We've accomplished enough for today. Please be at my house tomorrow morning around 10:00 a.m. We'll spend the day there. And thanks for your help. I'm sure Wharton is going to like the watch we've selected."

The next day, Kristina arrives at the Wylde's home as instructed. Charlotte has arranged that on those days that she wants Kristina in Sands Point, Kristina is to take the train to Great Neck, where Charlotte's chauffeur will pick Kristina up and bring her to the house. Kristina is in awe of what she sees as the car pulls into a three-quarter of a mile long winding driveway. She feels like Rebecca, when the second Mrs. De Winter first arrives at Manderley. Charlotte greets her at the door, with a brief touch of Kristina's shoulder and a "Welcome to my home," and then, with a sweep of her arm: "Come. Let me show you around."

Charlotte proudly displays her house, walking Kristina through some but not all of the 23 rooms, but spending extra time showing her the tile-designed pools, rival to the one at the Ritz hotel in Paris, the private beach and the stunning vista visible not only from the beach but from different locations in the house. Charlotte makes no comment on the incredible pieces of antique and designer furniture displayed in virtually every room, nor the original oil paintings and tapestries that adorn the walls, nor the magnificent sculptures that stand under carefully placed spotlights or in front of floor to ceiling glass windows. No comment is necessary and the cumulative effect of such wealth once more threatens to overwhelm Kristina.

After this tour de force has been concluded, Charlotte takes Kristina to one of the drawing rooms, which Charlotte tells Kristina will now serve as their workspace. As Charlotte sits down with Kristina, Charlotte says: "Okay, now to work. I need to set up a number of lunches and dinners for the next two months, some with my friends and some with William's colleagues and clients. I also want to plan some shopping trips. And finally, I need to attend some meetings for charities with which I'm involved."

"How would you like to proceed?" Kristina asks.

"I'm going to give you all the names and other details you need. Then you can use my computer to get the contact information and, after you've arranged something, please enter it in my calendar. At the end of next week, walk me through every appointment and engagement you've arranged. Of course, at any time ask me any questions that you feel necessary."

"Will do. I'm anxious to get started."

"Also, I have a number of things I want to do in Manhattan the next two weeks, which I will tell you about and which I want you to go to with me."

The rest of the day is spent with Charlotte giving Kristina the information Kristina needs to arrange Charlotte's schedule. And most of the rest of the week and the following week is spent with Kristina making the calls and sending the texts and emails needed to set up the numerous appointments and engagements that Charlotte has requested be made. Kristina works from her apartment most of the time, but meets Charlotte three afternoons to accompany Charlotte on one of her shopping jaunts. Charlotte and Kristina get along very well, as you would expect in this "honeymoon" phase of their relationship, with Charlotte continuing to praise Kristina's taste and judgment. But it goes beyond that; Charlotte has an intuitive genuine fondness for Kristina.

On Friday of the second week, Kristina calls Charlotte and, in a conversation lasting almost two hours, reviews all the arrangements she has made for Charlotte for the next two months and what remains to be done. Charlotte is delighted: "You've done a great job. I can't believe how many things you've already arranged and how much wasted time you've saved me. Next week, I'm going to have you come to Sands Point and stay for dinner one night. I want William to meet you."

That night, Jeff and Kristina are at his apartment having an intimate evening together. He asks her what her feelings about the job are now that she has completed her first two weeks, and she thoughtfully responds: "So far, so good, I guess. But other than making lots of appointments for her and going shopping with her, I'm not sure yet what else she'll be wanting me to do. We seem to get along well. Hard not to, when she's constantly thanking me or relying on my judgment. But she clearly belongs to a club of privilege in which neither you nor I are or will ever be members, so there's always that gulf between us that I'm not yet comfortable with."

"Let's see how it plays out," Jeff responds. "It sounds pleasant enough for now. And certainly it's exposing you to stuff you'd probably never otherwise see."

With that, the rest of their evening is spent snuggled in front of the TV watching part of a movie and then in bed "watching" each other, while they engage in activity that does not require any watching (except if you get your kicks from viewing porn).

CHAPTER XIII

As promised, but belatedly arranged, Kristina is to meet William for the first time tonight over dinner at William and Charlotte's home. It's the end of the third week of Kristina's employment, William having been too occupied until now to find the time to be introduced to Kristina. The truth, of course, is what has been keeping him busy these many nights and days is more him "occupying" Vanessa than working at Wylde Capital, more "wild" then "Wylde" one might say, were one trying to be clever.

His time spent with Vanessa these past few weeks has not been as pleasurable as he would have liked. Although he remains enraptured by her, consumed with her sexuality, her charm and her intelligence, an alarm bell has rung, rousting William from his dream-like reverie, as Vanessa has made it increasingly clear that she is not content with the role of mistress-lover and wants a timeline for her to move into the larger part of being his wife.

William is not reacting well to this new source of pressure in his life. It's the last thing he needs, particularly now, when there are serious rumblings as to the possibility of his being nominated to be the next Secretary of the Treasury, a rare honor for a person not birthed by Goldman, Sachs or some other old-line financial behemoth, and something William would value above all else in his life and for the rest of his life. His safe harbor with Vanessa is flashing warning signs of a possible storm headed for the port.

Wrestling with this turmoil, he thinks to himself that if only he could find a way to be rid of Charlotte, in a non-scandalous way, of course, all his problems would be solved. A contested divorce would be too nuclear; it would blow up everything he'd worked so hard to attain and, most certainly, his chance to be the next Secretary of the Treasury. "If only Charlotte were dead," barks a demon voice from his dark side. In business, William is laser-focused and often ruthless as a byproduct of that, but he's not an intentionally cruel or unkind person, so that seemingly unthinkable wish for Charlotte's demise is quickly suppressed, although it will never be entirely dismissed. To the contrary, like Taylor Swift's romantic relationships, it will surface from time to time with persistent frequency and escalating intensity.

For now, the thought of her death having been banished, the only solution he can think of is the temporary patch that crossed his mind when Charlotte first told him of her intention to hire a personal assistant. He must encourage Charlotte to rely on this person as much as possible, to make her a full-time companion and not just an employee. This would be a big help in keeping Charlotte off his back, freeing his hands to spend even more time with Vanessa, in partial assurance to Vanessa that they will indeed have a future together.

It is with this in mind that William has agreed to meet Kristina at dinner tonight — he needs to assess her suitability to engage, no, enthrall Charlotte (if such a thing is still possible). The table is festively set for three, with fruit-patterned plates, hand-painted cutlery, and hand-cut, crystal wine and drinking glasses. There are two bottles of Chateau Lafite Rothschild 2010 in wine holders on the table, centering a plate of Beef Wellington. Salmon ceviche starters have been placed at each setting. A side table contains a choice of sacher torte and strawberry rhubarb pie for dessert. Charlotte has gone to great trouble (or at least her cook and maid have) to try to make this a special evening.

William greets Kristina's arrival with a warm handshake and a slight hesitation before saying: "Welcome. I've heard a great deal of positive things about you from Charlotte. I'm glad to finally meet you." The hesitation William has had in uttering his greeting is the result of his being ill-prepared for how physically striking Kristina is.

"Thank you, Mr. Wylde. A pleasure to meet you," responds Kristina in a nervous tone, almost a vocal curtsy.

"Call me William, please. Come, sit down," he says soothingly. "Would you like a cocktail before dinner?"

"No, thank you."

"Feel free. Charlotte's chauffeur is driving you home so you can imbibe without concern."

"I'm not much for hard liquor. But I do like wine."

"Then wine it is," he says, with a glance and slight gesture towards the dinner table where the Chateau Lafite Rothschild reposes. "Shall we?"

Charlotte has remained uncharacteristically quiet during this brief exchange of pleasantries, but, as William pours the wine, skittishly chatters: "Kristina is an impressive young lady. She graduated from college as a philosophy major, so she's quite intelligent, but she's been a model and has an excellent sense of fashion and design."

Handing Kristina a glass of wine, William responds: "Charlotte doesn't often lavish praise on people, no less people who work for her. I'm delighted that you and she already have such a good relationship."

"Thank you. I am too."

Terrific," William enthuses. And with a cocktail in his hand and glasses of wine in Charlotte's and Kristina's, he raises his glass in the air and toasts the two of them, saying: "Let me paraphrase a favorite movie line of mine from 'Casablanca,' a movie you're too young to have seen, Kristina, I'm sure: 'Here's to the continuation of a wonderful relationship.'"

Kristina laughs as she replies with a slight blush: "I just saw that movie the other night with my boyfriend. He's been showing me some movies that are favorites of his that he used to watch with a good friend when they both were younger."

"How old is your boyfriend? My age?" William asks, only half-jokingly (the other half being wistful thinking).

"Not old. Jeff is 29. Just a few years older than I am."

"And he watched 1940s movies when he was a teenager?"

"Yes. He and his friend, Simon, grew up together. Simon had a passion for movies, so they'd often watch video tapes or dvds of old movies rather than just play Nintendo or PlayStation games all the time."

"I don't mean to be impolite and please don't answer if my question makes you uncomfortable, but are you and Jeff in a serious relationship?"

"They are," pipes in Charlotte. "They've been together for about a year now."

"That's great," William insincerely mouths, while thinking to himself that Kristina's boyfriend may present an obstacle that will preclude Kristina from ever becoming a steadfast companion for Charlotte, no matter how much Charlotte likes her. He, not Charlotte, will be Kristina's primary focus and Charlotte requires full-time, 24/7 attention.

As they dine and engage in more small talk, William is preoccupied with his thoughts. It seems from her comments as though Kristina likes Charlotte well enough, although how much he cannot gauge, nor can he guess what effect constant exposure to Charlotte may have in eroding those good feelings. William decides that he'll just have to let this all play out and reassess things a few months down the line. As they are in the process of being served their dessert, Wharton, an unexpected visitor, appears.

Wharton, now age 28, is William and Charlotte's oldest child. He's extremely good looking, movie actor handsome, having inherited his features from Charlotte. Unfortunately, he inherited very little from William, certainly neither William's intellect nor ambition. Wharton's personality is best described as that of a playboy, but he's also a snob, a bully and quite reckless. He's the product of the family's wealth, Charlotte's personality, and William's emotional and often physical distance.

Having drunk, snorted, and slept his way through college, Wharton has continued to play at life. Even the trust fund with which Charlotte's parents have annointed him — $50 million, payable $1 million quarterly, commencing at age 21, and paid until the earlier of his death or the exhaustion of the principal amount — and his lavish townhouse (a graduation present from Charlotte and a reluctant William), are insufficient to sustain his lifestyle. Most recently, he's twice wasted away the seed money he borrowed from William to start up new business ventures with some of Wharton's college buddies. If William could disown Wharton, he would. He views him entirely as the spoiled product of Charlotte's indulgence.

Wharton wasn't always the wastrel he's become. When he was a child, Charlotte doted over him, spending a great deal of time doing fun things with him, helping him with his early grade school homework and even attending some of his after-school sports activities. But as time passed, things changed. Charlotte's time spent with Wharton substantially diminished, as it now had to be shared with the time she spent with his two younger siblings and the ever-increasing amount of time she spent on pampering herself.

By his age ten, Charlotte had all but abandoned the nurturing role she'd played in his early life, now making all too infrequent guest appearances, replaced, instead, by a nanny and tutors and an always critical, hardly ever praising, William. Nothing Wharton did ever seemed to be enough to please William, who always told him he could do better, work harder; whether it was a sport Wharton played or the grades he got in school. Without a counterbalance from Charlotte, Wharton withered under the pressure, the best of him replaced by the worst of him, distilled into what he now has become.

Since apparently no matter what he did or how hard he tried, he couldn't measure up to what his father demanded and expected of him, Wharton concluded that he would just enjoy all that he had and the hell with the rest (and his father). He was helped along this path by his mother's constant approval or apologia, as the case might be, for everything he did (or at least everything he did that she knew about) and his own near death experience at age 15, when he was in a car accident while being driven home by his friend's mother. The accident left his friend and his friend's mother dead and Wharton with an abiding fear of his own early demise. "Enjoy the day" and "live for yourself" became his mantras.

Although two self-absorbed personalities can never truly bond, Wharton retains a connection of sorts with Charlotte. At a minimum, he knows how to play Charlotte, so from time to time he confers a figurative quick peck on the cheek to remain in her good graces. Otherwise, he has no tolerance for Charlotte's insecurities and emotional demands and avoids her as much as possible consistent with his financial needs.

"Thought I'd surprise you, Mom. Hey, Dad, I didn't think you'd be home this early, it's only 7:30 P.M," Wharton says with a chesire cat-like smile. Turning towards Kristina, he continues, without a pause and with what he intends to be Don Juan-like swagger (but sounds like the offensive, demeaning pick-up line that it is): "And who are you? I'd have come much earlier if I'd known you'd be here."

"Oh, Wharton," Charlotte coquettishly responds, charmed (the only one) by him, as usual.

"Wharton. Nice to see you," William responds, with far less enthusiasm.

"This is Kristina, my assistant," Charlotte says, as Wharton bends over to kiss Charlotte's cheek.

"Your assistant? How nice. That's something new."

"Not so new. She's been working for me for three weeks now. But I haven't heard from you in a while, except for a few text messages."

"Sorry about that. I've been busy. Been caught up in a few things."

"Sit down and have some dessert with us. Are you hungry?", Charlotte asks.

"Not really. But a piece of cake would be nice."

Charlotte summons the maid to bring another plate, fork and coffee cup. Wharton proceeds to cut himself an over-sized slice of sacher torte, which he rapaciously attacks, belieing his 'not really' response of a moment ago. In between bites, he says: "I'm just here to say hello. Can't stay too long." Then, turning towards Kristina: "I'm headed back to the City in a little while. Do you live there?"

"Yes. In Brooklyn."

"How did you get here, today? Did you drive?"

"No. I was working here with your mother today. So I was picked up in Great Neck by the chauffeur."

"Great. No problem then. It will be my pleasure to drive you home. It's a great opportunity for us to talk and get to know each other a little."

A reluctant Kristina hesitatingly responds: "Thank you."

Before she can say anything more, William somewhat forcibly intercedes: "Let Harold drive her home, that's his job. I'm sure Charlotte would enjoy a little more time with you."

Trying to conceal his disappointment, Wharton responds: "Okay. I guess you're right. Anyway, since you're home and I'll be staying a little longer, I have something I want to ask you."

"Business related, I presume?"

"Yes."

After he rises from his chair, William places both hands on the back of the chair, nods at Kristina and says: "I've very much enjoyed meeting you. I don't think Charlotte could have found a better person to be her assistant. I'm going to excuse myself and talk some business with my son." Then to Wharton, he instructs: "Let's go into the other room, Wharton. Then you can spend some time with your mother after we speak."

"Okay, pops," Wharton answers. As he gets up from the table he looks at Kristina as if she were another piece of cake to be hungrily devoured, and says: "I hope to see you again soon. Indeed, I'm going to induce mother to invite me the next time you have dinner here."

As William leaves with Wharton in tow, Charlotte says to Kristina: "Wharton is just a flirt. Ignore him, dear."

"I'm not offended. To be honest, I'm used to getting unwanted attention. You must be too. When I was modeling, it was a constant bother. Too much so, I'm afraid. It almost ruined me. It's not an issue now. But it really is time for me to go home. Thank you so much for the wonderful meal. I hope I made a good impression on Mr. Wylde."

"You most definitely did. He told you so. Goodnight, now. See you 10:00 a.m. at Cartier Monday morning. I need some new jewelry to wear for some of the gala events that William has asked me to attend with him. This is still confidential, but it looks possible that William might be nominated to be the next Secretary of the Treasury, so he needs to be even more publicly visible than he already is. You would think the social media attention that he already receives from palavering with the talking heads about economic and political issues would be enough. But he says it's not."

Kristina leaves, the recipient of air kisses from Charlotte, to be driven home by Harold. Jeff will still be awake and she can fill him in on her evening at the Wyldes. Then they can turn to the more important part of the evening for both of them, the feeling of well-being that physical intimacy between lovers brings.

Voices are raised between William and Wharton, which Kristina does not hear as she leaves, but which is an all too familiar drum beat to Charlotte, one to which she's compelled to listen whenever William and Wharton are together. Already, Charlotte feels the onset of the migraine that this type of confrontation always brings. She'll try to head it off with a Percocet now rather than wait and need two pills to quell the throbbing later.

"I 'loaned' you $3 million just a year ago, for you to invest as seed money that you and your friends were using to start a business. You were supposed to pay that back over the next three years from your quarterly trust fund distributions. I haven't seen a penny back. Your business is no longer a 'business' and now you want to talk with me about borrowing even more money for a new business venture? Forget it. Go spend time with Charlotte. Pretend I didn't have the misfortune to be home when you came to surprise your mother."

"It's not my fault that the business failed. Reputation management is a big field. We were developing computer programs that we thought would leap frog us miles ahead of the existing competition. Getting bad content about a company off the front pages of search engines and replacing it with good content that we create about the company, projects to generate huge year-over-year returns. We just miscalculated the cost and time to fine-tune those computer programs and then, as we were running out of money, the cost of our acquiring customers for our product became prohibitive."

"So, another failed business venture. That's the bottom line. Why don't you find a meaningful job — you have the means that most others don't: a Harvard degree, some social position, looks, sufficient money, and connections. So network and find something meaningful to do with your life. Make something of yourself."

"Same speech. I'm sick of it. The only work I want to do is be my own boss in a business I help create. My trust fund distributions are only $4 million a year. Not enough to create a business. You're my father and a billionaire. Get off your high horse. Help me out when I need you to — without the lectures. If I lose the money, so what. You have more than enough to spare."

"You're a spoiled, arrogant brat. Your mother has done some job on you. I worked hard all my life for what I have. I didn't inherit money or grow up with money like you and your mother did. Look at Willis and Wilma. They work. They do something meaningful."

"I've had enough. Sorry I asked. You don't even know what I have in mind but you reject it and me out of hand," Wharton says as he storms out beet red in the face.

As he heads for the door, Charlotte attempts to intercept him, calling out "Wharton. Please stay. Don't leave angry. Speak to me. Maybe I can help you with whatever you want."

"Another time, Mom. I'm sorry. Dad did his usual number on me. I'll call you in the next few days and we'll arrange to meet for lunch next week or the week after. We'll talk then. Love you."

CHAPTER XIV

For most truths, the truth lies in between. Put another way, there are three sides to every story — left, right and the truth. Such is the story that is encompassed in long-term relationships. But that's not the story that exists at the beginning of those relationships. At the beginning, there is only one truth, one story. Two people meet, the physical and emotional attraction is compelling (no one cares which comes first, the chicken or the egg), and the only truth is that they are in love.

What often follows, follows here, and, accordingly, Jeff proposes to Kristina, with ring in hand and an ear-to-ear grin on his face. She eagerly accepts and this evening their sex is extra-special, more intimate and intense if that were even possible.

It has been two months since Kristina had dinner at the Wylde house with William and Charlotte. And it's about the same amount of time that Kristina and Jeff have been living together in Jeff's now somewhat cramped Brooklyn apartment, with a view of the world-renowned Greenwood Cemetery (not a view to be cherished by any but the very young).

The apartment was big enough for Jeff, but with Kristina living with him, that has changed; they have just started the process of looking for an affordable larger apartment, one with more closets so as to better house Kristina's growing wardrobe, an unexpected perk provided by Charlotte as part of Kristina's employment. It seems that almost every week during the three months that she has been working for Charlotte,

Kristina has come home with more clothes that Charlotte has insisted (over Kristina's sincere protestations) on buying for her when Kristina accompanies Charlotte on one of Charlotte's full-day shopping binges.

Jeff has had occasion to meet both Charlotte and her husband. He's spoken with Charlotte several times in the course of Charlotte picking up or dropping off Kristina at their apartment. It's clear from these conversations (and from what Kristina has told him) that Charlotte has a deep affection for Kristina and has come to rely on her very much. It's also clear to Jeff that Charlotte is snobbish, self-centered, and incapable or, at a minimum, not used to, making decisions or doing much without someone's help.

His impressions of Charlotte were crystalized in a recent telephone conversation with her on a Saturday morning. "Hi. Is this Jeff? May I speak to Kristina, please?" Charlotte asked somewhat breathlessly.

"Sorry, Charlotte. She's not home. Try her on her cell," he replied, by now recognizing Charlotte's voice.

"I have, but she doesn't answer. Where can she be? I need her help on something rather important."

"She may be on the subway. Just text her or leave her a message. I'm sure she'll call you back soon."

"Would you do that for me, please? I'm late for my beauty parlor appointment. I need to get rinsed and styled before William and I go out to a fund raising event tonight. William told me we'll be sitting at Jamie Dimon's table, so I have to look my best."

"You always look great, Charlotte. I wouldn't worry about that."

"Why thank you, dear. You're so kind. But a woman my age, you know, must devote some of her time to doing the things that are necessary to maintain her appearance."

"I won't keep you. I'll text Kristina to call you."

"Thank you. Please tell her it's urgent. I need her help in deciding what dress and jewelry I should wear tonight, and William's not home. I'm meeting him in Manhattan at the dinner."

"Will do," Jeff responded, thinking to himself, as he ended the call, does she really need Kristina to pick out what to wear?

Jeff has only spoken once to Mr. Wylde and that was when Jeff and Kristina were invited to join William and Charlotte for a drink at the Harvard Club in Manhattan a month ago. Jeff had seen William interviewed on some CNN program that Kristina had been watching (at Charlotte's suggestion — "Dear, William's on TV again this evening. I'm sure you will want to watch the program with Jeff.") and William was quite impressive, although Jeff was not all that certain he fully understood what Mr. Wylde was saying. But Jeff had never talked to William until they met at the Harvard Club.

After obligatory pleasantries and some casual conversation, and with a second round of drinks for William and Jeff in hand, William took Jeff aside and said: "I understand that you and Kristina have been living together for a month now. Congratulations. You've got a wonderful young woman in her."

"Thank you. I know. I'm a very lucky guy."

"Charlotte has come to rely on her a great deal and is very fond of her. We wish you both the best."

"Thanks."

"You told us earlier tonight about your background growing up and your job. You seem a bright and personable person, so I assume from talking with you that you don't intend to sell cars forever."

"I make decent money doing it and I don't dislike being a salesman. I enjoy talking with all different kinds of people," Jeff responded, defensively and somewhat offended.

Picking up on Jeff's response, William replied: "I understand. It's a good job in many ways. I only mean to say that I think that you should consider other possibilities, something that might be more of a challenge to you and provide an even greater financial reward. If I can be of any help in that regard, please don't hesitate to let me know."

"I'm open to exploring other opportunities, I just haven't figured out what as yet. I'm no genius, but I do have a valuable person-to-person skill set and I'm willing to work hard."

"Good to hear. We have to head out now to some charity function that I was roped into co-sponsoring, but I'm sure I'll see you again soon. It was a pleasure to meet you."

They all said their goodnights to each other and departed the Harvard Club, the Wyldes off to their social function and Jeff and Kristina to a movie, despite being grossly over-dressed for it.

As they strolled toward the Regal Cinemas on 42nd Street, Jeff feeling the loosening effects of a little too much drink with too little food, they stopped to eat a slice of pizza, and Kristina, not usually prone to gossip, did: "William was quite charming tonight and seems to be a lovely man on the occasions I've spoken with him. But I don't know if there's something gone wrong between him and Charlotte. For the past few weeks, he's been spending most of the weeknights sleeping at their Park Avenue apartment."

"Probably some big deal he's working on. I agree that he's charming, also very impressive. But I found him a bit overwhelming. He kind of turned his nose up at my being a car salesman."

"Well, I love my car salesman very much. And he can do that forever if he chooses to."

"Thanks, babe. Love you too. And you can continue to be Charlotte's personal assistant as long as you want, if that's what you want to do. 'Tit for tat,' I like to say."

"Oooh. I like it when you talk dirty to me."

"Anything that makes you happy, my love. I aim to please."

"Speaking of making someone happy, it seems that I may be the only one that's making Charlotte happy these days. Not only is

William away all week, but she rarely sees or speaks with her children and, when she does, most often she's unhappy afterwards."

"Well, that's not your problem, it's hers. All you can do is do your job as best you can."

"It's not that simple. Charlotte sometimes complains to me about them and I feel very sorry for her. I like her. She's insecure, pampered and very needy, but there's a kind side to her. She seems to care very much about her children's well-being and is always kind to me. She treats me almost as a friend, or even in her eyes another child."

"That's good then. Maybe that explains her generosity towards you, her buying you all that stuff that she wants you to have and knows that you can't afford. But you've gotten me curious. What has Charlotte said to you about the Wylde progeny? Give me the down and dirty."

"She has complained that Wharton only calls or comes around when he needs something. Willis, the second child, is a doctor and, although Charlotte is proud of him, she dislikes his wife, whom she views as a social climber. I'm not sure why, but she once in anger said to me about Willis' wife, after a telephone call with her: 'Just like her kind. Out for money and position, that's all she cares about. Not my Willis.' And Wilma, the youngest child, I met her once. Seems very lovely. Works in cancer research. But she lives with a woman, Bess, that Charlotte despises, tells me she's a low-life drug peddler who's dragging Wilma down."

"Wow. That sounds like quite a crew. A lot of toxicity. I hope it doesn't come in on you and poison the job."

"Doubt that it will. I can take care of myself, thank you very much."

"I know you can. But I prefer it when we take care of each other — in the way we like best. So why waste the rest of the evening with a movie?"

Rhetorical question, so no answer needed. Just between the sheets activity. A more rewarding expenditure of their energy. A most happy ending to the evening that started with the Wyldes at the Harvard Club.

And here they are, one month later, engaged to be married and absorbed by each other, enjoying the prospect of the happy times they expect their life together will bring. The start of their story has no in-between. But in time that will come, as it always does. It's always just a matter of time.

CHAPTER XV

The sun is setting as Donna arrives at her sister's Sands Point mansion. They rarely speak, no less have sisterly tete-a-tetes. That they have little in common except for having been conceived and birthed by the same parents, has been readily apparent to Donna since at least her early tweens. But Charlotte has extended an unexpected invitation to dinner: "Donna, it's Charlotte. Remember me? Your sister. You never call or text so I'm calling you. I'm not sure why I bother, but I guess it's noblesse oblige. Only joking, dear. So come to dinner here. 7:00 p.m. this Wednesday," is the message Charlotte left.

Donna texted her acceptance, but cannot fully figure out why. Maybe, at best, a curiosity on her part to see what lies beneath the surface of Charlotte's invitation (there must be some underlying motive, there always is). Or at worst, plain and simply, another example of Donna's life-long submissiveness to Charlotte — "whatever Charlotte wants, Charlotte gets, and little Donna, little Charlotte wants you."

With little pomp but a lot of suspected circumstance, Donna arrives and, after an obligatory hug and air kisses from Charlotte, they nestle in the sun room, where drinks are served to the backdrop of a beautiful sunset. On the rare family occasion that they get together, Donna steels herself with a Valium an hour or so before. Today, for some reason, she has not.

"Isn't this just lovely?", Charlotte cries out, sweeping her arms up in front of her as she emphatically gestures. "What a beautiful time of day and a lovely view over the water."

"Yes, it is," Donna meekly replies.

"Here's to us, the Houghton sisters. All the best," Charlotte proclaims as she raises a glass of champagne in a grandiose toast.

Donna nods her acknowledgement of the toast as she tips her glass and sips, thinking uncomfortably to herself that this is Charlotte playing to an audience of one. Unfortunately, me. Then, with perfect timing (how Charlotte has orchestrated this precise moment Donna cannot figure out), a maid rolls in with an art deco serving cart containing several small hand-lacquered trays of hors d'oeuvres, a display that wouldn't be out of place in a royal palace.

As Donna vociferously attacks the hors d'oeuvres in an effort to calm her nerves, and Charlotte starts on a second glass of champagne, Charlotte maintains the almost one-sided conversation, condescendingly asking: "How are you? Are you seeing anyone that I should know about?"

"No. There's no one special in my life right now. Certainly no one worth talking about."

"Do you still like teaching? I guess the one good thing about your job is that you have a lot of spare time to travel or do other things. Frankly, I never understood why you decided to teach in the first place. And in the Bronx. To those types of kids. But you always were a do-gooder, I guess," says Charlotte, rambling on lest an awkward silence descend, but without regard to the unthoughtful, unkind nature of her comments.

With her mouth still partially full with an unfinished duck paté toast point, Donna replies, taking a deep breath and with a half sigh: "I still like it very much. I know you don't understand why, but I do."

Pretty much ignoring Donna's response, Charlotte prattles on: "I don't know how you can teach those unfortunate children. You're white and privileged. You're the enemy. Aren't you afraid?"

"No, I'm not. And I am quite able to effectively teach them."

"Well, at least you're not teaching in college. I can't understand what's going on there. I keep reading about the need for a 'safe space' and a prevailing 'rape culture.' Being in college today sounds like serving in a war zone."

"The idea of needing a 'safe space' at college is political correctness at its absurd worst," Donna quickly replies, happy to be able to turn the conversation towards something less personal than Charlotte's ill-informed view of Donna's life and the children she teaches. "It's become a real problem that college students only want to listen to others who share the same opinion on a topic as they do. It's in large part a function of social media, where it's become easy to just be fed and fueled by like-minded people. But college, at least, should be an environment where all opinions on a topic are heard, not just the opinions a particular group wants to hear."

"You sound very professorial. Maybe I'm wrong and you should be teaching at college," jokes Charlotte. "But then again, you would have to cope with the constant harangues from students, both female and male, about 'rape culture' issues. Who would want to put up with that nonsense?"

"It's not nonsense," Donna responds. "It's a very serious issue, not just in college but in the world outside. Read the news. The 'casting couch' mentality has to be permanently discarded."

"Oh, come on," Charlotte replies. "Get real. From the beginning of time, women have relied on good looks and sex to get what they want — a husband, money, a career. That's never going to change; it's been genetically engineered since Adam and Eve."

"You've always relied on your looks but that doesn't mean women who don't want to should be subjected to doing the things that you're

STEPHEN M. RATHKOPF

willing to do to get what they want. The formula for anyone, male or female, should be intelligence and effort, not good looks and sex. Countless men have been outed for using their positions of power to compel women to provide sex in exchange for advancement of one kind or another."

"But that's a fair bargain. Most of the women in the news weren't actually raped, No physical force was used to bring them to the hotel room or keep them there, or to hold them down on the couch. That's rape. Anything less than use of physical force or a rape drug is nothing more than a contract: an offer and an acceptance of the offer."

"You're talking bullshit," Donna explodes, in a deep masculine-sounding voice. "You may see nothing wrong with fucking whomever you want to get whatever you want, but the rest of us, those that work to accomplish something, do."

"Okay, calm down, Donna," a flustered Charlotte replies, waving a hand of surrender in the air. "I didn't mean to get you so angry. I never heard you speak in such a harsh tone of voice before. It's not like you."

There's a welcome pause in the conversation (break in the battle, might be a better description) as Donna stands up and excuses herself, saying she needs to use the bathroom. A few minutes later, Donna returns, her composure regained. Charlotte and Donna have a salad, polish off the hors d'oeuvres and continue to talk, mostly about Charlotte's family and her assistant, Kristina.

Donna says: "I'm sorry that you're having issues with the children. I've been meaning to call them myself, just to say hello and catch up. But I'm glad you like this girl, Kristina, so much."

"She's proven to be a gem. She's invaluable. William has agreed for me to ask her to move in here with her fiancé. I've met him several times and he seems a nice young man. We'll give them the two rooms in the east wing of the house."

Donna should be surprised at this, but isn't. Even though as far as Donna can see Charlotte has no real need for an assistant in the first place, every queen needs her court and now Queen Charlotte the First shall have a lady-in-waiting and a knight to call her own.

"Good for you," Donna says, not really meaning it, as she stands and prepares to leave, happy to be heading back to the emotional safety of her home.

"Before you go, I have a favor to ask," Charlotte says.

Donna is on instant alert, waiting for the boom to be lowered. She's not escaped without the true purpose of this evening's invitation being revealed. "Yes," she suspiciously inquires. "What is it?"

"I think you'll really enjoy doing this and you certainly have the spare time. I've been selected to be chairwoman of the annual gala fundraising dinner for the Long Island Children's Museum. Obviously, given my other social commitments, I don't have the time to do all the organizing this will require, but you do, and it's a charity that benefits children. So there you have it. Perfect for you. You love kids and this is for their benefit. Please agree. I'll use my and William's connections to get potential donors to attend but need your elbow grease to handle all the details and coordination needed to make the gala a success."

Donna is beside herself. Completely taken aback. The nerve of Charlotte, she thinks. The unmitigated gall. Typical Charlotte. Charlotte will sparkle at the event, shining in the limelight because of the spectacular evening that Charlotte has ostensibly arranged, while Donna will remain hidden in the background, her time, effort, and abilities applauded by no one. The story of Donna's life whenever she is involved with Charlotte, dancing like a puppet on a string to the tune of "Me and My Shadow."

For a second time this evening, Donna erupts, not able to restrain herself. This time far more forcibly than before (indeed, from ever before). In a chilling, deep-throated Mr. Hyde-like voice, she wags her finger at Charlotte and screams: "No. Not me. Not ever again. I will not let you abuse me like this. No more," as she moves close, almost face to face, nose to nose, with Charlotte.

Charlotte is dumbfounded and, while stepping quickly backwards, inveighs: "Donna. You're scaring me. Keep back. What's going on with you?"

Donna doesn't answer, but, instead, muttering to herself under her breath, turns away from Charlotte and rushes towards the door and, with a red face and angry glare, growls as she storms out: "I've no interest in being your servant. You have Kristina for that. Leave me the fuck alone or you'll be sorry."

CHAPTER XVI

What if you were poor and were offered $50 million to do something that you are told would result in your going to prison for three years of your life — easy answer, "yes." No matter what you were asked to do short of murder, rape, incest, pedophilia or some other gruesome act. But what if it was the last three years of your life? Different answer, correct? So everything is relative, isn't it?

That is what I think to say, but don't, to Jeff and Kristina after they have enthusiastically told me their "good news" — they are moving into the Wylde's Sands Point mansion, where they will occupy two rooms in one of the wings of the house: a master bedroom with en suite bathroom and an adjoining room that they can use as a living room. They'll also have use of the kitchen located in that wing.

"I can't believe how lucky we are," gushes Kristina. "Charlotte said that if Jeff and I live in their house, it will benefit all of us. Instead of Jeff and I moving into a larger apartment together and having to pay rent, we can save that money if we live with them. Their house is spacious enough that we won't be in their way. And she said that by my not commuting to and from her home, there'll be more time for me to be with her."

"The house is enormous," Jeff excitedly, almost gloatingly, chimes in. "You should see it, Simon. A large central section and an east and west wing. 23 rooms in all. An indoor/outdoor pool and a private beach. Not too shabby, old buddy."

"Sounds like maybe I should rent out my whole house and move in there too," I reply with a tinge of envy. "They probably wouldn't notice."

"Or if they did, they might think you were just a handyman that someone had hired to work there that day," Jeff jokingly retorts. "Yeah, perfect. Thinking you to be a handyman. The way the world should be. I move up to a world of riches and you remain with the hoi polloi of our youth."

"Thanks a lot. Some friend you've turned out to be. I'm definitely going to write you into my next book in a very noticeable way and then have the pleasure of killing you off in the most macabre manner that I can concoct."

"I'll enjoy reading your book while munching on my caviar and eating foie gras paté."

"Maybe that's the way I'll kill you off. Choking to death on a caviar-filled, poisoned cracker."

Kristina interrupts our boyish banter, saying: "Enough, guys. I'm hungry. Let's go out and celebrate."

As we leave, I don't express the reservation I have to all this that gnaws in the back of my mind. On the one hand, admittedly some-what coveting their situation (not to mention jealous of their real good fortune — each having found their partner for life), but, on the other, thinking that living in a billionaire's home with my fiance's employer might become too costly an intrusion on my privacy no matter how much money it enables me to save.

At dinner, after we've moved on to topics other than the Wyldes, I realize that I don't really know what Kristina does working for Charlotte Wylde, other than accompany her on shopping trips and help her pick out stuff. So, writer that I am, with my complete command of the English language, I cleverly choose my words (not), and belatedly inquire: "Kristina, what do you do for Ms. Wylde other than help her pick stuff out when she shops?"

Of course, what I say comes out wrong and sounds condemnatory, and Kristina responds as you might imagine: "If I wasn't in such a good mood tonight and didn't like you so much, I might be insulted by your question. I've come to do a lot of different things for Charlotte over these past few months, not just accompany her on shopping trips. I manage her extremely busy social calendar. I go with her to take photographs of scenes that she says she may want to paint. And I'm doing a lot of historical research for a memoir she's thinking of writing about growing up with her prominent parents."

"My apologies. I didn't mean to get your hackles up. I should have asked differently. It's just that any time you've talked about the job in my presence, it's pretty much only been about going with Charlotte to one fabulous place or another. To be honest, I wondered why she needed you to move in with her for you to do that."

"Short answer, she likes me, has come to rely on me and she wants to help Jeff and me out. I've become her companion, not just her employee. By the way, managing her schedule is a real challenge. She has to attend a lot of functions with her husband, I have to schedule charity stuff she's involved in, lunches with friends and family, then she has doctor appointments, gym, tennis lessons, and on and on. And she wants me to accompany her almost everywhere she goes if she isn't going with William or meeting with one of her children. So far, it's been a fairly rewarding job — I get to meet lots of well-connected, wealthy people, and do things I would otherwise never have a chance to do,"

"In any event," Jeff says, "we're moving in with a one-year time frame in mind. Between what we both earn and the $30,000-$40,000 or so we'll save in not paying rent or utilities for a year, we should be well on our way towards a down payment on a condo apartment somewhere."

"A man with a plan. Sounds like a good one, the way you just put it. And based on what Kristina just said, her job sounds a lot more exciting than my sitting alone day after day in the house I grew up in while I work on writing my next book."

"Hey," Jeff responds, "You're doing A-okay. Don't cry for me, Simonina. Your current book, 'A Guileless Death,' has gotten decent reviews and you told me that it's selling pretty well. I even saw it prominently displayed in the window of that new mystery bookstore you told me about, 'Sherlock's Tomes.'"

"I wasn't complaining, just babbling a bit. Yeah, I'm encouraged by all that. I may be working myself into a real career. At least I hope so,"

As we get ready to leave the restaurant, Jeff signals for the check and says: "This one's on us. It's our celebration and so it's our treat. We're moving in next week. I'll text you the address."

As we walk out, I say to Jeff: "On a sad note, you're leaving Brooklyn for that foreign and far off land, Sands Point. I'll miss you. It'll be tougher to get together, given traffic and how far out on Long Island that Sands Point is."

Jeff responds with a slight laugh: "True, in part. But I guess we forgot to mention that Charlotte promised us free use of her chauffeur to take us to and from the City whenever she's not needing him. So continuing to get together as often as we like won't really be all that difficult."

"Good news," I happily respond. "Love you guys." On that note, Kristina kisses me good night and our evening ends. It's still somewhat early, so I head to "Udderly Yours," an Atlantic Avenue bar several blocks from my house, which inexplicably has become one of the Brooklyn "in-crowd's" haunts because of the paintings of cows in funny clothes that adorn the brick to brick walls and the large cow-shaped glasses in which their very creative alcoholic libations are sold. I've been occasionally seeing Patricia Connelly, the blond from the gym, but, as always, am on the hunt for bigger and better game. When will I grow up? Jeff has. It has to be my time soon.

CHAPTER XVII

Jeff and Kristina have been very happy this first month of living in Sands Point with the Wyldes. Kristina and Charlotte have become stuck-together-like-glue companions, with nascent overtones of a mother-daughter relationship. On those occasions when William has been home, mostly on the weekends, William has spent time talking with Kristina and Jeff, but particularly Jeff. Jeff has come both to respect and like William who, despite all his wealth and having the command presence of an Army general, has certain down-to-earth qualities that soften his edges.

Kristina and Jeff have more than adequate freedom despite living with the Wyldes and far more luxury than they would have if they didn't. Their spacious east wing accommodations are far from where Charlotte and William dwell and, on the nights they spend at home, they seldom see Charlotte. On the nights they go out, Charlotte's chauffeur takes them if they want him to, but they are self-conscious about using him too often, lest they lose all their friends. Showing up at a Brooklyn restaurant, bar or movie theatre in a chauffeur-driven Lincoln Continental is not the best way to endear yourself to your still struggling to get along millennial playmates.

The one exception to their reluctance to flaunt their new-found fortuity is where Simon is concerned. Jeff derives special pleasure in teasing Simon and Simon enjoys it almost as much as if the chauffeur, the Sands Point mansion and Kristina were his. Best friends forever are best friends forever, and only wish each other the best of everything forever.

"Hey, Simon. Want a ride?" Jeff loudly calls out as he rolls down the back passenger window and the chauffeur slowly pulls the car over to the curb where I'm waiting outside my house.

"Slumming again?" I respond. "So nice to see someone as successful as you is still willing to visit the old neighborhood and spend time with old friends. Oh right, it's Kristina that's responsible for all your prosperity. Your only success is in somehow having convinced her to marry you."

Jeff opens the door and I climb into the back seat, plopping down next to Jeff. "Where's Kristina?" I ask. This is her car, not yours. You're just her escort, the court jester."

"Ha, ha, ha. No wonder you're so successful as a writer. You have quite a way with words."

"Kidding aside, where is she? We'll be late for the theatre. I don't want to miss any of the show."

"She and Charlotte are walking along the Brooklyn Heights promenade. As you know, Charlotte is considering trying her hand at oil painting and Kristina is taking some scenic photographs for Charlotte to paint. We're headed there to pick them up and then into Manhattan."

"I've really wanted to see 'Hamilton.' I can't believe Kristina got Charlotte to invite me to join you. $800 per ticket is crazy."

"Charlotte can well afford it. And where Kristina is concerned, Charlotte continues to want to please her. Kristina hardly ever takes advantage, almost never asks for anything. But when Charlotte told Kristina she was going to take us to see 'Hamilton,' Kristina asked if you could come as well and said that we would pay for your ticket. Charlotte replied 'Nonsense. If you want your friend to join us, I'm happy to pay for another ticket.' That's the good side of Charlotte."

"Has Charlotte shown a bad side, now that you've been living there awhile?"

"Not really. But according to Kristina, now that we're living there, Charlotte is confiding in her more frequently and Kristina is becoming a little uncomfortable with Charlotte airing out her dirty laundry."

"Oh, that sounds intriguing and very soapy. Could be good book material for me. What kind of skeletons in her closet has the very upper crust Charlotte revealed?"

"Kristina doesn't go into any great detail with me, but it involves Charlotte's less than perfect relationships with William and their children. I've previously told you as much as I know. All in all, Kristina likes the job a great deal. I think she won't admit it, but being constantly exposed to the affluence in which the Wyldes bask and the trickle-down benefits it bestows on us, is a big factor in her enjoyment in being Charlotte's assistant. Speaking for me, it's an A+ job as far as what it is enabling us to do."

"I'm seeing 'Hamilton' tonight as a result and that's about as trickle-down an effect as trickle-down can be. Proves President Reagan was right."

As we drive to pick up Charlotte and Kristina, I ask Jeff more questions about living with the Wyldes, but Jeff has little more to add except to tell me about a very recent conversation he had with William. Last weekend, over a drink while Kristina was still dressing to leave with Jeff to meet some friends, William asked Jeff about Jeff's job, but not in the usual casual, not really interested way that older people often ask their adult children's friends. Jeff tells me: "William raised the topic again of how I liked selling cars. I told him that the money from salary and sales commissions was decent for someone my age who lacks a masters or other post-graduate degree and that I enjoyed the constant person-to-person communication that's the main part of my job."

"So then, what?" I impatiently interrupt, as the car approaches the end point of the Heights promenade where we're to pick up Charlotte and Kristina.

"Hang on," Jeff responds. "William then asked me: 'Do you have any aspirations toward doing something else, something even more rewarding for you, both financially and personally, in the future?' As I did when we first met, I told him: 'Sure, I've been thinking about it a lot, ever since I first decided to propose to Kristina. We don't plan on living with you and Charlotte indefinitely, and we want a family sooner rather than later, so I need to find something with more money and better long-term viability.'

"He then said: 'You know, opportunity is all around you here, in this environment. For example, I'm an available resource you haven't yet tapped. I mentioned that to you the first time I met you, at the Harvard Club. You should think about how I might help you.'

"Before I can respond, Kristina belatedly makes her grand entrance and, as we are already running late, I have to rush out with only a lame 'thanks' in response."

To this recantation, I emphatically respond, with more than a little bit of urgency in my tone: "Opportunity knocks, dude. You've a chance at a big ask-and-get. Act on it."

"I know. I've discussed what William said to me with Kristina more than once already this week and we've come up with nothing for me to suggest to him so far. I'd appreciate your input. Let's find time for the two of us to talk this coming week. And don't suggest I be made a partner in Wylde Capital. This is a for real conversation that needs to lead to something that might make sense for me and is not absurd to William."

"I know. Believe me, I will take this very seriously. But have you spoken to your mom about it? What does she suggest?"

"No. I feel it's too early for me to discuss it with her. She has too high an opinion of my abilities. Also, I sense a bit of resentment on her part with regard to Charlotte, whom she's never met and only talked to a few times, but seems to dislike. I'm not sure why,"

"What has Barbara said that leads you to that conclusion?"

"Nothing directly critical. Just an occasional 'well, she can afford it' when Kristina tells her about something Charlotte has bought for her. Or when I told her how great it was that we would be living in the Wylde's Sands Point home, she commented: 'Money gets what money wants,' at the same time as saying how happy she was for us."

As I'm about to respond, the car stops, Charlotte and Kristina get in and the topic of a Wylde-assisted new career for Jeff is tabled for the rest of the evening. (Unbeknownst to Jeff, William was more ingenious than magnanimous in what he offered to Jeff — he wants to keep Kristina close to Charlotte for as long as possible, so he can be freer to spend his time with Vanessa. Tying Jeff to the Wyldes should be a big help in achieving that goal.)

"Thank you so much for including me this evening," I say to Charlotte as soon as she settles in her seat. "I very much appreciate it."

"My pleasure," she responds. "Kristina has told me of your close friendship with Jeff since you were children and I take this as an opportunity for us to get to know each other a little. Now that Kristina is living with me, I'm sure we will see each other more often, certainly when you come to visit Jeff at my house."

Our drive to the theatre is replete with small talk, idle chatter about podcasts concerning some possibly innocent person who has been wrongfully imprisoned, the best Instagram "likes," the latest celebrity pregnancy, and some funny memes, catfishes and trolls, all of which is a foreign language to Charlotte, one in which she has taken very few lessons, certainly nowhere enough to be remotely fluent.

As anticipated, we all love 'Hamilton,' although Charlotte complains that she couldn't understand the hip hop lyrics during the first 10-15 minutes of the show. I thank Charlotte again, as I head for the subway home to Brooklyn while Charlotte, Kristina and Jeff wait for the chauffeur to pick them up to take them home to Long Island.

"Your friend, Simon, seems very nice," Charlotte says to Jeff and Kristina as Simon walks away. "I'm glad he joined us. Please feel free to invite him to visit you at our home as often as you want. If you need Harold to pick him up or bring him back, he's available for that if I don't need him."

"As usual, we very much appreciate your offer. You've been nothing but kind and generous to us," Kristina gratefully and sincerely responds. Charlotte nods her head in brief acknowledgement of Kristina's gratitude, a gesture an observer might think to be almost imperial in nature.

CHAPTER XVIII

Barbara Muss can't believe what she's hearing. How stupid and reckless can her husband of 33 years be? That's now a rhetorical question, unfortunately, because the only current answer is an emphatic "plenty!" After learning what he's done, has she ever truly known him?, she asks herself, afraid to say it aloud.

She's long come to accept that Dan's ego requires her to play second fiddle to his instrument, something she's been willing to pretend to do, a fair exchange for the peace and harmony necessary for her to maintain a nurturing home for Jeff, the true center of her universe. Even with Jeff out of the house and living with Kristina in Long Island, old habits die hard, but she's been getting ready to kill this one off and the time to do so may be now.

"How could you do this? If it's discovered, we'll be destroyed. All of us, not just you," she plaintively pleads, choking back tears of anger and frustration. "Stealing from your employer. I can't believe it," she shouts. "How could you?"

"Take it easy, Barb. It will all work out," he sheepishly responds, very unlike himself. Tall, broad-shouldered, in still physically good condition, with a thick head of blond hair, and square-jawed solid features, like the face of a boxer who has never been hard hit, quick to temper, particularly after he drinks too much, Daniel Muss is not taken to soft words and almost never to apologizing. Not for anything.

Although never physically abusive, he's often verbally abrasive, to the point that persons of lesser substance than Barbara and Jeff might buckle. Barbara is yin to Dan's yang, but formidable and demanding in her own way. She met Dan in college, both of them athletes on their college's teams, he on the football team and she on the tennis team. She was a talented student and a whiz at chess; he was an academically challenged student with a talent for winning at his fraternity's nightly poker games.

They fell in love, pledged their troth, and then his National Guard service as a medic led to him being activated for the Gulf War. He was patriotically proud to serve but never shipped overseas, Desert Storm over almost before it began. Jeff was born soon after, his conception hastened by the prospect of Dan and Barbara's anticipated separation.

Barbara is a mistress of manipulation, skills birthed in the cauldron of her own childhood home and honed by her prowess at tennis and chess and her job with Children's Services. Without realizing it, she follows many of the principles espoused in Sun Tzu's "The Art of War." Dan can bellow and bluster, but he rarely blows the house down. Barbara twists and turns with the wind and eventually ends up where she intended.

As with most people, there's a dark and secretive side to Barbara. Date raped her senior year in high school, she's never revealed this to anyone. Just absorbed the blow and moved on, but not until first taking a baseball bat to her former date's kneecap and daring him to tell anyone the truth about how his injury was incurred. And before she met Dan, poker, not just chess, was her game. She made quite a bit of money playing with the frat boys her first two years of college. Once she and Dan started to date, she decided she'd rather have Dan than the money she was winning, so she professed to be bored with the game and smartly left the poker playing (and bragging rights) to Dan.

As the primary object of her affection and attention from the day he was born, Jeff has been the beneficiary of Barbara's deft maneuverings and all that Barbara has to bestow, which is quite a lot, given that, for the most part, she's a loving individual, very perceptive and a person concerned about doing the right thing. To a great degree, Barbara has pushed Dan to the sidelines of Jeff's life, without either Dan or Jeff (or even herself) realizing it. And all three of them have been to the better for it. However, tonight is not a night for the usual, not an evening for Barbara to bob and weave, to pretend deference while she plots her course. Tonight is a night for confrontation.

Dan continues, still in apologetic retreat from Barbara's wrath: "I only told you because it's been weighing heavily on me these past few weeks and I didn't want to keep it a secret from you any longer."

"I appreciate that," she responds uncurling her tightly-closed fists, as she starts to regain some emotional balance. "But I wish you'd never told me. Whatever possessed you to do this in the first place? You've earned good money as a senior property manager for XRX real estate. With my salary and yours, we've gotten by well enough."

Gaining back some confidence, he explains: "Our retirement money is not growing quickly enough. We won't be able to live the way I want to with just that and social security when we want to retire. So I took a chance to fix that for us. The idea of an unauthorized documentary about the secret lives of famous TV game show hosts sounded great. Still does. As the last $100,000 invested needed to finish the film, I'll get back at leave five times my money in just a few months, once Netflix or some other streaming service buys the documentary. That's why I altered the rent and expense records for the properties I'm managing. There'll be no problem putting the money back and correcting the records before anyone knows what I've done. I did it just after the company closed its fiscal year and the annual audit of the company's books for the new fiscal year is not for another 15 months."

Barbara lets out a big sigh, not of relief but of angst. She's having a hard time processing what Dan has done. By unburdening himself, he's weighted her down, much as a philandering husband does when he decides to come clean to his wife to salve his conscience. This is worse. She'll live in dread until the money is repaid, and what if something goes wrong? She has to find a way to push that from her mind.

"My life is crumbling all around me," Barbara cries out despairingly, once again fighting back tears.

"I regret what I did, but as I just explained, it will all work out and our future will be secured. Your life will be fine. It's not crumbling around you."

"You don't understand. It's not just this terrible thing you did. It's Jeff and Kristina too. We're losing them. Charlotte Wylde has latched onto them and now is taking them away from us. I hardly see them anymore or even hear from them since they moved to Sands Point. And do you see some of the things that Charlotte has bought Kristina? We can't compete with that type of money."

Dan doesn't know what to say to this unexpected outburst. He's not felt there was anything different in his relationship with Jeff and Kristina post-Charlotte. Then again, his relationship with them is as it was when Jeff was a boy living at home: not indifferent, certainly he loved Jeff, but he never made Jeff's problems his responsibility to resolve or mitigate, that was a role co-opted by Barbara.

Dan for a second time tonight attempts to placate Barbara, this time with regard to her just expressed feelings about Charlotte's effect on Barbara's relationship with Jeff and Kristina: "I think you may be over-reacting to the situation. The kids won't be living there forever. It's temporary. The Wyldes have invited us to dinner at their house this weekend and, once we spend the evening with them, I think you may feel differently."

Days later, Dan and Barbara are driving out to Sands Point for dinner with Jeff, Kristina and the Wyldes. Barbara has splurged on a bottle of Johnny Walker Blue Label as a dinner gift for the Wyldes. The

$180 she's spent is way beyond the Muss house-visiting budget, but she wants to impress the Wyldes.

Even on a Saturday night, traffic is bad and they arrive a half-hour late, in truth more attributable to the time it took Barbara to decide on what she wanted to wear than to the crush of traffic. Barbara has managed to push Dan's perfidy to the corner of her mind and this evening her focus is on getting a deeper understanding of what she's contending with as regards Charlotte and what she needs to do to prevent any further weakening in her relationship with Jeff and Kristina.

Dan and Barbara are warmly greeted at the door by Charlotte, who kisses both of Barbara's cheeks and then cups Dan's hand in a lingering, soft handshake. As Charlotte walks them towards the sitting room where William and cocktails await, she says: "Jeff and Kristina will join us for dinner later. I thought it would be nice if the four of us first get acquainted a bit before they come over."

"That's a wonderful idea. We've heard so many good things about you from the children, that we've been looking forward very much to meeting you and your husband," Barbara politely but distractedly responds, as she surreptitiously glances at the paintings, sculptures and ornate furniture that dot the hallways and rooms they are passing by. If the opulence of her surroundings is not off-putting enough to Barbara, there's always the designer ensemble that Charlotte is wearing to make Barbara feel ill at ease.

They enter the sitting room (which to Barbara seems to have been a quarter mile from the entrance to the house) and after introductions to William are made, the cocktails are served, and some preliminary small talk (the weather, the drive out, how long married, etc.) is finished, the Wyldes and the Musses try to find common ground beyond Jeff and Kristina. That's difficult, given the very different worlds they inhabit.

"I understand that you work with disadvantaged minority families and try to protect the unfortunate children of those families from being harmed," Charlotte says to Barbara, intending to be complimentary, but sounding racist and condescending instead.

"The children and families I deal with are not all minority. With some of the families, the only disadvantage the children have is an abusive parent," Barbara somewhat heatedly replies, offput by Charlotte's comment.

"Of course. I know that. I was only referring to the majority of the children you work with," Charlotte retreatingly responds.

William swiftly interjects: "You do very valuable work, Barbara. What about you, Dan? What do you do?"

"I supervise the management of large commercial properties, mainly class A office buildings, but also some regional malls. I know what you do, of course. Your reputation and that of Wylde Capital are highly regarded by anyone in business. I even think your company might hold some of my employer's debt."

"And you, Charlotte? What do you do?" Barbara duplicitously inquires, in her sweetest tone of voice, knowing full well from Kristina that Charlotte is one of the "ladies who lunch."

Proudly, as if it were full time, meaningful employment, Charlotte responds: "I do a great deal of charitable work and, of course, am required by the nature of William's business to attend many dinners and social events to help him network."

"She's a big help to me," William adds. "Charlotte can charm the pants off even my most bitter enemy. She's my Mata Hari, coming away with valuable information which her target never meant to let slip."

"You're the only one I try to charm the pants off, William dear," Charlotte coyly responds, while Barbara holds back the reactive grimace forming on her face, a grimace stemming not only from what Charlotte has just said, but from the fact that Dan has been almost openly ogling Charlotte's cleavage during the exchange.

Discussions about William and Charlotte's children, politics and world events follow, and then it is time for dinner, Jeff and Kristina having joined them at the tail end of the cocktail hour, just in time to listen to the state of the world lament that most older people seem to have, regardless of their economic status.

Charlotte and Barbara have taken each other's measure and have temporarily, at least, established détente. Charlotte thinks Barbara is beneath her station, certainly not a person she'll see except in the context of Charlotte's relationship with Kristina and Jeff. Barbara thinks Charlotte is what she expected — frivolous at best, vacuous at worst. But each of the women, for their own reasons, silently vow that in the future they'll be on best behavior and as outwardly friendly with each other as possible.

The conversation at dinner is considerably facilitated by the presence of Jeff and Kristina, with a great deal of focus on funny stories that Jeff and Kristina tell about what they have seen and done and about their friends. This induces William and Charlotte and, to a lesser extent, Barbara and Dan, to contribute similar stories of their own.

Towards the end of the evening, Jeff and Kristina are asked about their plans for the future and when they intend to get married. Kristina advises that they are thinking of getting married sometime in the mid-Fall and moving out of the Wylde's home at some point soon after that. She says that she intends to continue as Charlotte's assistant even after she's married and they move out. Jeff advises that he's been thinking about what William said about possibly changing jobs, but he's not yet decided on what else he might want to do.

After an effusive (but not heartfelt) thank you to the Wyldes for a most enjoyable evening and delicious dinner (lobster newburg appetizers, French country casserole entrees and ile flottante for dessert), Barbara hugs Jeff tightly, then kisses Jeff and Kristina as she and Dan take their leave and head home.

On the drive back, after an extended, thoughtful mutual silence, Dan says: "They seem like decent people, although I must say I was uncomfortable by the casual display of such great wealth." Barbara cattily responds: "There was nothing casual about Charlotte's display. Not in how she spoke, as if everyone should share her level of riches and those who don't, are somehow beneath her. And not in how she dresses or was made up. She certainly doesn't hesitate to display her body or highlight her beauty."

"You're just as beautiful, Barb. We're just not rich."

"Yeah, thanks. But I'm not. I know that. I do okay in the looks department, but she's really quite stunning, even for her age, and maybe especially for her age. If only her personality even remotely approached her physical appearance."

"I didn't feel that way about Charlotte," Dan replies, "and I liked William. For all his fame and money, he's a down-to-earth type of guy."

"I'm not so sure that he's down to earth, as that he made an effort to appear to be down to earth. Time will tell, but if he were down to earth he couldn't co-habitate with Charlotte, who lives amongst the stars."

"She's not that bad. I think you're being unfair. You need to give her a chance, you only just met."

"I'll try. For Jeff's sake. On another note, did you catch what Jeff said? Apparently, William has been talking to him about Jeff possibly changing jobs. Jeff has never discussed that with me. Has he talked to you about it, so this is another secret you were keeping from me?"

"No, he hasn't. And I thought you were getting past your anger at what I did. Obviously, not. I regret it and I'm sorry, but what's done is done. I can't change it."

"It will take me more than several days to get over the fact that my husband is a thief," she cruelly replies. "Several years, or never, are more likely."

The rest of the drive is taken in frosty silence, as Barbara contemplates the torrent of change swirling around her, threatening to sweep away the comfortable nest she's built for herself.

CHAPTER XIX

"Kristina, what events have you already scheduled for me for the Fall?" Charlotte inquires as she sips tea, pinky finger raised, from her fruit-patterned fine bone china cup, delicately balancing the saucer on her lap on top of her Dolce & Gabbana striped skirt.

"A lot. You're going to be very busy. Do you want me to go over them with you now? Or I can just print out a list for you to look at later."

"Now, please. William has just told me that he has some more events that he wants me to attend in connection with his possible nomination. I need to know what's already on my calendar."

"Okay," Kristina replies. She opens her computer and reading from her notes, says: "Well, you have the New York City Ballet Fall Gala and the Metropolitan Opera Opening Night Gala, both in September, the Rubin Museum of Art Gala and the Rita Hayworth Alzheimer's Gala, both at Cipriani restaurants in October, and then also in October is the Lunch Box Fund Annual Fall Dinner, sponsored by Prada, the New York Women's Foundation Fall Gala and Bette Midler's Hulaween Costume Gala.

"I didn't realize that I'm committed to so many October events already. I hope the events William wants to add aren't in October."

"Do you want to go over your November events as well?"

"Yes. But before I forget, William is purchasing a table for us to attend the Metropolitan Museum of Art's Costume Institute Benefit. It'll be in May. Please find the date and put it in my calendar."

"Oh my," Kristina enthuses. "I've seen pictures on the Vogue website of the famous people attending, with the women wearing the most beautiful gowns."

"Yes. It's the major social event of the year. I'll need your help in selecting my gown. I want heads to turn when I walk by. But it needs to be tasteful. I'm too old to compete with the Miley Cyrus types."

"I think you still can, Charlotte," Kristina sincerely exclaims, without intent to flatter.

Charlotte slightly blushes and says, trying to be modest: "Maybe with the proper gown and accessories, some diamond jewelry and the right Christian Louboutin shoes. But let's stay focused. What have you scheduled for me in November?"

"In November, you have the American Cancer Society Financial Services Cares Gala, the Museum of the Moving Image Salute Gala and the Time 100 Gala. Nothing else before Thanksgiving."

"We're going to have a great deal of shopping to do in the next few weeks," Charlotte frets. "I can't be seen wearing the same clothes or jewelry twice. One other thing. I just remembered. Please be sure to sign me up for the Hat Lunch Central Park Conservancy benefit in May. It's fun. Everyone wears crazy hats and my friends and I try to outdo each other in silliness. Except for Hulaween, we never get to kick off our shoes and let loose."

Just then, the maid enters and advises Charlotte that Wilma and Bess have arrived. Wilma, age 23, is Charlotte's only daughter and youngest child. Charlotte has smothered Wilma from birth, foisting all of her insecurities and foibles on Wilma, rendering her meek and uncertain, without either Charlotte's beauty or sense of entitlement. Making matters more difficult for Wilma, was that until she outgrew it in her late teens, she suffered from a mild case of Tourette's syndrome — blinking eyes, throat clearing and occasional inadvertent jerky movements.

On the plus side, Wilma is not unattractive and is academically gifted, probably having her father's genetics to thank for the latter. Her innate ability and inclination to learn have been facilitated, no doubt, by an unconscious need to find a "safe space" from Charlotte. Presently, Wilma works in a cancer research laboratory at Mt. Sinai Hospital. Her bent towards medical research was the result of an attraction she felt for her female biology teacher who, prior to teaching, had done several years of medical research and imparted her love for it to Wilma. Like her siblings, Wilma does not want for money (except maybe Wharton, who spends everything he can lay his hands on), as all three Wylde children have been gifted with identical $50 million trust funds by Charlotte's parents.

Living more than well on her trust fund, Wilma is quite content working for little salary at something she likes. She lives in Williamsburg, Brooklyn, with her lesbian lover, Bess Tully, and the bloom is far from being off the rose. Here again, the adage "opposites attract" proves true. Bess is neither insecure, meek, nor a child of wealth. She's been good for Wilma, imparting a sense of confidence and even a little daring in her, partially eradicating the shadows of Wilma's childhood.

Bess grew up an only child in a middle class neighborhood in Sheepshead Bay, Brooklyn. Her mother's death, when Bess was in her early teens, drove a stake through her working father's heart, from which neither he nor Bess ever recovered. Her father lost his salesman's job in a pharmaceutical company as a result of the deep depression which followed and thereafter worked only sporadically. To make extra money, Bess hooked up with the local toughs and started peddling marijuana to her classmates and in the neighborhood. A decent student, she could only afford to attend City College of New York, a free tuition school. But this proved to be an advantage. While in college, she expanded her by now successful sales career, having gained a new pool of people to whom she could sell her wares. Tuition being free, she could begin to build a small reserve for a possible rainy day.

It was a very good day for Bess when she met Wilma Wylde. Within weeks of meeting at a gay bar in Soho, Bess moved in with Wilma in her luxury, eight room high-rise Williamsburg condo gifted to her by her parents. Charlotte knows and accepts that Wilma is a lesbian but believes that Bess is not the right life partner for her. From the first time that Charlotte met Bess, Charlotte sensed that she would drive Wilma away from Charlotte and steer her in a direction that Wilma was not capable of navigating.

Unbeknownst to Charlotte, her fear is well-founded. At least once, Bess has tried to convince Wilma to steal chemicals from the lab in which she works, so that Bess can deliver the chemicals to a drug cartel in exchange for the high-profit fentanyl pills and other opioids Bess sells. Although Wilma is confident that she'll ultimately be able to get Bess to stop dealing drugs, she's not as yet succeeded. Wilma can well afford to support the both of them but Bess can't accept the largesse, both because she's too proud and because she'd no longer be dominant in the relationship. What Charlotte does know is that Wilma is no longer dependent on her, that Bess almost fully occupies Wilma's life, and that there's little room at the inn for Charlotte. Only an occasional vacancy, too few and far between.

As the maid withdraws, Wilma and Bess stride into the room walking hand-in-hand. "So nice to see you today, Wilmsy," Charlotte says, then continues, attempting, but failing, to sound sincere: "I didn't realize you were joining us, Bess, but you're always welcome." Kristina rises from her chair, says hello to Wilma and Bess and as she leaves, reminds Charlotte: "You have a 3:00 P.M. salon appointment this afternoon, so we need to leave by 2:30 at the latest."

Addressing Wilma and Bess, Charlotte says: "Sit down. Make yourselves comfortable. We've plenty of time. Lunch will be served in the central parlor room in a few minutes." Once they're all seated, Charlotte continues: "So girls? Anything exciting?"

"Not really, Mom," Wilma replies, in the usual subservient tone of voice she uses whenever she's speaking with her mother. "Work is fine. One of the research projects I'm working on at the lab shows real promise, so I'm excited about that."

"That's nice, dear," is Charlotte's apathetic reply. "But remember, you need to be very careful working with all those chemicals and cancer germs, who knows what you might contract if you're not. I do wish you'd work at something less dangerous."

"There's nothing dangerous about what Wilma does," Bess disdainfully remarks, a dismissive smirk on her rotund face.

"So you say," Charlotte grimaces. "I'm her mother and have been taking care of her for a long time. I know what's good for her and what's not."

"Mom, please. This is silly. I'm not giving up my job," Wilma protests. "I do important work, work that may eventually save lives."

"Ok, darling. I don't want to dwell on this. It's just a mother's opinion, which, predictably, her rebellious child chooses to ignore."

Oh, my God, Bess disgustedly thinks to herself. What bullshit. Charlotte, the poor suffering victim. She's a fucking soap opera queen. But Bess holds her tongue, not wanting to turn the already strong undercurrent of hostility between Charlotte and Bess into an aerial battle with no winners and Wilma the biggest loser.

Directing her next question at Bess, Charlotte snidely asks: "What about you, Bess, dear. What job are you working at these days?"

"I'm making ends meet. I'm still working a few nights a week as a fill-in bartender at a couple of the Soho and Chelsea bars. My latest gig is as a weekend hostess at "Laugh-At-Me, Me, Me," a new comedy club in the meat packing district that draws in some of the A-listers late at night."

"That sounds very interesting," Charlotte blandly responds, while thinking to herself how could such a brash, dumpy, unattractive person be a hostess anywhere? Charlotte accepts that Wilma is a lesbian, but Wilma is pretty and smart, so why couldn't Wilma be attracted to someone like herself?, Charlotte wonders.

"Actually, it is. Wilma meets me there some nights and we've had drinks and hung out with a bunch of celebs, Nicki Minaj, Jared Leto, Gigi Hadid, just to name a few. We have a lot of fun and it's good for Wilma to break out of her shell from time to time."

"To each his own. Those are not people with whom I would choose to spend any of my time. But you young people have different tastes. Nowadays, I suppose vulgar is in and gentility is out. So who am I to judge?", Charlotte responds, judging nonetheless, notwithstanding her ostensible abdication of that role.

From this less than promising beginning, their conversation during lunch continues to traverse a bumpy road of disagreement, with them bickering over any number of things: Bess' off-hand mention that she and Wilma smoke pot together (no surprise to Charlotte, who suspects Bess does much worse than just smoke pot), Bess' hatred of the police, whom she claims are either inherently, or trained to be, prejudiced against all persons of color even when they are themselves persons of color, Bess' advocacy for free colleges, in short, any topic Bess initiates for discussion.

For her part, none of these bothersome subjects were anything in which Charlotte wanted to partake. More light-hearted fare was what she had intended to be served: gossip about the Wyldes' relatives and friends, the latest in fashion, maybe some recent theatre performance that Charlotte had attended. But for some reason, largely Bess' doing, they've ended up at a much different buffet.

Wilma has remained relatively quiet during lunch, with Bess engaging Charlotte in most of the conversation. As coffee is served, Kristina enters the parlor to remind Charlotte that it's almost 2:30 and that they'll need to go soon. She tells Charlotte that she'll meet her at the front door in five minutes, says a polite goodbye to Wilma and Bess and then walks out of the room.

With that, Wilma says: "Mom, before you leave, one thing. There's something Bess and I want to mention that we hope will please you."

"Your father is parading me at some important business thing tomorrow night and I can't miss my salon appointment. I hope this won't take long. I wish you had mentioned whatever it is earlier, instead of our talking about some of the things that we did."

"This won't take long. It's just that Bess and I want to have a baby together, with me as the birth mother. We just wanted to give you a heads-up that you may soon have a pregnant daughter and that you and father might be grandparents much sooner than you would have thought."

A startled Charlotte, unable to suppress her feeling of dismay, maybe terror, at this unwelcome news, exclaims: "I'm too young to be a grandmother and you're too young to be a parent."

"I'm not too young. You were younger when you first gave birth. And I would think you'd be happy to have a grandchild."

Regaining her balance, Charlotte responds: "I'm sure I will be. I just think you should wait a few years, until both of you are more settled."

Of course, what Charlotte has just said is not what she actually means. What she means is: you and Bess have only been together about a year, I intensely dislike Bess, she's no good for you, and I hope the two of you break up in another year or two, so don't have a baby with Bess at all. Also driving her objection, and what she touched on in what she first spontaneously blurted out, is that she's too vain to want people that would otherwise be dazzled by her still youthful beauty, to view her through a different lens.

"Look," Charlotte continues, "I really need to run. We'll discuss this next time I see you, when we have more time. We'll make that the very first thing we talk about." With that, Charlotte goes over to the still seated Wilma, lightly kisses her on the head, waves a half-hearted goodbye to Bess and rushes out for her appointment.

Wilma and Bess look at each other, and with Charlotte gone, Wilma says: "I really thought she'd be happy."

"I told you she wouldn't be. Your mother wants to keep you a child so she doesn't have to share you with anyone. She can't deal with the fact that you're a grown woman. If you have a baby, she's lost you, not only to me but to your child as well."

"She'll come around. She wants what's best for me. Let's give her some time. I shouldn't have sprung it on her just as she had to leave. It wasn't fair of me to do that."

"We don't need her blessing. It's our lives and our decision, not hers. Anyway, let's go. There's still time to do something more pleasurable today than this lunch has been."

As they head out towards their car, Wharton drives up in his Bentley with a few of his friends. They've just finished playing in a polo match somewhere in the Hamptons and Wharton is using his parents' home as a way station for he and his friends to grab some drinks and snacks, maybe take a swim, before they continue on to the City.

"Wilma, Bess, I'm surprised to see you here."

"We had lunch with mother."

"Trust it was as much fun as having lunch with mother always is," Wharton sarcastically responds, with a cock-sure grin on his face.

"As to be expected," Bess mumbles under her breath.

"This is a fortunate coincidence," Wharton proceeds. "I was meaning to call you, Bess. I need to speak to you about something."

Wilma shrugs her shoulders and angrily says: "No need to speak to me, your sister. It's Bess you need to speak to. Let me guess. You need some more drugs and want Bess to sell them to you."

"Wilma, let me talk a minute alone with Wharton."

"Why?" Wilma questions. "I know you're still selling drugs, even though I've begged you to stop. How can we have a baby if one of its parents is a drug dealer? Wharton can buy what he needs elsewhere. And better, too, if he just stopped buying it at all, from anyone. Maybe then he'd grow up."

"Hey. I was buying pills from Bess before the two of you ever met. Don't cut off one of my main sources of supply," Wharton cavalierly responds.

Wilma, eyes tearing, frustrated and angry, looks sorrowfully at Bess, so Bess, who loves Wilma, decides that now is not the time to negotiate a transaction with Wharton, and that, although she has no intention of ending her lucrative opioid business, maybe she should no longer sell to Wharton, says to Wharton: "Let's defer this for now. Wilma and I need to talk privately and then I'll call you."

Wharton, being Wharton, can't take the signal, no less accept Bess' spoken words, so he carries on, undeterred and insensitive: "This will only take a minute. I'll pay cash now and arrange to pick the stuff up from you tomorrow."

"No," Bess firmly replies. "I told you, I'll call you tomorrow and we'll talk then. Bye."

As she starts to walk away, Wharton grabs her shoulder, spinning her not too gently around to face him, and attempts to bully Bess, saying: "Wait a minute. You're here. Let's talk now."

Wilma gasps as Bess puts her head down and, with closed fists, surges forward towards Wharton until they are chest to chest (or, more accurately, her chest to his navel), and, lifting her head, furiously responds: "Keep your hands off me, you snotty prick. Touch me again and you'll regret it." With that, Bess turns, takes Wilma by the hand and says: "Say goodbye to your jackass brother."

A tearing Wilma and a furious Bess drive off, leaving behind an embarrassed Wharton and his polo-playing friends, who've seen their friend dressed down by a Brooklyn lesbian toughie half his size.

CHAPTER XX

Kristina, Jeff and I are sitting around my house, having a drink in advance of going out for dinner. Nothing fancy, just shakes and burgers at R Burgers R Best, the latest Yelp-promoted fine dining establishment for the cost-conscious burger devotee.

We're waiting for Patricia to arrive. I've been dating her off and on since we first met at the gym. As much as I want her to be my significant other, I know that she's not. Although the sex (the "on" part) is great, the companionship is just okay (we operate in too disparate, incompatible spheres — hers is wealth management, mine is fiction creation), but for now she makes us a foursome, when I need the comfort of being in one. Even if it's more mirage than reality.

As we pass the time, the conversation turns to what I will be writing next, since my latest mystery has just been published. The modest success of my last book has motivated me to step up my pace and try to churn out two to three mysteries a year.

"I hope you have better ideas than the hard-boiled detective story you started to read to me when we last talked about your so-called career," Jeff says jestingly, with a broad smile.

"That's criticism I can ignore, since it's coming from a pusillanimous pussy," I shoot back (I'm not always as politically correct as you might think), and, with a smile to match Jeff's, I add: "And in case that's too difficult a word for your extremely limited vocabulary, it means you're a spineless, chicken-livered, weak-kneed dolt. What happened to the real man inside you — the one that used to respond to 'guy' stuff? What has Kristina done to you?"

Kristina laughs: "I've brought out the better side of him — something someone needs to do with you. Joking aside, Simon, I read 'A Guileless Death' and now 'Curtain Down, Die Stage Left' and liked both of your books. In your latest one, I especially enjoyed the romance between the chorus dancer and the lead detective, whose wife has just recently divorced him. I'm really interested — what's your next book going to be about and will those characters be in it?"

"Yeah. 'Curtain Down, Die Stage Right'", Jeff interjects. "A perfect sequel. Then he can write 'Curtain Up, Die Off Stage,' and then a whole series of James Patterson-like repetitive books. Those will sell for sure. Patterson's certainly do."

"Jeff," she pleads. "Stop. I really want to know. Simon, tell me."

"I'm working on several ideas. Not sure yet which I will go with."

"So, what for example?" Kristina asks.

"I'm considering a mystery that I call 'The Cereal Bowl Contretemps.' It starts with *'I seem to have misplaced my cereal bowl. It's white and says chocolate on it. If you have seen it, can you return it to me?' This was the last office email she ever sent. Her cereal bowl was never found, but a day later her strangled, brutally mangled body was.*"

Kristina stares at me like a deer caught in a car's headlights. For the moment, she can't figure out whether I'm joking or serious and is unsure how to react. Before she can say anything, I immediately spout out: "I'm only kidding around."

"I knew that," Kristina says, although I'm almost certain that she didn't.

Jeff pipes up: "I don't think you did. It sounds dumb enough for Simon to have written it."

"Ha, Ha," I respond.

Kristina plows forward: "Come on, Simon. Please," she begs, "What are you working on?"

I do have a few plot ideas that I am batting around (grappling with, is more accurate), but I hate to discuss them — they never sound like much until a book is actually finished and the final product read. Not that anyone often asks me. But this is starting to change. My book sales are growing amid good reviews from Publisher's Weekly, Kirkus, Bookmarks and Goodreads. So I probably should be less flippant and more serious when discussing my writing and I tell Kristina: "I'm considering several possible story lines at the moment. I haven't targeted anything in particular yet, because the world is so bizarre that it's difficult to choose from the miasma of lunacy."

"Look at all the crazy shit that's going on," I continue, with some emotion (she asked for serious me, so here he comes): "A man in a wheelchair robs a bank at gunpoint and escapes, rolling off down the street away from witnesses; a wi-fi enabled Barbie doll is a security threat. A predatory hacker gains control of the voice and 'talks' to a child; a local boy selling lemonade at a roadside stand just outside his home is stopped by police because a cranky neighbor complains that the child needs a license from the town; a diplomat wife's husband beats her up to near death but he can't be arrested because diplomatic immunity extends to the spouse of a diplomat. Any of these incidents could be used as the basis to formulate a really good mystery. Hard to decide which one to forage."

"You asked for it," Jeff says flinchingly to Kristina, then, looking at me, says: "Now that you've blown off steam, are we to gather that your creative pot is still simmering and that nothing has yet boiled its way to the surface?"

"Yes and no," I respond to Jeff. "A few taken from the headline stories have held my attention."

"Like what?" Kristina interjects eagerly, with continued genuine curiosity.

"A soldier flying home to California from her service in the Middle East learns, upon landing, that her service dog, which, because of its large size, had to be flown in a different commercial airline's cargo hold, is dead. On close inspection, it becomes clear that the dog has been injected with some type of poison. The distraught soldier, with the assistance of her still-serving overseas army friend, sets out to solve why the dog was killed. At the end, the denouement is that the dog was mistaken for another dog that was transporting narcotics in its stomach for a cadre of junior army officers dealing synthetic black market drugs."

"Interesting," says Kristina as Jeff stays silent (for once).

Oh, oh, I think. "Interesting" is just another one of those empty words or phrases. To a creative person, "interesting" affords as little comfort as "sorry for your loss" or "our hearts and prayers are with the families" provides to a bereaved person.

After a brief pause and a chance to reconsider, I tentatively continue: "In case you want to hear the other plot I have in mind, here goes. Remember the 16-year old kid who drives drunk and kills four people. He basically gets off by his lawyer asserting an absurd 'affluenza' defense, that is, the kid's wealthy parents coddled him so much that he didn't understand the consequences of his actions. He's tried as a juvenile and given an incredibly light sentence of two years' probation with the condition he not drink and that he perform 100 hours of community service. He's caught drinking on his friend's Instagram photo and flees to Mexico with his mother to avoid being put in jail for violating probation. Flash forward several years, and the judge, the prosecutor, the defense attorney and the wealthy parents are all murdered one by one. At the end, the big reveal: the murderer is not a member of one of the dead people's family, but the kid. He's in fact quite insane and kills them all because he blames them for ruining his life."

"I like that one a lot," Kristina asserts with enthusiasm and a big grin. "I think it would make a really good book."

"I hate to say it, but, since we are being serious, I agree," Jeff says. "Reluctantly," he adds.

"I'm a hit. You love me, you really, really love me," I respond, reverting to my non-serious, more usual nature as I mimic Sally Field and paraphrase her famous Oscar speech.

We all laugh and just then the doorbell rings. It's Patricia, and I'm saved by the bell from further scrutiny of my inner sanctum.

I get a brief kiss on the lips, Jeff and Kristina get "I'm sorry I'm a little late" and we all get going for our burgers and shakes, and maybe to go clubbing somewhere afterwards. Some of Jeff's Lexus customers are well-connected and, through them, Jeff has been able to gain access to several of the clubs most desired by we millenials. A welcome perk of his job.

CHAPTER XXI

It is a rainy Tuesday night, a few days after the Wyldes and the Muss family have had dinner together. As is his wont on weeknights, William is spending the evening in the arms of his inamorata, more specifically tonight in the valley between her breasts, licking and sucking on her aroused nipples while rubbing her clitoris, getting himself sufficiently aroused to penetrate her without the aid of the Viagra he needs on those increasingly rare occasions that he and Charlotte have sex. His performance with Vanessa tonight is spot on, and he wishes he could take a curtain call, but despite her urging, he's not been able to give even a short second performance in some 15-odd years and, mind over matter, no matter how sharp his mind is, it does not sharpen his matter.

As they lie together afterwards, a contented William reaches for the television clicker to turn on one of the cable talking-head shows that he likes to watch and often is on, but a troubled Vanessa places her hand on his wrist and stops him, saying: "Let's talk for a minute, please."

William rolls towards her, gently cups her chin, and as he stares lovingly into her eyes, tenderly says: "What's on your mind?"

"I don't want to become like Charlotte, a nag or burden to you. And I know I've said this to you before. But I need more from you than being your mistress. I need to know that I'll be your wife."

William attempts to mollify Vanessa, soothingly telling her: "You know that I love you very much. I want us to marry some day. When it's possible. It's just..."

Vanessa emotionally interrupts William in mid-sentence, blurting out: "It'll soon be a year that we've been seeing each other. I want a real family, children. If you're never going to provide me with that, just tell me, it's better we end this now, while I'm still young enough to find someone else I can share my life with. You mean everything to me, but you'll be leaving me no choice."

A shaken William, ambushed by this sudden, unexpected post-coital ultimatum, is not sure how to respond, but Vanessa has sat up and turned away from him, sobbing, her body trembling, obviously requiring an answer to her plea, and he wants to give that to her, to provide her some sort of assurance and comfort, so he answers: "I love you very much. I want us to live together and have a family. It's just that I need more time to arrange for this to happen."

"This is not one of your business deals to be 'arranged,' to be 'negotiated,'" a very upset, still crying, Vanessa despairingly responds: "This is far from the first time that I've told you how I feel. If you love me as much as you say, you'd have left Charlotte by now. We'd be living together openly and planning on a family."

"You're being unfair. You know I love you and want the same things for us, but I've told you, I need more time to make it happen. So continue to give me the time and trust in me."

Somewhat appeased, a teary-eyed Vanessa embraces William, as she whispers to him with mixed emotions of surrender, plea, demand and fear that are almost completely genuine except for the fact that she knows how to play her cards even at her relatively young age: "I'll do as you ask. I'll give you, it, us, more time. But please understand. I can't continue like this indefinitely. I need to know for certain. I need you to act, one way or the other. And it needs to be soon."

While this soap opera-like scenario between William and Vanessa is unfolding, Charlotte, unaided on this occasion by Kristina, is in the process of folding, that is to say, bending over on her knees while entered from behind by William's new and youngest business partner, the cocky (in every sense of the word) and quite aggressive (thankfully for Charlotte) Clifford Thurston III. What Charlotte no longer receives at home on a regular basis from William, she has no trouble or compunction in obtaining elsewhere. Even if not so openly so, what's good for the goose has always been good for her gander, well before the time that role reversal became the norm, not the variant.

Young master Clifford is just the most recent in a discrete number of mostly short-lived couplings that flatter, amuse and physically satisfy Charlotte from time to time, she having long recognized and accepted the philandering nature of her husband. Wealth has its privileges, one of which for Charlotte is to be sexually satisfied whenever she feels the urge, which is still an itch she quite often feels the need to have scratched.

William is indifferent to her comings and goings except when he needs her to be somewhere for sake of appearance purposes, knows that she (like he) sleeps around and has long accepted it, even welcomed it in some perverse way. Kristina by now must at least suspect that Charlotte is having affairs, but Kristina is not one to talk out of school. Charlotte's children are distant from her, no matter how often she tries to close the gap, and she doubts that any of them would even care one way or the other. And as to Charlotte's friends, all of whom are as pampered as she, and many of whom are having or have had their own illicit couplings, extra-marital liaisons are a badge of honor if discovered or revealed, not a scarlet letter, the details to be shared (the who, when, where and why, but not the what or how).

It is thus that Charlotte is free to carry on such bedroom antics as she sees fit, just not to flaunt what she does, because embarrassing William publicly is the only sin she can any longer commit as far as their marriage is concerned. And she does not intend to sin, but to stay married to William until death do them part. He's a bright light, a still rising star, and his prominence enhances hers. She's happy enough as things stand. When they were younger and just starting out, she never would have believed she could (or would have to) settle for how she now lives. But the erosion of their life together, largely the product of her narcissism, neediness, sense of entitlement and lack of purpose (although aided by William's focus on acquiring fame and fortune at the sacrifice of almost all else), has been a fast-moving process and before she could fully realize where they were heading, their journey had ended.

The latest in Charlotte's broken band of lovers, Clifford Thurston III has much more in mind than just a one-time pleasurable lay of a still beautiful older woman, his enjoyment heightened by both the fear of discovery and his mistaken notion that in fucking Charlotte, he's getting back at William. Clifford has decided to play a slightly longer game, a dangerous one to be sure, but he has a strategy with possible alternative endings, all of which he hopes will lead to a win that will ensure his future success at Wylde Capital or, if need be, elsewhere.

Clifford comes from a socially prominent and politically well-connected family, once very rich, now not very, but still with tentacles attached in all the right places. Clifford is not particularly bright but as part of the "old boy" network gained (better put, "gamed") admission to Yale University, where he was invited in his senior year to join Skull and Bones Society, where other young scions reposed.

After Yale, Clifford used his family's connections to obtain a position as analyst at a large investment bank, where he toiled long hours for three years, struggling mightily but eventually mastering the job. With his newly-acquired skill in analyzing companies and their potential profitability, and the assistance of one of the older Skull and Bones Society members, he moved from the advisory side to the trading desk of the investment bank, where he scored some quick successes, aided by inside information unlawfully fed to him by a few of his boyhood and college buddies.

Buoyed by a moderate but decent trading track record, good looks, a fair measure of self-confidence and his family's vast network of connections, he decided that his next step towards recapturing the wealth of his forbearers was to work at a hedge fund, where the appetite for risk, and his chance for reward, would be far greater than it was at his current stodgy investment bank employer. So it came to be that little less than a year ago, William Wylde was convinced by one of his hedge fund's largest institutional investors, to bring Clifford Thurston III into Wylde Capital with the title of partner (but, in reality, an employee who could be fired at will).

This shotgun marriage has not turned out as expected by either Clifford or Wild Bill. Without the easy access to insider information that he previously had but which is now much harder to come by because of recent stronger governmental enforcement activity and Wylde Capital's internal monitoring procedures, Clifford's trades as a whole are barely breaking even, no less achieving the minimum 20% yearly return on investment that Wylde Capital targets. On top of that, Wild Bill is a demanding task master, closely second-guessing everything that Clifford does and highly critical of most of Clifford's decisions. Clifford's partnership is hanging by the single thread that less than a year's employment is too short of a time for Wylde Capital to fire him in a manner that will not upset Clifford's institutional investor patron.

That Clifford has managed to bed Charlotte shortly after first meeting her at a Wylde Capital table taken for a charitable event, is the only good luck he's had so far as regards Wylde Capital. He hopes to parlay this into securing his position or at least making his exit from the company palatable to uninformed observers and future employers. In short, he intends to continue sleeping with her and ingratiate himself to her in every way possible, at least for now, so that later on he has a viable end game for Wylde Capital: if necessary, he can let William know that he's been sleeping with Charlotte and threaten to embarrass

William by going public with it (secret bedroom camera video available upon request), in which case, either Clifford keeps his position for as long as he wants or William assists him in locating an equivalent position elsewhere. Alternatively, if William fires him, Clifford leaks the video and claims that the only reason he was let go from Wylde Capital was his affair with Charlotte. In all events, he intends to make Charlotte a valuable chip for him to play.

Charlotte has no end game in mind in coupling with this handsome, attractive young lover. For her, Clifford is just another salubrious experience, one she would not hesitate to repeat a few more times. For a young person, he's a very skilled lover and his stamina is something she's not encountered in quite a long time.

CHAPTER XXII

"Did you see 'Shark Tank' recently?" I ask Jeff. "Program after program, people parade ideas for new businesses, most of which sound pretty good even when none of the sharks invest."

It has been almost two weeks since William urged Jeff to consider how William might be able to help him if Jeff wanted to apply himself to something other than selling cars. This evening represents a second attempt by Jeff, Kristina and me to come up with something that Jeff might want to do where William could be of assistance.

"I don't get why you can't come up with anything better than what you have so far," I continue. "Jeff, help us out here. It's your life, your future."

"I know what I am and what I'm not," Jeff responds, with characteristic honesty. "I'm a salesman. I like dealing with people and they like interacting with me. So I just need to figure out what I'd rather sell and how, if at all, William can help me."

"We went through this exercise a few days ago and came up with nothing. Nada, zilch," I say. "That's because we weren't thinking out of the box, and not big enough. So I decided I'd better apply my creativity to your future and save the day."

"Oh, great savior of mine, go forth and save my day."

"Done. Ever hear of Horn & Hardart? Or the Automat?" I inquire.

"I'm not selling soap to laundromats," Jeff responds, only half jokingly.

"What is an Automat?" Kristina asks.

"I was looking at a picture book of old Brooklyn before we were born, when our parents were young. I saw a picture of a store called 'Horn & Hardart Automat' and was interested, so I did some research on it."

"And," an impatient, disinterested Jeff quizzically asks. "What is it? Get to the point, please. I'm starving and want to eat."

"A perfect segue. Basically, before McDonalds, Burger King and their progeny, there were the Automats, the original fast food restaurants, serving freshly made on the premises food in automated vending machines. You'd put a Horn & Hardart token in the slot, turn the knob, the window in front of the food you had selected would pop open, and then you'd reach in and remove the food you wanted and bring it to a table where you'd sit down to eat it."

"So, what's that mean for me? Are we going to one of them now to eat?", a confused Jeff, scratching his head, asks as he half-rises from my couch and pretends he's about to walk out the door.

"Jeff, sit down, let Simon finish. He's being serious. He has an idea. Let's hear it," Kristina scolds.

"There was a whole series of these Automats, all over New York City and in other cities, and they were very popular. But the last Automat closed around the time we were born. So it dawned on me, when I finished doing some more research on them, that these Automats were fast food before any of the current fast food places, but the mistake they made that eventually led to their restaurants closing, was that they didn't open enough restaurants, or, more specifically, they didn't open a series of smaller restaurants in the type of locations that McDonalds, Burger King and the other fast food competitors target."

"I'm still not sure what you're driving at," Jeff says.

"Think big, I said before. One more thing to know, the inside of the stores had a very art deco look. A back wall with rows and rows of small steel-framed windows which contained the food, the kitchen hidden in back behind the food windows, the floor was all checkered black and white tiles and the furniture was stark, with a steel trim deco look. Let's revive the concept, maybe use or, if we have to, buy, the name 'Automat.' And then dress you up in a black tuxedo, take your picture and make you the spokesperson for Automat, its face."

"You're going to turn me into a younger version of Col. Sanders? That's your grand idea," an incredulous Jeff excitedly shouts as he jumps out of his seat, looking at me in disbelief. "And what would I do besides have my picture taken and plastered around, something you could use much better looking models to do?"

"You'd help raise money for the company. Help sell Automat franchises and be in charge of all company relationships with customers and franchisees. That's a big job, an important job, and a real career, big money, and a good application of what you said you are: a salesman, who likes dealing with people," I enthusiastically answer, continuing: "We just need William to buy into the idea and give you some start-up capital to get this off the ground."

Kristina, who's been paying close attention to what I've been saying, rushes over to me, hugs me and, with a broad smile, says: "I love you. What a great idea." Turning her face towards Jeff, with her arms still around me, she continues: "This would be perfect for you, Jeff."

Jeff hesitantly responds: "I need to think about this much more than the few minutes I've had in listening to Simon lay this out. I want to do my own research on these Automats and about how franchises work. It's definitely a big idea. I just don't know whether even if I get comfortable with it, I can get comfortable with asking William for the amount of money I would need to start me off, if I can even figure out what that amount is. And why in the hell would William back me, as opposed to someone more experienced in the restaurant business, even if he liked the idea?"

"Let's cross the 'William' bridge after you see whether you like this for yourself as a possible career," I counter.

"Okay. Now can we go eat? I've a splitting headache that needs to be fed," Jeff playfully pleads, lightening the mood and eager, for now, to change the subject. "We'll talk about this again in a few days, after I've had time to do my research and think about this some more."

As they leave to eat, with that resolve in mind, there are other conversations being had by people in the Wylde family orbit regarding their own plans for the future, all of which also involve, in one way or another, the family's wealth.

Melody and Willis Wylde are eating sushi dinner together at the kitchen table in their elegant Tribeca townhouse. Willis would have preferred Chicago-style pizza from Deep Dish Nirvana, but Melody is hell-bent on their eating healthy, if no other reason than to maintain her figure. He has no complaints in that regard, so sushi it is. Melody is in the process of trying to convince Willis that now is the time for him to begin to plan for a future beyond that of being a primary care physician in a small five-person medical group.

Willis is the Wylde's middle child. Now 26 years old, he graduated on an accelerated basis from NYU Medical School and completed his residency a few years ago. Although a very skilled and talented young doctor, that he is a member of his practice group at such a young age is probably as much attributable to his buying the small Soho building in which the group houses its offices as his diagnostic and treatment abilities.

As a child, Willis was sickly. At age two, he had his first of many fever convulsions, at age five, rheumatic fever, and at age 13, mononucleosis. In between, he caught more than his fair share of high-fever colds, bronchitis, flu, gastroenteritis, and other debilitating childhood illnesses. Charlotte is proud of Willis being a doctor, even if she herself wouldn't want to spend her life in close contact with people who are ill, but worries that given Willis' own medical history, he's made a bad choice of professions.

Willis has a wild streak, the product of too many days spent ill as a child and confined to his bed. Despite the displeasure of both his parents, he got his first tattoo when he was only 15 and several more before he turned 19. It was at age 19 that for the first time he slept with one of Charlotte's "friends," but it was far from the last. By the time he was 23, he'd shared the bed of several more. He's quick to jump to the aid of a friend in distress, and in doing so, has had his fair share of physical altercations, some quite violent.

Like his siblings, Willis has a $50 million trust fund which, as is the case with Wilma, should be sufficient to ensure his future given his relatively unpretentious life style (of course, "unpretentious" might not be appropriate to describe a life style that includes living in a mortgage-free townhouse (his graduation present) with a Maserati convertible and Harley Davidson custom-built motorcycle in its two-car garage).

Willis is married to a 25-year old woman he met during his final months as a resident doing rounds at the hospital. Melody Mendelson was being treated in the emergency room for a badly twisted ankle, but it was Willis who was struck down. Melody is from a Long Island Jewish family of modest means, but there's nothing modest about her physical appearance. Her pixie-like face, with button eyes and up-turned nose, is set off by a trim body that over-highlights her more than subtle breasts. Until she met Willis, she'd used her physical attributes to little advantage, never achieving the acting career to which she aspired, restaurant hostess and occasional high-priced escort being as close as she got.

Melody is more than a touch venal, more than a little ambitious and 100% opportunistic. Willis was a prize worth her being captured by. It didn't hurt that he's sexy in his own way (even without the aura that wealth can exude) and clearly a mostly decent, well-intentioned person. She's never been head over heels in love (although she many times has been heels over head), but Willis, she thinks, is someone whom she can come to truly love. She has real feelings for him, but

Melody being Melody, at least some of that derives from the life she believes his family's wealth can provide.

The lavish wedding (and wedding gifts) with which she and Willis were bestowed was a good first step along her anticipated highway to Paradise. She glowed with happiness as she walked down the long, winding, elegantly designed Stanford White staircase at the Metropolitan Club at 60th Street and Fifth Avenue, a club built by JP Morgan and William Vanderbilt. No Leonard's of Great Neck wedding for Melody.

But Melody's looks, ambition and obvious power over Willis do not sit well with Charlotte. Nor does the fact that Melody is Jewish. From her pedestal of privilege, Charlotte views all Jewish people to be inherently money-hungry and unscrupulous and Melody is no exception. Charlotte's anti-semitism was learned at the foot of her father, who, when he first started in business, was partners with two men, both Jewish. Just as their company was at the cusp of being acquired, Gordon Houghton discovered that he'd been cheated by his partners, who'd conspired to secretly cut a lucrative deal for themselves to Gordon's exclusion. When the acquisition fell through, Gordon found someone to back him and bought out his eager to sell, duplicitous partners. He never forgot and made sure Charlotte wouldn't either.

As they're finishing their sushi, Melody says: "I don't want to sound like a nagging wife. It's just that I think you'd do much better with your life, help so many more people and be even happier, if you would plan to open a Willis Wylde Medical Center. I'm certain that your father would give you the money or raise it for you."

"I know you're only looking out for my best interests. But I'm not suited, and don't want, to oversee the operation of a major medical center. I'm happy as things are."

"I'm not saying you should do it now. I'm just saying you should start to think about it, see what William thinks."

"I'm not ready to talk to him about the possibility, since I don't think I'll ever want to undertake something like that. It would be too much administrative work and not enough time spent treating patients."

"At least keep an open mind. You can hire people to do most of the administrative work. That doesn't have to fall on you. Just think about it some more. Then see how you feel."

"I very much doubt I'll feel any different. But, okay. That's fine."

"You are such a 'goody two-shoes.' How could you ever marry someone like me?" Melody flirtatiously inquires, bending slightly forward towards him, just far enough so that her décolletage can't help but become the main focus of his attention.

"Hey. Don't distract me like that. I want to finish my dinner. Don't get me started on demonstrating at least one of the reasons that I married you," he responds, smiling at her while pretending to be annoyed.

"There's something else I want to discuss with you tonight. I've become bored volunteering my time for charity work. What do you think about my starting a business dealing in art?" Melody has a background in art education and summered for two years during college working as an intern at the Whitney Museum.

"That sounds terrific. I'm sure you'd be good at it. You've got a great eye and good sense."

"We have room here in our house to display the first few pieces that I buy. Then when I buy more, I can open a gallery. I'll be another Wylde that makes money. You should see how little was paid for work by Lichtenstein, Warhol and Basquiat when these artists first started out and then compare that to the prices being paid for their work now. A Lichtenstein original oil in the 1970s could be bought for a few thousand dollars at most, now tens of millions at best..."

"Stop," Willis cries out, "I'm at your mercy. You're preaching to a believer."

"Sorry. I got carried away. I've been considering doing this for a while. Just haven't got my nerve up yet."

"Why are you concerned about this at all? We can afford at least $1 million/year to invest in art. It won't hurt us badly if you make mistakes."

"I can start with the million. But I really don't want to try to guess on completely new artists, those just beginning their careers. It's too tough a race to call, with way too many horses in the starting gate."

"Since when are you a horse racing fan?" he laughs.

"There are some things you obviously still don't know about me. My dad liked the horses and I often went with him to the track or watched with him on TV. I got very good at picking winners. That's how I picked you," she jokes (or not). "Any way, kidding aside," she continues, "I want to buy the work of artists who already have established reputations but whom I believe are still far from the apex of their careers. That will require $20-30 million over a few years, not the $2-3 million we could safely risk from your trust. We'd have to ask your parents for the money, and I'm pretty sure Charlotte won't be receptive, she'll think I'm just another money-hungry Jew."

"No she won't. That's crazy."

"Well, she makes anti-semitic comments to me all the time. A few days ago, she referred to 'Jewing someone down' when she mentioned something about people bargaining with street vendors. Another time she told me the most awful joke. She asked: 'Do you know the difference between when a Jewish boy becomes a man and when a Protestant boy becomes a man?' Then she answered: 'At 13, a Jewish boy says a prayer and becomes a man, but a Protestant boy that age goes to a prostitute to become a man. In one case just another worthless prayer; in the other, a prayer answered.'"

"That's just Charlotte talking without thinking. A bad habit of hers and she most certainly is insensitive more often than any of us would like. Come up with a budget for what you want to do or a few examples of what you might want to buy and I'll talk to my mother about this before you ask my father for the money. I'll neuter whatever objections she might have. And anyway, I'm sure my father will listen to you with a completely open mind no matter what."

"You're a doll. Love you to pieces."

"Talk is cheap. I finished my dinner and am ready to eat the dessert."

At approximately the same moment as Melody straddles Willis' lap and starts to unbutton his shirt and unzip his pants, Wharton can be found pacing back and forth like a lion in a cage, except his cage is the townhouse gifted to him by his parents. He's thinking to himself about how to convince his father to give him the $7 million he needs in order to purchase the Long Island team in the MLL league or a Brooklyn team in the new professional lacrosse league being formed.

Many of Wharton's friends played lacrosse in college, as did he. Sports and entertainment are where real money can be made, he thinks to himself. Leisure time has increased dramatically and playing video games, interacting on social media or watching streaming video series can only go so far. Polo is too much a sport for only the wealthy, three-man professional basketball is too far along with TV contracts in place, women's pro beach volley ball is for ogling only, but lacrosse, like soccer, is played in high schools and colleges throughout the country and these two sports, he's firmly convinced, are where real money can be made.

He has to finish putting his business plans together, and then approach his father again. Hopefully, he can get the money from him, notwithstanding the failure (through no fault of his own, of course) of the prior business ventures which his father funded. Anyway, his father can well afford the money that Wharton needs. It's chump change to William, even if Wharton were not his eldest son and rightful first in line to inherit.

The final performer in tonight's Wylde family playhouse is Bess Tully. Bess is in the process of trying, one last time, to convince Wilma to steal some chemicals from the Mt. Sinai laboratory where Wilma works so that Bess can trade them for opioids from the drug dealers with whom Bess does business. Bess has a regular cadre of customers who buy opioids, including fentanyl pills, from her. Her existing customers' needs for these pills are increasing at the same time as her customer list is growing, and both events are occurring exponentially.

"Please, Wilma," Bess urges. "You can easily slip into one of the laboratory supply rooms and remove the chemicals undetected. I only need you to do it once. It will give me extra creds with my suppliers and a valuable edge to ensure my getting an increased amount of better quality product to sell."

"Forget it. I won't do it. You need to stop selling drugs. Period. End of discussion. I've repeatedly told you that I have more than enough money for both of us, now and forever."

"I don't sponge off anyone. I pay my own way. It's that way or I take the highway. And I've told you that repeatedly as well. So 'yes' or 'no' to helping me out?"

"No," Wilma shakily responds. "I don't want to lose you, but I won't help you sell drugs, commit a crime, not ever, not even for you. And how will we raise the child we want if you're going to continue to be a drug-pusher?"

"Let's drop this. I should never have brought it up again," a truly repentant Bess says. "I love you and don't want to force you to do what you don't want to do. As to my dealing drugs, it won't be forever. I'll figure a way to move on to something else, something legitimate. But for now, let's just agree to disagree and get on with our life together, including having a child. I'm not doing anything that's so terrible. I'm just a pharmacist who doesn't require a prescription. Like a pharmacist, I don't sell to children. I draw the line there and always will."

With that, Bess embraces Wilma, and they retire to the boudoir to repair their spirits by engaging in the pleasures of the skin.

CHAPTER XXIII

Wharton has decided that lest the opportunity be lost, he must move rapidly to try to obtain the money he needs to buy a professional lacrosse team. His best opportunity is the Long Island team in the existing league and he's decided to focus on that. Over the past few days, he's cobbled together a business plan with the help, of all people, of his father's newest partner, Clifford Thurston, whom his mother somehow volunteered to him for the job when Wharton first mentioned his idea to his always supportive (always manipulable) mother.

Wharton has come to dinner this Sunday night to make the big reveal to his father, who has reluctantly agreed, as a result of Charlotte's continued pestering, to give Wharton a chance to pitch him about the new business in which Wharton and a few of Wharton's friends are planning to embark. Wharton believes that with Charlotte on his side and this business plan in hand, William will be receptive to the venture despite the argument they had a few weeks ago, where William told him that from now on Wharton had to make good on his own without any more money from his parents.

"You have to give Wharton another chance, he's your son," Charlotte has passionately pleaded as a prelude to this evening. "I know that he has his faults, but at least he's trying to make a go of it in business, even if he's failed at it in the past. He's still young and trying to find his way. You can't judge him against Willis and Wilma, who are very different people than Wharton, but not without their faults too."

"I've no confidence that this new business venture of his will turn out differently if I once again make it easy for him by giving him the money he wants. Let him go out and raise it from his own friends and connections, he certainly has enough of them. If he raises the money on his own, that's the first big step he can take towards achieving something with his life that he can take pride in. I didn't work hard all my life so that I could shelter idle children who just want to play at it."

"You're being cruel, William. I don't see how you can treat Wharton as if he were a bastard child. A few million dollars is meaningless to our life, except to the extent it can make things easier for one of our children."

"Taking the easy path is taking the road to failure. Wharton for once needs to succeed at something by working hard to obtain it. Less polo playing and nightclubbing and more industriousness is what's required."

"Oh, William," she quivered, with a foreboding sense of hopelessness at winning the day. "You're really upsetting me. You need to change, even more than Wharton. He has time to mature, but you have no excuse for your attitude towards him."

To this last comment, a disgusted William harshly replied: "Enough of this, already. I've agreed to hear him out. I'm just telling you not to bank on me changing my mind."

"I banked on you when I let you sweep me off my feet and onto my back. I banked on you when I gave you most of my $250 million inheritance to help you start up Wylde Capital. You've taken what I've lovingly given you and run away. You've no patience for me. You don't spend much time with me, except to trot me out as your shiny, first place winner's trophy. And you're almost never in my bed. There, I've said it. My life with you has become dreadful." With that, Charlotte fled the room crying, heading to her bedroom to lie down, but not before taking a Xanax and the two Percocets that her now throbbing temples required.

With that backdrop, the curtain rises on what Wharton hopes will be his magic hour. Dinner goes relatively smoothly, attributable in large part to William holding his tongue while listening to Charlotte and Wharton make small talk, Charlotte telling of her adventures with Kristina at various Soho and Chelsea boutiques and galleries, and Wharton of some of what he considers the humorous exploits (follies to William) of he and his friends. William's contributions to the table talk at dinner center on topics of the day that are far more serious, but which are quickly brushed aside by Charlotte and Wharton, who've no appetite for meaningful discussion except for the post-dinner conversation which is soon to occur.

"Did you read about the most recent school shooting?" William asks. "Five killed and eight high school students wounded. This violence has to stop."

"Do we need to discuss this at dinner?" Charlotte decries. "We so seldom dine the three of us, that I'd rather we not talk of such depressing things, things that certainly would never occur in our family or the family of anyone we know."

"The shooter came from a very fine family, both parents were college professors and their two older children a lawyer and a scientist," William replies, but does not press the point any further, since he always has a keen sense of his audience, and tonight is no different. Other topics, which William twice attempts to insinuate into the dinner conversation so that it will consist of more than a potpourri of frivolous blabber, meet a similar fate of profound indifference (at least in part because William makes his opinion sound like the sermon on the mount).

"One of my employees was arrested today. He posted naked pictures of his now ex-girlfriend which resulted in her losing her job as a teacher. This type of revenge porn is just another example of the broader bullying that seems to define the social media sites these days. We need governmental regulations to spell out reasonable policing metrics for the content that Facebook, YouTube, Instagram and others distribute."

"The woman should have known better than to take naked pictures of herself or to allow them to be taken," is Wharton's snarky response. "And I don't see the need to legislate content controls on social media — we don't need Big Brother watching over us."

As William is about to engage with Wharton, Charlotte once again plays the role of perfect party hostess, saying: "Please, let's not get into this tonight. Let's just enjoy our dinner."

Later on, William makes one last, half-hearted attempt to talk about a topic of substance, this time, presidential executive orders, but Charlotte's deep frown and look of consternation when he raises the subject is all the "discussion" he needs to abandon this and any other effort to divert the dinner conversation to anything of interest to him.

As dinner ends and the maid removes the remnants of dessert and coffee, William and Wharton adjourn to the library. They sit down in catty corner brown leather, high-backed club chairs, and William, looking over at Wharton, sternly says: "I know you're here to talk to me about a new business venture of yours. So I turn the floor over to you. I'm ready to hear what you have to say."

"Dad, here is a business plan for my purchasing a professional lacrosse team in Long Island in an existing league. There's a market research report attached to the business plan. When you read these materials, you'll see the efficacy of what I propose to do. Two of my friends will partner with me, but I need $3.5 million for my share of the initial start-up costs and another $3.5 to cover projected first two-year operating losses."

"Leave the materials with me and I'll review them over the next few days and give you my comments. Hopefully, I'll have few comments to make and the ones that I have, will be helpful to you."

"Thanks, Dad," Wharton happily responds. "And after that, I know you'll be convinced to back my play."

"Not with money," William forcefully responds. "Just with my best business advice after I read what you've left with me. I already told you the last time we talked that the Wylde spigot has run dry for you. I've no interest in providing you with money for any business you become involved with, at least not until you've made the business a success and are looking for growth capital."

Wharton turns a variety of colors in just a very few seconds and then, with barely controlled rage, bolts from his chair, and says: "I should've known I was wasting my time, that I can't count on you when I need your help."

"You're not making your case by stomping around like a spoiled five year old," William steadily replies. "I'm going to help you, but in the best way possible, with a critique and sound advice on the plan."

"Okay, Dad. Thanks. I appreciate that so very much," Wharton bitingly shouts, no longer even remotely in control of his feelings.

As he storms from the room, Charlotte approaches to try to calm him down, but to no avail. Before he reaches the front door to head home, he stops and says to Charlotte: "Love you, Mom. But him? How can you tolerate living with him. He so clearly cares so little for us."

Charlotte has no stomach to do battle tonight with William over what has just occurred, indeed, she has little fight left in her at all as regards William (except, of course, when it comes to staying married to him). She will go to bed, take the Oxycontin pills that provide her with escape and think happy thoughts, about the good things in her life, the heads that still turn her way with admiring glances when she walks by, the Architectural Digest home she lives in, the apartment in London and estate in Carmel, both of which she visits on occasion, the wealth and social position she enjoys, the friends she spends time with, her massages, workouts, salon visits and shopping forays, the physical satisfaction that her latest lover, Clifford, supplies, and the close relationship that has developed between her and Kristina, filling the void left by the atrophying relationships with her three children.

CHAPTER XXIV

After his disastrous conflagration with William, Wharton determines that his best course of action is to adopt whatever changes his father suggests he make to his business plan (his father's business acumen will at least be of value to Wharton) and to seek the money he needs from Charlotte. Maybe, for once, she'll summon enough resolve to act in a manner contrary to William's wishes.

So it is that less than a week later, Charlotte is having lunch with Wharton at Le Bernardin, enjoying a leisurely tasting menu while Kristina has taken the chauffeur to run a bunch of errands for Charlotte: dropping off earrings to be returned at Tiffany's, picking up Charlotte's new gold and diamond bracelet that had just been sized at Cartier and purchasing art supplies for Charlotte at Picasso Shopped Here.

At what he deems a propitious between-courses moment, Wharton leans close to Charlotte and implores: "Mom, I need your help. I want you to loan me the $7 million that I need to buy a professional lacrosse team, since dad won't do it."

"Wharton, you know I want to, but I can't. William's in charge of our family's finances, always has been and always will be. I can't fight him on that, I don't have the strength," she defeatedly admits.

"You have joint access to the family accounts and plenty of money of your own, you inherited $250 million for god's sake," he exclaims in frustrated response.

"You know that I don't do well handling any type of business affairs, and my only proclivity with money is to freely spend it, mostly on myself," she counters, in an effort to make light of an uncomfortable conversation. "Your father and I have an unspoken arrangement. I can pretty much spend what I want on myself or gifts for you or others but not make any business investments, those are for William to decide."

"So consider this a gift for me, not an investment. Anyway, what will he do, kill you? Please, Mom, just this once. Really help me out."

Shaking her head in humbled defeat, she whispers: "I just can't. He'd make my life miserable, totally intolerable."

Disappointed but not yet wholly discouraged, Wharton makes another stab, this time taking a different tack: "You know, mother, let's be honest. I'm the oldest child and dad has always been hardest on me. He treats Willis and Wilma far differently. From the day I was born, he's second-guessed and criticized virtually everything I've ever done."

"That's just not so," Charlotte vehemently protests, notwithstanding that she knows it to be mostly true.

"Look," Wharton continues, "Willis is a doctor, Wilma has a career in scientific research, both have partners. This is my chance to have a business, to accomplish something for myself. Dad liked my business plan, he only had a few comments, so why can't I get the money? If not from him, then from you?"

"I just can't do it, Wharton. Even if I wanted to, almost all my inheritance money is tied up in Wylde Capital investments. But I promise I'll speak with William about it this weekend and do my best to convince him to give you the money. Let me try. I still have my ways with him, at least some times."

Accepting his Waterloo, but not yet ready to head for Elba, he hopes that Charlotte is true to her word, that she carries his colors into battle and prevails with William. But anticipating that the odds of her victory over William the Conqueror are slight, Wharton decides to go to plan B: he will approach Willis and Wilma and see if he can

128

shake free $2 million from each of them which, with what he can muster from his own money and borrow against his trust fund, should produce the amount he needs.

As Charlotte and a dissatisfied Wharton are drinking their double latte and decaffeinated cappuccino coffees, Kristina arrives to take Charlotte to her 4 P.M. therapy appointment. Not even Kristina's appearance in a tight, hip-hugging, booty clinging mini-skirt and bright green top with a deep V neck can lift Wharton's spirits, although it does serve to slightly elevate a part of his anatomy. His foul mood notwithstanding, he cannot overlook the opportunity to toss another pass at Kristina: "Harold is here. Why not let him drive Charlotte to her appointment without you? That way, you can stay here with me for a while so we can talk. We need to get to know each other better, now that you seem to be coming part of our family."

Charlotte immediately quashes Wharton's suggestion: "No. I want Kristina with me. My therapy session can be very taxing and sometimes I need to talk to her afterwards. She has a knack for comforting me when I need it."

"Some other time, Wharton. I'd love it. Maybe when you're next at the house. That way, the three of us, you, me and Jeff, can talk together and you can get to know both of us a little better. I'm sure you and Jeff will hit it off," Kristina responds, with the ease of a matadoras twirling her cape and gracefully pivoting her hips as the bull rushes past.

A second defeat of sorts for Wharton today, but not one he can take to heart since his effort with Kristina was middling at best. He retains intact the egocentric delusion that if he puts his mind to it, he can successfully seduce any heterosexual or bi-sexual woman, married, engaged or single, Kristina included, such is his unique combination of physical appearance, charm, wealth and good breeding (Wharton, a true legend in his own mind). He'll shelve for now any further thoughts about a campaign to woo Kristina (certain that he will bed her once he applies himself more thoughtfully to the task) and concentrate on his more immediate issue: convincing Willis and Wilma to lend him the money he needs.

Wharton calls Willis to arrange to meet him after work at the "Looney As A Toon" Club in Chelsea, one of the places where Wharton and his friends pal out. It's a members-only club in which indulged spawn of privilege can wallow to their extreme in private rooms where naked bodies lull around unabashed (but not untouched) amid a sea of trays laden with assorted pills and multiple lines of cocaine, all available for a night of entitled bacchanalia.

Only self-destructive Wharton can explain (if even he could) why he has chosen this as the place for a serious discussion with Willis about money, but he has: "Hi, bro. It's me. Can you meet me after work today? I need to talk to you about something."

"I'm meeting Melody for dinner with some friends. So my time's tight today. Why don't you just tell me over the phone what you want to talk about?" Willis responds.

"I'd rather have some face time. We haven't seen each other in several weeks. What time is your dinner?"

"7 P.M."

"So, it's 3:30 now. Instead of going home, finish up at work and meet me at 5:00 and then you can meet Melody for dinner at 7:00."

"Okay," Willis hesitantly replies.

"'Looney As A Toon,'" 28th and 10th Avenue."

"Okay. Never heard of the place. But I'll meet you there."

"It's a fun place. Cartoon characters from Looney Tunes decorate the joint."

"What is Looney Tunes?"

"Ever see 'Who Framed Roger Rabbit' or 'Space Jam'?

"No."

"Take my word for it, you'll like the fun vibe the club has. See you there."

Wharton arrives a few minutes after the appointed time and finds Willis and Melody already there, waiting for him in the reception area just inside the entrance to the club. After Wharton and Willis shake hands and Wharton gives Melody a hug, they sit down together at a table in the corner of the club's main floor cocktail lounge.

"It's been far too long," an outwardly composed, insides churning, Wharton glibly begins. "And Melody, this is a very pleasant surprise. Good to see you."

"Thanks," she responds with a wry and wary smile. "When Willis told me about your call, I figured I'd tag along, get a chance to see you and this club you told Willis about."

"Glad you came. Let me end the suspense and get right to the point. Then we can spend the rest of the time, before you have to leave, just catching up and gossiping about Charlotte and William, and their newly adopted daughter, Kristina. I'd like you to lend me $2 million as part of the money I need to purchase and operate a professional lacrosse team. Dad has vetted my business plan and even though he thinks it has a real chance of success, he won't give me the money I need for the business."

"Why not?" Willis questions.

"He says that I need to do this without his help. He thinks if I do, I'll show him I'm a man, not just a grown boy. Something like that."

"To be fair, Wharton, he has given you money in the past for business ventures of yours which failed. So maybe that's his reasoning."

"Right. No confidence in me," Wharton balks: "People fail at something without it being their fault and certainly without it meaning that if they failed once, they will fail again. This business is going to be a winner, I know it. I really do. It's been very carefully researched and thought out, even to Dad's satisfaction. But because it's me, his black sheep child, he won't lend me the money."

"I'm not sure how to respond to you on this. I need to think about it and talk it over with Melody."

Melody speaks up, squelching Wharton's request in no uncertain terms: "I want us to be up front with you. There's no need for Willis and I to talk this over. I'm planning on starting a business, buying and selling art, and we'll need the money for that." Turning towards Willis, she looks at him in a manner that requires no interpretation on his part and continues: "Willis. I just don't see how we can lend him the money if I'm going to start up my business. And you know how very much I want to do that."

Willis picks up Melody's cudgel: "Sorry, Wharton. She's right. Melody and I have been talking about this for a while now. I'm even going to need to go to Dad to see if we can borrow some money from him for her business."

"Oh, you'll probably have no trouble getting what you ask for from him. He likes you, he just doesn't like me," Wharton petulantly declares, then, after taking a deep breath and expelling it, he says: "I'm not angry at you two. Just at dad. Forget that I asked you to lend me money, and let's just catch up. It really is good to see you. Both of you."

The time remaining is spent in family gossip and casual commentary, "you look lovely, as always, Melody"; "what do you think about our Kristina and her fiancé living in our home?;" "did you notice that Charlotte seems to be getting a lot more migraines lately? I wonder how bad things are between her and William"; "what happens to our lives with the spotlight we will be in if dad is nominated Secretary of the Treasury?"; "have you spoken to Wilma lately?"; "when are you two going to make me an uncle? Willis would be an uncle already if I were married to you, Melody"; "You know they both have lovers, don't you?"; "Have you noticed the beautiful clothes that Kristina always wears? Charlotte has bought most of them for her."

As Willis, Melody and Wharton polish off the last of their several drinks and drain the remnants of their gossip, Willis' parting gesture is an attempt to offer some comfort to Wharton, optimistically encouraging him: "I think dad will change his mind and come through for you if you don't give up. We'll be seeing him soon and I'll say something to him about it. Maybe that will help."

"Thanks. You've always been an optimist but maybe with you and Charlotte in my corner, he'll change his mind. I damn well hope so. This is such a great opportunity, to get in on the ground floor of what'll be the next great professional sport. With a few more teams in the league, we can garner a cable contract and once the games are televised, the sky's the limit and I'll own the only New York based team."

On that note, hugs and kisses all around, Willis and Melody wobble off to meet their friends for dinner, a little late and a lot sloshed.

CHAPTER XXV

"I'm going deaf by marriage," William declares to Charlotte, after having had to listen to her go on at length about Wharton and Melody. This is a rare weeknight that he's dining at home (and verily regrets it), Vanessa attending some business event with the CEO of one of her public relations clients.

Yesterday, Charlotte had lunch with Willis, whom she had invited to join her for a "quick bite," having "not seen you in ages," we just "must make some time to spend together." Lunch with Willis went quite well at first; he seemed happy to see Charlotte and share stories with her about his patients (no medical ethics violated) and the other doctors in his physician group, and she was happy to chatter on about the social events she'd attended, the book she was going to write about the Houghton family history, what a great help to her and lovely person Kristina was, and how exciting it was that William might be nominated soon for a very important governmental position. So, for a time, they both carefully avoided any hot-button topics.

Willis was the first to slip off the slope with his mention of the fact that Melody, being somewhat of an art connoisseuse, intended to make money by buying and selling art, possibly in a gallery of her own branded by her name. Try as she might, Charlotte could not hide her disapproval of the idea or, unfortunately, her dislike of Melody, although try very hard she didn't: "That's Melody, for you. She's certainly ambitious, just like the rest of her people. Make money off

William's back, the Wylde name in business, a reputation that he's worked so hard to establish. And what does she really know about art at her age? Not enough yet to make a successful business of it, I would say."

"Mom, what's with you? What do you have against Melody — that she's Jewish? Is that really it? Because what you just said — that she's 'just like the rest of her people' — sure makes it sound like it."

"I admit that I'm not a big fan of Jewish people in general, nor was my father. I wish them no harm but I don't want to do business, or be in business, with them. But my problem with Melody is just that I believe that she's not right for you in the long run. She's too ambitious and won't let you remain what you are: a kind person, always looking to help others, and a loving and lovely son."

"Thanks. But I'm no angel and you're pissing me off. There's no shame in Melody wanting to have a career and make money. Melody wants to accomplish something, and dealing in art is what she's chosen. Just as I've chosen to be a doctor."

"Let her have children, as I did and most women of quality do. Having married you, she has enough money, so let her accomplishment be raising children. She can make money, if that's what she wants, after they've grown up."

"You're completely out of touch with reality," Willis heatedly responds, his temper flaring and his voice rising. "Women today have children and a career at the same time. Your own mother was in the vanguard of that, for fuck's sake." Calming down a bit, he continues, "Melody is just another modern woman — beautiful, smart, loving and ambitious. Those qualities are what make her the person I love."

Backing off an argument that she saw she couldn't win, certainly not by the type of direct attack that she'd just advanced, Charlotte offered a peace pipe, saying: "Maybe you're right, Willis. Maybe I am out of step and have been unduly harsh in my opinion of Melody. I need to examine this through your eyes. I love you and if she makes you happy, then that should be good enough for me."

"Thanks, Mom," Willis gratefully replied, not recognizing that deceit could possibly, and did, lie beneath those conciliatory words of promise. "You should know, I intend to ask dad to help Melody out and lend us some money for her to start her business. I hope you'll support my request. I'm just waiting until Melody is ready with a plan on how much she needs and how she intends to spend it, so dad can see that this is not some lark, but well-thought out. That's important to Melody and to me."

It's the combination of Charlotte's effort to convince William to lend Wharton the money he needs to buy a professional lacrosse team and her attempt to put a kibosh on William possibly giving money to Melody when she requests it, that has led to William's pronouncement that Charlotte is making him "deaf by marriage."

"Please, Charlotte, I didn't go out of my way to come home to have dinner with you tonight so that you could bombard me all evening with how you want me to behave with regard to Wharton and Melody. I don't want to hear any more about it."

"You need to listen to me for once. You hear me, but you don't listen. Wharton is a little wild and at times has been irresponsible, it's true. But he's making an effort to change, can't you see that? If he gets involved with this lacrosse team of his, he'll be able to be all the things you say you want him to be."

"We've been over and over this," a weary William responds. "He needs for once to do this completely on his own, without any money from me. A good idea and well-thought out business plan can always find financial backing. And I don't see that he's making any effort to change. He's as wild and irresponsible as ever, obviously still doing drugs too, in case you haven't noticed."

"He's your son. The $7 million means nothing to you. You donate more than that to charity each year. So give it to Wharton," she passionately pleads, one last time. "I'll make you a promise. If you do this and Wharton ever again asks for money from you that you don't want to give him, I'll fully support your decision. I'll never again try to get you to change your mind."

"Even if I believed you'd honor your promise, which I don't, I'm firm in my decision. This time he needs to raise the money elsewhere and not get it from me."

"Then I'll give him the money. I'll write him the check."

"No, you won't Charlotte. Not if you want to continue to have the life our marriage provides you."

After a long pause, Charlotte dejectedly surrenders: "Alright, William, I give up. You win, as always. But if you're not giving money to Wharton for his venture, you most certainly can't give money to Melody for hers. That would be devastating for Wharton."

William replies: "Melody's idea of buying and selling art sounds feasible. From what I can tell, she has good taste and a head on her shoulders. The issue of whether I agree to give Melody the money when she actually asks for it, which I might add has not happened yet, has nothing to do with how it may or may not affect Wharton."

"I don't think you see the real Melody," Charlotte fires back, loosing all her cannons. "She married Willis for the Wylde name and money. When his lust for her wears out, he'll see her for what she is. Then what? You'll just have given her money for nothing — wasted it on her."

"Where is this coming from, Charlotte? Take a pill, for God's sake. You've gone off the deep end."

"I'm right. You'll see. She's going to make Willis unhappy some day. We can help him if we don't help her. If she sees that she isn't going to get money from us, either she'll settle down and be a real partner for him or she'll leave him for a different prey. Either way, he'll be better off in the end."

"I can't take any more. I'm done. You need to think about what you're saying and what is driving your opinion about Melody. I'm going into my den to listen to the news and then I have some work I need to do on a speech I've been asked to give next week. Before I go, I was waiting for the right moment to surprise you, that's why I came home for dinner with you tonight," William lies. "But since there obviously isn't going to be a right moment, I want you to know that the rumors about my possible nomination to be the next Secretary of the Treasury weren't unfounded. I've had discussions with the administration and should know for sure soon."

"How wonderful for you, William. Congratulations," Charlotte perfunctorily replies. Look at what you gave up for it, she thinks but does not say, as she heads for her bedroom and the comfort of her pills.

CHAPTER XXVI

Simon and Jeff have diligently scoured the internet and completed what they hope to be a comprehensive analysis of the idea that they and Kristina discussed about a week ago — an Automat-type restaurant business.

Although online purchases of meals have dramatically grown over the past few years and are fast becoming a routine part of many people's daily lives, they've become convinced that there's still a thriving market for the grab-and-go food that McDonald's, Burger King and their competitors provide, particularly if healthy alternatives to the usual staple of burgers and fries, fried chicken, and fried fish are available. And that's what the restaurants they have in mind for their business would be: retro-styled, handsomely furnished, art deco grab-and-go restaurants offering not only hamburgers, frankfurters and fried foods, but salads, grilled foods, vegetarian selections and other healthy, weight-conscious options, all set inside walls of clear glass food-containing windows to which a customer could walk up, insert a vending machine restaurant coin and remove the meal of his or her choice. William has opened a wide door of opportunity and Simon, in coming up with the idea, has pushed Jeff through it.

So it is that Jeff has arranged to meet with William at Wylde Capital's Park Avenue South offices. He's bringing with him some basic data sheets that he and Simon have prepared about fast food restaurant operations, franchisor-franchisee dynamics and operating issues, and some very basic spread sheets of cost to construct and open, and expense to operate, an Automat-type restaurant.

Wylde Capital's offices consist of the entire top floor of an art deco building constructed pre-war but since upgraded to state of the art technology. William got a great deal on the lease when a law firm that was the prior tenant of that 50,000 square foot space went belly up just three years after it finished paying for renovating and elegantly redecorating its offices. The 70-lawyer firm's collapse was attributable to two of its five senior-most rainmaking partners unexpectedly departing for the greener pastures of an international 900 attorney firm, where they were promised to earn two and one-half times their current share of the profits at Shapiro, Hussein & O'Rourke, the firm they'd helped found 15 years ago. (Proving once again, that even loyalty has its price.)

Wylde Capital's reception area is even more grand than Jeff had imagined. A floor to ceiling glass window takes up the entire back wall of the eight-chair, leather-seated waiting area, the Wylde Capital name is emblazoned in a neon-lighted blinking logo set behind a massive dark Cherrywood reception desk located on the left wall of the waiting area, and large, very colorful Julian Schnabel plate paintings hang both on the wall opposite the reception desk and by the elevator bank. Behind the reception desk sit a young man and young woman, both in their early 20s, he looking as if he were one of People Magazine's selections for Sexiest Man Alive and she as if she had recently been on the cover of Sports Illustrated's swimsuit edition.

Upon arrival, Jeff is quickly ushered into William's corner four-windowed office, so rapidly that he barely has time to disguise the look of wonder that had caused his jaws to drop and eyes to bulge when he first got off the elevator. Seated in a high-backed, ornate chair behind his elegant 19th century antique hand-carved mahogany partner's desk, William looks more like a king on his throne in days of old, than the very savvy, cunning and knowledgeable modern businessman that he is.

William cordially greets Jeff and beckons him to take a seat at the large glass-topped, circular working table in the back corner of William's office. As William sits down next to Jeff, Clifford Thurston enters his office and introduces himself to Jeff, "Hi. I'm Clifford Thurston, one of the partners here. William has asked me to sit in on the meeting, if you don't mind." That Clifford has been asked by William to participate in the meeting is the result of Charlotte suggesting it to William when she learned of Jeff having asked to meet with William and why. In doing so, Charlotte had dual purposes in mind: to help Jeff with any business analysis William might require of him and to possibly advance Clifford's career at Wylde Capital.

"A pleasure to meet you," a duck out of water, visibly nervous Jeff replies.

Assessing Jeff's anxiety, William attempts to put him at ease: "I'm glad you've thought about what we talked about a few weeks ago and I look forward to hearing whatever it is you want to discuss with me. Please proceed at your own pace. Clifford and I have plenty of free time this morning, so no need for you to rush through anything."

"Thanks, Mr. Wylde."

"William, please. Always William to you."

"Okay. In a nutshell," a slightly more at ease Jeff says, "my idea is to form a company called Auto Eats and pattern it after the old Horn & Hardart Automat restaurants, but make it a fast food operation akin to McDonalds and Burger King and for Auto Eats to own and operate a few restaurants but franchise most of them to other operators. I've brought data sheets and spreadsheets to go over with you and pictures of some of the Horn & Hardart Automats that existed in the 1950s and 1960s."

"Before you say anything more, it would be easiest if you first give us a few moments to look at what you brought with you," William says, as he holds out his hands for the papers, takes them and then spreads them out on the table in front of him, while Clifford gets up and walks to the side of William's chair to look over William's shoulder at the documents. After several minutes have passed, Clifford retakes his seat and William turns towards Jeff and says: "Very impressive. Really. Did you prepare these materials all by yourself?"

"No," Jeff readily admits. "My friend, Simon, the writer, was a very big help. We did this mostly together."

"I don't know what thoughts Clifford has, but this looks to me like a very interesting concept, one that you've supported with statistics and information that warrant a deeper analysis of the cost and potential return on investment."

"I agree, William," Clifford eagerly responds. "Why don't I work on preparing a deeper analysis, as you just suggested, then I'll go over it with Jeff and we'll submit it to you."

"Sounds right," pronounces William. "To be clear, Jeff, is your intended role in all this to be the head of this company?"

"Yes and no. I'm a people person, not a numbers or operations guy. So I would have you help me hire people to perform those roles and while they'd let me know at all times what major decisions they were making, I'd pretty much leave them alone to perform as they see fit. My role would be to be the face of the company for the media, to interact with Auto Eats' employees and customers to the extent any problems arise and to find suitable franchisees and establish strong, continued good relationships between these franchisees and the company."

"Comments, Clifford?," William inquires.

"None, not yet. Let me do the analysis required and let's go from there. The first step is to drill down and see what hard rock we hit, if any, that might prevent us from going forward. If all systems are go, then we can proceed to the next step from there."

"How long do you think you need to prepare the analysis?" William asks.

"One to two weeks. I'm working on a few other matters that require my immediate attention and I don't want to give them short shrift."

"Okay. Let's target late August." Turning to Jeff, William gives him a figurative pat on the back: "Well done. Tell your friend Simon that as well. See you at home this weekend. Any interest in going golfing with me on Sunday? One of the regulars in my foursome can't make it."

"Growing up in Cobble Hill, I never got exposed to golf. We had schoolyards, not golf courses, except some makeshift mini-golf, of course. My sport is, or at least was, basketball. So I think I'll use a basketball term to say 'I pass.' But thanks very much."

William, with a laugh, responds: "Well, you're presently a denizen of Sands Point and we revoke your passport if you don't play golf — let me set you up with a few lessons with our club golf pro, and then see how you do and whether you like it. Pretend I'm your godfather and that it's an offer you can't refuse."

Thinking to himself that William may well, in fact, be his godfather, since he's living with him and might be being backed in business by him, and intrigued by the opportunity to try a new sport, Jeff readily accepts the carrot and agrees to take up the stick (in this case a nine iron).

Once outside the building, Jeff calls an anxiously waiting Kristina to tell her how his meeting with William went.

"Hi, babe.

"Hi, yourself. So tell me. How did it go?"

"It went better than I ever expected. He liked the whole thing, complimented me and is having one of his partners, Clifford Thurston, doing some more analysis to see if what Simon and I worked on actually pans out."

"That's great," Kristina gushes, her enthusiasm only slightly dampened by the fact that she now knows that Charlotte and Clifford Thurston are having an affair and she worries what impact that might have on the start-up of Jeff's business were William to find out in the near term.

"When I get home we'll go out and celebrate," an exuberant Jeff announces.

"I've a better idea. Let's stay home and celebrate. There are things in life much better to do than eat food," Kristina playfully replies.

"Can't wait to find out what that might be. I'll be home early today. Think I'll take the rest of the day off."

"Love you."

"Love you back."

CHAPTER XXVII

"I need my pills, Kristina, a Xanax and an Oxycontin, and a glass of ice water, please. I'm a bundle of nerves today. This Children's Museum Gala has been a real trial for me. I never realized what a burden being chairwoman of the event would turn out to be."

"I'll bring the pills right down," Kristina says as she hurries toward the large circular staircase that leads up to Charlotte and William's adjoining bedroom suites. As she starts walking up the steps, Charlotte calls out: "While you're up there, please go to the safe in my bedroom and bring me the larger of the three jewelry boxes marked with the 'Harry Winston' name. I want to try on the diamond and pearl earrings and matching necklace that are in there that I think I'll wear tonight."

It takes but three minutes for Kristina to return, pills in one hand and jewelry box cradled with the other. She places both on the coffee table in front of the floral-patterned silk couch on which Charlotte is reclining, embroidered throw pillows under her head at one end and her bare feet on top of the other.

Kristina goes to the kitchen to bring Charlotte a glass of water and, as she walks back with the water into the main floor sitting room where Charlotte reposes, Charlotte sits up and complains: "I can't believe I have to go out tonight, feeling as badly as I do. But I simply must. William committed us to this casino night event." After taking the glass from Kristina and swallowing the pills, Charlotte continues: "It's a fundraiser sponsored by one of his largest institutional investors, a pension fund, and Cary Larson, the senior investment adviser for the pension fund, specifically asked if I'd be coming. William says he has eyes for me and that I should feel complimented, but not enough to do something rash with one of his business associates. I need to flirt and charm, but duck and weave if anything more than flattery comes my way."

"You're a very beautiful woman, so that's no surprise," Kristina replies, then pauses and says: "I hope I'm not out of line with what I'm about to say. I've noticed that lately you seem very stressed and that you're taking pills more frequently than you used to. I'm worried about your health and that you might be over-medicating yourself. If there's anything I can do to help reduce the strain you've been under, please let me know."

"Thank you, darling. I really do appreciate your concern, but I'm not over-medicating. I'm only taking what I need, what's been prescribed for my various illnesses. And you're always a big help to me. I don't know how I'd manage without you. Just look at what you've done to help me put together the Children's Museum Gala next month. I don't know why the Gala is making me so nervous. I guess it's just that I want it to be a huge success."

"It will be, I'm sure. Maybe it's also other things that are making you so upset," Kristina innocently suggests, as she sits down next to Charlotte.

"You're right. It's a great many things, all piled one on top of the other. My life's becoming a shambles. William has always had a wandering eye and I've accepted his many infidelities as being just part of his basic make-up. As far as I could tell, none of them really meant anything to him beyond the physical. But that has changed; he seems very distant these past months, almost never home any more, certainly not since you and Jeff moved in with us, and frequently displeased with me when he is. Then there's Wharton. He's angry at William for not giving him some money that he asked for and that has carried over to Wharton not coming around or calling me very much anymore. We used to be close."

The flood gates open, Charlotte breathlessly lets flow a non-stop recitation of the litany of other ills that now litter her life: "Willis and Wilma are very dear to me, but my relationships with them have been fractured by the partners they've chosen. Willis married a fortune hunter. She's Jewish, you know. So no surprise there. Already she's trying to get millions from us, not even married to Willis for two years. I can't stand it. He's such a good person. She'll ruin him.

"And then my Wilma. We were inseparable. Now, there's Bess in her life. They're living together and want a child. Bess is from the streets, low class, claims she makes money as a bartender and hostess. I know that she makes most of her money selling drugs. Wilma confided that to me, but said Bess is a good person and Wilma is getting her to stop. Wilma is an innocent lamb whom Bess will slowly devour until there's nothing left of the daughter I raised."

Having spewed out her many trials and tribulations to Kristina, an emotionally exhausted but momentarily relieved Charlotte rests her head on Kristina's shoulders, while a still silent, somewhat stunned Kristina puts an arm around her shoulders in an attempt to comfort her. After a moment, Charlotte, in a soft, low voice, adds: "Now you know all my secrets, not just about my sleeping with Clifford Thurston."

Having heard much more than she ever expected when she commented about what might be upsetting Charlotte, Kristina realizes that what Charlotte needs beyond the medication her doctors have prescribed is a better therapist than the one she's presently seeing. Kristina is no substitute for that and has no desire to try to be one; it's a role well beyond her pay grade.

"So, it's quite a mess, as you can see," Charlotte dispiritedly concludes.

"This will all work itself out," is all that Kristina can think to say. A handy platitude to offer, a placeholder, until Kristina has time to sort through how all these newly shared confidences might impact her in her job, a job that she has, to this point, very much enjoyed. "I'll help you as best I can."

"I know you will, Kristina. I'm counting on you. Even just your presence is a comfort to me. No more for now, dear. My head's still splitting. I need to rest for a while if I'm not to make a fool of myself tonight. I need a warm compress and a dark bedroom. I'll see you later."

"Do you need me to bring you anything upstairs?"

"No. Just wake me at 6:00 P.M. I'll need the time to make up and dress. We're leaving at 7:30 for the benefit."

Kristina acknowledges Charlotte's instruction with a bow of her head, turns away and walks towards her quarters, hoping that Jeff will be there. She'll keep Charlotte's confidences, but not from Jeff. Charlotte has laid too large a burden on her shoulders for Kristina to bear alone. She has no choice but to share this information with Jeff, as it may come to roost that it greatly affects their lives.

CHAPTER XXVIII

"In ten years, the world's supply of helium will be exhausted. Is that nuts, or what? No more inflated party balloons on birthdays," are the first words I say after Jeff and Kristina sit down next to me at my corner table at Lulu's Lair, the latest in-place, where the elite meet, greet and eat while texting to each other across the table.

"That's our greeting?" Jeff replies. "Ok, I can't believe that I'm falling for this, but I'll bite. 'Why is that?' the straight man asked, waiting for delivery of the punchline."

"No joke this time. I just read about it. Helium is produced by the radioactive decay of underground rocks and most of it just floats away into the atmosphere. We're left with what's trapped in the earth's crust, and China is rapidly using that up as a liquid coolant for manufacturing."

"There'll always be floating balloons when you're around. You're full of enough hot air to bridge the gap," Jeff quips, as Patricia slides down to sit in the chair next to me, having successfully navigated her way to and from the ladies room without, she tells us, having been subtly groped more than twice. You'd think that these days unwanted touching need only be at defcon five on a woman's radar, but apparently not.

I'm still dating Patricia, but I'm not sure where, if any place, we're headed. She has a sense of humor that seems to be in sync with mine — in other words, she laughs at all my jokes, even when she's heard them more than once. That she also has not lost any of her curves and is eager for me to navigate them, only strengthens her case. I'm finding that sex and laughs, in no particular order as long as not simultaneously, are quite an engaging mix. I'm not a sexist pig, so it's also appropriate to acknowledge that Patricia is quite intelligent. (I note, however, that I think of this quality last, and mostly as a defensive after-thought.)

Having caught the tail-end of Jeff's comment, Patricia asks "what've I missed?"

Kristina jumps in with: "Nothing much. Simon has just been educating us on the imminent disappearance of helium from our lives."

"Sorry I missed that," Patricia jokingly grimaces, while affectionately placing her hand on my arm. Addressing Kristina, she says: "Not to change the subject, but it has been weeks since we all last got together. Simon is a sphinx when it comes to getting information from him. I ask him 'how's Kristina doing?' and he replies 'ask her yourself when we see her.' So, I'm asking. How's your job going? Do you still like it?"

Kristina hesitates, then thoughtfully responds: "I do. Pretty much. Sometimes it's interesting, sometimes it's fun, sometimes it's both and sometimes it's not so great. Yesterday was one of those not so great days."

"In what way?"

"I spent the entire day accompanying Charlotte to a bunch of designer flagship stores and mostly stood around while she tried on, browsed through or marveled over a vast array of merchandise, none of which an average person could ever afford to buy. My sole productivity for the day, if you can call it that, was that I helped her decide which of the three $19-$21,000 Birkin bags she had selected she should purchase."

"Sounds like fun to me," Patricia enthuses, and then continues: "How's Charlotte as a person, is she easy to work for?"

Although tempted to share more, to be more forthcoming about how more complicated her job is starting to become, Kristina cannot in good conscience betray any of Charlotte's recently shared confidences.

She cares too much for Charlotte to gossip about her, to treat her emotional problems as a topic for casual conversation. She does, however, reply: "Charlotte's a very complex person, both kind and entitled. I've become more than just a personal assistant to her, she treats me as family. That has its good and bad points, as you can imagine."

Eager to hear the latest progress report on Auto Eats, I try to cut further discussion about Charlotte off at the pass: "The good outweighs any bad as far as I'm concerned. All hail the newest wealthy Wylde, called to the queen as her lady-in-waiting. I expect your inheritance will be large. So please remember your friend, lowly surf Simon, when you receive it, and be sure to bestow some of your riches on he."

I'm always so quick-witted, I think proudly to myself, even though no one has laughed or even cracked a smile. More like blank looks telegraphing their thoughts that "Simon can be just a superficial jerk sometimes." But writers can't afford to let bad reviews stop them (bad book sales are a different matter), so I'm not intimidated and I carry on: "So Jeff, what's the latest with you and William?"

"Nothing new on Auto Eats yet," Jeff responds. "I should be hearing back soon. I saw William when I was getting a golf lesson he arranged for me at his club and he was on the practice range. I asked him where things stood and all he said was that he's expecting Clifford to be reporting to him on it soon. That was Sunday."

"Fingers crossed," I say.

"What about you? How are you spending your time now that I'm not around as much to help fill the voids in your pathetic life?" Jeff jokingly asks me, with an undercurrent of concern that only I can detect.

"Oh, I get by, even without a little help from my friend", I banter. Then, more seriously, I say: "Truthfully, I miss our hanging out together. But things are good. The sales on my newest book have been even better than expected and I'm pretty far along on the first draft of my next one."

Before I can say anything more, Patricia interjects: "And now he has me around, also on the 'things are good' side of his life's ledger."

I was contemplating (but not certain) about next mentioning Patricia as a person who cheered some of my days (more accurately, some of my nights), but she's beaten me to the punch. I'm backed in a corner, trapped into having to affirmatively acknowledge Patricia's statement if I want to continue our relationship. The only thing I can come up with is to lamely say: "No doubt about it," and turning my head towards Patricia, offer the bon mot: "You're the best thing in my life since Krispy Kreme donuts."

"And I'm much healthier for you than the donuts," she responds. "Our morning workouts together in the gym, if nothing else."

'I prefer our workouts together at night," clever to the end, I rejoin.

"Enough of this mush. You're both making me sick," Jeff responds.

"I think it's sweet," Kristina says.

"To each his own," Jeff comments, then leans towards Patricia, with his chin jutted out like a cop about to grill a suspect, and says: "So tell us, ma'am, what about you? What wealth are you managing these days? You may be out of a job soon, you know. All wealth is going to be sucked away into a thickening fog of taxes."

Patricia laughs, and responds: "It's going to disappear for some people well before taxes make it go 'poof.' I try to steer those who want high risk-high reward investments to hedge funds like Wylde Capital or Pershing Square or private equity funds like The Carlyle Group or Blackstone, companies with a track record of profitability. But some of our clients don't follow our advice and, instead, borrow from us so that they can roll the dice on some friend or relative's lame-brained scheme."

"Now you've hooked me. Examples, please."

"The names will never cross my lips. But some of the stuff the idle rich have invested in, against our advice, run the gamut from a start-up company claiming to have invented a new revolutionary cryo-freeze technology that will put cemeteries out of business, to a company whose business plan is to sue Google, Amazon and other large technology companies for allegedly infringing some worthless foreign nation patents the company has recently purchased, to a company which is going to clone people to harvest organs and prolong life to an average age of 300 years old. I could go on. But you get the idea."

"Egads," Jeff laughs. "You have a hell of an interesting job. Beats selling cars, that's for sure."

"Hopefully, you won't be selling them much longer," I say. "Auto Eats awaits you if you can reel Mr. Wylde in now that he's taken the bait."

"I don't want to reel him in. I want him to fully believe in me and the Auto Eats business plan; if he doesn't, I don't want him to invest. I can find something else to pursue with or without him."

"I hear you," I say, as I raise my glass of Amstel Light in an anticipatory toast of good things to come. "Best of luck to you, buddy."

Our foursome evening ends with a plethora of more drinks and delicious bite-sized food and a very hefty check not so easy to swallow. We say our goodnights and promise to get together again soon. As I leave, I pull Jeff aside and tell him I'm confident that William's response is going to be an "all systems go," even if I don't necessarily feel all that confident. But that's what good friends do for each other. Support and encourage each other, and wish each other only the best. And we're not just good friends, but the best of friends. Always were and always will be.

CHAPTER XXIX

It's mid-September. A little less than four weeks after our Lulu's Lair dinner. Jeff and Kristina are here with me at my house for drinks, before we go to a movie together. It's been an eventful time for all concerned.

Patricia and I are no longer dating, no less a sometimes couple. We had a big row over commitment. I was not ready to step to the plate and swing for the fences with Patricia as my teammate. She just wasn't my soulmate, no matter how hard I tried to believe she might be. That she laughed at my jokes turned out to be more superficial than genuine, and politics, religion and our disparate careers were too great a divide for us to traverse. I want what Jeff and Kristina have. I have obviously matured, at least to that extent. Or maybe not. Who knows? I certainly don't.

Patricia was not happy, to say the least, as this was her second break-up in a little over a year, each time with someone in whom she had invested substantial emotional capital. I apologized as best I could, but the words were empty shibboleths, and no consolation to her. "It's not you, it's me," is so common, even if true, as to be of no value at all. I will miss her (did I mention her body and how great the sex was?), but I needed to move on before I was caught in a quagmire of my own making from which there'd be no easy escape.

Jeff and Kristina's lives are faring much better. Talk about understatements.

William has decided to move forward on funding Auto Eats, although instead of the immediate franchise business that Jeff and I outlined, he's going to take it slower, one step at a time. Jeff is to open one suburban company-owned restaurant in Melville, Long Island to see how it performs. If the restaurant's sales are good and it has a strong, repeat-customer following, then Wylde Capital will fund the opening of three or four more company-owned Auto Eats and, after that, the franchising of 20-30 more restaurants in the tri-state area.

As you would imagine, Jeff and Kristina are very excited, but also apprehensive. There are risks involved for Jeff. He'll be giving up a job he still enjoys in exchange initially for overseeing the operation of a single restaurant, a role which he may neither be suited for nor enjoy. Although he'll draw a salary in the first year comparable to his Lexus earnings (thank you, William), if the restaurant is not successful, then were does that leave him? Answer: unemployed. Not a great start to married life.

Oh, yes. Did I fail to mention it? Jeff and Kristina are soon to be married, and that's a story in and of itself. They had decided they would have their wedding in the late Fall, a small, intimate affair at a night club in Williamsburg that doubles as a rental hall for weddings and other affairs. Kristina's mother died when she was a teenager, her father died six months after she graduated college and she has no siblings. Her only living relatives are an aunt and uncle and two cousins, all of whom live in Oklahoma City, and only the aunt and uncle were planning on attending. As their gift to Jeff and Kristina, Barbara Muss had offered that she and Daniel would pay for the wedding, something she very much wanted to do for her son and his soon-to-be bride, whom Barbara has come to adore.

Even though Jeff and Kristina are living a distance away in Long Island, Barbara and Kristina have grown very close. The "kids," as Barbara refers to them, frequently come to dinner at her house. Sometimes, Barbara invites me (her other "kid") to join them. On occasion, Barbara and Kristina meet in Manhattan and go to a theatre matinee together or browse through Chelsea art galleries, Soho clothing stores or the small number of still-remaining specialty book stores sprinkled around Manhattan. Barbara's tribe has increased. From Jeff has sprung Simon and now Kristina. Barbara's love, advice and concern extends to us all, and we reciprocate as best we can; she is loved in return.

Alas, the best laid plans of mice and men, in the words of the poet, "gang aft agley," and so it was with Jeff, Kristina and Barbara's wedding plan — it went awry. Some would say for the better, but not as far as Barbara is concerned.

When Kristina told Charlotte about her wedding plans, Charlotte talked to William and, with his blessing, made another offer that Jeff and Kristina couldn't refuse. "Kristina, dear, what you and Jeff have planned sounds very nice, but William and I would like to provide you with a much grander memory of your wedding day. William has spoken to the Tata Group's CEO, it owns the Pierre Hotel you know, and arranged a December wedding for you at the Pierre. We'll pay for everything, of course, including all expenses to attend for those relatives and friends of yours living in Oklahoma City that you wish to invite."

"Thank you. But this is really too much for us to accept," was a nonplussed Kristina's initial reply after regaining her ability to speak. But after much back and forth, a still overwhelmed Kristina's response was whittled down to just "Thank you," a beyond generous offer reluctantly accepted but conditioned, of course, by her saying that she needed to speak about it with Jeff. She did, he did, and they did — accept the wedding at the Pierre, and so it came to be.

Kristina and Jeff shared their happy wedding news with me, but also the reasons for their hesitation in having accepted Charlotte's offer. On the one hand, Kristina feels that they're taking advantage of the Wyldes in accepting such a gift and, on the other, that she may become trapped by doing so. I asked her why she felt that she might become trapped, and she explained: "It's just that I'm not sure how long I may want to keep working as Charlotte's assistant. It's becoming more complicated. She shares with me many of her secrets and problems, and there are a lot of not so great things in her life that are distressing her. These carry over into my job. I like her, I'm concerned for her and on balance still very much enjoy being her assistant, but there may come a time that I want out. How can I quit after she'll have done so much for us? And this is on top of William starting Jeff off in business."

I told her that the Wyldes could well-afford the $300,000 or so that I guessed the wedding might cost and, if Kristina and Jeff were to become trapped by anything, it was Auto Eats, not the wedding, that set the trap.

Jeff disagreed with my assessment of their situation, at least as far as Auto Eats is concerned, his view being: "If the Auto Eats trial period proves out to be successful, William has a profitable business, one which he's not likely to throw away because Kristina leaves her job. My mother had a lawyer friend of hers represent me in the contract I have with Wylde Capital, and I retain all rights to the Auto Eats trademark and business plan if Wylde Capital exits the business. So I'm protected no matter what Kristina decides to do."

We left it at that, nothing more really to say. Kristina is entitled to feel how she does about the downside to accepting such a gift, but it's of no consequence since they've already agreed to a December 15th wedding at the Pierre.

How did Barbara and Dan take all this?, you might ask. I did and Jeff's response was: "Mom was upset when we told her. She said that she'd spent a great deal of time in thinking about and helping us plan the wedding, all of which was now just wasted. More importantly, she wanted the wedding to be her and dad's gift to us, something special they could do for us that we would always remember and cherish. Dad's reaction was that a wedding at the Pierre is a once-in-a-lifetime dream come true that no sane person could turn down. Mom got over her initial disappointment, because the very next day after we told her about the new wedding plans, she called to tell us that, after speaking with dad, she had come to realize that she was wrong to feel the way she did and it was the right thing for us to be married at the Pierre. If that makes us happy, it makes her happy."

It's with this background, this confluence of life-changing events, that we find the three of us in my house, drinking some booze, smoking some weed and kicking back having some fun. Jeff teases me: "We liked Patricia, she was way too good for you. I was surprised you lasted as long as you did before she caught on to you."

Kristina jumps in to protect me, not yet fully on board with the give-and-take barbed remarks that guy friends with an excess of testosterone regularly exchange. "That's cruel, Jeff. I don't like that. I doubt that Simon is taking their break-up as lightly as he may pretend."

"I was only joking around," Jeff protests to Kristina. "That's how Simon and I always behave. We're brothers."

"Then behave more like sisters when you're around me," she implores.

Appropriately chastised but undeterred nevertheless, Jeff and I fake hug and break out laughing. I tell them how star-crossed they are and how truly happy I am for them (which I am) and they tell me how they wish I'd find someone to love but are glad that my writing career is going so well. (I have a new, aggressive agent and she's gotten me an advance from the publisher for my next, already half-written, book — a first for me, and any advance, no less $25,000, is quite a milestone in a 30-year old author's career.)

The pre-movie portion of our evening ends without our usual discussion of any or all of the political, economic, racial, religious, women's rights, immigration, healthcare, clean environment or police state issues that bombard us on a daily basis. We do find time, of course, to comment on the latest happenings in television and social media.

"Did you see 'The Bachelor' last night?" Kristina inquires.

"You have to be kidding," I exclaim, in fake outrage that she might think I would watch something like that. "I don't watch any of that junk, not 'The Real Housewives of Alcatraz,' not 'Survivor of the Very Crazy Masochists,' not 'American Idol' which I spell 'Idle,' not the latest Khardasian reality series, 'Kim's Quim Gets a Trim,' and not the game shows, except sometimes 'Jeopardy,' which I confess to watching, but at least it's semi-intelligent."

Ignoring my commentary, Kristina continues: "Jeff and I watched 'The Bachelor.' It's really fun. There's a great deal of human interest in it."

"Jeff only watches it to see how many of the good-looking women the guy gets to sleep with before he selects his supposed mate, so he can fantasize about what might have been had he not already met you."

"Jeff has nothing to fantasize about, I can assure you. He's played his fantasies all out with me," Kristina coyly responds while she scrunches her nose and sticks her tongue out at me.

"Let's not go there," Jeff says, "Some things I choose to keep private, even from you, Simon. To quickly change the subject, did you read about that judge who sentenced a guy who raped a 15-year old girl to one year's probation and some community service?"

"I didn't. How did the judge explain the reasoning behind his disgusting joke of a sentence?"

"The guy had a clean record, supposedly had learned his lesson and was unlikely to rape anyone else."

"Ha," I laugh, shaking my head. "What a fucking world. I bet the rapist is not a black kid from the ghetto; if he were, the sentence would have been very different."

"Bingo. You got it. The guy was a 23 year old Amherst College graduate and white, of course."

"I suspect some of the women's rights groups will be seeking to investigate. I'd check the judge for offshore bank accounts or recent purchases."

"That's already happening. But once the furor dies down and the social media spotlight turns off, I'll bet nothing comes of any of it until the next time the guy commits a crime, as he almost certainly will."

Having touched on these two disparate topics of the day (the "Bachelor" and the "Judge," a good title for a movie, I think), we proceed to rapidly purvey the latest news about movie star hook-ups and split-ups, wonder who's still willing to act in a Woody Allen movie, ignore Kristina's presence while we jabber about Cardi B, J-Lo, Lady Gaga, Kate Upton, Halle Berry, Heidi Klum and other women of the moment, and end our dithering with a fleeting conversation about transgender people, the latest minority group to catch the public's attention.

With that breadth of discussion behind us, our curiosity (and stomachs) fully sated for the night, we head out for our movie, a full-screen, remastered version of an old Jerry Lewis movie, "The Bellboy." They don't make them like that anymore. After we see the movie, Kristina comments "and for good reason."

CHAPTER XXX

The period between the Labor Day weekend and mid-September is not just eventful, but tumultuous for Charlotte, as her relationships with her children continue to deteriorate amidst a flurry of deeply emotion encounters. The first of these occurs on the day before the start of the Labor Day weekend.

Wharton and a few of his friends are heading off to Las Vegas for the weekend, a welcoming environment for the cocaine snorting, pill popping and profligate womanizing, not to mention excessive gambling, which increasingly dot, if not define, their privileged lives. To assuage his mother, who's bitterly complained that she hardly ever sees or speaks to him anymore, Wharton has made room in his very busy schedule of an idle rich, to visit her this afternoon, the day before he leaves for Vegas.

As they sit together in swimming suits by the pool this simmering end of August day, drinking large glasses of high octane Arnold Palmer (sometimes called a John Daly when vodka has been added, as it has been here, to the lemonade and tea), Charlotte asks Wharton to please put suntan lotion on her back.

As he smooths the cream on her back, he says: "Mom. You're completely tan. You look great, as usual."

"Thanks, dear. I try to keep in shape and look good. It's important to your father, especially now that he's so close to being nominated to be Treasury Secretary."

"You've succeeded," he says, playing to an audience he knows very well. "You look like a runway model half your age. Cindy Crawford and Christine Brinkley can't hold a candle to you."

"They're older than I. But I appreciate the intended compliment," she vainly replies, and then, after rapidly downing several sips of her Arnold Palmer, faces Wharton and asks: "Have you spoken to your father recently and patched things up between the two of you?"

"No. He is what he is, and for now, it's better for me to keep my distance. He may be suited to be a great Treasury Secretary, he's tight enough with money, but he's not a great father, he doesn't have my back."

"That's not entirely fair," Charlotte tepidly responds. "He's helped you financially in the past," she adds, not sure why she's attempting to defend William except that she'd like the two of them to at least reach a détente so that she'd get to see more of Wharton.

"Whatever you say, Mom," Wharton bitterly erupts, with genuine pent-up emotion that surprises even him: "But you can't close your eyes forever. It's always business first and the rest of us a distant last, unless we do something he can brag about, like Willis, the doctor, Wilma, the scientist, your looks, but me, the failed businessman, the hell with me. Cross me off the Wylde family list, I'm a last place disgrace."

Trying to convey to Wharton how much she loves him, Charlotte shakily responds: "Not with me. Not ever. You know how much I love you. I always have. You're irresponsible sometimes. But you're still young and feeling your way. I've confidence in you."

"I know you think you mean that, that you have confidence in me, but words are just words. If you did, you'd lend me the $5 million I still need. I can buy the lacrosse team if you do, it's not too late."

"I just can't. I can't go against William on money matters. I've tried to convince him to give you what you need. Maybe I can try again."

Giving up the ghost, Wharton surrenders, but not without one last feeble try: "Okay, Mom. I appreciate that. I just wish I could convince you that you lending me the money is the right thing for you to do, even if dad won't do it."

Wharton excuses himself to go to the bathroom, and instead of using the bathroom by the pool, walks into the house to use one of the inside bathrooms. When he returns, his pupils look strange and his nose is running. As he and Charlotte discuss less confrontational topics, Wharton keeps jiggling his legs and becomes hyper-talkative, to the point where even Charlotte, who usually does everything possible to have a blind eye to his conduct, is compelled to ask: "Are you still doing drugs, Wharton? Snorting cocaine? Is that what you did just before, when you went inside to the bathroom?"

"I do what I need to do to have fun, to enjoy life. It's no big deal. You must have done plenty of drugs too, when you were young," he dismissively responds, retaining enough of his faculties to refrain from saying what he's really thinking: Who the hell are you to condemn me for my recreational use of drugs? You can't go a day without an opioid.

Ignoring his comment about what she did when she was young, she continues to admonish him, angered by his cavalier attitude: "Whenever I see you lately, you seem to be 'having fun,' as you put it. So much 'fun.' Too much, as far as I'm concerned. Maybe it's a good thing that William didn't give you the money."

Agitated and strung out, he loses the restraint that he'd exhibited just seconds ago and hurls a stream of harsh truths, inadvertently disclosing something that he didn't mean for Charlotte to know: "Wake up, Mom. Drugs are totally mainstream. And it's all in the family. You take pills every day. Hell, do you know from whom my friends and I get most of our stash? Bess! So do you think Wilma and Bess aren't also doing drugs? And Willis, the doctor. Think he doesn't pop some of his pills too?"

Charlotte is aghast, horrified at what Wharton has just revealed. "My god. I knew Bess was no good. That she was still selling drugs and that she would be toxic to Wilma, sooner or later. But that she has the audacity to sell them to you, to be the main supplier for you and your friends? She's just scum of the earth, something to be wiped from the bottom of my shoes."

Starting to come down from his high, and jolted to his senses by Charlotte's harsh reaction, Wharton attempts to walk back his hastily spoken words: "I didn't really mean everything I just said. I was angry. My friends and I don't really buy most of our drugs from Bess. Only occasionally, and she sells them to us only as a favor to me because I badger her to do it. She's really not a bad person at all." Wharton has tried to put his cat back in the bag, not because of any affection he has for Bess, but because it's not in his interest to have Charlotte go on a rampage against her. Were Bess to discover he was the cause, it would eliminate Wilma as a possible source of money for him.

And Wharton needs money, more so now than in the past. Not only to buy the lacrosse team, which is still a possibility, but failing that, he may need it to pay off his gambling debts, which are almost to the point where his yearly trust fund stipend and whatever he can wheedle from time to time from Charlotte, are insufficient to both maintain his present lifestyle and pay his mounting debts. He's seen too many James Bond movies, and Baccarat Chemin de Fer is just not Wharton's game.

Wharton dives into the pool, both to cool his heavily perspiring body and hopefully avoid further heated argument, while Charlotte moves to the edge of the pool, where she sits dangling her feet in the water, still fuming over Bess and upset with Wharton. Despite a lengthy swim, nothing topside has improved, so Wharton gets dressed and fabricates a reason to leave, telling Charlotte that he's late to meet his friends and has to go. As he departs, he says: "Don't be upset. It only makes you ill. I love you. I'm fine. And, really, Bess is a decent person." Before she thinks to tell him it's not safe to drive home, Wharton has fled the coup, so a very rattled Charlotte heads to her bedroom medicine cabinet to take something to settle her nerves.

By the time he arrives home, Wharton realizes that he should call Bess and give her a quick heads up about what he's just let slip to Charlotte, and apologize to her. Bess takes it well, says that she can handle Charlotte, but in the course of the call, sarcastically says: "I would've thought that you had enough to talk about to Charlotte, what with William having just put Kristina's fiancé in business, without the need to mention my business."

Wharton explodes in fury: "What the fuck. When did that happen? Charlotte never said a word about it. What business — did the fucker have him buying my lacrosse team? I wouldn't put that past dear old dad."

"It just happened. Wilma told me. Some fast food restaurant business."

Wharton shuts the call off, heaves the phone onto the couch and proceeds to beat his fists against the wall, screaming: "Cocksucker. Motherfucker. My father's a fucking bastard and my mother a useless piece of shit." For the next hour, he can't get out of his mind how better his life would be if his only living parent were Charlotte, or, maybe better still, if he had no living parents at all.

CHAPTER XXXI

On this Wednesday after Labor Day, Charlotte has arranged to have dinner with Bess and Wilma at Wilma's duplex condo apartment. They dine in the open kitchen with a window view of the Williamsburg Bridge and the Manhattan skyline. Charlotte's pretext for the evening is "I've not seen you, Wilma, in far too long. I miss you. Let's have dinner together, Bess too. I wouldn't want her to feel left out."

The subtext, of course, is quite different. Unaware that Wharton has alerted Bess that she needs to be on guard against Charlotte, Charlotte intends to surprise Bess by confronting her in front of Wilma about her selling drugs to Wharton and his friends. By doing so, she hopes to demonstrate to Wilma how loathsome a person Bess is and how little regard Bess really has for Wilma.

After finishing their sushi omakase meals that Charlotte has arranged to be delivered from Notso, Chef Hirohito's three-star (not so cheap) signature restaurant, and having concluded a bevy of obligatory conversational small talk: "How's the job?", "What've you been doing?", "How's the Children's Museum benefit coming along?", "How do you keep your skin so clear?", "Did you read about the latest police shooting?", "Did you see the Netflix documentary about how the melting icebergs will affect coastal cities?", "How about that innocent person released from prison after 24 years of wrongful incarceration?", "Your hair looks so lovely", "What color is your lipstick?", Charlotte turns to the main dish of the evening — Bess' head on a plate.

"Bess, are you still making a living working as a bartender and hostess?" Charlotte disingenuously inquires.

Knowing what's about to come, Bess attempts to parry the anticipated attack. "Yes and no. Truthfully, I'm also still selling drugs, mostly marijuana but some other stuff on occasion." Bess then lies, as she adds, as a supposed after-thought: "No heroin or meth, nothing dangerous like that."

"It's bad enough you sell drugs at all. Wilma told me she was getting you to stop. But I know for a fact that not only have you not stopped, but you've been selling drugs to Wharton and his friends. You're their main supplier, for God's sake. How little regard you have for us. Are you poisoning Wilma and Willis with that junk as well?"

"It's recreational stuff, not harmful or addictive to the average person, no more than alcohol is. Any way, you take plenty of pills every day, Percocet and Oxycontin included. If your concern is my disgracing the family, look in the mirror first."

Charlotte answers, flustered, but not so much on the defensive as infuriated by the parallel that Bess has attempted to draw between them: "I have physical conditions that require medicine. There's no disgrace in that. But let's call a spade a spade. You're a drug dealer, plain and simple, taking advantage of people's weaknesses. If that's not disgraceful enough, you have so little regard for the family you've become a part of, that you willingly endanger the health of my children, your family members, by peddling your toxins to them. Shame on you."

Turning her wrath on Wilma, Charlotte continues: "And you, Wilma, how did I raise you? Certainly not to live with a criminal who makes a living endangering people's lives. If you can't get Bess to stop, that's all the proof you need as to what your relationship means to her. Mutual, reciprocated love it isn't. More like the rot of lust, dependence and habit."

"Are you done, Charlotte?" a now seething Bess shouts back. "From the day Wilma and I met, you've had your guns out for me, to shoot me down, kill off our relationship. Is it because I've had to scrape to earn a living and wasn't born to money like you and your children were? So I'm not like you and the other Wyldes, a member of the top 1% of the one-percenters, and you can't abide Wilma and my mixed marriage, not in your family, the elite Wyldes, not if you can prevent it."

Wilma, who's remained silent but hardly calm through all this back and forth between the two people who've been most important in her life, can no longer stand to bear witness to this war of hurtful words, so she angrily calls out: "Please. Both of you. I can't listen to any more. Mom, I love you. But you need to leave now. I'll call you tomorrow. I promise. Bess, I love you very much. But we need to talk once Charlotte leaves." Turning towards Charlotte and placing her hand beneath her arm, she almost lifts Charlotte from her seat and, ushering her out the door, voice quivering, she says: "Good night, mother. Speak to you tomorrow." As she closes the door, she turns to Bess and says: "We need to speak, now." And so they do.

Undeterred by her only days apart bitter quarrels with Wharton and with Bess and Wilma, on Friday Charlotte heads off for her previously planned evening with Willis and Melody, a golden opportunity for her to accomplish a trifecta of calamitous clashes, although that's not her intention, only her result.

They dine at Del E Tante, enjoying, among other specialties, the veal in tuna sauce appetizers and the orecchiette with duck sausage entrees, polished off by a coconut and dark chocolate tartufo, which Charlotte declines to even taste, since "I've eaten way too much already. I've got a busy social calendar this Fall. I have to be able to fit into my gowns without busting the seams."

Willis, sincerely and well-intentioned, responds: "Mom, you look great. Stop worrying about busting your seams — the only thing that will bulge are envious eyes when people see how gorgeous you look when you're dressed to the nine."

"Thank you, Willis. I'm just not so sure that's so."

Melody, less sincerely, offers Charlotte a compliment of her own: "I hope that I look anywhere near as well as you do when I'm your age, Charlotte. But I don't think that's possible."

"Thank you, Melody. How very sweet of you to say."

After dinner, they drive to Tribecca to Willis and Melody's apartment, to which Melody has insisted Charlotte come so that Charlotte can see the paintings and sculptures that Melody has recently purchased to decorate their home. After her disturbing encounters with her other children, Charlotte needs this evening with Willis to be different. So far, it's been very pleasant, no mention by Charlotte of anything of substance about Wharton or Wilma, and Melody not having said anything that triggered an angry response from Charlotte.

As they wander through the apartment, holding glasses of dessert wine from which they sip from time to time, Melody proudly identifies each new work that she's purchased and provides a thumbnail description of that work's special features, the artist's background and, unfortunately, the bargain-basement price at which she was able to obtain it.

"This piece is by Linda Holland," Melody says, pointing to a three dimensional, colorful pop-art construction hanging in one of the hallways. "Her work has been displayed in several museums and I acquired this piece from someone who desperately needed money because of an illness in his family. It's worth at least $75,000 and I only paid $37,500."

After showing Charlotte two more of Melody's well-purchased acquisitions, they stop in front of a large abstract work that's been painted in animal blood, and which takes up the entire wall between two windows in a guest bedroom. As Melody explains the work and the artist, Charlotte is by now only half-listening, until Melody effusively says: "This painting is probably the best bargain and most valuable of everything I've bought. Not only do we love it, but eventually it can be the start of my art dealership business. Based on the other prices that have been paid by Fortune 500 companies for his work, this painting is worth $425,000 and I got it direct from the artist for only $175,000. He needed money for the renovation he was doing on his studio, and I was 'Johnny on the spot.'"

Charlotte shakes her head in disgust and almost involuntarily mutters: "Everything's a bargain. You're prouder of that than of owning the work."

Melody, taking instant offense at Charlotte's remark, angrily responds: "There's nothing wrong with negotiating a price. Everyone does it, or should do it if they don't. There's nothing shameful about trying to save money. I didn't grow up in a wealthy family. I know the value of money and the pain of not having it when there's something you need or want that you can't afford."

Trying to head off a brewing confrontation, Willis raises his hand in the air, palm out, and calmly says (although he doesn't believe it): "Melody. I'm sure Mom didn't mean it the way it sounded."

Melody responds: "Unfortunately, I think she did." Melody then faces Charlotte and asks: "What is it that you have against me? This isn't the first time you've said something nasty to me."

"I don't have anything against you, Melody," Charlotte fabricates. "It's just that I find it distasteful for you to take advantage of other people, the way you just described. If someone needs money, don't take advantage of that. If you want something enough, then pay what it's worth." Charlotte pauses and then tacks on, "Also, you demean yourself when you bargain to buy something. It's almost like you're begging."

"That's absurd," Melody explodes. "Who thinks that way, except someone like you?" Not content to leave it at that, Melody decides to have it out with Charlotte. "I think behind all your talk about it being disgraceful for me to bargain, lurks a strong whiff of anti-semitism."

Willis once again tries to avert disaster but, before he can say anything, Charlotte lashes back: "I'm not anti-semitic. But let's be honest — Jewish people do have a propensity to over-emphasize money and to unnecessarily haggle over every little thing, and every last penny."

"That's enough," Willis shouts, infuriated by what Charlotte has just said. "Mom, you are fucking prejudiced, Melody is right, and it affects how you treat her. So you better cut it out, or you won't be seeing me any more."

After a long silence, which affords everyone an opportunity to cool down, Willis says, "Let's call a truce and, since you both love me very much, let's end tonight with you each promising that, in the future, you'll make a real effort to get along with the other. That's what I need and what I'll expect."

Having been appropriately rebuked, Charlotte and Melody exchange perfunctory apologies and withdraw from their field of combat, more accurately, Charlotte retreats to the safety of her chauffeur-driven car and Melody into the arms of her loving husband. With Charlotte gone, a still fuming Melody says to Willis, "I love you very much. But your mother is a supercilious, anti-semitic bigot. I'll try my best to get along with her, for all our sakes. Thank God you are who you are and nothing like your mother."

An apologetic Willis says, "I love you too. I know you'll make an effort. I don't know what's gotten into her. I don't remember her ever being this bad when I was growing up. It could be the effect of all the pills she takes for her various conditions. She won't talk to me about it. But I won't let her mistreat or demean you, no matter the cause."

Melody and Willis end the evening in bed together, arms (and other parts) wrapped around each other, while Charlotte's evening ends with her alone in her bedroom, with her fingers wrapped around a prescription bottle from which she takes an Oxycontin pill to swallow.

What is William's role in all this recent drama in Charlotte's life? He's a bit player, at best. As to the only happy event, Charlotte's plans for Kristina's wedding, he's fully on board. He approves of the lavish wedding that Charlotte intends to bestow, as it serves his purpose: to keep Charlotte focused on something or someone other than him and, to that end, to find a way to get Kristina and Jeff to continue living in Sands Point after they're married. That William likes Jeff and to some extent has taken him under his wing, is a bonus. William failed with Wharton, but Jeff is of more malleable material, and William wants to see if he can help Jeff become what he couldn't accomplish with Wharton: a success in business.

As to the conflicts Charlotte has had with their children, William knows little. Every effort by Charlotte to engage William and obtain his opinion about any of it, has been dismissed by William with uncaring platitudes: "I'm sure you can handle this, Charlotte;" "Just be patient. It'll all work itself out;" "She didn't really mean that;" "He'll come around, find himself one of these days;" "Don't take things so seriously."

Neither pills nor platitudes offer Charlotte sufficient comfort. That, she thinks, she'll have to derive from Kristina, more a child to her now than the children she bore and raised.

CHAPTER XXXII

I'm sitting at the dinner table at the Muss family home, a place very welcoming and comfortable for me, although I've not been here very often in the past few months. It's a Sunday night in the last week of October, and at the table are Jeff, Kristina, and the patriarch of the family (at least by name and sexual identity), while Barbara is in the kitchen putting the finishing touches to the cracked spaghetti dinner of which we're about to partake.

I've not seen Jeff for a few weeks, although we've texted each other and spoken a few times, but not for long about anything of substance. I've a lot of catching up to do, I imagine. "So fill me in you two," I say, while we wait for Barbara to mix the sautéed peas and onions and crispy-fried chopped bacon into the boiled pasta, which she'll then top off with heavy cream, parmigiana cheese and a variety of special spices. "Heavy on the nutmeg, please," I gleefully cry out to Barbara before Kristina or Jeff have had a chance to respond to me.

"Always for you, precious. Always heavy on the nutmeg," Barbara answers, smiling as she looks back over her shoulder at me.

Jeff says, laughingly: "If you're done orchestrating the preparation of the pasta, Simon, we can dish."

"The food will be ready in about three minutes, so save your 'dishing' until after you finish the food I'm about to put on your plates," Barbara shouts.

"Deal," Jeff says, speaking for all of us.

Barbara may not be Italian, but I'd match her cracked spaghetti against the finest pasta that any Italian chef (or mother) can prepare. The garlic bread, endive and anchovy salad and homemade pistachio ice cream are the perfect accoutrements to the meal. We talk very little, our gluttony having rendered us, at least temporarily, unable to speak, lest food rather than words spew from our mouths. We're able, however, to manage a more than occasional appreciative "hmm," "yum," or contented sigh, loud pleasing music to Barbara's ears.

"Well, you all gobbled that down quickly enough," a visibly happy Barbara says as she gets up to clear the table. "I'm glad you enjoyed my dinner."

As we get up to take our plates and utensils into the kitchen, Jeff's father stops us: "Barbara and I will do the clean-up. You three go into the living room and talk. You're our guests this evening. It won't take us long to load the dishwasher and then we'll join you." Offer made and eagerly accepted, we make ourselves comfortable and begin to catch up.

"Jeff, tell me, what's the latest with Auto Eats?" I ask.

"It's coming together very quickly. The restaurant should be open for business by March 1st, if not even a little earlier. I gave my two weeks' notice to the Lexus dealership last week."

"Wow. I didn't realize things had moved so far along. Will Auto Eats be paying you a salary before the restaurant even opens?"

"Yep. William has budgeted for Auto Eats to pay me this year, the same amount that I received last year for selling cars. But after that, I only get paid 70% of that amount as a base salary, the rest of my compensation will be dependent on Auto Eats' success."

"Why only 70%?" I ask.

"Because William wants to be sure I have 'skin in the game,' that I have something immediate to lose if Auto Eats fails and that I'm amply rewarded if it succeeds. So, in the second year of Auto Eats doing business, if the restaurant has done well, my compensation jumps to one and one-half times as much as I made last year selling cars. And don't forget, I also own 20% of the company."

"That's great. This is a chance of a lifetime for you and I know you'll knock it out of the park. Before I know it, I'll be ghost writing your autobiography, a modern day Horatio Alger story."

Jeff laughs nervously, and then says: "Who's Horatio Alger? It's a success story, I assume. Anyway, from your mouth to God's ears. I wish I was as confident about my succeeding at this as you seem to be."

Kristina pitches in, saying: "Simon and I both believe in you and so does Mr. Wylde. If he didn't, no matter how rich he is, he wouldn't be putting up a red cent, no less all the money needed to open an Auto Eats restaurant. Look what he did with Wharton."

I'm puzzled by this last remark; I don't know to what Kristina is referring, so I ask Kristina: "What happened between Mr. Wylde and his son?"

She replies: "Long story short. Charlotte told me that Wharton needed $5-7 million for a business he wanted to buy and run, a professional lacrosse team, and William refused to give it to him, despite Charlotte's urging."

"What was Mr. Wylde's reason?"

"Basically, that he has no confidence in Wharton, he thinks that Wharton lacks character. From what I can ascertain from Charlotte, even though she won't admit it, William is right. Twice William gave Wharton money to go into business and both times the businesses failed and the money was lost. Wharton is heavy into drugs, gambling and who knows what else. Charlotte is very unhappy about it."

"That's sad," I respond, "but not unusual. Successful father, idler son. What about the other Wylde children, same problem?"

"No. Willis, the second son, is a doctor. And their youngest child, Wilma, is a scientist of some sort; she works in a research lab."

"Well, two out of three. That's a higher score I suspect than in most extremely wealthy families. At least Charlotte has a good relationship with them."

"Not really," Kristina explains, "Charlotte doesn't like Willis' wife, Melody, or Wilma's partner, Bess."

"How come? I'm intrigued."

"The problems I think are mostly of Charlotte's own making. As regards Melody, Charlotte thinks Melody is an opportunist who has latched onto Willis in a grab for Wylde family money. Her perception of Melody may be colored by the fact that Melody is Jewish, and Charlotte has this thing about Jews, believes that they will do anything for money."

"Not quite an enlightened point of view and certainly not what I would've expected."

"I was surprised too," Jeff volunteers.

"What about the third kid. What's the story there?," I eagerly inquire, looking to get the down and dirty, to peek at the poop that lies beneath the glister — it's the schadenfreude in me.

"Bess deals drugs and is even selling them to Wharton and his friends. But I'm pretty sure that's only part of the reason Charlotte doesn't like her. From what Charlotte has let slip, I think Bess' aggressive, dominating personality, even if she didn't sell drugs, is the issue. Wilma is a warm, soft, somewhat shy person from what I can tell and she and Charlotte have always been close. I think Charlotte fears that Bess is so taking over Wilma's life that there soon will be no place left in it for Charlotte."

"Have either of you had any issues with any of the children?" is the next thing I ask, my seemingly insatiable curiosity continuing to steer the direction of this evening's conversation.

"I've had a brief but unpleasant incident with Wharton," Jeff replies. "He'd come to visit Charlotte just as Kristina and I were leaving. After exchanging brief 'hellos,' Wharton pulls me aside and says, 'I need to speak to you for a minute. I want to ask you something.' So Wharton and I walk several feet away from Kristina, out of her hearing, and Wharton, a little wild-eyed if you ask me, says: 'Tell me, Jeff. What's your secret? How're you able to get my father to back you in a business, one in which you have no experience or other qualifications to run, when he won't do even less than that for his own son?' I replied that he should speak to his father about that, not me, and walked away. He was still glaring at me as Kristina and I left."

"To be expected, given what Kristina told me earlier," I respond.

Kristina then says: "Since you seem to want a full reveal tonight of all the Wylde family secrets, at least as far as Jeff and I know them, I'll add to the hopper my recent conversation with Melody.

"Melody was at the house with Willis and while Willis and Charlotte were talking, Melody came looking for me. I was in our home office working on the final preparations for the Long Island Children's Museum gala for which Charlotte is the chairwoman. It'll take place the first week of December and should be a big success and raise a lot of money for the museum; I've certainly worked hard enough on it, that I can tell you.

"Anyway, Melody walks in and says, 'Sorry to interrupt but I'd like to talk to you about something.' 'Sure. What can I do for you?' I replied. Then Melody says, 'I know we don't know each other very well, but I've a favor to ask. I intend to start up a business dealing in art, maybe open an art gallery as part of it, and Charlotte seems dead set against it. I know from Charlotte how close the two of you have become. If Charlotte raises the topic of my art business with you, I'd appreciate you saying something in support of it.' I told her that I wouldn't feel comfortable doing that, since I didn't know enough of the details, but I'd be happy to meet with her another time and she could walk me through everything. Then I'd be able to be honest with her, and tell her if I was willing to do what she'd asked. She responded, saying: 'Thanks. I may do that. But on second thought, forget I asked. I doubt you can help change her mind no matter what. I'll do better just concentrating on dealing with William, one on one.'"

"This has turned out to be a most fascinating evening so far," I enthusiastically exclaim. "There are many irons heating in the Wylde family fire. Are there any other stories you have to share? About Bess? Maybe something about William?"

Jeff cuts me off, saying: "William has been unbelievably terrific. He seems to have taken me under his wing. We play golf together sometimes, even though I'm not all that good at it. But he encourages me, says I'm a natural athlete and all I need is more lessons and practice. After we finish playing, he takes me to the clubhouse and introduces me around. Says he wants me to have the type of social contacts I need to have in order to be successful. Once in a while, we have a man-to-man chat about life." Then in a low voice so he's certain that his parents, still in the kitchen, cannot hear, he says: "It hurts me to say, but I'm closer with him than I am with my own father."

Kristina jumps in to confer some accolades on Charlotte, saying: "If we're awarding medals, let's not forget to pin several on Charlotte. She has her bad points, she's snobbish, entitled, insecure and very needy, but with me she's mostly polite, kind, concerned and extremely generous and, in many ways, treats and confides in me like a favored daughter. My only real complaint is that because we live in the house, I'm always on call and I spend a great deal of time, day and night, talking her off the ledge about one problem or another. That William most week nights sleeps in their Manhattan apartment, makes it even worse in terms of the amount of occasions where I'm her only available sounding board."

Jeff says: "The job will be much easier after we're married and move out of their house. Then it will be more of a job with normal working hours."

"Speaking of getting married," Kristina gleefully emotes, "It's about time I finally get to tell you more about that — it's at the Pierre Hotel, ceremony in the Cotillion Room, cocktails in the Grand Foyer and dinner in the Grand Ballroom. You've never seen such a place. Go online. Look at the rooms. Charlotte has planned everything: the caterer, the menu, the flowers, the orchestra, all without the help of a wedding planner, just me. And because of William's relationship with its owner, the Pierre has waived its required minimum number of guests, so that there'll be just 60 people in total, and the cost, all in, will only be about $250,000."

"Only about $250,000?", Barbara, who just entered the living room with Dan in time to hear Kristina wax ecstatic about the wedding, exclaims in shock, quite angrily. "Only? You've got to be kidding. How could you even accept such a gift from them? William Wylde is funding millions into Jeff's business venture but he's doing it because he thinks he can make money off of Jeff's back. But the Wyldes have no reason to pay that kind of money for a wedding for you and the two of you never should've let them do it. We're not a family on the dole, that needs a handout."

We are shocked by Barbara's quite uncharacteristic outburst, particularly since she's known of Charlotte's wedding plans, although obviously not the cost, for some time now.

Attempting to calm Barbara down, Dan says: "I think it's very generous of the Wyldes to do this for Jeff and Kristina. I'm happy for them to have a wedding that we can't afford to provide. The Wyldes obviously have great affection for them and lord knows they can well afford the money. It's barely a drop from their very deep bucket."

Barbara glares at Dan, but in better control of her emotions, replies: "Maybe I'm overreacting in how I'm expressing myself. It's just that this doesn't feel right to me. Somewhere in there, you're losing your souls to the devil. No one gives a gift of that magnitude without expecting something in return."

"Mom, we love you very much, but you're wrong. This is a gift without strings from people who can well afford to give it and who are doing it because of the affection they have for us and we for them. Dad's right on this, on what he just said."

"I surrender. It's done already anyway. Too late to change. I'm happy that you're happy." Then, in an effort at levity, she adds: "One good thing. Our friends will think we hit the jackpot. I just hope they don't try to hit us up for loans."

Everyone smiles and the remainder of the evening consists of conversation that studiously avoids any further mention of the Wylde family. It does, however, include my being asked about how my life is going and my having the opportunity to brag a little. I tell them how I've made some mystery book best seller's lists (Amazon Kindle included), spoken on two podcasts, and attended several book signing events arranged by my publisher, including one at the large Barnes & Noble on Court Street in Brooklyn and, more importantly, one at the Strand in Manhattan. The result of all this, I explain, quite proudly, is that I'm starting to be able to enjoy some luxuries, including that of being occasionally recognized from my photo on the back of the hardcover and paperback versions of my latest book.

"And is there anyone special in your life these days, Simon?" Barbara wistfully inquires.

I respond "Unfortunately, not. But I'm still looking and definitely hoping." Brushing aside that bit of sincerity, the smart ass inside me can't help but contribute: "Not to worry though. My buffet table is quite large and I get to sample a wide selection of delicacies. Especially now that I've become successful."

On that note, our evening ends. Barbara hugs me to her as I leave and quietly whispers in my ear, "At least I still have my Simon."

CHAPTER XXXIII

This is becoming intolerable, a frustrated, angry, yet contemplative, William thinks to himself, as he sits in the smoking lounge of his Long Island mansion distractedly puffing on a Cuban cigar and sipping from a crystal-cut tumbler of 25 year old scotch whiskey, but deriving little pleasure from either. William is accustomed to resolving difficult situations, he's done that with regularity in his business life, quite successfully, but here the conundrum involves his personal life and hits too close to home for him to gain the prospective needed to find a propitious solution.

The toxic combination of Charlotte's all-pervasive sense of being to the manor born and her inability or unwillingness to do or decide anything by or for herself has become more pronounced with the passage of time, so much so that for William each day with her has become increasingly challenging if not completely insufferable. Having passed the mid-point in his life, exacerbating his disdain for Charlotte is William's desire to enjoy the fruits of his hard labor, the spoils of victory one might say, one of which is his being with Vanessa, not just for the sexual pleasure that she provides, as intense and exhilarating as that might be, but for the feelings of youth and vigor that he experiences whenever they are together, a sense that much more life lies ahead for him than behind. That Vanessa is pressuring him for an open, more permanent arrangement, future children included, has churned the already roiling fever of his discontent.

What prevents him from just divorcing Charlotte, as messy, unpleasant and financially ruinous as that might be?, he asks himself. After all, he won't be the first public person to walk that plank. Unfortunately, the answer to that question takes but a millisecond: his soon to be announced nomination to become Secretary of the Treasury. Under no circumstances is he prepared to allow that prize to be snatched from his grasp by the scandal and notoriety that a contested divorce from Charlotte will entail. Charlotte has made it clear, certainly in words, if not yet action, that any attempt he makes to publicly separate himself from her will result in a scorched earth response, her reputation (and his) be damned. Once again, the by now not so uncharacteristic thought "if only Charlotte were dead" forces its way to the forefront of his thinking. Even more so after the strident argument he had with Charlotte earlier this evening.

The fight with Charlotte was more the result of his squabble with Vanessa two nights earlier than anything else. He and Vanessa had just returned to her apartment after what he thought had been a very enjoyable dinner at Fresco by Scotto. Only in New York City would the family of a convicted labor union racketeer be welcomed with open arms (if not turned up palms) by politicians, wealthy business people and high society "blue bloods," all eager to show their respect by eating at the Scotto family's restaurant. Convicted or not, the Scotto patriarch, and his family, had the support of very powerful people and, to this day, more than 25 years after it first opened, the restaurant still attracts many of the rich and famous. As much as the food, the desire to see and be seen drives its success. This evening was no exception. Seated at the table next to William and Vanessa was Leon Black, CEO of Apollo, and his family. Across the room with some of her children was Angelina Jolie and the head of UNICEF. And, better yet, not a single Instagram or Twitter "influencer" in sight.

During the course of dinner, several people came over to say hello to William. To each of them, he introduced Vanessa as a business associate. Maybe he was just too tired, maybe he had too much to drink, maybe he was too busy exchanging perfunctory greetings with people that he knew or knew of him, maybe he was too focused on the rack of lamb and risotto he was consuming, maybe he was too engrossed in daydreaming about what he had in mind once Vanessa and he went back to her apartment, but whatever the reason, he missed the signals and so was unexpectedly bushwacked the moment they walked through her apartment door.

"That was a very nice dinner, wasn't it?" William blithely stated, as he put his arm around Vanessa to draw her close to him for a kiss and warm embrace.

"You've got to be kidding," Vanessa responded, as she forcibly pulled back, knocking his arm from her shoulder, and looking at him with venom in her eyes. "It was one of the most atrocious, most embarrassing nights ever in my entire life. I felt like a hooker. That's the message you conveyed to people and the way you made me feel when you kept referring to me as a 'business associate' all night."

"Well, how was I supposed to introduce you? I have to introduce you in some manner, so what would you have me say?"

"How about as your girlfriend, since that's what I am? Or even better, your fiancé?"

"You know I can't do that, not right now, probably not for another year, unless my nomination falls through."

"I love you, but I can't keep on this way, hiding in the shadows as if I've something to be ashamed for, or worse, that you're ashamed of me, of our relationship. It's not fair of you to ask me to continue this way."

"Vanessa, you need to understand once and for all how important it is to me to become Treasury Secretary, it's my legacy. I can do great things, beneficial things, in that office. The President and the FBI know of our relationship, that's no problem. I just can't go public with it until after I'm confirmed by the Senate. If I do, Charlotte will feel humiliated and she'll react by saying terrible things about me. The social media fallout from that will derail my nomination. You just need to be patient. I've told you more than once, I'll separate from Charlotte once I'm in office."

"You care more about becoming Secretary of the Treasury than you do about me. That's the bottom line to what you're saying?"

"No. You're deliberately misstating what I'm saying to you. I want you forever, for the rest of my life, but I also want to be the Treasury Secretary. I can have both, all it takes is for the person who loves me and wants us to share the future together, to let this play out, for at most another year. Then I can do what's necessary to make our future together a reality."

Placated but not satisfied, Vanessa, blotting with the back of her index fingers the tears nestled in the corner of her eyes, plaintively responded: "I'll try my best to do as you ask. But as rational as you seem to make it, I'm not sure that I'll be able to do that — just stand back and let another year go by."

William spent the remainder of that evening consoling Vanessa, embracing her while assuring her that they were going to have a bright future together, that oft times people had to sacrifice in the short term to gain in the long run, that it was not easy for William to play the charade his life with Charlotte had become, but he needed to do so, to make the sacrifice, just as Vanessa must sacrifice, a joint effort to achieve their shared goal of a happy life together. It was with the still flickering flames of Vanessa's plea from two evenings ago that William found himself having to damper what turned out to be a raging fire with Charlotte.

As they sat down for a drink before they were to meet some friends for dinner at the club, Charlotte (surprise!) complained: "I've barely spoken to you all week, William. It's bad enough that you sleep four or five nights in the City during the week, but now I think you're ducking my calls. I end up more often than not in your voicemail or with an unanswered text; it takes forever for you to get back to me."

"Let's try to have a pleasant evening tonight. We're meeting friends soon. Don't pick an argument for no reason. My work schedule hasn't changed, it's nothing new. I'm not avoiding or ignoring your many calls and texts. I respond as soon as I can. I have a business to run, one where all our money is at risk every day. You run the household and have Kristina to assist you. She's the one you need to lean on, not me. That's why we hired her and why she and Jeff are living with us."

"There are some things that are not for Kristina, some things that I need your opinion on," Charlotte replied, put off by his dismissive attitude.

"Like what?"

"Every day stuff. Which social engagement do you want me to accept? What day can I arrange for us to see any or all of our children?"

"You don't need to call or text me several times a day for those types of questions. Keep a list, for God sakes, and do it all at once, at the end of the day. I promise that I'll respond much more quickly, probably immediately, if you contact me that way."

A now furious Charlotte, face thrust forward, eyes blazing, flayed William: "Not everybody's like you, organizing their lives with lists, living by lists. Was it on your list each day whether you'd sleep with me that night? If so, I seem to have dropped off your list for the most part these past few years."

"I don't know why you seem intent on picking a fight with me this evening. As to sleeping with you, we've had an open marriage for a very long time. There's nothing new in that," William unabashedly dissembled. (Good thing for him that Vanessa was not a fly on the Wylde's parlor room wall.)

"The point of an open marriage was to enhance our sex with each other. You were always my best lover. That's all disappeared. You've disappeared, first almost no sex and now almost no you, you're not present at all, not physically in our marital home, nor even by phone or text, and most certainly not emotionally. You can't be bothered with me any more. Leave it to Kristina, is your new mantra. You've become the nowhere man in my life, except when you need to trot me out to charm your business associates or political compatriots. We might as well be divorced as things stand now."

William saw an opening and took a misguided chance: "If that's the way you feel, why don't we get divorced? Be done with your suffering with me. Maybe a divorce will help make you happier, free to find someone new with whom you can better share your life."

With more vehemence than William would have thought Charlotte capable of, she blasted back: "You can forget about a divorce. I won't have people think you cast me away, traded me in for a newer, sleeker model. I know you've been seeing someone, probably very young, and sense that she's managed to get her hooks in you. I'm no fool. But I won't be embarrassed, that's what a divorce would do, embarrass me, announce to the world that the very successful William Wylde has no further use for me. I'll expose you for what you are if you ever try to do that to me. And if the public humiliation you'll suffer isn't enough, please remember my family inheritance helped get you started in Wylde Capital and I'm entitled to all that back and half of everything you own, have or earn, now or in the future. And that's just for starters."

With this argument descending to the depths of his personal hell, William decided that a well-timed retreat is the better part of valor: "This conversation has gone off the rails. It's my fault. I've no desire for a divorce; I was just responding in anger to what you said. You still know how to push my buttons. But let's level the playing field; I know you've been sleeping with a same someone for the past few months, identity unknown and I don't want to know; so nobody has been cast aside, we're each just continuing with our open marriage compact."

Surprisingly, an emotionally exhausted Charlotte responded well to William's attempt at apology and the evening at the club went smoothly enough, all things considered. After they returned home, William told Charlotte that he was not sleepy, that he was going to have a cigar and drink and that he'd see her in the morning.

And so he sits in his smoking room revisiting Thursday's drama with Vanessa and the bitter words exchanged tonight with Charlotte, trying to figure his way out of the maze of lies and half-truths that now define his personal life, the biggest of all being the lie that he's been telling Vanessa: that he'll divorce Charlotte after he becomes Secretary of the Treasury. The truth is that, for a variety of complex reasons, tax-related and otherwise, he cannot ever untangle the serpentine financial affairs of Wylde Capital to give Charlotte her inheritance back and half of everything else in the context of a contested divorce. To do so would not only destroy Wylde Capital as a company, but dissipate a substantial portion of their personal fortunes. This, too, William is not willing to do, not even for Vanessa.

CHAPTER XXXIV

"'Backwards and in high heels.' Do you know what that phrase refers to?" I ask a puzzled looking Kristina.

"I've no clue," she responds.

"That's because, unlike moi, you're not a student of classic old cinema," I smugly but teasingly state. "Fred Astaire and Ginger Rogers are a famous movie dance team. They...."

"I know their names," Kristina quickly submits, "even though I've never seen any of their movies."

I continue, ignoring the interruption: "Astaire and Rogers made nine musicals together in 1933-1939. Astaire is widely-renowned as one of the greatest dancers of all time, but feminists point out that Ginger Rogers did everything he did, and that she did it backwards and in high heels."

"Your point?" a still curious Kristina asks.

"I'm coming to that. Despite being the other star of those movies, she was paid far less than Fred Astaire and even less than some of the male supporting actors in those films. So, my point is that here we are, almost a century later, and it's still the case that women are being paid less than men in similar jobs. So why was Charlotte surprised, and Wilma shocked, to learn that Wilma was being paid less than the two male laboratory scientists in her research group at the hospital?"

Kristina pauses and, thinking aloud, responds: "I think Charlotte probably never thought anyone would dare take advantage of a child of hers, that the Wyldes were above the fray. And from what I've been told, Wilma is something of an innocent, not to mention that money has never been a concern of hers, having grown up with a trust fund and the Wylde family resources."

It is a few days after Thanksgiving and two weeks and three days before Jeff and Kristina's wedding. "Coronation" would seem a more appropriate word, given the grandiose event that Charlotte has conceived and she and Kristina have orchestrated. There are none of the last-minute pre-wedding jitters or glitches that are typical as weddings draw near, in large part, of course, because money has been no object and the Wyldes are paying for everything.

We've met at my house for some three of us "alone" time before we head off to Jeff's parents' house for belated Thanksgiving leftovers. As has become our custom, we spend much of this time gossiping about the Wyldes. If curiosity kills the cat, it's a good thing I'm not a cat, because my curiosity is the engine that once again drives much of the discussion. The more I've learned about the Wyldes, the more fascinated I've become. They seem to define dysfunction and I can see a possible book in this for me somewhere down the road.

"Tell me more, tell me more," I eagerly sing the lyric to 'Summer Nights,' "did Wilma walk out the door?"

"Not yet. And I don't think she will. She's not very spirited when it comes to standing up for herself, certainly not from anything I've observed those times she's been with Charlotte. Charlotte bosses her around and Wilma mostly just remains silent. The only times that I know of where Wilma has ever stood up to Charlotte are those occasions when Charlotte has attacked Bess or berated her to Wilma. If anything happens with Wilma's job, it will because Charlotte will have asked William to intercede and do something about it."

"What about the rest of the Wylde family, any juicy tidbits for me there?" I gleefully inquire as I mimic rubbing my hands together in greedy anticipation.

Not amused by my continued flippant wit, Kristina reprimands me: "I don't mind talking about the Wyldes with you because it's hard to avoid and we're family. But what's going on among the Wyldes is not a joke to me. I think the problems the Wyldes have with each other and with their children are very sad and not something to be laughed about."

Properly admonished, I'm about to reply when Jeff leaps to my defense: "You know that's just Simon's way. He tries to make light of almost everything, but he doesn't mean it unkindly. It's just how he copes with and processes things."

"Sorry that I jumped at you, Simon. I know that about you. As you can tell from how I just reacted, what's happening in their family is troubling me. I see what's going on, or I hear it from Charlotte, and I want to make things better for her somehow. But I haven't figured out what I can do, other than just listen and be a person to whom she can unburden herself."

Jeff adds: "That 'listening' part of the job is beginning to take a toll on Kristina. On the other hand, given all the benefits and opportunities her job has provided us, it's a small price to pay."

"It is. But I'm the one paying it," Kristina points out, looking at Jeff. "As long as it remains a small price, I can handle it. I console her as best as I can and try to reduce her dependence on pills. But I can't say that I've succeeded very well. She frequently takes Percocet for migraines and Oxycontin or Xanax at other times for other ailments, real or imagined."

"Don't take this the wrong way, but it sounds like Charlotte is another victim of opioid addiction," I say.

"I think so too. I don't know what, if anything, more I can or should do about it beyond what I'm already doing — which is telling her she's taking too many pills. Obviously, William already knows about this but I can't see that he's done anything to help her."

"Not to switch topics too quickly, but since Kristina just mentioned William — Jeff, how are you getting along with William and Auto Eats? Any problems?"

"None. He couldn't be more supportive or complimentary. The restaurant is on target for a March 1ˢᵗ opening. And he's still spending time mentoring me and introducing me to people. So, absolutely no issues for me with William."

"Sounds like you're well on your way to your first of many multi-millions. I'll be able to point to your Time Magazine cover picture and say, 'I knew him before he wore that top hat, tuxedo and eye monocle, when he was just one of us.'"

"Don't worry," Jeff laughs, "I'll never forget you. As long as I'm in charge, there'll always be a job for you at Auto Eats. We need people like you to clean the tables and sweep up the floors."

"Thanks, dude. I know I can always count on you, we're best friends."

"We're going to be late to mom and dad's. We should get going," Jeff says.

"A minute more, please," I urge. "Kristina, Jeff told me what a great job you've done with that Children's Museum gala, that close to $2 million has already been pledged and the gala is still a week away. Congratulations."

"Thanks. It was a lot of hard work, what with the wedding coming up and all, but the result makes me very happy. Publicly, Charlotte is taking all the credit, but privately she can't stop thanking me."

"One more thing before we go. Has Barbara cooled down about Charlotte's having taken over the wedding planning and paying for everything?"

Kristina answers: "It would seem that she has, but there was at least one flare-up between Charlotte and Barbara over it." Before she can say anything more, Jeff cuts her off: "No need for the gory details. Let's just say that Charlotte could've allowed my mother to play at least some role — pick the flowers, select the band, something — but she didn't. She told Kristina that she was concerned that Barbara would be too focused on cost and unwilling to spend the money needed for, as Charlotte put it, a 'first class wedding.'"

"Charlotte may be right on that," I respond. "But still she could have made some accommodation so that Barbara would feel better about everything. Couldn't the two of you have done something about that?"

"Maybe. But the bottom-line is that although we love my mother very much, I need not tell you, it was easier to let Charlotte do everything if that's what she insisted on, than to have to deal with the fallout from Barbara and Charlotte clashing over wedding details. We very much want the wedding Charlotte has envisioned. We'll make up it to Mom in other ways."

"You know. I never thought to ask this before. Are any of the Wylde family attending the wedding?"

"Just William and Charlotte," Jeff responds.

"That makes sense," I remark as we get up to put on our coats. "Kristina hasn't been officially adopted by Charlotte yet, so the three 'Ws' aren't officially her siblings. By the way, who but some high-faluting blueblood thinks to alliterate the names of all of her children?" On that note we leave, with my having only succeeded in gaining more of an 'ugh' than a chuckle with my clever departing words. Good thing I'm not trying to make a living as a comedy writer.

CHAPTER XXXV

We arrive at the Muss family home (less than a block away from me) just a few minutes late and are warmly greeted at the door by Barbara who ushers us in as she points at the dining room table, where majestically atop sits a platter of delicious-looking and even better smelling homemade honey maple ham, a serving plate with cut-up turkey wings, legs and thick-sliced dark and white meat, a bowl of freshly mashed potatoes, and an even larger bowl of marshmallow-topped baked sweet potatoes. No vegetable yet in sight, this looks like my kind of meal. Leftovers, indeed. But I certainly don't mind having been so happily misled. I should've suspected it. Barbara always had happy surprises for us, all throughout our childhoods.

"Sit. Eat. While it's hot. You're a little late. I should have guessed you would be, given how far you've had to travel to get here from Simon's house," Barbara jokes.

We virtually rush to the table, beating both Dan and Barbara there, not yet having given Dan even a perfunctory greeting. As Dan lowers himself (plops might be a better description) into his chair, he says: "Nice to see you all. Jeff, looks like you're putting on a little weight. Eating well at the Wyldes, I see. Good for you." Without intending to be either sarcastic or facetious, I suspect, but being both, he concludes with the pronouncement: "Let's eat."

"Thanks for the compliment, Dad, I can always count on you for that," Jeff responds, with a sigh of barely concealed resignation. This, however, does not prevent him from reaching over the table and filling his plate full from the cornucopia spread before us.

As Dan and the three amigos (two amigos and an amiga?) chow down as if we're hungry cowboys who've just returned after a lengthy cattle drive, Barbara asks me: "How's your family, Simon? Have you been in touch with them recently?"

This almost causes me to lose my appetite (but, of course, it doesn't), since discussing my family is never a favorite topic of mine. I think maybe Barbara asked me this to throw me off my game and slow down my gluttonous behavior. But she can't really be afraid we'll run out of food, can she? After a brief pause, so that I can finish chewing and swallow, I reluctantly reply, as if my teeth were about to be pulled: "They're fine, thanks. In good health and happy living off mom's inheritance. They travel a lot, mainly Princess cruises to the Caribbean. They always told me how much they loved watching 'Love Boat' and 'Fantasy Island' before I was born, something I never could understand since I watched the syndicated re-runs a few times and thought the shows sucked. But I guess they're living their dream: sailing on the 'Love Boat' to their fantasized islands."

"You sound awfully bitter, Simon. Don't you think it's time you cut your parents some slack?" Barbara criticizes.

"Sorry, you're right. It's not like I see or even speak to them very often. At this point, I suppose it's time to let go of any anger I might have. So what if my mother emotionally deserted me from birth and they both physically left me the first chance they had?"

"After that, dare I ask you? And Felicity? How's she?"

"My sister's good. Finishing college, dating around, no one in particular. She's a communications major, hopes to land some type of media-related job. She's a volunteer on some local politician's campaign, so she's getting some on-the-job training and experience. We speak but, given both the 10-year age gap and the physical distance between us, it's tough to have as close a relationship as we might like."

"Hopefully, that will become easier once she graduates from college. And as you both get older, the age difference should become less important," Barbara offers consolingly.

Changing the subject, since we have dwelled on my less than stellar family relationships as deeply as I'm willing to go, I say to Barbara affectionately: "It's your turn to deal, Mrs. M. Be honest, are you still happy as a social worker at Child Protective Services? Kudos to you, if you are."

"For the most part, I am. I think I continue to make a difference for at least some of the families I cover. That's the best you can hope to do in this job. It's hard to describe how good I feel when I do succeed."

Kristina compliments her: "I don't know how you do it, Barbara, seeing physically and emotionally damaged children every day and dealing with their abusive parents. I really admire you. You don't at all seem burned out by the job. Every time we speak about it, you talk about the job with love and passion for it."

"The most difficult part for me is the danger I often face in confronting a parent, when I tell him or her that I may remove the child from the household if the abuse continues. These are really bad, violent people, and some of the threats of bodily harm made against me are chilling. But I'm no coward, so I just shrug it off and do my job."

Dan adds, "If we're being honest, we still need the money Barbara earns. She's achieved a seniority and pension level that she can't carry over to a different position in city government or elsewhere."

"How can you say that? You make it sound as if we're desperate for money," Barbara angrily berates Dan. "If I came to dislike the job, I'd quit and we'd get by quite well with what you earn and what I'd be paid at a new job."

"I was just stating a fact. I didn't mean it to sound like we're in dire straits. But we're certainly not the Wyldes. We're not even a distant planet in the same financial universe. The kids need to remember that.

It may be hard for them to do, given the wedding they're about to receive, courtesy of Charlotte and William."

"You're not upset about that, are you Dad?" Jeff asks.

"Not at all. I'm very happy about the wedding. And I'm happy about the Auto Eats business that William has financed for you. If I could afford to do those things for you, I would. But I can't, so I'm glad that the Wyldes are doing it instead."

Barbara shoots Dan a fiery look that I may have been the only one to see, and then turns to Kristina and asks: "Are any of the Wylde children attending the wedding? Charlotte hasn't shared the guest list with me except to tell me that everyone on the list I gave her has been invited and are attending."

"Funny, Simon asked us the same question just before," Kristina responds. "The answer is, no. This is a wedding for our families and friends, not theirs, even though they're paying for it. Of course, William and Charlotte will be coming. We welcome that; in many ways they've become like family to us."

Barbara presses on, marching to the beat of a drum I'm not hearing: "How's Charlotte's relationships with her children. Is she close with them?"

"Not really. Some issues she's having are with the children themselves, others are with their spouses or partners."

"Well I know that she and her sister, Donna, don't get along at all," Barbara states.

"How do you know that?" Kristina queries, with a puzzled look on her face.

"I had lunch with Charlotte in mid-November, at my request, to go over all the final details of the posh bash she's throwing for you, so that even if I had no input on any of the preparations, I'd at least know what to expect. I didn't want to be embarrassed if our friends or family asked me anything about it. Towards the end of our lunch, which was not all that pleasant I might add, Donna showed up. I was surprised, since Charlotte had failed to mention that she was meeting her sister after lunch to go somewhere together.

"We still hadn't finished either our coffee or the argument we were having, so Donna sat down to join us. Charlotte encouraged me to finish what I had to say in front of Donna, so I did. Basically, that you were my children, not hers, and that although I appreciated her and William's generosity, I very much did not appreciate her having excluded me from any part of the wedding planning. Nor did I appreciate her not allowing Dan and I to pay for at least some small part of the wedding, maybe the rehearsal dinner, if nothing else.

"Charlotte responded, as only she can, nose figuratively stuck up in the air, without regard to my feelings, and not at all, even the slightest bit, defensively: 'I only wanted everything to be first class for them.'

"Before I had a chance to tell her what I thought about her holier than thou, supercilious remark, Donna sprung to my defense, a champion bearing my colors. She told Charlotte that she had no right to have excluded me from the wedding process to the extent she apparently had.

"Not to make this too long a narrative, we had a few more minutes of heated conversation. Then, just as I was calming down, ready to put this all behind me after having gotten it all off my chest, Donna reacted to something Charlotte said to her about minding her own business, with an almost frightening emotional outburst, shouting, in a deep, very strange voice, how Charlotte couldn't expect to continue to treat people the way she did without suffering the consequences, that Donna was sick and tired of Charlotte and everything about her, that she wasn't going to take shit from her any more and that maybe no one would have to, she could see to that. Then Donna stormed out, without a further word but shaking her fists in the air.

"Fortunately, by this time the restaurant was mostly empty, so we didn't have to put up with too many annoyed, sympathetic or curious stares from patrons at nearby tables. Charlotte apologized to me for

Donna's behavior, saying: 'This was never like Donna until recently. Now, for some reason, the last few times we've seen each other, our time together has ended with this type of eruption. I think she may be having a breakdown. That's what teaching public school in the Bronx can do to someone.'"

We have all listened attentively (well, except for Dan, maybe, whose eyes are half-closed and who might be lightly snoring) to this account with varying amounts of discomfort, since it's clear that Barbara's feelings have been hurt by Charlotte, but also that Charlotte's life is in disarray, knowing what Jeff, Kristina and I know about the Wylde family dynamics.

What follows is a half hour of wedding event small talk, during which my attempt to veer the conversation towards less dangerous topics is to no avail. With the wedding day so close, and Jeff and Kristina so excited about it, there simply is no way to avoid the iceberg, this despite the warning we were given by what Barbara just told us about her lunch with Charlotte and Donna.

As the wedding talk filters down, I think we might have managed to forestall disaster and keep the good ship "Pierre" afloat without rocking the boat. But then Barbara, in an emotion-laden voice, turns to Kristina and Jeff and says: "I want you both to hear, really hear, what I'm about to say. I preface it by telling you that I've made peace with you getting a wedding fit for nobility. But if I don't say this to you, I don't know who will. You've been dancing to a piper's tune these past several months, being gifted extravagantly by the Wyldes. But there'll be a heavy price to pay if you continue skipping merrily down the road. Move out of the Wylde's home soon after you're married, just as you've said you intend to do. Kristina, continue to work as Charlotte's assistant if you enjoy it; otherwise quit and do something else. Jeff, if Auto Eats is a good business, then great. But, if not, don't go into another business with Mr. Wylde. Find a job you like without his financial support. I love you both very much but I can't protect you, you must take steps to protect yourselves."

I have remained atypically silent. I'm sensitive to what Barbara has just advised. I share her misgivings and have no wisecracks on the tip of my tongue. The bounties bestowed by the Wyldes on my best friend and his soon-to-be bride have to have strings attached, if nothing else, the atrophy of values and alteration in personality attendant when things come too easily and unearned. Danger lurks ahead for my friends; will they take another bite from the apple, notwithstanding Barbara's warning that it's poison fruit? Who knows what I would do if I were exposed to such Medusian temptations.

Jeff and Kristina react by telling Barbara how much they love her and that she need not worry, that they fully understand how fortunate they've been. They assure her that Charlotte is in no way a surrogate mother (ironically, the very role Barbara plays in my life), just a most generous benefactor of whom they have no intention of taking advantage.

"But you already have," Barbara replies. "You've accepted this ultra-expensive wedding they offered you. And who knows what they might tempt you with next? There are no free rides in this life. You both have to know that."

"Mom, this is a one-time gift that they can well afford, and this is our once in a lifetime, very special day. They didn't gift us this wedding for any other reason than all the help Kristina has been to Charlotte and that they are billionaires, so they can afford it. In a way, it's the same kind of thing they do when they make a substantial donation to a charity, just that this time we're the recipients of their generosity."

"I think this dialogue has played itself out," I exclaim, my first words since earlier this evening. I want to end this conversation before it can become any worse. I'm joined in my opinion by an unexpected source, Dan, who apparently has awakened in time to second my suggestion. I only surmise this, because the only words he actually says are: "Barbara, isn't it time for dessert? We finished the food a long time ago."

The pumpkin pie and red, white and blue buttercream cake that Barbara has baked go a long way towards helping me block out the not so sweet taste that lingers from the acidic admonition that Barbara has delivered. I don't imagine that this is true for Jeff or Kristina. The evening ends with Barbara packing up pie and cake to go for each of her three children and nothing more being said about "Beware the Wyldes bearing gifts."

CHAPTER XXXVI

"Quite a bash, my friend," I extol to Jeff (as if he had anything to do with the wedding except for putting on a tuxedo and showing up).

"Thanks," a distracted, partially drunk Jeff responds. "I'll catch up with you later. Kristina just told me it's time for our first dance as a married couple."

As he rushes off, already exhibiting the traits of the stereotypical female-dominated, long-married man, I can't help but gaze in wonderment at my surroundings. Overhead, crystal chandeliers cast a warm glow on the European-inspired Grand Ballroom, awash in cascading standing flower arrangements. Circling the room are well-spaced round tables set with purple tablecloths and matching linens, gold plated cutlery, gold leaf trimmed plates and colorful orchid centerpieces. In the center of the ballroom there is an eight-piece orchestra and ample space to dance. I feel like a prince at a ball or an impoverished flower girl looking in from the outside, I can't quite decide which. Maybe at different times, both.

Earlier in the evening, before the Cotillion Room wedding ceremony (at which I most definitely felt like a prince), I consumed more than my fair share of a wide array of fancy finger foods in the Grand Foyer (Blowfish Surprise, anyone?). Of course, I also took full advantage of the pre-ceremony time available to position myself in front of the vodka bar in order to most expeditiously sample its multicultural offerings.

As to the wedding ceremony itself, what most called out to me was how absolutely lovely Kristina looked in her hand-embroidered, off-the-shoulder wedding gown and the adoring looks exchanged throughout between her and Jeff.

With a drink in my hand, as I wait for the orchestra leader to "strike up the band" for Jeff and Kristina's first dance, I can't help but glance at the dinner menu adorning my place setting. After all, it's almost been an hour since I last ate anything. I see that the main course will be a choice among Dover sole, chicken Kiev and steak au poivre. I wonder if I'm limited to only one entrée or if they at least allow a surf and turf. I recognize that this is wishful thinking and I will have to make a Sophie's choice.

After Jeff and Kristina start their dance, they're quickly joined first by Jeff's parents and then by Kristina's aunt and uncle. I didn't know that Jeff could waltz. Of course, he can't, he only thinks he can, so the rhythm is changed to a slower moving (more accurately, barely moving) cheek-to-cheek entanglement. I am unaccompanied at the wedding, although invited to bring someone. I have no significant other and would feel more depressed and alone to be with someone for whom I have no deep feelings. Jeff and his parents, and now Kristina, are my family and this is an occasion for me to share with family only.

I have spent time chatting with Jeff and our friends, and with Barbara and Dan and certain of their friends, some of them casually known to me since childhood. I was introduced to Kristina's aunt and uncle and, of course, I made certain to go over to Charlotte and William and thank them for all the kindness shown by them to Jeff and Kristina, of which this wedding is the most generous example one could ever imagine. They were most gracious in their response and Charlotte was effusive in expounding the virtues of Kristina and Jeff and how she considered them part of the extended Wylde family. Throughout the evening, William and Charlotte did not so much mingle as hold court, William frequently cornered and fawned over by virtually everyone in attendance, and Charlotte the center of a vortex of masculine admirers.

In the time I spent with Barbara and Dan, it was clear that they still had very different attitudes about the wedding. Dan was delighted, so much so that on occasion I overheard him bragging to his friends about the food, the ambiance, the service, indeed the elegance and tastefulness of everything, as if he had a hand in it. Barbara, however, was subdued throughout, neither overtly unhappy nor outwardly enthusiastic about anything. As far as I could tell, she spent only the minimum time appropriate speaking with Charlotte and William and, in the snippets of conversations with her friends that I overheard, seemed to be trying to focus the conversation away from any discussion of the wedding itself and on to other subjects.

Kristina approaches me, takes my hand, gently pulls me up from the table and affectionately whispers in my ear: "We'll soon be cutting the cake. It's time for toasts. So please be ready."

I sit back down and rapidly finish off the remainder of my Dover sole and steak au poivre (I stole the steak from Jeff, since he was too busy being a consummate host to notice) and polish off the rest of my tumbler of vodka. I'm now adequately prepared for my moment in Jeff and Kristina's spotlight.

The toasts are announced by a few chords of music and a "ladies and gentlemen please raise your glasses" from the orchestra leader, followed by the traditional clinking of champagne-filled flutes (as the sound loudly reverberates, I mischievously envision the simultaneous shattering of several of these delicate, pricey objects d'art).

My time has come. Dan has completed his toast, welcoming his friends and family, thanking William and Charlotte and praising the qualities that define Jeff and Kristina. William has toasted the happy couple, saying how glad he is that he and Charlotte have been able to help out (false modesty becomes William, I would note) in arranging this wedding for Jeff and Kristina, whom they consider like family. And Kristina's uncle has delivered a short, best wishes toast of his own.

As I stand to speak, cognizant of how much more of a significant role Barbara and Charlotte have played in Jeff and Kristina's lives than their husbands (and guessing that the same is true for Kristina's aunt), my inappropriate for the occasion first words are: "I see that the women's rights movement has not yet reached the Hotel Pierre this evening. Four men, and no women, delivering the toasts. But I'll speak for all women and all non-gender persons, of all races and religions, whether present here tonight or not, when I say 'Congratulations, Jeff and Kristina.' To you, Jeff, I've never had, and never will have, a better friend than you've been.....up to the moment you met Kristina. Since then, not so much. But forgive and forget, I always say. Turn the other cheek. And believe me, if I'd met Kristina first, I wouldn't even remember your name, no less invite you to my wedding. I'd definitely turn both cheeks...away from you, as I rushed to Kristina. Who wouldn't choose spending time with her over spending it with you? Now, as a famous comedian once said: 'But seriously folks.' Seriously, Jeff and Kristina are each the best of their species and together unbeatable. They're my family and always will be and I'm privileged to have them in my life and to be in theirs. I wish them the best of everything for all years to come. Please raise your glasses and drink to their love, health and happiness forever."

With that, I walk over and kiss Kristina and hug Jeff. A few minutes later, the five tier butter cream and marzipan wedding cake is cut by the bride and groom, who lovingly smash large pieces into each other's face while being photographed doing so, and who then pose for additional face full of cake pictures (a wedding tradition that definitely should be dispensed with — #starving people in third world countries).

The considerable amount of cake that remains notwithstanding this blasphemous destruction, is served to all we eager (how can we still be hungry?) guests. After everyone has finished and the evening ends, there is still some cake left over. Dan unabashedly asks for a container of some kind to take home some cake (has this man no shame?), so, what the hell, so do I (I know that I have no shame). Boxed cake in hand, Dan, I and Barbara (not thrilled to be with her box boys) say our goodbyes and depart for home together. We share the limousine that Charlotte and Kristina have arranged for us. All the way home, Dan is ebullient, telling us how much he's enjoyed the wedding, and Barbara mostly silent. I'm torn by my own thoughts about how life moves on, things change and a person needs to adapt, and about how I've not lost Jeff so much as gained Kristina. Now I just wish I could add a significant partner of my own to the mix. But I'm still young, just past 30. So I need to be patient. It will happen, I'm sure of that. At least I think I am.

CHAPTER XXXVII

Spring has sprung, inflicting on us the usual unpredictable March weather: the snow of lingering winter, the cold, numbing heavy rain of mid-late March and the sprinkling of warmer, sunny days soon to become our norm; sunny days, brighter dispositions, I always say.

Jeff and Kristina don't need sunny days to brighten their dispositions this early spring day, as they excitedly tell me about their St. Barts honeymoon. Everything is "aces" for them at the moment.

Of course, pessimist (or is it realist) that I am, I think to myself that it all could change in an instant, without warning. A person leaves the door unlocked to run out to the corner bodega to buy a container of orange juice, too lazy to go to the bedroom to get the keys. One minute later the person returns, only to be mugged and robbed by someone who entered the house in that unguarded moment in time. A triathlete, pronounced by his doctor to be in perfect physical condition, dies at his desk in his office from a massive stroke suffered the day after his annual checkup. I could go on and on with such examples, but what's the point? We all know that shit happens. No need to damper their spirits by reminding them of that.

"We had a fabulous honeymoon, thank you very much," Kristina coquettishly exclaims as she turns her face partially away from me, chin down, and bats her big eyes at me, eyelashes aflutter.

"Please, ugh. I'm not interested in your sex life. Just the other stuff," I say in mock disgust throwing my hands up in the air. Truth be known, pervert that I am, I wouldn't mind reveling in what I'm sure would be a very exciting peep show. I do watch Pornhub, Hamster and Redtube from time to time. It's not only my mind that I like to stimulate.

"The 'other stuff' was also terrific, as you so elegantly put it, once we finally were able to get away," Kristina says. With all the tumult and excitement after the announcement, the day after their wedding, of William's nomination to be Treasury Secretary, Jeff and Kristina had to postpone their honeymoon so that Kristina could help Charlotte prepare to play, as Jeff describes it, the role of 'First Lady' in waiting. A ton of new clothing to be bought, a frenetic bevy of new, last minute social engagements to be made in January and February, some politically motivated by William and others purely for bragging rights by Charlotte, and a sudden frantic determination by Charlotte to make progress on her family memoir, kept Kristina crazy busy. And while Kristina was occupied with all that, Jeff had focused on what needed to be done to prepare for the March 1ˢᵗ opening of the first Auto Eats restaurant, in Melville. It wasn't until after the opening, that they could go to St. Barts.

"The white sand beaches were magnificent, beyond description," Kristina continues.

"You wouldn't think so, given the many shops she dragged me to," Jeff laughingly complains.

"I just looked, window-shopping only. Going with Charlotte to one designer shop after another must have rubbed off on me, that's my only excuse," Kristina playfully banters in response.

"Best of all on St. Barts," Jeff proclaims, "were the restaurants. It has to be some of the best food I've ever eaten. Our dinner at La Bouffe was extraordinary. Spiny lobster, vegetable cannelloni and wahoo tartare, what's to say? At Rol-e-Bel-e, the ceviche was outstanding, and the two specialty cocktails we each downed were works of art. Then we ate...."

"Basta. Enough. No mas," I shout, adding with a broad grin, "since when did you become such a foodie?"

"You asked for details and I was giving them to you, buddy, at least the non-x-rated ones," Jeff replies, pointing his finger at me and taking his best shot (unsuccessfully, I would note) at being witty.

Addressing Jeff, I say: "I imagine that Barbara was thrilled that everything turned out so well, I know how important it was to her that her gift be enjoyed."

"Yes. Paying for our honeymoon took the edge off her not having been able to provide the wedding."

"Changing the subject, you guys seem very 'up' today, anything else that you want to share with me? Kristina's pregnant, even if it's not by you? Auto Eats is going public, road show next week to launch its initial public offering?"

"As usual, you're way off the mark, Kemosabe, at least for now. But we do have some good news to share. Since you mentioned Auto Eats, you should know that it did gang busters business these first weeks, even while I was away, so much so that William just told me that if the Melville restaurant continues with strong numbers through the summer, he'll accelerate the growth plan to fund the opening of more Auto Eats restaurants."

"Wow. That's really great. I don't know what to say, except congratulations. Let's hope the restaurant continues to do well. "

"Thanks, Simon. I owe you for this. Big time."

Kristina dives in, unable to restrain herself from disrupting this rare exchange of honest spoken sentiment between Jeff and me: "Also, you won't believe it, but William and Charlotte have just offered us a $100,000 bonus if we don't move out and I continue to work for Charlotte for one more year. They said that they're offering this to us because it's now almost a year since I started working for Charlotte, that I've proved to be invaluable and that since the next 12 months will be the most hectic and disruptive in their lives, they want to ensure that I stay 24/7 available to assist Charlotte. With the bonus and what we are saving by not paying rent, in a year's time we'll have the down payment needed to buy a really nice apartment. So it's a win-win all around."

"That's some offer. No wonder you're excited," I say, trying to sound more enthusiastic about it than I am.

"Yes. And it's not like we don't enjoy living in such a beautiful home; we've enough privacy in the living arrangements, at least for now. When we have a child, that will be a different story. But living one more year in the lap of luxury so that we can buy a place of our own, we don't see a downside," Kristina gushes.

Always the pessimist (here I go again, but this time not thinking to myself but saying it out loud), I offer some slight words of doubt in response: "Last time we talked about your job at any length, just before the wedding, I recall you saying that Charlotte's pill abuse and emotional demands on you were starting to make the job less desirable. So you'll be committing yourself for a year to a job you might not continue to want."

"I don't think I ever expressed any reservations I had about the job anywhere near as strongly as you're making them seem," Kristina defensively corrects me. "The concerns I expressed, in the scheme of things, are minor, not major, so in no way a deterrent to accepting this offer."

Jeff leaps in with his take on things, suggesting: "And if things change, if the job evolves to the point where the bad outweighs the good, Kristina can quit, we'll forgo the bonus and we'll still be better off financially than if we hadn't stayed on."

"I stand down. I didn't really mean to crap on your parade. I was more thinking aloud than anything else."

"And I didn't mean to jump at what you said," Kristina replies. "It's just that when we told Barbara yesterday that we'd be living another year with the Wyldes and why, she became quiet, didn't say much, and seemed more upset than happy about it."

I know why Barbara reacted as she did, and can't imagine that they've forgotten Barbara's post-Thanksgiving admonition about the corruptive effect of overly-generous gifts, but like Barbara, I choose to remain skeptically silent, having already said enough. So, instead, I inquire: "And how did Dan seem with it?"

"He said that we should jump at it, that it was an offer we should immediately accept, if we hadn't already done so," Jeff replies. "I think maybe if my mother didn't seem as excited or at least encouraging about it as we expected, that might in part be because it shared the limelight with our telling her how great our honeymoon had turned out to be. And I guess that she's still concerned that somehow we're being led down a garden path by the Wyldes' money."

As we leave the bar we've been in and head out to meet some friends at the movies — who can resist a big screen, double feature, colorized revival of "The Thing From Outer Space Meets the Thong from Inner Space" and "Santa Claus Captures the Martians" (only kidding, we're going to the Film Forum to see the 1956 classic science fiction flick "Forbidden Planet, a favorite of Jeff's and mine) — I give Jeff and Kristina a warm hug and again apologize for being a bit of a Grinch. In my mind, however, not to mention in my gut, I think that we're all underestimating Barbara's warning and the seductive power of great wealth.

CHAPTER XXXVIII

Charlotte's fear that Bess' influence on Wilma will be toxic has not, on balance, proven to be true. As time has passed and their relationship deepened, Bess and Wilma have each had a mostly salutary effect on the other, two disparate personalities blending more towards the center. In Wilma's case, she's started to open up, experiment a little, react to some things instead of remaining silent and, most importantly, become more assertive and protective of herself. That she has substantially distanced herself emotionally from Charlotte is a positive for Wilma (although perceived, of course, as a negative by Charlotte).

But not all of the change in Wilma has been to the good. When Wilma discovered that a newly hired male colleague, with less educational qualification and little experience, was earning more than her for the same type of research work, the new, "improved" version of Wilma neither accepted it nor permitted her overbearing mother to intercede with her employer on her behalf. Even though the money as such was of no consequence to Wilma, the matter of principle was, particularly since despite her excellent work evaluations, her salary had never been increased in the three years of her employment. So she acted to rectify the injustice. But what she did was too much Bess and too little Wilma.

Since she worked side by side with both of her male colleagues, it was not difficult for Wilma to alter the data and otherwise subtly sabotage some of the studies the new hire was conducting, the end result being that he was fired for his supposed incompetence after only five weeks' employment. She timed her request for a substantial raise to his departure, and was financially rewarded for her perfidy.

In her zeal to prove to herself her new-found independence, she'd acted without consulting Bess but with the expectation that Bess would applaud her bold action. That she had donated all of her raise to charity, did not make what she'd done any less reprehensible, either, in hindsight, to herself, or to Bess, once Wilma told Bess what she'd done. Bess would've praised Wilma's devious cruelty had Wilma acted out of necessity, but the fact that she had not, that she'd no need for the money, was at the heart of Bess' unexpected condemnation. Wilma's self-flagellation was rooted in the simple fact that she'd been so easily able to sink so low. What else might she be capable of?

Despite the many beneficial changes in Bess that her relationship with Wilma has effected, she's not stopped dealing drugs, an occupation which has now come to endanger the lives of both of them.

CHAPTER XXXIX

"I'm sorry that I put you at risk. I never intended for this to happen. Forgive me. But please, I really need you to do this for me," Bess desperately begs, looking up at Wilma, a hand on each of Wilma's shoulders, gently holding her captive to Bess' plea.

Bess has just finished relating in painful, agonizing detail, the mess that Bess has created, "mess" being too soft a description for what has transpired.

For many months Bess has ignored Wilma's laments that, if she cares at all for Wilma, she need once and for all stop dealing drugs and find a safer, respectable career to pursue. But dealing drugs has become second nature to Bess, a part of her fiber. At the beginning, like the Walter White character in "Breaking Bad," it was a matter of survival, in her case her own, not her family's. As her business grew year to year and her opioid profits spiraled upwards, she, too, like the fictional Walter White, transmogrified, no longer content to make enough simply to get by, but now seeking to attain real wealth, in her case to accumulate enough money so that while still relatively young, she'd be able to kick back and enjoy it.

It was her drive to acquire money that initially drew her to Wilma, even more than the feel of Wilma's flesh. Having learned from Wilma the first night they met that Wilma worked in a Mount Sinai research lab, Bess viewed Wilma as a mark she could exploit. Savvy black market business woman that she'd become, Bess immediately concocted a scheme whereby if she could manipulate Wilma into stealing some chemicals, specifically some or all of the ingredients that could be used to manufacture fentanyl, Bess could then give them to one of the cartels which were her sources of supply in exchange for product that Bess could sell.

It was on their third date that Bess, very much attracted to Wilma but still eyeing her more as possible stooge than life-time partner, first floated her idea about Wilma becoming complicit in Bess' drug business. A shocked Wilma responded: "What? You've got to be kidding. I'd never do such a thing. I'm leaving."

As she headed towards the door, Bess stopped her and convinced Wilma to give her a chance to explain, saying: "I'm sorry. Don't walk out on me. It's just that I saw this as an opportunity for us both to make some real money, maybe enable us to afford an apartment together if things continue to go as well between us as they have."

Anger abating and somewhat appeased, Wilma accepted Bess' overture: "You've not yet been to my apartment, we've only gone to yours, and that was deliberate on my part. I never take a date to my place the first few times we're together. I feel comfortable enough to take you there tonight and to tell you some stuff about my life that I haven't told you, but which anyone who sees where I live would instantly realize. I'm extremely wealthy. Money has never been a concern of mine, not as a child nor now. I work at the lab because I want to make a difference in the world and being a research scientist is my way to do that."

After spending that evening enjoying the bed in Wilma's apartment (not much time spent on the views), Bess decided to file her scheme away and just enjoy the relationship. As things between them cemented, their mix curing very rapidly, Bess moved in with Wilma, and for the first time got a real taste of what being wealthy meant. Not just the size and location of Wilma's luxury apartment, but the cultured way in which she'd furnished and decorated it.

One night, after having lived together for several weeks and having fallen deeply in love, emotionally not just sexually connected, Wilma tenderly placed her hand to Bess' face, and offered: "If we're going to be life partners, you need to make my apartment yours, and not just a transient place where you have some drawers and closet space for your clothes. I want you to change anything you want to change, new furniture, new art work, we'll do it to our mutual taste."

"I love you too," Bess responded. "The stuff you have is okay with me for the most part. And I can't really afford to spend much on re-doing what I'm already pretty much okay with."

"You know money is not an issue. I can more than pay for anything you could possibly dream up. I want the apartment not just to be pretty much okay with you, but to reflect our shared tastes, our union, our life together, our commitment to each other," an emotional Wilma tearfully replied.

"If we're going to have a life together, I have to pay my fair share. You've already contributed this mansion-like apartment to our pot. From here on, we need to be 50/50 on everything. We'll never be truly partners if we're both living off your trust fund. It would make me feel subservient, inferior to you, and, as much as you may not think it, there would always be a faint voice in the back of your head, murmuring 'she's a parasite, she's living off of you.'"

"Never. I'd never feel that way. It's silly, what you're saying. What should I do with the money if not spend it on the both of us?"

"Well it's how I feel. So, not silly to me, not the least bit. If you want me, then you get a person who insists on pulling her own weight. You can give your trust fund money to charity for all that I care. But I'm not your charity case."

It was that ongoing thorn in the side of their happiness, the tug-of-war between Wilma's trust fund money and Bess' need to earn her own way, that drove Bess to do what she did and that had led to her tearful resurrection of her long dead and buried, filed away and almost forgotten, request that Wilma steal the ingredients needed to make fentanyl.

What Bess had done in her thirst to accumulate a pot of gold of her own seemed clever, very cutting edge, way ahead of the curve as far as relatively small-fry drug dealers are concerned. Seeing the fluctuations in the value of bitcoins, not to mention that paying and being paid in bitcoins went a long way towards preventing someone engaged in criminal activity (as Bess so clearly was) from being caught, Bess went on the Coinbase website and opened a bitcoin wallet for herself.

It took her no time at all to set up the wallet on her mobile phone and make the first of her many purchases of cryptocurrency. In only a matter of weeks, all of her drug profits were situated in her bitcoin wallet, from which she now made all of her drug purchases. Bess had successfully availed herself of the ability to better conceal her illegal conduct while at the same time being able to speculate in this wildly volatile currency.

Easy peasy it all was until it wasn't, until it turned horribly wrong and extremely dangerous. As the price of bitcoin continued to escalate, Bess was suddenly flush with an aggregate $2 million in bitcoin currency, so she decided to bet the farm, placing it all down on an extremely large order for oxycodone and fentanyl pills with a new to the United States Mexican cartel. The product was delivered, but when Bess went to her cell phone to make the payment, she discovered that her bitcoin wallet was empty, $2 million in bitcoin yesterday had become zero today. Her cloud-based account had been hacked. Now, she had no money with which to pay the cartel, and, even though relatively new on the scene, it already was not noted for its patience, sympathy or mercy, only for the swift justice it meted out to someone who messed with it. Nor would it let Bess simply refuse the delivery and turn the pills back for the cartel to sell to someone else. That would be bad business for the cartel. It had plenty of supply but not yet enough people on the ground to sell it all.

Worse for Bess, was that Wilma had taken Bess' words to heart and irrevocably directed that her quarterly trust fund distribution for the next three years be paid $250,000 per quarter to her and the balance to St. Jude's Children's Hospital and two other cancer charities. Now Bess could not even swallow her pride and ask Wilma for the money, because Wilma no longer had it.

The cartel will be reasonable, it has told Bess. Having done its due diligence on Bess before agreeing to sell her $2 million in drugs, it knows where Bess lives, with whom she lives, and that Wilma is William Wylde's daughter. It has given Bess one month to pay for the pills, which it's holding onto as collateral until Bess pays in full. And now the price is $3 million, not $2 million, since it's only fair and reasonable for the cartel to receive interest for Bess' delay in payment. Oh yes, did the cartel fail to mention it to Bess? If the $3 million is not paid within 30 days, the cartel will execute both Bess and Wilma, maybe live on You Tube, as a warning to others who might think to renege on an agreement they made with the cartel.

This is the burial grave that Bess has dug for them which she needs to find a way to skirt. As Wilma's shock at what Bess has told her wears off, anger edges in and then steams over, until it reaches a boiling crescendo, as Wilma, stomping around, stops, points her finger at Bess and shrieks: "That's it, once and for all. You'll never deal in drugs any more or we're done. I can't let you ever again bring this into our lives."

"I promise. If we get past this, I'm out. I'll find another way to earn a living. I really will," a very frightened Bess earnestly and contritely responds.

"I'll ask my parents for the money. I'll go out to Sands Point today. I'm sure they'll agree to give it to me, certainly under these circumstances."

"Please don't do that. They'll pay the ransom but it will be the death of me, at least as far as you and I are concerned. Your mother already hates me, but up until now, not enough to deliver an ultimatum that it's her or me."

"I would choose you. So who cares?".

"I care. If you're estranged from your family because of me, it would eat away at us, I just know it. Over time, it might even split us apart."

"That's only in your head and it's the least of our worries. Over time, if anything, so long as you're not selling drugs again, any rift with my family will heal. Anyway, we have no choice."

Hesitantly, Bess replies: "Please don't get even more upset than you already are, but I just want to toss this idea out there, to think about it. There is another choice; you can steal the chemicals from the lab as I once asked you to do, when I didn't know better." Before a visibly outraged Wilma has a chance to respond, Bess adds: "It's a one and done thing. I'm sure I can figure out a way with you where the missing stuff can never be traced back to us."

"I won't do that. Never. You know me, so you know that. You're not thinking straight, not now and not when you bought $2 million of pills from a cartel. If you had ever given me the slightest hint that you had escalated your drug business to that degree, I would have stopped you right then and there, told you it's me or your filthy business. I'm telling you that now, for sure, in no uncertain terms. I've closed my eyes too long, so I guess I'm partly to blame that our lives are now at risk. I'm going to my parents. End of discussion. I leave the distinction of being a criminal solely to you."

With a defeated, hang-dog look, Bess surrenders and retires for the evening. This is the first night living together that they will not share the same bed; Bess will occupy the one in the guest bedroom, her doghouse for the evening. Wilma offers no objection, since she's had enough of Bess for tonight. Wilma knows her parents will give her the money, so she's not worried about the cartel's death threat. What does concern Wilma, very much so, is whether this incident will mark the end of things for Bess and her. She loves Bess and can't bear the thought of breaking up, but she doesn't know how Bess will react to being rescued by her parents, Wilma's ultimatum and having to live off Wilma's trust fund, at least for the next couple of years, but maybe longer.

CHAPTER XL

Franklin looks at himself in his bathroom mirror this morning and can almost see the smile he feels inside. His meeting with Shirley Duzz last night went even better than anticipated. His hiring of her was well-worth the expense incurred in obtaining the information she reported.

"So, what do you have for me?" an eager Franklin inquired. Ever cautious, he had, as in the past, requested that they meet face-to-face rather than her report to him by phone, and has previously instructed that she keep no record of any kind of her investigation.

"Charlotte's drug dependency has continued to worsen, to the point where, plain and simple, she's an addict."

"And you know this how?"

"From speaking with some of the household help. Do you want more detail on whom I spoke with or what they said?"

"No. Not necessary, if you're sure."

"I'm sure. No doubt about it."

"Have you learned anything else to tell me?"

"Not from speaking with the employees. But I followed Charlotte for three randomly selected days and on one of those days she spent the good part of the night in a hotel room with a man, who I then discovered was one of Mr. Wylde's partners. I'm pretty sure they weren't playing chess all evening."

"Great work," Franklin gleefully exclaimed, then continued: "Is that it? Anything more?"

"Not really," she replied, then added, as an afterthought, "Unless you care to know what drugs she's hooked on."

"Just out of curiousity, sure," he disingenuously responded, since he intended to ask, and very much wants to know, if he's to execute the plan he has in mind.

"Percoset and Oxycontin."

"Do you know how she gets the pills?"

"Apparently by prescription from multiple doctors."

Last night's conversation is invigorating Franklin this morning. He's fixated on figuring out a way to cause Charlotte to overdose and he already has something (more precisely, someone) in mind. Achieving his goal will not be a job for Ms. Duzz. Her services for him as regards the Wyldes have been concluded with the $10,000 (literally under the table) cash payment he made to her last night.

He needs a different type, even more discreet, "professional" to achieve his desired result. Franklin has employed the services of one of the leaders of Los Amigos de la Muerte in the past, the head of their assassins unit, and this is a job for her. One meeting, arranged by burner phone, is all it will take. And Franklin will arrange that meeting in the very near future. Daniela Sorrano is not particularly attractive, but she is poised, educated, smart, and very, very deadly. Together, they will finalize a course of action and she'll see to its (and Charlotte's) execution.

CHAPTER XLI

"That's one time too many, one pill too often for me. I'm out of here and out of your life," an angry Clifford rants at Charlotte. During the six months that Clifford and Charlotte have been carrying on their affair, her drug dependency has worsened, causing her to be happy, sexy, loving and giving, one minute, doped up, crying, demanding and withholding too many of the others. "I became your lover to share your fantasies, not to subject myself to your drug-fueled whims and whimsies. I'm just not going to deal with your shit any longer."

"Please, Clifford," Charlotte begs, grabbing his arm to prevent him from leaving their hotel room. "I'm sorry," she moans, sagging to the floor on her knees, her head spinning from the Oxycontin she recently ingested. "Don't leave me. Things are so bad for me right now. I really need you. I'll do better. I promise."

"I'm sorry Charlotte, but you've become an albatross around my neck," a still angry, callous Clifford replies, not even offering to help her get up off the floor. "When we started our relationship, it was all about sex and having fun together. Open your eyes," Clifford urges, sternly admonishing Charlotte. "Now it's no longer fun, and sex has become an afterthought to time spent trying to bandage your emotional wounds."

Charlotte's eyes are flashing. She's risen from the floor while Clifford is speaking and now, not only her body, but her back is up.

"How dare you speak to me this way. Who the fuck do you think you are?"

Clifford stops in his tracks, surprised by Charlotte's uncharacteristic vituperative outburst. Charlotte continues, fiercely and viciously attacking and demeaning Clifford, while slightly slurring her words: "You're going to put up with my shit, as you so crudely refer to our having any meaningful conversation, for as long as I want. If I only wanted a hard cock in me, I would've dropped you for someone bigger, harder and more inventive a long time ago."

"If you had any chance that I'd reconsider, your little speech just now clinches it. We're most definitely done, whether you like it or not."

"If I don't like it, and I don't, there'll be consequences for you that you won't like, I can assure you of that."

"Now you're threatening me? So go ahead, do your worst. What do you think you can do to me?"

"For starters, I'll tell William. He'll be furious and throw you out of the firm. He won't tolerate your presence knowing that he's been sharing my body with one of his minions."

"He won't care. Why should he? You've told me that you have an open marriage and I know that you do."

"This is different, my carrying on with you, and for so long. We don't embarrass each other and this will humiliate him, the thought that his young partner had the audacity, not to mention bad judgment, to poach the boss' wife. No, he won't like that at all."

Things have not gone well for Clifford at Wylde Capital. He's managed to improve his lackluster performance just enough so that William has not asked him to leave the company. The problem is that he's done so by violating the law (as he did at his prior employment), trading more than once on insider information that he's obtained from his socially-connected pals. Unfortunately, he has not yet covered his tracks on his most recent, very profitable, illicit transactions. If he's fired, his trades will be audited as a matter of company policy, and his criminality undoubtedly uncovered. His social connections (and secret sex video of Charlotte) being what they are, he could survive having his ass kicked to the curb by William Wylde (he's called Wild Bill for a reason), but not under the present circumstances, not if he could be found out and charged with insider trading.

Mustering up as much bravado as he can in the face of Charlotte's surprise attack, he responds, with a veiled threat of his own: "I don't think you'd do that. And if you do, maybe I'd be fired, but maybe not. After all, these are sensitive times for William, with his nomination presently before a divided Senate."

Unaware of Clifford's video, Charlotte retorts: "The FBI has already spoken to us as part of the vetting process, and the President was aware of our marital arrangement when he made the nomination. No one cares about this kind of stuff anymore, certainly not the senators. They won't be quick to cast stones, given their own glass houses. William will most definitely rid himself of you, and it won't be a soft landing."

Now it's Clifford who's desperate, although he can't afford to show it. He can't let Charlotte go to William, the consequences are too dire. Backtracking as best he can, he says: "Look, despite what I said, I have real feelings for you. You know that. I said what I did out of frustration and concern. I meant it to be a wake-up call for you. I was willing to lose you that way if that was the price I had to pay for you to get yourself better."

If she weren't in fact addle-brained by virtue of her most recent opioid intake, Charlotte would easily have seen through Clifford's feeble excuse for his callous words and hurtful conduct. But even if she had, she would still not be prepared to let him go. Whether he stays willingly or by compulsion, she needs him nonetheless. He's someone other than Kristina who can provide Charlotte with comfort. If the only comfort he provides is sexual, she'll settle for that for now, it's better than nothing at all.

Walking two steps towards Clifford, she stretches her arms out wide in an olive branch gesture, signaling for him to come to her embrace, as she says: "I'm not addicted to anything. I just have bad migraines and anxiety-depression. But I'll cut down on the medication. You'll see. I want us to be happy together."

So they embrace, all supposedly forgiven by each of them. Their armistice is celebrated by mutual victory laps. There's nothing better than make-up sex. One and a half hours and two orgasms later, as they lie in bed together, still sweat-covered and redolent of sex, Charlotte still needs more, but now it's only talk she craves: "I'm sorry for being so crazy earlier tonight. It's just that it's been a terrible week for me. I can't begin to tell you."

This is a "come to Jesus" moment for Clifford which he readily accepts, not out of true belief, but out of his necessity to forestall a breakup with Charlotte long enough for him to cover his tracks at work. So he fakes concern and, with the charm of a snake oil salesman, soothingly encourages her: "Tell me. Maybe I can offer you some advice or help you some other way."

"This week, it's all been centered around Wharton. Against William's wishes and without his knowing it, about a month ago I gave Wharton $5 million towards his share of the money needed to start up a new business with some of his friends. They were going to buy a professional lacrosse team. At the last minute, after contracts had been finalized, another group swooped in and purchased the rights to the franchise from the league.

"I didn't learn this until this week, when Wharton came to see me and revealed that not only has he lost the team, but he's gambled away a good portion of the money I gave him. I can't tell you of the many fights he had with William trying to get the money in the first place. William was adamant in his refusal, said it was time for Wharton to grow up, to make it on his own.

"I pleaded with William several times to change his mind, but he wouldn't. And he warned me not to go against him on this, not to give in to Wharton. But I did. I couldn't bear to see how unhappy Wharton was. I thought if I gave him the money, he'd show William how wrong William was about him. That Wharton had just been unlucky in business before and this time he'd succeed. When Wharton promised me that he'd stop taking drugs once he launched his new business, that it would be time then for him to concentrate on work and not engage in idle play, I wired the money to Wharton from a small personal account that William doesn't remember that I have. I keep my 'mad money' there, about $10 million.

"I realize now that I made a huge mistake and William was right to not have given him the money. Wharton explained to me that when he lost the deal as he did, at the very last moment, after he was all but certain that the team was his, he reacted poorly, became an emotional wreck, and needed to do something dramatic to get out of his funk. So he and his disappointed buddies flew to Macao for a week of fun and games in the gaming capital of the world. Wharton lost close to $1.5 million at the tables before he came to his senses and returned home."

Thinking (hoping) that Charlotte has concluded her tale of woe, Clifford blithely pronounces: "He'll grow up, sooner or later. He's still young. And let's be honest and keep things in perspective. The money of yours that he lost gambling is not really of any consequence. You probably spend more than that every year just on gifts to people."

An agitated Charlotte responds: "You don't understand. I haven't told you everything yet. Once Wharton told me what had happened, I knew that William would eventually find out and thought it was better if I told William the whole story now, rather than he find out later. When I did, William was furious. When he threatened to leave me, I made it clear that I'd never go down without a fight. A big, bruising one. As much as I enjoy you, Clifford, I need William. We've a long history together and I'm heavily invested in him. I'm not prepared to let go of him. Not now or ever."

Trying to sound sympathetic, Clifford, with sham tenderness, says: "It will all blow over with William. You'll see. Just give it some time. As to Wharton, hopefully both you and he have learned a lesson and can move on from that. Again, just give it some time."

"I hope you're right. But I can tell you that there's one thing that time will most certainly never heal, that I'll never forget or forgive — Wilma's partner, Bess, is entirely to blame for Wharton's drug-fueled Macao fiasco. For some time now, she's been giving Wharton easy access to the drugs that he and his friends abused while there."

Talk about denial, Clifford thinks to himself. An opioid addict criticizing the source of supply rather than the user. Keeping these thoughts to himself, he responds in deceitful agreement: "You're right to be furious about Bess. Selling drugs to your son, her de-facto in-law, there can be no excusing that."

Charlotte feels good, she and Clifford are back in step. She swears to herself that she'll make good on her promise to Clifford, she'll cut down on the medications. Only take them if absolutely necessary. Exhausted, both physically and emotionally, she falls asleep with those as her last waking thoughts. Clifford's last thoughts before he sleeps are not as peaceful; he needs to figure out a way to free himself from Charlotte's clutches, as he now believes, based on what has occurred this evening, that she may never willingly let either he or William go.

CHAPTER XLII

"Things are getting dicey at the Wyldes," Jeff says to me as he and I share some rare these days "guy" time at our favorite bar in Brooklyn, the one on Atlantic Avenue with the ax throwing in the back and karaoke singing up front every Friday and Saturday night, the Ax Me Ouch.

It's a Thursday night in mid-June, so the bar is not very crowded and we can hear ourselves talk. I know that I'm still a young guy, so maybe I need to get my hearing tested because in most bars, restaurants and other public places I find the noise level such that, unless I'm standing or sitting very close to the person talking, I mean right next to them, not opposite them across the table, I'm reduced to reading lips, and I don't do that very well. I read somewhere that restaurants play very loud music not because they want to give you a blaring headache so you'll leave more quickly and they can turn the table, but because studies show that if there's music playing, customers will eat more food than if the restaurant is quiet. Go figure it!

Anyway, here we are, best friends since birth, sharing our lives as best friends do. Most people would say they pity couples that don't have children, because they're missing out on experiencing one of the greatest pleasures in life. I say that about people who do not have a true best friend. Fortunately, I do.

"Dicey. In what way?" I ask.

"I don't know where to start, there's been so much going on over there lately."

Kristina doesn't like to talk too much about the Wyldes, even though it's a topic we can't avoid when the three of us are alone together (is that correct, can you be "alone" if you're "together," I wonder?), she feels it's disloyal, that she's betraying the Wyldes' confidences after they've been so generous to her and Jeff, including, most recently, offering a $100,000 bonus if Kristina stays as Charlotte's assistant for 12 more months, an offer accepted about three months ago. So three down, nine more to go.

Since it's just Jeff and me who are "alone together" tonight, this is an opportunity for me to get the real lowdown. I like learning about the comings and goings of the Wyldes because it's like watching a soap opera or telenovela without the guilt you feel when you do. "Just start, already," I say impatiently, my interest peaked.

"Okay. And this is really something that you need to keep confidential. I'm not kidding. Wilma came to Charlotte about ten days ago telling her that she needed $3 million in 30 days or she'd be killed by some drug cartel."

"What," I exclaim. "Wilma? The cancer research scientist?"

"Charlotte was so distraught that she couldn't stop crying when she told Kristina about it. Apparently, Bess is still dealing drugs, couldn't pay for a large shipment she ordered, and now a cartel has threatened to kill both Bess and Wilma unless they come up with the money."

"I assume the Wyldes are paying it, of course."

"Yes and no. Apparently Charlotte's first response was 'over my dead body. Let Bess get herself out of the mess she's made. As far as I'm concerned, she's no good and never will be.' Wilma responded 'You don't understand. The dead body will be mine, not just Bess', if you and dad don't pay what they're demanding.'

"So naturally Charlotte told Wilma, 'We need to speak to your father. He'll deal with this' and, after Wilma tearfully explained the situation to him, he was furious, but told them not to worry, he'd handle it. He said that he wouldn't pay the cartel a single penny because he couldn't afford to ever be in any way connected to some Mexican drug cartel, it would be the end of Wylde Capital, whose investors would scatter to the wind. But he has a powerful Mexican family as one of his investors and they'd take care of it for him.'

"That's the Wyldes for you," I say in wonderment. "The kids make a mess, William cleans it up, one way or another."

Jeff stops me: "There's more to this story, pal. You jumped the gun. After William told Wilma what he was going to do, Wilma thanked him for taking care of this for her and Bess and told him that Bess had made a solemn promise to stop trafficking in drugs. But William, so enraged at Bess is he, that he told Wilma that he didn't believe that Bess will ever stop and that he didn't say anything about taking care of this for Bess. He has to think about Bess. And no amount of Wilma's tears or impassioned pleas could move him from that position."

"So what did he decide? That was ten days ago."

"We don't know. He refuses to tell Wilma or Charlotte anything other than that he's spoken with whom he needed to speak and that Wilma is no longer in danger."

"So Bess has been left worrying about whether she'll be killed?" I ask incredulously.

"That's the long and short of it."

"That's incredibly cruel," I say.

"I would guess he wants to teach Bess a lesson, but that she's also out from under the threat. He knows how much Wilma cares for Bess. And even without that, I don't think it's in his nature to let them kill Bess, when it's easy for him to prevent it."

"I guess we'll know in three weeks, when the 30-day clock will have run out," I respond, as usual trying to make light of the situation. "You weren't kidding when you said things had gotten a little nuts at the Wyldes."

"I wasn't, and there's lots more. Wharton won't even acknowledge my presence if he sees me when he comes to the house to visit Charlotte.

He resents William helping me with Auto Eats. But he's just a prick, no matter what. His most recent misadventure was to piss a shitload of money away gambling in Macao with his druggy, wealthy buddies."

"Define shitload," I say.

"About $1.5 million."

"That's a shitload by anybody's definition. By this time, though, I guess the Wyldes just accept that from him. It's his own trust fund money that he's squandering."

"In the words of the immortal Bard, 'Aye, there's the rub.' It seems that it was money that Charlotte gave him so that he could embark on a new business venture. Whatever deal he thought he had fell through and he drowned his sorrows by pissing away a large chunk of the money Charlotte had given him."

"I'm going to make a guess here," I venture. "William was not very pleased when he found out."

"Right on the nose you are, old friend. Particularly since William had refused to give Wharton the money and Charlotte had gone behind his back in doing it."

Shaking my head slightly side to side, I laughingly say: "Well, at least there's one child that probably hasn't been a problem recently, Willis, their doctor kid."

"Again, yes and no. Like Wilma, he seems to be a very decent person from everything Kristina tells me about him. But his wife, Melody, that may be a different case. Charlotte dislikes her because she thinks she's a fortune hunter who married Willis for the Wylde's money and there may be some truth there. A few days ago, talk about bad timing, when she and Willis were having dinner with Charlotte and William, Melody told them that she wanted to open an art gallery on Fifth Avenue and asked them to lend her $15 million to launch her business."

"There's nothing so terrible about that," is my reaction. "They have more than a billion dollars and they can't take it with them. So with

Wharton, I understand he's basically, as they might say in olden times, a 'useless fuck-up.' William wants him to stand on his own two feet for once and succeed at something. But what's the issue in lending the money to Melody?"

"Mostly Charlotte's feelings about her, I suspect," Jeff responds. "Charlotte's immediate reaction was to turn her down, questioning what Melody knows about being an art dealer or owning and operating a gallery. But William interceded, asking Melody if she'd prepared a budget as to how the money she was requesting would be spent. She responded that she had a rough budget on start-up and operating costs. She told him that of the $15 million she'd requested, $12 million was to buy art. She wants to buy from up-and-coming artists whose best works are in the $100,000 to $500,000 price range.

"William at first seemed receptive to the idea, but then asked whether she couldn't skip the gallery for now and just be an art consultant to wealthy people. He offered to make introductions for her if she'd want to do that. He told her that after doing that for a few years, she could build up a client base and then open a gallery. He'd loan her the money if she did that.

"But Melody was not content with that, and continued to press for the loan, ending her request by telling him that it would be named the 'M & W Wylde Gallery' and that she'd already identified a perfect location for it. William responded that he needed to think about it some more, but strongly suggested she follow his advice and first work as an art consultant."

"How do you know all this, in such great detail?" I ask Jeff. "Is the Wylde house bugged and you've listened to the tapes?"

"Charlotte gives poor Kristina a word-by-word description of everything that goes on with her and the family. How else would I know?"

"Intrigue at the royal palace, read all about it," I hawk, as if I were a newsboy in London back in the 1890s. "This is all too much. How are you and Kristina dealing with the fallout?"

"Nothing bad for me. For Kristina, however, not so good. More and more she's been complaining to me about how smothering Charlotte has become, and how she spends a significant portion of each day having to hold Charlotte's emotional hand. As I said, Charlotte confides everything to her. It's very stressful for Kristina."

"Well, Kristina better do her best to hang in there. If she can, you'll be set up to buy a place of your own in less than a year."

"It hasn't reached a critical point yet and hopefully it never will. But you know how it is when you go for an MRI and they tell you not to move for 45 minutes once they slide you into the tube. What's the first thing that happens? All the time you're in the machine, all you can do is think about not moving, how much longer you'll be stuck in this medical coffin, and that you can't wait until it's over and you're taken out. Well we've been starting to think like that about Kristina's job. Hopefully it doesn't come to the point where Kristina feels she can't hang in any longer and must get out."

"At least not until you've bagged the $100,000 carrot that they've dangled," I reply, with the usual tinge of envy I feel whenever I consider how fortunate Jeff has been in these past 15 months that Kristina has been working for Charlotte.

"Any more delicious gossip for me?" I jocularly inquire, confident in my belief that there certainly could be nothing more that Jeff could possibly recite.

To my surprise, he replies: "I've saved the best for last."

"I don't know about that. Wilma's life being threatened and William's reaction to it would seem to be the topper to me," I sarcastically respond.

"Well, in its own way, what I'm about to tell you has a compelling gravitas of its own. Have you ever heard of 'The Giving Pledge?'" he asks.

"Vaguely. Fill me in."

"When Bill Gates left Microsoft, he and his wife, Melinda, formed the Bill & Melinda Gates Foundation. Around that time, Gates announced that he would be dedicating a substantial portion of his $100 billion fortune to support a variety of philanthropic causes. So far, he's already donated more than $50 billion to various charities. He proceeded to convince a substantial number of other super-rich people, such as Warren Buffet, to do the same, that is, make a public pledge that they're dedicating a substantial percentage of their fortunes to philanthropy.

"Now, there's another billionaire who will be making the Giving Pledge. You guessed it — William Wylde. He told Charlotte that since the children each have mortgage-free luxurious homes and trust fund income of $4 million a year for their entire lifetime, that should suffice as a financial safety net for each of them. He said that Willis and Wilma have jobs they love and are content with what they have. Wharton doesn't deserve anything more. So he decided to make the Giving Pledge and has promised that 85% of their money will be donated to several charities and charitable foundations upon or prior to his death.

"It has created quite an uproar in the family. Charlotte is aghast at the thought. She wants not only all of her personal fortune but all of William's to be available for their children and hopefully grandchildren, even though she has no intention of giving anything much to Wilma or Willis until they shed themselves of their undesirable partners.

"Kristina told me that Charlotte and William had a huge argument about it, which Charlotte told her about through the intervals when Charlotte could lift her head off Kristina's lap and stop hysterically sobbing. Apparently, William not only pledged most of his own money to charity but a good portion of Charlotte's Houghton inheritance as well. When Wylde Capital was formed, Charlotte invested most of her personal fortune in the funds it managed. The profits earned on Charlotte's money over the years have gone into trusts managed by William and, as trustee, he has the power to donate all or part of that money to charity, which he has now just done. Charlotte's original inheritance, less various fund fees, remains, but it's tied up in long-term, illiquid Wylde Capital investments and not available to the children for many years to come.

"The kids did not take the news well, I'm assuming."

"I'm told that Wharton stormed out of the house cursing at William, and even Willis and Wilma were unhappy."

"You'd think 15% of what I'm guessing is closer to $2 billion than $1 billion, even whether that does or doesn't include Charlotte's money, would be enough of a pie to divvy up on the deaths of their beloved parents," I declare, as I shake my head wondering how much money the children of the rich really think they need.

Jeff says: "Yep. It should be. But remember, there's no guaranty that William will give any of the remaining several hundreds of millions of dollars to any of their children, either now or in his will. And I've no idea how much they spend each year to support their households and the other extravagances they enjoy, but it must be $20-30 million a year at a minimum."

"Ah, the problems of the rich," I utter, as I let out a soft, commiserating moan. "I have to tell you, Jeff, this has been a treasure trove of murder mystery material that I fully intend to incorporate in the book I write after I finish the one I'm working on. But don't expect any thanks in my acknowledgment page. I don't want to open myself up to a lawsuit by any of the misbegotten Wyldes."

"You do your best work when you plagiarize. So you should let people know that you've 'plagiarized' a family's life, that way more people will buy the book," my wiseguy friend replies.

Except for a short discussion in which Jeff tells me with great pride how well the Auto Eats restaurant is continuing to do, we spend the rest of the evening discussing sports, politics and social media, none of this conversation as titillating as when we talked about the Wyldes.

CHAPTER XLIII

On the same mid-June day as Jeff gossips with his best buddy Simon about the Wylde family's troubles, Vanessa is about to add another to the growing pile.

"I'm pregnant," a hesitant but unrealistically hopeful Vanessa reveals to William, just a moment after he's removed his suit jacket and hung it on the back of the restaurant chair on which he's just sat down. She's been waiting anxiously for a half-hour for him to arrive and can't constrain herself any longer, eager to relieve herself of her burdensome secret.

Gobsmacked, William responds: "I don't know what to say." He pauses, looking vacantly into her tear-filled eyes, "I really don't."

"How about you're happy for me? For us," a disappointed Vanessa prompts.

"Happy? You're kidding, right? Did you really think I'd be happy about this? It's the worst possible time. If this comes out before the Senate votes, it'll squash my nomination. I can get away with having an extra-marital affair, but not a pregnant girlfriend. Certainly not if Charlotte finds out. How did this happen? You're supposed to be on the pill."

Shocked by William's cruel thrust, with raised voice, an extremely upset Vanessa heatedly responds: "It happened by you putting your penis inside me and ejaculating. I didn't hear any complaints from you all the times you were doing that. Do you think I stopped taking the pill so I could pressure you into marrying me? That I'm a conniving tramp?"

Having had a moment to recover from his initial shock, William tries to calm things down and avoid a confrontation in such a public venue. In a conciliatory tone, he leans over to her, affectionately puts his arm around her shoulder and says: "I'm sorry for the way I reacted. I didn't behave well. We'll figure this out together and do what's best."

Softly crying, wiping tears from her eyes, she, too, apologizes: "I didn't mean to get so angry and attack you. It's just that I didn't think you'd respond as you did. I thought you might even welcome us having a child together, you know how much I want one, and that Charlotte would have no choice but to give you your freedom once she knew."

"You don't know Charlotte. She'll feel shamed and degraded and she'll strike back to hurt me any way she can. As long as we play to the public as having a loving marriage, whatever I do outside our marriage is fine with Charlotte. But if she knew that I'd fallen in love and was having a child with you, she'd try to crucify me."

"What can we do?," a distraught Vanessa sighs. "I'm not going to kill my baby. I'll never do that."

"I don't know. I'll figure something out. I just need some time in which to do it. How many weeks pregnant are you?" William asks, his ability to reason still intact despite this potential tumultuous upheaval of his apple cart.

"Six at most, I think. I just tested myself this morning. I missed my period about two weeks ago."

Trying both to comfort her and prevent a further discussion which he's unprepared to have, he assures her, "Okay, then. We still have plenty of time to work through this."

"It's a wonderful thing that I'm having a baby. The only thing you need to figure out is whether you love me as much as I love you, so that you're ready to embrace that."

After a skip-the-appetizers, one course meal hastily eaten, with little further conversation, they ride back to Vanessa's apartment, distractedly holding hands in the back seat of William's limousine. Contemplating a happy future and misreading what William is thinking, Vanessa leans over towards him and whispers: "You know, it wouldn't be the end of the world, would it, if you're not the next Treasury Secretary? I know how much it means to you, but we'd have a child and a life together as a family. Then who cares how Charlotte reacts or what she does?; she can't really hurt you."

Without thinking, William briskly retorts: "Being Secretary of the Treasury means everything to me. I'm not willing to lose my chance at it." Tempering the severity of his outburst, he more calmly attempts to explain: "You're still young. I'm in my 50s. I don't mean this to sound egotistic, but I've worked a lifetime to attain a certain prominence. Even if I'm willing to forego being Secretary of the Treasury, I'm not eager to have Charlotte publicly disparage me, make me look like a fool incapable of managing his private life. That's not good for me personally and certainly not good for my business."

"What means everything to me is for us to be together and for me to have our baby. But now, based on what you just said, the only thing I'm sure of is that I'm having our baby," Vanessa heatedly responds, unable to contain her emotions or restrain her tears.

"We'll be together. Just give it time. Once my appointment is confirmed, Charlotte won't have the same incentive to publicly destroy me that she has when she thinks she can take away something that she knows I want so very much. After I'm Treasury Secretary, I'll divorce her no matter what she might do. It's a risk I'm willing to take and a sacrifice I'm willing to make. It's a fair exchange for having a new life and family with you." These are the deceitful words that William so smoothly, soothingly mouths, backtracking from what he previously said, but not the reality of his situation. Charlotte will destroy him no matter when he might seek a divorce. And there are (unknown by either Vanessa or Charlotte) complex financial issues (not to mention his need for public adoration) which preclude William from ever seeking a divorce that Charlotte would contest.

"I don't know how long your nomination will take to be approved, but our baby is coming in eight months, so that's our timeframe. I know this is a horrible thing to say, but maybe we'll get lucky and Charlotte will overdose on the pills you've told me she takes, that would solve everything."

"I don't wish Charlotte dead. I still have feelings for her and want her to find happiness without me," William rotely mouths, while thinking to himself: Vanessa is right. Charlotte's death, by overdose or otherwise, would be a perfect stroke of good luck. Given his present circumstances, this wouldn't be horrible at all and William has never been one to just leave things to chance. He needs to give this some serious thought.

Back at their Sands Point home, Charlotte, like William, is in the process of weathering some seismic upheavals of her own. Wilma has insisted on seeing her this morning to talk about Bess. She's on a mission to convince Charlotte that Bess is deep down a good person, the right life partner for Wilma, and that rather than continually disparage Bess, Charlotte needs to be more supportive of their relationship.

After hugs and kisses, Charlotte and Wilma sit down side by side on one of the couches in the sun room, facing each other, holding hands. A visibly distraught Wilma says: "I know that dad is going to protect both Bess and me from the cartel, regardless of what he said. That's not why I'm here. I need to make you understand that Bess and I are forging a life together. We intend to get married, have children, be a family. I'm here because I believe in Bess and want you to be more open-minded about her, to get to know her better, to give her a chance to show you the type of person she really is. This constant tension between you and Bess is tearing me apart. Please don't make me choose between the two of you, because that's what it's coming down to, and I don't want to have to make that choice."

"She's a drug dealer," Charlotte exclaims. "You'll come to your senses when passion wears off, as it always eventually does. Look at what she's already done to you, put your life in danger. You need to open your eyes. Mine have been wide open from the day I first met her. I know exactly who she is. She's a person without values who's after your money and is going to drag you down to her level so you can wallow together in the muck of her life."

"That's not true, Mom. You need to understand her. Bess can't accept living off of my money, she needs to pay her own way. If she doesn't do that, she feels we can never truly be equal partners. That's admirable. Unfortunately, she's made money selling drugs since she was a teenager, a great deal of money, actually. After this mess with the cartel, Bess has promised that she's done with it forever. But what she did with the cartel only happened because she was trying to surprise me. She had amassed enough for one large transaction which, if successful, would have given her a substantial enough stake to do what I had asked: stop dealing drugs once and for all. Then her plan was to go back to school for a masters in business and find a legitimate career to pursue. Now that all her money has been lost, to prove to me that she's going to keep her promise, she's swallowed her pride and agreed to let me pay for her masters degree."

Skeptical, unforgiving, unreceptive and unbending, Charlotte coldly says: "She's out of the drug business because the cartel will kill her if they find that she's still dealing drugs. That's the reason, not what you've romanticized."

"She's out of the business because she loves me enough to give it up. She knows that after what almost happened, if she ever sells drugs again, we're through, no matter how much I want us to be together."

"She's not the right person for you, Wilma. She's after your money no matter what she's told you. You'll see," Charlotte persists. "I'm your mother. I've always known what's best for you and how to protect you. This time's no different."

"I'm not a little girl any more. I can take care of myself."

"By almost getting yourself killed?"

"That's why I came this morning. I know how terrible a thing that was. I'm still shaken by it. So is Bess. But I came to ask you, plead with you, to give Bess a chance despite what happened."

Charlotte pauses for a moment, looking at Wilma, and then threatens: "Let's see how Bess deals with what I'm about to say. Please understand that what I'm going to do is for your own good. I'm going to change my will so that if I die at a time that you and Bess are married or living together, you get nothing from my estate. And if the two of you remain together while I'm alive, I'll never give you a penny."

"I don't care about your damned money and neither does Bess," a frustrated Wilma declares. "Do what you want with your money. I have more than enough without it. But you need to treat Bess better, not be hostile towards her, if you want to avoid pushing me out of your life."

After Wilma departs from her unsuccessful attempt to broker a truce for Bess with Charlotte, having achieved not even the slightest hint of possible compromise from Charlotte, Wharton arrives for a tete-a-tete of his own, requested by his mother. After air-kisses on both cheeks and a brief discussion of Wharton's possible summer plans, Charlotte gets down to the business she wants to address with Wharton, her purpose for having asked him to come see her this afternoon. "Wharton, you know how much I'm worried about you. You seem very unhappy lately. What can I do to help you?"

"Nothing. I'm fine. You helped me when you gave me the money I needed. I'm so very sorry I gambled so much away, but I was so disappointed in losing out on my deal that I lost control of myself. That doesn't usually happen. You saw me at my worst. Things are okay now. No need to worry about me."

"I don't think you're telling me the truth. You almost always seem angry or unhappy when we speak. And from what I can see, you're doing drugs way too much and running with too wild a bunch of friends."

"Everyone my age smokes pot, pops some pills, snorts some cocaine. But it's not to excess and I'm not out of control. If you want to know why I seem angry or unhappy, it's because of the way dad treats me. He treats Jeff as if he were his favored son, and me, his oldest and real son, as an outcast."

"I think he just wants you to prove yourself to him, but I really can't defend it. We have plenty of money and if you need money for something, if your trust fund isn't enough, why shouldn't we give it to you?"

"Thanks, Mom. I know you're always in my corner."

"I am. But I'm also in your corner when I tell you that I think you've a drug problem and need to get some help."

After a disbelieving, caustic stare, Wharton lets loose an angry rant: "Is this a joke? A fucking cosmic joke? You're worried about me taking too many drugs? Should we go open your medicine cabinet? There's a year's supply of stuff for me in there, I bet."

"We're here to talk about you, not me. I have medical conditions and doctor's prescriptions for what I take. You're doing it for kicks. If you continue, you'll wreck your life and never be able to climb out from under the rubble."

"This is ridiculous. If my acquisition of the lacrosse team had gone through, my life would have been perfectly fine and we wouldn't be having this conversation. Some other business venture will pop up soon, I'm sure, and if I can get dad to treat me like a son and not continue to throw me to the curb, then things will be good. So you can stop worrying about me. Worry about yourself, and how dad treats you."

"Your reaction just now, the angry manner in how you're speaking to me, proves my point. I have reason to worry. You used to be sweet and gentle when we were together, now most often you're bitter and abrasive, saying hurtful things to me."

"This conversation is going nowhere good, Mom. I'm leaving. I love you, appreciate your intentions, but I'm out of here."

As he gets up and starts to leave, Charlotte calls out: "Before you leave, I have something more to say. You seem high to me on something right now, as we've been speaking. If you don't get counseling and help yourself, and I mean soon, I'll be changing my will and disinheriting you until you do."

"Then maybe I should take steps to do away with you before you have that chance," a furious Wharton replies as he rushes from the house.

CHAPTER XLIV

"I need your help. I did something and I'm in trouble," a downcast and ashamed Dan says to Jeff, as they sit together in the parlor floor living room of Jeff's parents' house. Barbara is not home from work yet and Dan has asked Jeff to meet him this afternoon because he needs to discuss something with Jeff that he can't do over the telephone. An alarmed Jeff has left work to meet with his father and, after a quick hug and brief greeting, Dan has started to unburden himself.

"What, Dad? What did you do?"

"I stole some money."

"You stole money?" a flabbergasted Jeff disbelievingly cries out. "I can't believe it. You? The 'follow the rules' general of my entire life?"

"I had hoped for a little more sympathy and a lot less sarcasm. This is tough enough for me as is," Dan pushes back, disappointedly. "I'm asking for your help."

"Okay, sorry. You're right. It's just the shock of what you said. I'm listening. Tell me what you did."

After Dan explains how he jiggled his company's property management books to embezzle $100,000 to invest in a documentary about TV game show hosts, he continues the narrative of his misbegotten adventure to a slack-jawed, silent, incredulous, critical son: "I thought the documentary would be sold within six months at most and then I would correct the records and return the money, with no one the wiser. I don't know how I could've been so stupid. I saw the chance to make a lot of money quickly, to build a bigger nest egg for our retirement, and I acted on it. But to this day, I can't explain how I could let myself and my family down just for a chance at some easy money."

As a mortified Dan pauses to take a breath, to swallow his shame, Jeff speaks: "And now it's gone wrong, apparently. Exactly how bad a fix are you in?"

"I'm about to get caught. Next month the company is going to audit the management records for the properties I oversee. The regular fiscal year audit is a year away, but the company just announced a change in its policy and I'm the first lucky recipient of a spot audit."

A suddenly more sympathetic Jeff responds: "How can I help? We haven't saved up anything like that much money for me to give you. Don't you and mom have enough in savings? What about in your retirement plans?"

"If we did, I wouldn't be talking to you about this. We make ends meet, but have never been able to save very much, just enough to pay for your college education after you lost your scholarship. Barbara's government retirement plan is untouchable and all the money in mine has been invested in small ownership percentages of various company-owned properties, which I can't cash in until I reach age 65 or five years after I leave the company's employ."

"I never realized things were so tight financially for you and mom."

"We've managed okay, at least until I went nuts and fucked up."

"I'm really sorry, Dad. Does mom know?"

"She knows what I did. She's been pissed off at me for months now, but that's none of your business, that's between her and me. But I haven't told her yet about the surprise audit. I wanted to speak to you about it first, to see if I could get your help in finding a way out before then."

"What is it you want from me? I wish Kristina and I had the money. We've got about $40,000 saved and I can give you that. Can you borrow the rest from friends, maybe?"

"What 'friends' would you suggest? They don't have the money and, even if they did, they're not just going to lend it to me without a good explanation. No. What I'd like you to do is find a way to get it for me from the Wyldes, without telling them why or even that it's for me. Just make up some reason that you and Kristina need $100,000 and then, once you get it, give it to me. Maybe borrow it from Auto Eats."

"I can't do that. Even if I would be willing to lie for you and concoct some story. I wouldn't be able to get the money, not now."

"Why not?" Dan pleads.

"I haven't told you and mom yet, but Auto Eats is in trouble. In July, some customers at our restaurant apparently got food poisoning from a contaminated franks and beans dish that we served. We only learned about this yesterday, when Auto Eats was sued by some money-hungry, publicity-seeking lawyer, who went to the press before coming to us. Mr. Wylde is furious that this lawyer has mentioned Wylde Capital's controlling ownership interest in the company and has accused Wylde Capital of cutting corners to make a profit at the expense of consumer health." Jeff continues: "So right now, various town, county and state agencies are planning to do inspections of our restaurant, and the money Mr. Wylde had lined up to fund the expansion of our business is no longer committed. Obviously, I can't get any money from Auto Eats or from Mr. Wylde for anything right now, even if I were willing to lie about the reason I need it."

"Please, son. Help me here. You can figure something out. I'm sure you can. Speak to Simon. He's always been the clever one. Tell him what I did; he'll keep it to himself, he's a member of our family."

A dejected Jeff, hurt not only by what his father has done but what he's said about Simon always being the 'clever one,' says goodbye to his father, promising: "I'll speak to Simon. We'll try to figure something out. But I can't see what. The only thing I can think of is to tell Mr. Wylde what you did and ask him to bail you out."

A prideful Dan vehemently responds: "No way. Never. I'd rather go to jail for my mistake. I won't beg someone like William Wylde to help me. Not under any circumstances."

"You might have to change your mind about that. Talk to mom about the audit and then see how you feel."

"I don't need to talk to her to know how I feel. I won't ask him for a get-out-of-jail card. It's too high a price for me to pay."

Dan's disturbing revelation is not the only troubling conversation this hot and humid early August day. Wiping his brow with his monogramed white linen handkerchief, Wharton is feeling scorched by heat wholly unrelated to the time of year.

"Are we going to have to break some bones here, Mr. Wylde?" asks one of the Atlantic City casino's "debt collectors" in the parking lot outside the casino. "You've run up quite a tab here and in our Vegas casinos, and it's time for you to pay up on the $2.3 million you owe us. We've cut off your credit, don't make us cut off anything else."

"I'll pay. No need to threaten me," a high-as-a-kite Wharton nonchalantly responds, while slowly swaying back and forth on unsteady feet. "I'm good for it. I'm a Wylde. I'll give you $250,000 next week, and the rest over the next year or two. Not to worry."

"'Worry' is our business, Mr. Wylde. As far as we're concerned, you're snorting our money away. Our employer is very unhappy with the present state of its union with you."

"I just told you. I'll pay $250,000 next week. Then the rest over the next two years. That should be acceptable."

"What's acceptable is that by the end of next month you pay half of what you owe and the other half within three months after that, plus, of course, the interest you owe, which is one percent per month until your debt is paid in full."

STEPHEN M. RATHKOPF

"You're just fucking with me. That's tough guy bullshit from the movies and it won't fly with me. No way I pay that kind of interest and I can't pay you the principal amount that quickly."

"Yes, you can and will, pretty boy. Or you might not be so pretty any more. Just go home and ask your daddy for the money. He'll soon be Secretary of the Treasury and can print it for you if he doesn't want to use any of his own billions on you."

"I have my own money but you'll just have to wait longer to get it. I'm not some patsy you can just intimidate. I'll pay as I promised and that's it. You can take that to the bank. Tell that to your employer."

Without warning, Wharton doubles over and crumbles to the ground from a swift, powerful punch delivered to his mid-section by the shorter of the two nattily-attired "debt collectors" with whom he has been talking. As Wharton simultaneously gasps for breath and expels the contents of his recently digested meal, the second of the two "gentlemen," the one who has been threatening Wharton, leans over him and mouth to Wharton's ear, whispers: "You can take that to the bank. And more deposits to follow if you don't pay as I think I hear you saying you now agree. You do agree, don't you?"

Wharton, still writhing in pain, mumbles some indistinguishable response, words that he himself doesn't know what he's saying.

"I'll take that for a yes. Payment of one-half of what you owe by September 30th, at the latest."

As they walk away from Wharton, leaving him on the ground still heaving, gasping and wheezing, the taller of the two enforcers chortles, almost to himself: "That was fun. The most enjoyable part of this job for me is when we get to bring one of these wise guy playboy types down to earth. Teach them a lesson they never learned in boarding school or at Hahvahd."

Wharton is not the only Wylde child left gasping in shock today. Willis, too, has been floored, in his case not by a punch, but by the pile of unpaid bills that Melody has managed to amass without Willis realizing it. "You're first telling me about all this now?" Willis exclaims, unable to moderate the overwhelming combination of exasperation, frustration and disappointment that he's experiencing. What were you thinking, Melody?"

A weeping Melody replies, "I was only thinking of us. Of how I could get you to embrace the vision I had for our future."

"So you engaged architects, conceptual artists and designers to draw plans and prepare renderings for a clinic I don't want and for an art gallery that my father is not ready to fund? And if that was not enough, you ordered samples of various types of marble and quartz for counters, woods for paneling and stones for columns, all without telling me any of what you were doing?"

"I knew that if I told you, you'd object, and that then I might never get a chance to convince you that you were wrong. I thought by doing all this, showing you how your clinic and my gallery might look, I could win you over and then we'd be united on what we asked for when we next broached the topics with your parents."

"But almost $1 million for this. What a waste."

"It's not a waste. Look at how wonderful this all can be. You need your own medical clinic to run. And I need my art gallery. You have to help me convince your father to give us the money for both of these things. I know he'll do it for your clinic, if you just ask him to."

"I told you, I'm happy doing what I do. I don't want any clinic, certainly not for the immediate future. And you just need to wait on owning a gallery. Just do what my father suggested, first work for a few years as an art consultant to gain experience and a client base."

"What good is William's money doing just sitting there, when just a little of it could do so much for us. He can't take it with him."

"It's his money, not ours. And he's not taking it with him; he's done the Giving Pledge for most of it. We're lucky to have the trust fund from my grandparents. That's more than we need. Or at least it would be if you didn't spend it as quickly as you have been. I've left the money matters to you. But now that I've been forced to look at what's been spent, I have to ask how much clothing and jewelry do you need, how much traveling do you have to do?"

"Gallery or not, I'm trying to get my art business off the ground. I need to look and play the part of a Wylde to woo possible clients and I need to travel to identify possible up-and-coming artists. We also have social obligations that we have to meet, charities that we have to contribute to, and clubs that we need to be members of. Every penny of our $4 million is spent every year. Your salary certainly doesn't contribute much, which is another reason you need to run your own clinic."

"Listen to you, Melody. You can't make ends meet on $4 million a year. That's absurd," Willis says. After a moment of strained silence between them, Willis suppresses his anger sufficiently to be able to get up from the table where they've been sitting and walk around it to Melody, where he puts his arms around her shoulders, bends over and lightly kisses her cheek in an effort to prevent this conversation from escalating any further.

Melody means everything to Willis and there's little he wouldn't do to make her happy. True, that on occasion, where opportunity presented itself, he's strayed from the marital bed (is it genetic?, he often wonders), but those forays are no reflection of his feelings for Melody. He loves her dearly. Melody has her secrets too and that she might be playing him to achieve a goal has never crossed Willis' mind.

His effort at conciliation has apparently been successful, as Melody, sounding contrite, looks up at him and says: "I'm sorry. It's just that I want more for us; we're both capable of accomplishing great things. I'll try to be patient and give things time to develop. And you're right, of course; there's no reason we can't live exceedingly well on the trust fund if I'm just more careful in what I'm spending our money on." With that, Melody and Willis hug, kiss and ostensibly make up, all forgiven and forgotten, at least by Willis, but not by Melody. Instead,

Melody's words have been carefully crafted to facilitate a safe retreat from a battle field Melody intends to soon re-enter, this time with a better strategic plan to win her war.

Charlotte is the enemy Melody must first defeat. She's confident that in short order after that, she can win over William (who has a bit of a roving eye for her) and Willis. It's not patience but action that is required. Her first step has misfired. Her next won't. She loves Willis in her fashion, but love in Melody's world goes only so far, it's the Wylde family money that carried her over the threshold in Willis' welcoming arms. And that's the spoils of war to which she aspires. She needs to find a way to be rid of Charlotte. The sooner the better. And permanently. She has some ideas about how to do that. Now she must pick one and act on it.

The youngest Wylde child is also in the heat of battle this not so fine day. Her opponent is Bess; better put, it's Bess' lifestyle. In actuality, of course, although Wilma doesn't fully realize it, it's also Charlotte, who has always maintained a close hold over Wilma and still has her at least partially tied to her emotional apron strings.

"I can't keep partying so much with you, Bess. I've got to go to work every day, and my job requires that I be fully alert and attentive."

"I get it. You're a very important person, a research scientist, the apple of Charlotte's eye, while I'm only a low-life, fun-seeking drug abuser," Bess fires back.

"Fight fair. I'm not saying that and I don't think of you that way, and you know it."

"Well, that's what Charlotte says to you about me and what I think I'm hearing."

"I'm not Charlotte. I'm your partner, the person who loves you and wants to have a child with you. I'm only saying that so many late nights out and all the drugs we've been taking have become too much for me."

Bess angrily responds: "I've stopped dealing drugs and I have to make money. Bartending suits me best and, when I work the night shift, I have the opportunity to play afterwards and have some fun. I want to share that play time with my partner."

"Weekends, ok. But not week nights. I can't do it anymore. And I'm not willing to spend nights alone while you're out doing that without me."

"Bullshit. That's your mother in you speaking and holding you back from enjoying yourself. You've too much of Charlotte in you, too many of her insecurities and baseless concerns. You've got to rid yourself of her to be happy. I wish I could do that for you, for both of us."

"I'm happy just being with you, here at home. And it's not just the late nights I'm talking about, but the drugs you do when we party. I can't plan a future with you if you substitute abusing drugs for dealing them. My mother is right about that, when she says that a life with a drug abuser is no life for me."

"That's a laugh. Charlotte, who takes pills as if they were M&Ms, warning you about living with me because I use drugs to party. Did you ever see a re-run Christmas time of 'The Honeymooners'? 'Har, har, hardy, har, har.'"

"Forget Charlotte. It's just me asking you, begging you, less late nights and go easier on the ecstasy and oxycodone. Better still, give up bartending and go back to school like we discussed. Get your master's degree in business."

"I'll make the effort to party less if you make the effort to loosen up and enjoy things more. But as to the rest, I don't have the money to pay for me to go back to school. And I won't take yours. I'm not willing to be your paid escort, only your equal partner."

"Now who's being foolish? Paying for you to get a degree is an investment in our future. Consider it a loan you can repay from all the money you'll earn down the road. We already agreed on that, or at least I thought we did."

"I'm happy at what I do. At least for now. I'm not built to work some stuffy office job. I'm an entrepreneur. I succeeded in my drug business until I got unlucky, brought down by a Black Swan event. I don't need a business degree — I already earned one in the streets. I'll come up with something else to pursue, but for now bartending as a stopgap is fine. I meet a lot of people and make a lot of connections that may prove valuable for me. So please, stop being Charlotte with me, and just be you. Don't just love me. Accept me for who I am. Don't try to change me more than you already have."

Nothing more to be said, Wilma and Bess cease fire and make love, not war, but Bess can't help herself from thinking, afterward, how perfect things might be if she could somehow get Charlotte out of their lives forever. And she has a plan in mind as to how to do it. Pills, glorious pills.

CHAPTER XLV

"What a fucking kick in the head," I say to Jeff, very much shaken by what he's just told me. I can't believe it. Dan, a thief. Not someone married to Barbara. And how badly must Jeff feel about his father? True, they were never close growing up; Dan was way too much of a ramrod for either of us, at least that's what we always thought. Well, there's most certainly been a bend in the stick, if not a complete break.

"According to my dad, you're the 'clever' one. Not sure what that makes me, but any ideas you have would be greatly appreciated," a clearly wounded Jeff woefully utters, then sadly continues: "This is particularly difficult since it come just on the heels of our happy news that Kristina is pregnant. Talk about the ups and downs of life and bad timing."

"I wish I could come up with something. The only thing I can think of is for you to disregard what your father told you and ask the Wyldes for the money. Have you discussed this with Barbara?"

"I promised not to. Dad said he doesn't want mom to know how bad things have suddenly become. Apparently, she's been consumed by anger and concern since he first told her what he did and he doesn't want to increase the strain on her. He says there's nothing she can do any way, except worry some more and continue to excoriate him."

"Then go to Mr. Wylde and ask him for the money. I don't see any other choice."

"I don't feel comfortable doing that. Ever since the lawsuit was brought against Auto Eats a few weeks ago, he's given me pretty much of a cold shoulder. He blames me, says I should've had better food management and employee training measures in place, that if I had, we wouldn't have served customers spoiled food. Today, another tainted food lawsuit was filed against the company and I think it may be the death blow to Auto Eats. William already has threatened to close the restaurant, not so much because of the potential liabilities, we have insurance to cover most of that, but the bad publicity about Wylde Capital being its principal owner. And even if William were willing to let Auto Eats continue in business, the bad press surrounding these lawsuits will keep customers away. Looks like I'm back to selling cars. Not the right time to tell William that my father is a crook and ask him to give me $100,000 to cover his tracks."

"I'm sorry about your father, but, to be honest, I feel even worse about Auto Eats. You were doing so well. All that good social media vibe you got when you first opened up, influencers taking selfies at the restaurant, has all gone to waste."

"I screwed up. I took on more than I could handle. I was supposed to be the outside guy, the face of the company. Instead, I played the role of manager of a fast-food restaurant when I should've hired someone with the necessary experience to do that. If I had, food wouldn't have been left unrefrigerated long enough to spoil."

"You're being way too hard on yourself. You weren't afraid to take a chance at something new and almost made a success of it. That's something to be proud of."

"I don't feel very proud at the moment. Not of either of the Muss men. Wylde Capital took a chance on me and I let William down; he lost a lot of money because of my mistakes."

"Don't dump yourself in the same garbage heap as your father. The character defects and sins of your father aren't yours. In time, you'll see that I'm right and you'll appreciate how far you took Auto Eats. This won't be the first time Wylde Capital lost some money, and relatively little when you realize that a single Auto Eats restaurant is probably by far the smallest investment Wylde Capital has ever made."

"What I feel worst about, of everything, is the effect on my mother if dad is arrested and she has to endure the shame of it, not to mention people's suspicion that she knew and condoned what he did."

"What about Kristina asking Charlotte for the money? They're still very close, aren't they? Given how generous Charlotte has already shown herself to be where Kristina is concerned, she probably will give her the money, maybe not even mention it to William."

"There's a problem with Kristina doing that. Her feeling about continuing to work for Charlotte has been changing. She says that Charlotte has been taking more pills than ever, is having wild mood swings as a result, and that being with her has become like riding an emotional rollercoaster, with Kristina an unwilling passenger. And it's not just the mood swings that trouble Kristina. Charlotte could over-dose and Kristina doesn't want to be party to that."

Simon quickly responds: "I know this doesn't help your father, but maybe it's time for the both of you to move out of Tara and leave all the Wylde's baggage behind. Get on with your lives the way they were before you met the Wyldes. You've already been rewarded with a lavish wedding, substantial savings, and experiences you'll cherish forever. It's been almost all upside until now. So why stick around while things crater?"

"I'm ashamed to admit this, compadre, but it's a one-word answer: 'greed.' You jumped in before I had finished what I had to say."

"So? Go on."

"So, Charlotte is as excited about Kristina's pregnancy as she was about our getting married. She's told Kristina that she feels almost like this will be her first grandchild and she wants to provide everything possible for us and our baby. She's going to give us a $1 million gift when the baby is born and is going to change her will to provide a $10 million bequest for our child."

"Holy moly, great balls of fire," I declare, while shaking my head and rolling my eyes in an exaggerated gesture of wonderment, although I'm not sure it's exaggerated. "The answer to my question isn't 'greed,' it's 'common sense.'"

"Yes, but that may also be the answer to the question of whether Kristina should ask Charlotte for the $100,000 for my father. Given the present state she's in, who knows how Charlotte might react? Except for your ticket to Hamilton, Kristina has never asked for any of the things that Charlotte has given her. If she asks, maybe Charlotte comes to look at Kristina differently, to doubt her sincerity and question her motives in working for Charlotte these past 17 months, and so she changes her mind about the gifts she's promised."

"So, if you stay and weather the storm, you get $1 million, plus the previously promised $100,000, but if you leave before the baby is born, you are both unemployed with a bun in the oven and without either the baby gift or the 12-month bonus."

"You got it. My dad's problem is just one part of a rather complex puzzle that we have to address."

Always the mystery writer, where death lurks on every page, I reply: "Of course, if Charlotte were to die tomorrow, there's a $10 million bonus in the pot and it would be immediate Valhalla for the present and future members of the Muss family, not to mention all of the Wyldes supposedly mourning at her wake. If I were writing your story, I'd have someone kill her off."

To that rather flippant (usual for me, I need not remind anyone) comment, a downcast Jeff replies: "Maybe Kristina or I should just switch out one of her pills for something more lethal, one of the fentanyl pills you told me about a long time ago. That would do the trick, I imagine."

STEPHEN M. RATHKOPF

"It would, and you probably could get it from Bess," I joke, trying to alleviate Jeff's pain and help lift the cloud that hangs over his Pig-Pen."

"Kristina and I have a lot to think about. Let's leave it at that for now."

As we break off, I think to myself, would I ever seriously consider becoming Jeff and Kristina's saviour, take their matters into my hands and slip Charlotte a loaded gun, in this case a single-shot fentanyl pill? They mean that much to me. Not only Jeff and Kristina, Barbara too. They're my true family, all I've really got. Is it enough to cause me to kill someone in real life, even though I could justify (or at least rationalize) it as assisted suicide? Or is my killing people limited to the fiction I write as opposed to the fictions I pursue in my life?

CHAPTER XLVI

Charlotte's week is bursting its seams and she's about to be overrun by the weight of it, too much for even her pills to shore up.

On Monday, it's Wilma pushing back against Charlotte, appalled by yet another ill-tempered, malignant comment Charlotte has made about Bess. "Stop trying to break us up. Enough already. I wish I could just get you to stop."

"I'm only doing what a mother should, trying to protect you, shield you from your mistakes. If you stay with her long enough, she'll eviscerate everything good in you, leaving you the wanton wreck that she is."

"I can't keep having this fight with you. This is the last time. If you don't give up this unholy crusade once and for all, then I'm out of your life regardless of whether you're out of mine."

"I'll stop. It's falling on deaf ears anyway," Charlotte retreats in apparent defeat. "But be sure Bess understands that what I've threatened, I'm now doing — I'm taking you out of my will and dead or alive, as long as the two of you are together, you'll never see another dollar from me or your father. With that said, I surrender."

Charlotte, of course, hasn't surrendered. Once Wilma has had a chance to tell Bess what Charlotte has said, Charlotte intends to confront Bess with an offer that she's confident Bess won't refuse — $5 million to leave Wilma, paid $1 million up front and $1 million each of the next four years on each one-year anniversary date. Charlotte desperately needs another ally in her life, and Wilma sans Bess is the most likely candidate.

That evening, Charlotte and Clifford have another in their continuing string of acerbic arguments, the latest triggered, yet again, by Charlotte's pill-induced histrionics and unadulterated need for attention. "You don't need a lover, you need a lengthy stay at the Betty Ford Clinic," an exasperated Clifford unkindly declares. "On the outside, you're a beautiful woman but inside, you're a mess. We used to spend our time making love; now we spend it with me listening to you complain how horrible your life has become, how William, your children and your sister continue to disappoint you, and how your only comfort is the 'wonderful' Kristina and me. Not the foreplay I signed up for. The harsh truth, Charlotte, is that you derive most of your comfort from the pills you wallow in. You've become an addict and need to get treatment."

Overwrought, crying and hugging herself, head bowed as Clifford delivers these devastating blows to her teetering psyche, a desperate Charlotte implores: "I'm not an addict, not as you mean it. I just take medication and only as prescribed by my doctors. I need you, Clifford. I'll do whatever it takes to keep us together."

Remembering that "whatever it takes" includes her not so long ago threat to reveal their affair to Wild Bill and almost guarantees the discovery and probable criminal prosecution of his illegal trading activities, Clifford, as he has done in past arguments, decides to dial back his disgust: "What it takes, for starters, is for you to cut down on your pill consumption. If you'd just do that, things would be so much better. We could build back from that to how things used to be."

But Charlotte's mood has swiftly shifted, deeply offended by Clifford's emphasis on the words "for starters" and the overall demeaning and condescending way in which he's been upbraiding her: "You know what, Clifford? I'm not going to take this from you. How dare you talk to me like I was some addict prostitute whose only role in life is to pleasure you? You'll give me what I want and thought I was getting — a compassionate lover. Compassion was the foreplay that I signed up for. That's what's my 'for starters.'"

Seeing no way out this night, only ruin, Clifford apologizes in a tone and with a look of faux sincerity. "I care very much for you Charlotte. You know that. I'm only trying to help you. And to get things between us back to the way they were."

In control of neither her emotions nor her faculties, having taken an Oxycontin and Xanax two hours earlier, and wanting, no needing, to believe the genuineness of his words, she responds: "I also want us the way we were. No arguments any more. Let's both do our best. There's something very good between us that's worth maintaining. And not just the sex. Though no complaints there, from either of us, I imagine. Not on our good days."

With that having been said, Charlotte only opens her mouth the rest of the evening to embrace Clifford's lips or other parts of his anatomy, giving great pleasure to them both, fleeting as it may be. When Charlotte, in a more sober state, reflects on the evening, she'll be less sure of Clifford's good intentions. Clifford will need no reflection at all; Charlotte is sometimes still a good lay, but not often enough for him to want to remain her emotional pin cushion. He needs to find a way to be rid of her, and soon. In her current volatile state, there's a clear and present danger that at any moment she might reveal their relationship to William. He needs to eliminate this risk, because the risk is too great and the consequences for him are too lethal.

Wednesday begets a vicious confrontation with Melody. William has agreed to make time for he and Charlotte to dine this evening with Willis and Melody, and the four of them have indulged in the lobster creole and candied crawfish specialties of the latest celebrity-frequented, social media-praised restaurant of the moment, Chef Francois Schulson's signature establishment, "Francois du Orleans."

Charlotte has prepared herself for an evening with Melody by downing an extra dose of Xanax, so dinner conversation goes relatively well, despite Melody pushing her agenda of a clinic for Willis and an art gallery for her. Willis continues to say he's not ready to run a clinic, not at his age, and is happy for now just to practice medicine as a primary care physician, although he concedes that in a few years the idea of his own clinic may appeal to him.

Charlotte thinks to herself that Willis' new attitude towards a clinic shows how much Melody has already corrupted him, altered his values to more align with her less desirable, purely pecuniary ones. Charlotte holds her tongue, or at least the medication does, but it's wearing off, so better the evening ends soon so that the taste that lingers is mostly as pleasant as the food deserves.

Before the coffee is served, William excuses himself from the table, saying: "I've got to get back to the office for an overseas conference call. Lovely evening. I've taken care of the check. I'll think more about what you said, Melody, but I don't think the time is right. Certainly not for a medical clinic, which Willis says he's not yet ready for. But since you're so passionate about owning an art gallery, maybe I'll change my mind on that and fund the money for your gallery."

"Thank you," Melody excitedly replies. "Willis and I would really appreciate it if you do. It would make a big difference in both of our lives."

Charlotte visibly cringes, but remains silent, keeping her thoughts to herself. As they sip their coffee, waiting for three plantain chili-Nutella crepe desserts, a Chef Schulson specialty, Willis' cell phone messaging goes off. He texts a response and, as he stands, says: "Sorry, I also have to run. I've a patient having an epileptic seizure and I need to get to the hospital's emergency room; she's in an ambulance headed there right now."

"Why do you have to meet her there?" Charlotte asks, not wanting to be left alone with Melody. "Emergency room doctors can take care of her, can't they?"

"Mom, you know I'm part of a concierge practice. That requires that we provide 24 hour, seven days a week patient coverage. I'm the quarterback for all treatment for my patients. No choice. Got to go. I'm sure you two will be fine without me. You can split my dessert between you if you like," a blind and tone-deaf (not great attributes for a diagnostician) Willis casually responds.

If timing in life is, indeed, everything, the case may be proven here. Willis' departure and the expiration of the moderating effect of Charlotte's pre-dinner Xanax coincide at almost precisely the same moment, leaving Charlotte and Melody in each other's unfiltered company.

As they nibble at their desserts, Melody, having already won the day, plays on nonetheless: "I'm so happy that William is reconsidering funding the art gallery. It'll be so much fun and I promise I'll make it a real business, high-caliber and profitable, something to which you both will be proud to have the 'Wylde' name attached. I'd be happy for any advice you can give as I get the business started."

Charlotte reacts to the carrot Melody has offered by chomping at the bit and taking a bite out of Melody: "I've had to listen all night to you trying to weasel your way into our pockets. I know you, and have always known you, for what you are — a black widow spider. You've ensnared my son in your web and slowly but surely are inching him closer to his destruction. I'm going to do everything in my power to stop you from succeeding. Don't count on any inheritance from us. William has signed the Giving Pledge and I've decided to write Willis out of my will for so long as he's married to you. And if I have anything to say about it, rest assured that William will make you work a few years as he first suggested before he gives you any money for an art gallery. As unpalatable as it may be to a person like you, you'll just have to learn to be content to live off of Willis' trust fund."

"You'd view me very differently if I weren't Jewish," Melody snarls back. "That's what you've always had against me. You can't hide that stink any longer. Not from me. Certainly not when we're alone and can speak our truths."

"Here's my truth, young lady. You'll suck no money ever out of me or, if I can help it, from William, not while I'm alive and, once I change my will, even after I'm dead. We're in a no-holds struggle for Willis' well-being. Your only peace with me will be if you can content yourself to live within the means of Willis' income and raise my grandchildren, if and when you have any, to be like their father. That's what's best for Willis."

"I'm what's best for Willis. You just can't accept that you're no longer the primary person in his life. You've been supplanted by his wife. And yes, one who wants some more of the Wylde money. You can well afford to give it. You're the one who'll have to learn to live with that, if you want there to be any peace between us."

"Peace? I'll never give in to you, never let you into our pockets or trade on our name. You'll see, sooner or later, I'll expose you to Willis for what you are. Then you'll be through and out of our lives. Just watch, wait and see."

"You watch, wait and see. At the end of the day, I'll have the money I need and it will be you who'll be out of our lives, one way or the other. I'll see to that."

"Not so long as I'm alive."

"Then so be it."

"What is that, a threat? Are you threatening me?"

"Take it as you will. Down it with some more pills. Don't think that I don't know, that we don't all know, that you're an emotional wreck, surviving each day on the strength of the medications you're abusing. You do very little to conceal it these days. Do us all a favor, yourself included, take an overdose why don't you? You will eventually, whether you intend to or not."

"You're a conniving bitch," Charlotte screams as she abruptly stands up, turns and leaves Melody to her desserts, just or not. "But your schemes will fail. I'll see to that."

Charlotte's two partially full, soon to be emptied, prescription bottles week is topped off by a Friday late afternoon surprise visit from Wharton. Not completely a surprise for Charlotte, since a day earlier she'd received a call from a rough-voiced, shady-sounding character who reached her by pretending to be a friend of Wharton's. He'd warned her that she needed to speak to Wharton about paying off his gambling debts if she didn't want harm to come to him. Alarmed, she had twice texted and called Wharton, but he'd not yet responded until this unannounced visitation.

Brushing his cheek kisses aside, she escorts Wharton into a sitting room, where she plops him down into a plushly-cushioned, green velvet chair, separated by a small convenience table from the identical chair in which she sits. Then she leans over, touches his arm, looks him in the eyes (neither of their eyes being entirely focused, since both of them have taken pills of one kind or another earlier in the day) and with concern asks: "What's going on, Wharton? I've been trying to reach you since yesterday afternoon. I received a very unsettling call about you having gambling debts that need to be paid and you getting hurt if they're not."

"Guilty as charged, I'm afraid," a slightly stuporous Wharton rather insouciantly admits to his very worried mother. "I've had really bad luck at the casinos ever since Macao, lost far more than I realized over the past few months. I've stopped gambling and offered to pay what I owe in installments from my trust fund, but the casinos are insisting that I pay $1 million by the end of September and have sent some very rough characters to ensure that I do. So I need to get $1 million from you now, which I promise to repay you next year."

Angered by the flippancy of his words and his assumption that she'll once again bail him out of a jam, Charlotte rebukes him: "Drugs, gambling and carousing. That's how you spend your life. You're totally out of control. I didn't see that. Your father did, but I didn't. I've enabled your horrible behavior. But not anymore. I refuse to do it again now."

Her words have a sobering effect on Wharton, who pleads: "You have to help me. This one last time. They'll hurt me if you don't. I don't know how badly, but I don't want to have to find out. Please, Mom."

"I'll speak to your father. He can protect you from getting beat up, I'm sure. But that's all either of us will do for you."

"I don't know if dad will even do that much for me. He probably thinks it would be a good lesson for me to get beat up. I can hear his voice now, saying that 'it's time he's taken to the woodshed.' He's often shown how little he thinks of me, what a disappointment I am to him."

"I'm not going to get into a discussion about what your father thinks of you. It's beside the point. You need to know that you're on your own here and from now on, for the foreseeable future, until you're off drugs, stop gambling, find a job of some sort, and settle down with someone."

"That's a pretty tall order. So you're casting your baby out with the wash water. Is that the gist?" Wharton petulantly snips.

"No. The gist is that I'm showing you 'tough love' to help you get your life in order. I've let you twist me around your finger, take advantage of me because you know how much I love you. I still do. But now it's time for 'tough love.' No more money from me for anything. Not until you change your ways. And, if you don't change course, and quickly, I'm going to write you out of my will until you do. Next time I see you, you best be steady on your feet and clear-eyed or I'll put my lawyer to work."

"Thanks for nothing, Mom. Now, on top of everything else, I have two fathers in my life. Lucky me. And you're a fine one to talk about being steady on your feet and clear-eyed. That's a laugh."

Distraught by the conflagrations she's already had this week, Charlotte visibly recoils from this latest attack, but manages to stand firm: "This is about you, not me. If I don't see any progress from you in the next few weeks, I change my will and show it to you, so you'll realize I mean what I say."

A long-pampered and very spoiled Wharton thinks to himself, better that she were dead, that would solve my problems and hers, as long as it's before she changes her will. He storms out of the room with a "Thanks for nothing. Really appreciate it." As he gets behind the wheel of his car, fearful of the physical harm that might soon befall him, his thought of a swift end to his mother's life drifts to the possibility that one of the casinos' collection agents, the shorter one, might be an appropriate person to hasten his mother's demise, were it to be suggested to him in lieu of administering a beating to Wharton.

Driving home, what was at best a fleeting spark in the cauldron of a drug-infused temper tantrum, morphs into something more tangible, more compelling, something which he feels the need to more seriously consider. If she's no longer going to act towards him as the mother he's known but as another father to detest, maybe her death at his behest could be deemed, in his eyes at least, a justifiable homicide. It would put them both out of their misery, except he'd still be alive. A mercy killing in many respects. Hell, he could even do it himself if need be. It would be so easy and virtually undetectable. Just substitute a much stronger opioid for the one she thinks she's taking. Let her do the rest. A suicide or accidental overdose. No reason anyone should suspect anything else.

Charlotte, too, is having thoughts that, until now, were mostly foreign to her. Maybe she should take heed of what's being said to her. Maybe she's become too pill-addicted and a "vacation" in a private, sequestered rehabilitation facility is an appropriate step to take. Not now, while William's nomination is still pending, but later, once he's confirmed as Secretary of the Treasury and she's less in the public's spotlight. For now, she'll have to continue to muddle through the escalating family tensions as best she can and just be more mindful as to when and why she's medicating herself. She can do that. Yes, she can.

CHAPTER XLVII

Fortunately, thinks Charlotte, so far this Sunday has been a day of much needed rest from the horrible week she's just had. Her spirits sapped by the arguments she's had with her ersatz lover and supposed loved ones, her sole solace not found in the bottom of one of her prescription bottles has been her unrestrained excitement over Kristina's pregnancy. The plans she has in mind for Kristina, Jeff and their baby re-energize her, feeding her some of the strength she needs to tunnel past the continued disappointments in her life towards a new beginning, a first "grandchild" for Charlotte to love and fawn over and get things right.

With each crushing conversation this past week, Charlotte has rushed to Kristina seeking shelter, her port in the storm. An ever dutiful, sympathetic, compassionate and grateful Kristina has listened patiently and attentively and done her best to smooth things over. But her empathy and compassion have taken a heavy toll on Kristina, one that's fast becoming an unhealthy burden for a first trimester, new mother to bear.

The Humpty Dumpty all fall down portion of each of these heart-to-hearts has ended with an uplifted Charlotte in a manic stage, explaining to an emotionally exhausted not so receptive Kristina how wonderful things are going to be for Kristina and her soon-to-be child. "I can't wait until your baby is born," Charlotte enthuses. "I think it'd be great for both of us if you lived nearby. I'll buy a place for your family and you can live there rent free until at some point I gift it to you. We need to go shopping for maternity clothes. You'll be starting to show in another month or two. Not frumpy, off the rack stuff, you want to look pretty. I'll set up an appointment with one of my dress designers to see what she can do. You need to remain attractive for Jeff during your pregnancy and stylish clothes will help. In a few months we'll start to buy baby furniture. And we'll plan your baby shower. You must have one, you know. I'll invite some of my friends who sit on the boards of the better nursery and day schools. It's never too early to let them know about you."

Whenever Kristina has attempted to proffer even a soft word of protest, that the promised $1 million gift at birth is already more than sufficient, Charlotte has waved her off, saying: "You know you've become like a daughter to me. I consider your baby to be my first grandchild. I look forward to sharing your lives and helping your family in any way I can."

At Charlotte's invitation, Barbara and Dan Muss have arrived for a high tea this afternoon to celebrate Kristina's pregnancy. Barbara was initially resistant, seeing no reason for her to celebrate her son and daughter-in-law's happy event with Kristina's employer, but Dan felt otherwise, particularly in light of the elegant wedding and other substantial benefits the Wyldes had bestowed on Kristina and Jeff, not to mention the recent promise of a $1 million baby gift at birth, and convinced a recalcitrant Barbara to accept the invitation.

"Great to see you both again. And to celebrate another happy occasion for Jeff and Kristina," Charlotte says, as they all settle in at the dining room table for a London-quality high tea that would make even the Connaught hotel proud. Sterling silver, triple-tiered hand-embellished servers are stacked high with colorful, flavorable, artfully shaped finger sandwiches in classic British combinations. On separate stacked trays lie the desserts: English scones with clotted cream and strawberry preserves, green apple and chocolate mousse tart, carrot cake spiced with cinnamon and tablespoon-sized cups of English trifle.

After the obligatory exchange of questions about everyone's health and how everyone's been doing, and complimentary exclamations about the elegant repast that's spread before them, Dan, during one of the occasional digestive pauses in his gobbling down of more than his fair share of the copious sandwiches, ventures into the territory of meaningful conversation: "From what I read, William, your appointment as Treasury Secretary should be confirmed by early October. Congratulations. What an achievement. Your family must be very proud."

"We are," chimes in Charlotte. "But let's not jinx anything. The Senate still has not voted on it and, in politics, anything can happen. One bad word about William in the media could harpoon his appointment. Look what almost happened when those awful Auto Eats lawsuits got filed recently, and all William did was invest in the business."

Not knowing, and not wanting to know, whether Charlotte, for some reason, has just given William some type of veiled reminder of his vulnerability to her, William changes topic, responding: "Thanks, Dan. But today's occasion isn't to celebrate me. Charlotte has asked us together today to celebrate Jeff and Kristina's great news. So, let's raise our glasses and salute them with a toast: 'Congratulations. Good health. Best of everything.'"

"Thank you," Kristina quietly says. "Me too," adds Jeff.

Dan and Barbara join in the toast by raising their glasses, but, for different reasons, each of them remain distractedly silent. Dan is trying to figure out if and how he might approach William, or at least plant a seed, about a possible $100,000 loan (without, of course, disclosing the true reason why he needs the money). He's also engrossed in contemplative thought as to which of the array of desserts that sits a half-arm's length away he should eat first. Barbara is silent because she views herself and her family as prisoners of the Wylde's wealth and this sumptuous, opulent high-tea just another offering to stave off rebellion and escape. She's seen how Charlotte took over her son's wedding. She can only imagine what comes next, now that Kristina is pregnant. This high tea is no doubt just the first of many occasions that should belong to Barbara but which Charlotte will coopt.

Charlotte doesn't disappoint, filling the brief silence after Jeff and Kristina's "thank you" with an enthusiastic outline of the ambitious plans she has for Jeff and Kristina's future: "I don't mean this to be over-bearing in any way, and Barbara you're certainly invited to join me in any and all of this, but we need to help Kristina select appropriate maternity clothes, pick out baby-proof, high-quality furniture, plan a baby shower, and see the appropriate professionals, not just an obstetrician, but a nutritionist and a personal trainer as well. There's so much to do and much less time to do it than Kristina might think. I don't know how it was for you when you were pregnant with Jeff, but as a mother of three children, I very well know how too much time slips by when you're pregnant if you allow it to."

Kristina already has heard this from Charlotte several times, including the promise of buying them a house to live in which Charlotte has thankfully omitted from her list of things that need to be done, but this is the first that Barbara has heard any of this and it meets the worst of her expectations.

Losing what little appetite she had to begin with, Barbara battles herself to be tactful and controlled and addresses Charlotte in what she hopes is a non-confrontational tone: "You and William continue to be most kind and generous to my children. I know that they appreciate all that you've done for them and so do Dan and I. But many of the things you're planning on doing for Kristina during her pregnancy, I'd rather do for her, as Jeff's mother and her mother-in-law. As a parent of three children of your own, I'm sure you can understand my desire to embrace these precious moments for myself."

Having not thought even once about the possibility that Barbara wouldn't be delighted by Charlotte's offer that Barbara should feel free to participate with her in all the things that Charlotte was planning to do for and in anticipation of the baby, a very surprised Charlotte replies: "I'm not trying to take anything away from you, Barbara. But you can't afford to give them what they deserve and what I can provide. It's no knock on you and Dan, no badge of shame, that you're not wealthy. It's just a fact. Why deprive Jeff and his family of things they otherwise won't have? You can work side-by-side with me in planning everything. There's room enough for both of us in their lives. Just consider me an over-indulgent aunt, at worst."

"You're not a family member, not an aunt. That's the disconnect. You're Kristina's employer. A very generous one. But I need to be selfish here. I wasn't with the wedding. The birth of this child, my first grandchild, and the months that lead up to it are experiences I want only to share with Jeff and Kristina. If you're involved, I'll be shunted to the side with you leading the charge. All the things that you've just said leave no doubt about it. You offered for me to participate if I want, instead of asking me what I planned and whether you could play a role in any of it."

A flustered Charlotte is about to respond, when Jeff leaps in with an attempt to cut short any further escalation of hostilities: "Mom. Charlotte. There's room for both of you, roles each of you can play in the ensuing months. No need for a tug of war with Kristina and me in the middle. We're the ones that will be hurt, and our baby. This will all work itself out. Kristina and I will make sure of it. We have deep affection for Charlotte and William and, of course, Mom, we very much love and appreciate you and Dad. There's room at the table for everyone, just as there is now, seated here together."

William and Dan utter platitudes of assent and Charlotte and Barbara stand down, ostensibly apologizing to each other, but thinking otherwise. Charlotte thinking: Barbara is a jealous ingrate who should be delighted with what I plan to do for her son and family. Barbara thinking: there may be room for everyone at Charlotte's table, but not at mine. I'm his mother and I won't let her steal my joy again.

In the early evening, William and Charlotte are sitting together on the veranda overlooking the water, sipping vodka lime martinis, Barbara and Dan having left to spend some time alone with Jeff and Kristina. "Do you believe how Barbara spoke to me? The nerve of her. She's a jealous, petty bitch."

After a thoughtful pause which engenders a withering stare from his wife, William challenges Charlotte: "If you're asking me, I think Barbara's right to be pissed off. You're substituting yourself for her as Jeff and Kristina's parent. It's wrong-minded."

"Just like you. Never on my side. Not in more years than I can count. It seems that any time I say or do something that gives me pleasure, you shoot me down, rather than encourage me. I can provide Kristina with things that Barbara can't afford. That's all I'm trying to do."

Under pressure from a now pregnant Vanessa to make her a firm commitment about a future together as a family, William makes a snap decision that no time is a good time for what he's about to say, so propitious moment or not, he'll cross the Rubicon and take another shot at getting what he wants: "You're very unhappy Charlotte. So am I. What you just said, you're right, we're not in sync anymore, not for way too long a time. And clandestine liaisons can only salve so much. One way or another, in another month or so, I'll either be Treasury Secretary or I won't. The time has come for us to exit each other's lives. Let's do it amicably; let's divorce and permit each other to better enjoy the time we each have left."

Taken aback by what William just said, Charlotte perceives his words as a gauntlet thrown rather than a peace offering and, although knocked off kilter, musters her anger and spews forth a vitriolic response: "Over my dead body. That'll be when you 'exit my life,' as you so nicely put it. I haven't put up with your holier-than-thou, judgmental persona and, yes, your blatant philandering, to relinquish my reward. I've earned the social prominence I enjoy, soon to be the wife of the Secretary of the Treasury and who knows, you've always been an ambitious, driven man, maybe even First Lady someday if you play the cards right that you keep so close to your vest. Do you really think I'd permit a divorce? The finger of blame would always be pointed directly at me, marking me a failure, a dilettante, an object of pity, just another wife outpaced and outgrown by her spouse. It's 'till death do us part' for us, that's the vow we took and a vow you'll have to keep. If not, parting from me won't be such sweet sorrow. It'll be your reputation not mine that gets shattered. I'll see to that. Count on it."

Having opened a Pandora's box of threats and emotions, William quickly decides that he needs to shut the lid back down before much more can escape. Who knows what a volatile Charlotte might unthinkingly do if he doesn't. He can't afford even a hint of scandal these next several weeks.

William is between a rock and a hard place. Charlotte guessed correctly. He has political ambitions beyond Treasury Secretary and the money with which to accomplish them. But Charlotte is not the only one that might thrash his plans. Vanessa has warned him that once the Senate confirmation vote is over, she's not prepared to be a baby mama with a bastard child. She wasn't raised that way. She needs the sanctity of marriage for her and their child. If William is not prepared to fight Charlotte for a divorce, then Vanessa is prepared to do it for him.

William has not painted a pretty picture for himself, more painted himself into a corner. He's on the cusp of accomplishing things he never even imagined. He wants it all. Push come to shove, face to the mirror and truth be told, he wants both public office and a life with Vanessa. She stirs him the way no one ever has, except for Charlotte in their first few years together. But escape from Charlotte is nigh impossible, save for her death.

Having processed all these thoughts with computer-like efficiency, there's no pregnant pause before William feigns sincerity in his response to Charlotte's diatribe: "I see how unhappy you are. We are. I've been groping to make things better for each of us. In suggesting we divorce, I never considered that in this day and age you would think that an amicable divorce, one that I let you file for, would tar you with some type of scarlet-letter. I've no desire to do that to you. So let's both think about how we can improve the situation between us in a way that we both benefit."

Not at all placated by William's effort to avoid the crater edge he had pushed them to, Charlotte, shaking her head side to side in disgust, bangs her glass on the table, pushes her chair away and, as she hurls herself up, looks at him and snarls: "Whatever you say, William. Always the logical one, never emotional. But we're not yin and yang. We're superior to inferior, and it's what's made me sick all these years, I'm only starting to realize now. All the little and not so little ways you put me down, belittle me, treat me as inferior to the great Wild Bill. I'll leave the great man to his thoughts. But you can put a divorce out of them, once and for all. It isn't going to happen."

As Charlotte leaves, the only thought William has, as he watches her still shapely ass wiggle away, is that her physical beauty is no longer of any moment to him, overshadowed by the shallowness and ugliness that now define her in his eyes. While he won't admit, even to himself, that he considers himself a 'master of the universe,' he, in fact, does and, as such, believes that he's earned more at this supposed to be celebratory stage of his life than having to cohabitate with Charlotte and accommodate her never-ending complaints, demands and discordant remarks concerning everything and everyone in her life. He wants Vanessa full time, and Charlotte not at all. He wants Vanessa and his child, a second family, a chance to start his personal life anew. He has to make that happen, and soon, because if he doesn't, Vanessa may make good her threat to confront Charlotte herself, an action that will wreak havoc on everything he hopes to accomplish.

Charlotte hit the nail on the head when she said 'till death them do part.' Can he seriously contemplate making this happen? He's always carefully thought things through and then, once risk-reward has been properly analyzed, never been afraid to take bold steps if the reward justifies the risk. Is Charlotte's demise, the murder of a human being, his wife, the mother of their children, really something he's capable of making happen? It might be as easy as asking the question of the right person, 'Will no one rid me of this troublesome Charlotte?' Even easier, just himself change out some of her pills for a much stronger opioid, then she'd be doing it to herself and who would be any the wiser? These are not thoughts he wants to have, nothing the William he believes himself to be would ever remotely consider. He's not some brutal savage, is he? But he's considering this, he can't push these thoughts away, and this is the William he's become, whether or not he realizes it.

As William is processing the previously unimaginable, Charlotte has reached out to Donna, the only person she can think of to talk to about the bombshell William has just tossed her way. (What William said is not for Kristina's ears.) Donna and she might not be close any more (they never were, but that's a reality not permitted in Charlotte's world), but they're still sisters, bound by blood, genetics and a history together as children. Hers is not a topic for the telephone, so Charlotte has arranged to meet Donna at Donna's apartment the next afternoon, after Donna's classes are finished.

As they sit awkwardly together, Charlotte explains why she asked to see Donna and seeks her advice as to how best to deal with William. For good measure, since she's come here anyway, she throws in her spat with Barbara as a topic for discussion.

Having listened at length to Charlotte's recapitulation of these conversations, a perplexed Donna inquiries: "Why have you come to me? For William, you need to consult a lawyer, I would think. Or, screw his brains out if you can, you used to be good at that. And Barbara is absolutely right in the way that she feels. You're usurping her role, invading her space, and you need to cede back her territory."

"I came to you seeking a loving sister who'd give me some moral support, not one who'd be so dismissive of me."

"A loving sister? Moral support? You live your life in a fog of self-delusion, oblivious to anything you don't have the courage to face, which is pretty much everything. You and William haven't had a real marriage in years, you're trying to use money to seduce Barbara's children away from her, and we've never been 'loving sisters' because you've never been that to me. All you've ever done is make me feel small, not even a shadow in your light."

Shocked, Charlotte replies: "I can't believe you're attacking me this way, when I've just opened up to you, exposed how vulnerable I am, besieged by William, harassed by Barbara. And I've not told you even half of what else has been happening to me these past several weeks." Lathering herself up, she continues: "And what do you know about a 'real marriage' anyway? You haven't had a relationship of more than a few months, except with an abusive alcoholic who was your most recent beau."

Donna cringes at this last remark, visibly shrinking into herself, shoulders sloping downwards, head bowing, legs twitching, eyes losing focus until, without warning, she bolts upright, stands over a still seated Charlotte, wags her finger at her and then puts her face a hair's breadth from Charlotte's, and growls in a deep, ominous voice: "You're done abusing Donna. I'm going to make certain of that. You're soon going to have one pill too many rammed down your throat, if I don't strangle you to death before that."

Charlotte is beyond frightened, if there can be such a state, maybe almost scared to death a more approximate description of the terror she's experiencing. Now she's the one shrinking and shaking, which continues as she slides out of her chair and then dashes for the door, leaving in her wake a mumbling, muttering Donna talking to herself. Clearly, something is desperately wrong with Donna, but Charlotte has too many other, more immediate problems to worry about. She'll leave it to Donna's therapist to sort Donna out.

CHAPTER XLVIII

This mid-September day, temperature in the mid-70s, picture-perfect cerulean sky with few clouds and bright sun, is a day conducive to people basking outside, worry free or at least imagining that they are, enjoying the calm, lazy pace of a summer-like day so close to the stormy, frenetic tempo of the chilly days soon to arrive.

For Charlotte, however, this is just another dark, somber, spirit-depressing day, replete with unrelenting inner angst ameliorated only by her frequent ingestion of Percocet, Oxycontin, Xanax, you name it, whatever prescription she can wrangle from one of her many enabling physicians, each of whom has had a favorite charity or foundation handsomely enhanced by a monetary contribution from the Wyldes.

As Charlotte lies outside on one of her patios, partially spread-eagled atop an Eames fabric, patterned vintage rattan sofa, a cold ice pack that Kristina has brought her across her brow, she can find little respite from the hammering concerns that plague her. Her life has become an unhappy bollix through no fault of her own (of course). Her husband, her children, her lover, her sister and now even Kristina, have all let her down, rejected her or cast her aside in one way or another, and there seems to be no cavalry riding to her rescue.

As the cold compress and pills take effect, Charlotte attempts to assess the current state of things, imagining her life to be fodder for one of those TV programs that review the news of the week, "Last Week Tonight with John Oliver" perhaps.

In the tumble-dry of Charlotte's still-throbbing head, Bess is the first to spin out. Charlotte did what she had secretly determined to do a few weeks ago, after Wilma had made it clear that if it came to a choice between Charlotte and Bess, Wilma would choose Bess. Charlotte met with Bess and offered her $5 million to surrender her hold on Wilma and simply vanish from Wilma's life as quickly as she'd entered it. That didn't go well.

"Wilma and I are a couple, like it or not, and we're going to stay a couple," a fuming Bess exclaimed, rejecting Charlotte's bribe almost before Charlotte had finished offering it. "You're really evil, aren't you? You dominated and controlled Wilma all her life, filled her with your nonsense and insecurities to the point where her job was her only pleasure in life. I've helped her escape your prison and now you want to recapture her. Well you can't have her, she's mine by her choice. And by mine"

"We'll see for how long. I'm sure Wilma has told you that I'm going to disinherit her, so her trust fund is the only Wylde money that will ever be available to you. Sooner or later, you'll be back selling drugs, it's your nature, who you are, lower class, and I'll be right behind you, waiting for the chance to tip the authorities or, better still, have William remove his protection and let the cartel kill you. Or maybe I'll do that now, so it will be bye-bye Bess. Don't think I won't. I know what's best for my daughter and it's not you. I think you know by now that there's nothing I won't do to protect my daughter. So one way or the other, I'll see to it that you're gone."

"Not if you're gone first, you sanctimonious bitch. You've the nerve to threaten me? You've poked the sleeping bear. From now on, I wouldn't rest easy if I were you. Remember, I'm lower class, not high and mighty like you, so I've no moral ambivalence, no hesitancy, in ridding myself of an enemy, in this case you."

Nor have Charlotte's recent conversations with Wharton taken any turn for the better. Wharton seems to be headed completely off the rails, at best teetering precariously over the edge. Repeatedly in the past two weeks, he's asked, begged, implored, cajoled Charlotte to pay the $1 million installment of his gambling debt, threatening he'd be killed or take his own life if she doesn't pay it before the end of this month. Charlotte has continually refused, insisting that before she'll ever again give him any money, she needs to see him in better control of himself, off of drugs and gainfully engaged with something.

Her latest conversation with Wharton was by far the worst, ending with a hysterical threat from her ranting, once loving, son, something she'd have never believed possible: "You haven't disinherited me yet, mother, so wouldn't it be wonderful, a miracle of sorts, if you were to die before you did? That would certainly stay my execution, if not yours. I believe in miracles, do you? You know, sometimes a person can help make a miracle happen. Maybe this will be one of those times."

The Wheel of Misfortune playing in Charlotte's head spins round and round until it halts at the space marked "William." A few Sundays ago, William had had the audacity to suggest that they divorce. She hoped she'd squashed that idea once and for all. But although he hasn't mentioned it again, William, on those rare occasions when he's home, has barely talked to her at all, instead he just sits around or wanders from room to room, as if in a trance, like Hamlet, but obsessed with something other than his father's death.

She now suspects that his Sunday suggestion was just an exploratory foray, with William's full forces amassed and waiting to be launched on a "D-Day" that will occur shortly after his taking the oath of office. She must assemble her own troops and marshal her allies lest she be caught unprepared. She intends to force a retreat. There'll be no divorce — she has the armament and strength to prevent it.

Her thoughts of William slide over to Clifford, where trouble in what started out as paradise continues to fester. Clifford, the other man in her life, also wants out of their relationship. She's looked in the mirror and, as objectively as she can, has judged herself a still compelling beauty, so she's at a loss to understand why Clifford no longer sees the luster in her. Maybe, as he says, she takes too many pills and complains about things too much, but don't all women of any substance or position do that? She's still a keeper, all things considered.

In any event, she intends to have her cake and eat it too — she's not prepared to let either William or Clifford go and will fight hard to keep them both. She's communicated this to each of them as forcibly as she knows how, making it clear that an unexcused absence from her life will have grave consequences for all they hold dear: their reputations, careers, ambitions and finances.

A person Charlotte is more than willing to see exit her life is Melody. She'd shed no painful tears over Melody's disappearance, only tears of joy. What's wrong with her children?, she wonders. Wharton has no significant other and Wilma and Willis have both picked such losers. Willis is so good-natured, kind and innocent (Charlotte mistakenly thinks) that it was easy for such a quite outwardly-attractive young woman as Melody to bait, hook and catch him. Now that she has Willis firmly in her net, she wants to reel in the rest of his family so she can access the real catch she seeks, the Wylde family treasure chest.

Charlotte suspected this the first time they met. Her suspicion has long since turned to certainty, Melody having virtually admitted to Charlotte that she's after the Wylde family money. ("You have enough of it," she so brazenly declared.) Melody tries to cloak her naked greed in the guise that an art gallery and a medical clinic not only would benefit both Melody and Willis, but bring great credit to the Wylde family name. But Charlotte knows that these are but stepping stones for Melody, first steps in her path towards more money for other self-serving grandiose plans this fortune hunter will concoct. Charlotte has drummed into Melody that she intends to plug her road to riches, dead or alive, with changing Charlotte's will being just one piece of the blockade Charlotte intends to erect.

Usually last in her thoughts and definitely least, is her sister, Donna, who's been acting weirder and weirder over the past few months.

Where she used to be mostly docile in Charlotte's presence, she's now mostly hostile, even going so far as to have threatened Charlotte when she turned to Donna for some comfort and compassion after her distressing confrontations with William and Barbara. Charlotte decides to spend no time puzzling over Donna, that time is better spent thinking what to do with regard to Kristina.

Apparently swayed by what Barbara said at high tea that fateful Sunday, Kristina has started to object to some of what Charlotte wants to do for her and her family, telling Charlotte: "Jeff and I very much appreciate all that you want to do for us. The gift you've promised when our baby is born, there are no words with which I can adequately express how thankful we are for such generosity. But I think we need to let Barbara do the maternity shopping with me. And let's leave the baby shower exclusively to her, that's not very important to me; the wedding was, but not this baby shower."

As she mulls things over, Charlotte decides that it's best to let Barbara have these small victories, she is Jeff's mother after all. Anyway, Charlotte can buy Kristina other maternity clothes to wear in addition to whatever Barbara selects, and throw her own baby shower for Kristina with the "right people" for Kristina to meet and without inviting the Musses.

Kristina's baby may be Barbara's grandchild by blood, but it's one she'll have to share with Charlotte, who intends to be the baby's godmother. As godmother, Charlotte will make sure that this child is afforded all the advantages of Wylde family privilege, and, if Barbara wants what's best for the child, she'll have no choice but to step back and let Charlotte do what's necessary. It'll just take a little time for Barbara to adjust to this new reality, but adjust she will, of that Charlotte is positive. Charlotte will make that happen.

As Charlotte drifts off into the euphoric haven that her Oxycontin provides, she does so with the one happy thought she has just mustered, that she will be a godmother, a fairy godmother at that, and will reap the rewards that come with having a young family in your life.

CHAPTER XLIX

"It's quite a quandary," I say, listening to Jeff and Kristina weigh the pros and cons, vacillating about what's the best thing for them to do, the best course of action to take.

Kristina says: "Yesterday, Barbara and Charlotte almost came to blows arguing in Charlotte's sitting room over who was going where and when to baby shop with me. The opposing camps eventually made nice, after Charlotte was floored not, as I feared, by Barbara, but by one of Charlotte's now almost daily onsets of a migraine. Barbara felt bad and was conciliatory, even helping Charlotte up the stairs into her bedroom to lie down."

Even without the tensions over Kristina's pregnancy, Kristina has told me that she's finding the job less rewarding and increasingly difficult. She's still busy maintaining Charlotte's jam-packed social calendar and accompanying Charlotte to a bevy of appointments, even sometimes to Charlotte's visits with her children. But the book and oil painting and other special projects Kristina had been assisting on have all been abandoned or completed. Worse, a substantial amount of Kristina's time is spent listening to Charlotte confide intimate secrets about her children, her sister and now even William and Charlotte's lover, looking to an untrained, inexperienced Kristina for guidance and advice navigating Charlotte's very choppy waters.

Kristina continues: "If we can get Barbara comfortable with it, I don't mind at all the plans Charlotte is making for us and our baby.

Maybe Jeff and I have become greedy and are taking advantage of her, but we very much want the $1 million baby gift she's promised us."

"Who wouldn't?" I interject.

Ignoring my interruption, Kristina proceeds: "If getting that gift requires that we permit Charlotte to select and buy me maternity clothes and baby furniture and plan a shower, that's the cherry on top of the sundae. We've no intention of living in Sands Point after the baby is born, no less allow Charlotte to buy us a house, but we can kick that can down the road and deal with it later. Ordinarily, I would be able to continue working for Charlotte for another six months no matter how stressful the job has become. I still care for her very much and want to help her. What's making me want to quit, actually making me afraid to continue, is my pregnancy; it isn't good for the baby to sense that its mother has knots in her stomach all the time. I need our baby to feel it's in a safe and happy place."

"I don't think the baby's development in your womb is affected one way or another by how you feel emotionally," I offer my two cents, without any science to substantiate my opinion.

Jeff quickly shoots me down: "You're wrong. We've researched this on the internet. Strong emotions like those Kristina's experiencing can increase certain hormones in a woman's body, which can harm the baby's development."

"Then I don't see much of a decision to make, if that's really the case, if your baby's at risk."

"It's not that cut and dried," Kristina says. "I think Jeff and I could be letting our emotions color our thinking on how much we may be putting our baby at risk, that we may be overreacting to the science. Also, I can try to better maintain my equilibrium when I comfort Charlotte. I don't have to internalize her problems, make them mine. Listen with half an ear, as they say. It's not in my nature, but the reward is so great that I probably should make a better effort."

"And I'm unemployed at the moment, let's remember," Jeff adds. "In order to end the customer tainted food lawsuits, at the instruction of our insurance carrier, Auto Eats filed in bankruptcy last week and I need some time to figure out what I want to do. After my experience there, even with its having failed, I'm not eager to just go back to selling cars. If Kristina quits, it means we're both unemployed with a baby on the way, and the need to find a new place to live. We've saved some money, so we'd be okay for a while, but not for too long, maybe not long enough."

"And no $1 million baby gift or $100,000 bonus," I unnecessarily contribute.

"Yes, there's certainly that," Jeff responds. "And my parents are in no position to help. My father could soon find himself out of a job, if not behind bars, once the audit of his company's books is completed. We still haven't ruled out the possibility of Kristina asking Charlotte for the $100,000 he needs, but certainly can't do it, take the money and then have Kristina quit. We're not those kind of people. If we ask and get it, Kristina has to stay at least until the baby is born."

"And, of course, my aunt and uncle have no money, so they can't help us out," Kristina throws in.

"As I said before, quite a quandary."

"So, you've listened and we've put everything I can think of on the table. Any ideas?" Jeff asks.

Once again the jester, always the comedian, trying to lighten the mood, I reply: "You could have Kristina slip Charlotte a fentanyl pill or two. You'd get the $1 million and the $100,000 bonus and Kristina wouldn't have to put your baby at risk anymore."

"Not to mention the $10 million bequest for our baby that Charlotte promised to provide in her will," Jeff laughs, playing along with my gag. "If Kristina doesn't want to do it, I easily could — just slip a few fentanyl pills into her Percocet or Oxycontin bottles. I'm sure, from what Kristina's told me, that Bess would be ready, eager and willing to supply them to me. Or maybe even Wharton."

I play out the joke: "You know that I'd do anything for you guys. You might come under suspicion if you do it and then probably crack under pressure. But just ask, and I'll do the dirty work for you. The police will never get a confession from me." I'm joking, aren't I? Or am I? There's truth beneath every "joke." I wonder how much truth lies beneath this one.

"All this has been fun — Not," Jeff says. "Back to reality. Any suggestions, Simon? What do you think?"

"I think Kristina has to play this out longer. Try to disconnect herself emotionally from Charlotte, if she can."

"I intend to," Kristina replies. "But if I can't, then what? I can only give this a few more weeks, I think. Then, if I'm not doing any better with the stress, we're back to square one. What do I do?"

"I'd say 'suck it up.' Go for the money no matter what."

"Even if that means we might be damaging our baby? Never," Kristina bursts out, crying. "Not ever. Not for all the money in the world."

"So that's the answer, I guess," Jeff shrugs as he wraps a reassuring arm around Kristina's shoulders and draws her close. "We weren't completely certain how we felt, but in talking it out with you, Kristina's reaction just now leaves no further room for doubt. We give it a few weeks, Kristina makes her best effort, and then we have no choice except for Kristina to leave the job if things haven't gotten any better."

"Don't take slipping Charlotte some fentanyl off the table as an alternative, it's a better solution," is my parting shot at levity.

"Dude, I'm not sure how much you're really joking," Jeff responds, with only a half chuckle. "Truth be told, if we were different types of people, that might be the best solution."

"It certainly would be a final solution," I say. And with that offensive remark, I rush off, late to meeting my date for the evening, a model

I met at a recent book signing of mine. She likes mysteries and likes my latest book (which, like the prior one, has garnished some decent attention, good reviews and solid sales). Since turnabout is fair play, I should mention that I like models and I like this model, so I'm very much looking forward to our evening together. I'm still searching for a Kristina to call my own, my holy grail, and this evening's dish may be very much to my taste. We start off with a love of mysteries in common, so who knows, maybe that's solid earth from which to grow a relationship. It would help if I learned to take things more seriously, in other words, if I matured. I've passed the dividing line of youth and will be stuck in a danger zone if I don't soon enter the territory of adult.

CHAPTER L

"You need to let him go. Please. Not just for our sakes, for yours, too. Your marriage has been dead for a very long time; why hang on to it? On to him? You know he's only disdain and pity left for you. Why live every day with that?" an overwrought Vanessa pleads to Charlotte.

Vanessa is almost three months pregnant and William has made no discernable progress in getting Charlotte to agree to a divorce. Vanessa is not certain as to how hard William has even tried, given his intention not to take any action that might jeopardize confirmation of his nomination. Vanessa is certain about one thing, and that's that she means to have their baby and it will be born of married, or at least soon to be married, parents. That's how she was raised and what her mother, father and pastor expect of her. She's not let them down in the past (does sleeping with a married man count?) and doesn't intend to do so now.

Vanessa loves William and knows that he loves her. She's decided not to continue to be patient, as William has repeatedly urged, not to continue to be a spectator in her own life, a bystander to her future; the time has come for her to be a participant and to take action, regardless of what William thinks or wants. It's the combination of these thoughts, the heightened emotions of pregnancy and a false sense of optimism that's propelled Vanessa to confront Charlotte.

For her part, Charlotte was shocked when Vanessa called yesterday and explained who she was and said she wanted to meet. Charlotte knew William had a mistress, but this was the first time their unspoken compact, not to embarrass each other and that never the twain shall meet, had been broken. Charlotte was enraged by this breach in the etiquette of their marriage. That William had recently asked for a divorce was distressing enough, but that his arm candy would have the nerve to contact Charlotte directly was so offensive, so disrespectful, that Charlotte couldn't wait to meet her so that she could crush her hopes and dreams the way that William had long since crushed Charlotte's.

"You've some nerve," Charlotte declares. "Do you think the fact that you spread your legs for my husband gives you some sort of standing to come here and talk to me that way? That you can even guess at the bonds that bind William and me together? Your only bond with him, I can assure you, is your welcoming vagina. Soon he'll tire of it and discard you like he has all the rest of his frivolous dalliances."

"William and I have been together for a year and a half now. We're in love and I'm having his baby. You need to accept the facts and let us all get on with the rest of our lives."

"William is part of the rest of my life, whether he or you like it or not. 'Till death do us part,' that's the vow we made to each other and one I intend to make him keep."

A flustered Vanessa responds: "But why? What's left for you at this point in your marriage? Certainly nothing physical between the two of you."

"Everything is not about sex. Not any longer. I wish we still made love as we did when we were first married. But surprise. On occasion, William still reaches out to me for a taste of the past. I'll bet he didn't mention that to you," Charlotte replies, with some misplaced pride, then continues, "We've a history together, three children and, at least until recently, a cordial enough relationship, that's what left for me, that and the social prominence which I've attained and will not permit to be tarnished by a proclamation of an unhappy marriage. I deserve better than that. If William pursues a divorce, it'll be William's reputation that's blackened and his finances and ambitions destroyed, and, as his baby mama, you won't just be collateral damage. Get rid of your bastard child if you want, because I won't be rid of William."

Satisfied that she's accomplished her purpose in agreeing to this meeting, Charlotte cruelly dismisses Vanessa: "There's nothing more to say. You can leave my house now. At best, you're a foolish girl who got herself pregnant while consorting with a married man. Next time, use birth control and don't try to latch on to another woman's wealthy husband."

As a sobbing, near hysterical Vanessa rushes from the house, she shouts: "You're a vile, fucking bitch who should be put down. I can arrange that, just you wait and see."

Unbeknownst to either Charlotte or Vanessa, Kristina has been working in the next room and has overheard this entire relatively short, but certainly not sweet, conversation. Kristina thinks to herself, as much as she wishes that she didn't, that it would benefit everyone, including Kristina, if Charlotte were to die, sooner rather than later. Kristina has pretty much decided she must give up her job, even if it means foregoing her bonus and the $1 million baby gift. The stress in continuing to work for Charlotte has become too much. Charlotte's death would be providential for Kristina, to say the least. Then another unwelcome thought surfaces — how easy it would be for Kristina, who's become Charlotte's primary caregiver, to make it happen the next time Charlotte asks Kristina to bring her some pills. Just a slip on Charlotte's tongue is all that would be needed.

As much as she tries, and as fundamentally good a person as she is, Kristina finds it difficult to push this disturbing thought away. When she's needed to, she's done other bad things in her life: shoplifted, even traded her body. But, of course, nothing as terrible as killing Charlotte would be. Maybe it's Kristina's sympathy for Vanessa, after seeing how atrociously Charlotte has treated her, another new mother-to-be, that has triggered this thought but, whatever the reason, it's lodged in her mind, where it remains trapped for the rest of the day. Kristina is too ashamed of herself to tell Jeff what she's been thinking and how much it's troubling her that she's been thinking this way. She must keep this noxious thought to herself no matter how long it lingers, for fear that in revealing it to Jeff, she might initiate something that could destroy both of them. Unfortunately for Kristina, she recalls all too well the conversation she and Jeff had with Simon just a few weeks ago where Simon and Jeff joked about slipping Charlotte a fentanyl pill — a jest that seems far too real and disturbing in Kristina's present state of mind.

CHAPTER LI

Several days after Vanessa's encounter with Charlotte, Charlotte's body was discovered by her maid who, after receiving no response when she knocked on Charlotte's bedroom door late in the morning, entered the room to the discomforting sight of the sprawled, fully dressed, inert body of her obviously deceased employer. She fled the room, called 911, alerted the rest of the household staff and Mr. Wylde and then repaired to her living quarters to await the arrival of the police, disturbed more by the thought that she soon might need to seek new employment than by the death of the mistress of the house.

Were Charlotte the Ghost of Christmas Past, and not merely dead, what she would reveal to herself is that by her actions, she's left no one behind who'll truly miss her or whose life will not be made appreciably better by her absence in it. Many had the motive to want her dead, but neither the nerve nor moral bankruptcy to hasten what surely would sooner rather than later have been her death from natural causes, if "natural causes" were broadly enough defined to include a self-administered, unintended overdose or a fatal accident incurred while under too much of the influence of a drug of choice.

In the days immediately following her death, Charlotte's loved ones react as all but Charlotte might expect.

A skilled practitioner in the arts of pretense and obfuscation (he's become a politician, hasn't he?), William does his best to deport himself as a widower in mourning, while in private, with Vanessa, they happily celebrate the freedom they've achieved (although William worries whether the notoriety surrounding Charlotte's death might work to deny him Senate confirmation). Wharton does little to disguise his feelings, eagerly inquiring as to how soon his mother's will is going to be read. Melody and Bess can't stop smiling (although not while being questioned by the police), each for different, but compelling, reasons. Willis and Wilma are guilt-ridden but, they too, for very different reasons. As to Donna, all that need be said about how she reacts is that on the night of her sister's death, Donna had another one of her dreams, but this one stands out from the rest. In this one, it was Donna in the dream, not some unidentified man, and a person was murdered, most definitely Charlotte.

Among her litany of lovers, Charlotte's death has pleasured two of them and had no effect on the rest. Clifford revels in his newly-obtained freedom, one jail escaped from and another one apparently avoided, although none of his friends or business associates know exactly what he's celebrating. Franklin proceeds to put in play the plan he had formulated with Daniela Sorrano, immediately trumpeting — in tweets and posts, on podcasts and in news media interviews — that he doesn't see how someone who couldn't keep his own house in order is suited to oversee the economy of the United States. And no, he has no hard feelings or resentment towards William Wylde, the "At Home in Your Home" corporate contest notwithstanding; he knew Charlotte and shares in William's grief at the loss of such a fine lady. But it's a loss that could and should have been avoided had William paid even a modicum of attention. Having failed at that simple task, how can William be expected to succeed at the far more difficult job of juggling all the balls in the air that being Secretary of the Treasury requires? In casting his net, Franklin has also managed to ensnare the Wylde children and their partners in the bright spotlight of a media always looking for salacious gossip.

As is the case with all suspicious deaths, the police have examined the body, taken photographs of the scene, lifted fingerprints and otherwise forensically examined the room, the surrounding areas and Charlotte. Her body is being autopsied and a toxicology report is expected in four to eight weeks. The police are interviewing the immediate family and several other persons connected to Charlotte or who were in her presence or at the house the week before her death. The initial opinion, given that there were no signs of struggle, is that it was death by accidental overdose or possibly suicide, but no preliminary determination will be made until the interrogations and autopsy are concluded. In all events, the investigation will remain open until the toxicology report is received, and maybe even after that, depending on what the toxicology report may reveal.

What of Jeff and Kristina in all of this? They, too, are going to gain by Charlotte's end, financially as well as emotionally, they too are being questioned by the police, and, if Charlotte's death is determined to be a homicide, they'll be two of the prime suspects. They are guilt-ridden for good reason. Barbara and Daniel are not.

CHAPTER LII

"That she died from a drug overdose is no surprise. But since when did she start taking fentanyl?" I ask Kristina.

"I've no idea. Not a clue. I thought it was only Percocet, Xanax and Oxycontin, which is bad enough," Kristina replies.

The toxicology report is back, some six weeks after Charlotte's autopsy, and confirms the initial diagnosis: death due to a drug overdose, suspected (and now confirmed) to be fentanyl. With the tox report back, the police investigation has been completed. Death by accidental overdose is the official conclusion, case closed. Jeff, Kristina and I are conducting our own post-mortem in the sanctity of my living room.

Jeff and Kristina have hit the jackpot because Charlotte has busted out. One woman's poison has become Jeff and Kristina's meal. William has given Kristina a $150,000 severance payment and when little Simon is born (only kidding), they'll receive the promised $1 million gift. To complete the prizes behind window No. 1, Charlotte's will has been placed in probate and if the codicil executed two days before her death withstands the challenge from her disinherited children, Jeff and Kristina's baby will receive a $10 million bequest. Talk about stepping in shit, this is a sweet-smelling bucket full.

Always ready to deaden a conversation with an inappropriate joke, I propose: "Now that you've struck the Wylde motherlode, I've an idea on how you should invest some of your treasure. Let's produce a reality TV show similar to 'Americas Got Talent.' We'll call it 'New York's Got Beggars.' The three of us ride the subways and pick out the best hucksters pretending to be homeless and then they audition their pitches to a panel of judges and a voting home audience. The ultimate winner with the best patter gets a Las Vegas condominium and the right to hustle outside the entrance to the casino of his or her choice."

"As always, a great suggestion from Simon the Magnificent. But don't start counting our money. The codicil will be tied up in court with litigation for quite some time," Jeff responds with less cheer than I had hoped to elicit.

"I'm not a lawyer, but it seems to me that the Wylde progeny have no basis to overturn Charlotte's will."

"They claim that Charlotte was a drug addict and not of sound mind when she executed the codicil, and that she died from a drug overdose only two days later is proof positive."

"That's poppycock. Just sour grapes."

"Maybe. But our lawyer says it'll probably take years to sort out. If the codicil is overturned, we don't get the $10 million."

"No matter what, at least you'll get the $1 million baby gift. And you were able to give your father $100,000 from Kristina's severance payment, so you dug him out of the tough spot in which he got himself."

"Agreed. Bottom line, we're a big winner no matter what. Kristina had decided to quit and Charlotte overdosed the night before Kristina was going to tell her. We would've gotten nothing. That the codicil had been executed was a surprise. Kristina knew that Charlotte intended to change her will but not that Charlotte had already done it. Usually, she'd have had Kristina accompany her to her lawyer's office, but, for some reason, she didn't do that this time. I really hope the codicil stands up. We want the $10 million."

"Who wouldn't? To be human is to be greedy."

"Now it's Simon the Philosopher. Can't wait for your next iteration."

Kristina, who's remained silent throughout, puts a halt to any further banter by injecting a note of solemnity, more appropriate to a vivisection of Charlotte's death and its aftermath: "Charlotte was a lost soul who needed more help than I could provide. You asked me when she started ingesting fentanyl. I don't know. That's what I told the police, when they interrogated me."

"They seemed to conduct a pretty thorough investigation for an accidental death," Jeff says. "Questioned almost every family member and their partners."

"And William's mistress and Charlotte's lover, as well," Kristina adds.

"They interrogated pretty much everyone it would seem, including me," I say. "I had the misfortune to be visiting the two of you in Sands Point the day before she died."

"And even my parents," Jeff throws in. "They also were questioned for some reason."

"Just the police ticking off the boxes. That's what they do, particularly when the deceased is the wife of a prominent person," I knowingly respond, an authority on police procedures, mystery writer (have I mentioned that fact?) that I am. "And here, everyone in Charlotte's life, including you and Kristina, had a motive of one sort or another to want her dead, maybe strong enough to knock her off."

"Really?" an incredulous Jeff asks.

"Why do you sound so amazed? You already knew that from Kristina and to the extent you didn't, it's all flying free in the social media diaspora. Even the details of what police investigations uncover are not kept secret any longer; the public yearns to ingest the scandals of the rich or famous, and accomplished hackers continue to break down firewalls to feed that frenzy. William had a mistress. Turns out she's pregnant and he was trying to convince Charlotte to agree to a divorce. But Charlotte was steadfast in her refusal. Charlotte had threatened several times to disinherit her children, but none were aware that she had actually done that two days before she died. Wharton, in particular, was in desperate need of money to pay off some gambling debts that he had incurred. He was being pressured by some pretty unsavory characters. Charlotte had a lover, one of William's partners, who wanted to break it off but she was blackmailing him into staying together. Bess and Melody hated Charlotte and each would have benefited from Charlotte's death whether or not Charlotte had secretly changed her will. There was no love lost between Charlotte and her sister, who had some very bad arguments over the past few months. And, of course, you and Kristina and your family, all benefitted by Charlotte's death in so many ways."

To my surprise, Jeff somewhat angrily responds: "You recited those motives, including ones for me and my family, rather dispassionately, an interested observer looking at a storm a safe distance away. Kristina and I were too close to the epicenter to think about the motives anyone might have had to kill Charlotte, or reflect on what people might think would be ours. Anyway, no one did. She killed herself, accidentally. Possibly even on purpose. That's how unhappy and drug-dependent she'd become."

"I wasn't suggesting that she actually was murdered. Just playing the game in my head out loud. No one claims to have knowledge of her ever resorting to fentanyl to chase her blues away. Where did she get the pills from? No prescription. Maybe she got them from Bess, or even Wharton, but both denied it. Lots of people with motives, but no indication of any opportunity. No signs of struggle in her bedroom or on her person the morning her body was discovered."

"If someone killed her, he or she was very clever, doing it in a way it was not likely to be detected. So, no, I never really thought very much about people having motives, because I never considered that what happened might be anything other than accidental or suicide," Jeff says, apparently indignant that I had questioned his surprise at the fact that almost everyone in her life might be suspect in Charlotte's death.

"I've just been thinking hypothetically. Remember, I do this for my living, sketching out murder plots in my mind. We've a cast of characters worthy of a good mystery. And don't forget that female gang leader they arrested just a few days before Charlotte's death. She was caught with a bottle full of fentanyl pills as she was either coming out of or trying to enter the Wylde's home. Nothing was stolen, but she remained silent and was charged only with possession of illegal drugs. All that's missing for me to write a book is for me to determine the culprit and the method. Since the book in my head is fiction, maybe I'll make you or Kristina the one who somehow slips the victim a deadly dose of fentanyl. You're the ones with the most immediate financial benefit."

"If we're playing mind games", Jeff responds, seeming to get into the spirit of things but I'm not entirely sure, "you're not much of a writer if you select the murderer to be the person with the most obvious motive. In a good mystery book, something apparently alien to you, the person who did it is usually the least likely, not the most."

"So, Harold the chauffeur did it? That's whom you'd choose?"

"No. In my book, I'd choose you, Simon. We're brothers and you said you'd do anything for me. You know we'd be on the balls of our ass if Kristina gave notice and that Kristina was likely to do so at some point soon. You were with Charlotte the day she died. Alone for a few minutes, if I recall correctly. Maybe somehow you slipped fentanyl into her system or maybe switched out some of the pills in the bottle she had. You're my 100% solution."

"I'm not that good a friend. Your readers would feel let down by your ending. That's the problem with mysteries. So many endings. So many of them unsatisfying."

"I think we've played this out," Jeff says. "You can fictionalize whatever you want, but here, in the real world, I'm pretty sure we can all agree that Charlotte's death was most probably accidental."

"I agree. As the police have officially declared, case closed. No further Simon speculations to follow. Certainly not if by doing that, I'm making myself a prime suspect. Onward to glory you both go. We focus on the birth of a happy and healthy Muss child and the money with which to indulge him and his uncle Simon. I hereby reserve the right to base my next book on these extremely convoluted familiar relationships. A great title would be 'The Call of the Wyldes,' but then it wouldn't be fiction."

CHAPTER LIII

It was so easy to substitute the fentanyl pills for Charlotte's Oxycontin. About a week before she died, Barbara snuck into Charlotte's bathroom with a handful of fentanyl pills that looked exactly like the Oxycontin.

When Barbara had helped Charlotte to her bedroom after the bitter argument that afternoon a few weeks ago concerning Kristina's pregnancy and the selection of appropriate maternity clothes, Barbara was not burying a hatchet, but rather taking the first steps towards firmly planting one with a deadly blow in Charlotte's back. As Charlotte lay down and took her pills, Barbara removed one Oxycontin pill from the bottles she offered to return to Charlotte's medicine cabinet.

Several days later, Barbara had occasion to make a deal with the devil. This didn't bother her because she'd long ago decided, from the very day Kristina had announced that she was pregnant, that she'd do whatever was necessary to prevent Charlotte from continuing to use her wealth to kidnap and secure for herself, Barbara's son and family. She'd not devoted the better part of her life doting over Jeff, loving him, providing him with whatever assistance she could, guiding him into being the fine person he had become, to let Charlotte get away with that.

The devil with whom she dealt was the mother of one of the children under Barbara's care, whom the mother used as a punching bag from time to time when the boy did something to offend her on those occasions when she was sky-high on the opioids she sold for a living.

The bargain made was that in lieu of Barbara having Child Protective Services remove the eight year old from the mother's abusive household, mommy dearest would provide Barbara with 15 fentanyl pills in a color and shape identical to the Oxycontin pill that Barbara had removed from Charlotte's prescription bottle.

Less than a week after that, with pills in hand, Barbara made an excuse to meet with Jeff and Kristina in Sands Point, and, before she headed home, asked Charlotte if she'd mind if Barbara looked at her bedroom again, because she very much admired the décor and was thinking of redecorating her own bedroom, not with anything so elegant, lavish or expensive, but a more budget-conscious, downscale version of the room. Her sense of pride of ownership commanded ready agreement from an unwitting Charlotte, and a very witting Barbara used that opportunity to substitute the fentanyl for the Oxycontin, without even the slightest twinge of regret or second thought about it.

Barbara had no financial motivation in doing what she did. Her husband's dilemma or the money her children might receive were Charlotte to die weighed not a gram in the balance on her scale of justice. She only wanted to prevent the continued atrophy of the time, love and attention of her son and daughter-in-law, and continued erosion of their values, from turning into a mudslide that swept them and their child permanently away.

It's ironic that Barbara had never been told that Kristina might be on the verge of leaving her job. Had she known, Charlotte might still be alive, or at least Barbara not the cause of her demise. When Barbara did learn of Kristina's intention, Charlotte was already two days past her expiration date. Nevertheless, Barbara "non, je ne regrette rien." For all her years, Jeff had been her one true love, the focus of her being, and a loving mother's love is unconditional; in Barbara's unfortunate mind, that meant she'd do anything to protect her child, even if it meant violating the most basic societal (and her own) standards of moral propriety. To the victor belong the spoils.

I learn all this by accident, initiated by a slip of the tongue Barbara made one night when I was about to leave Barbara's house after another Muss family Sunday night dinner. Jeff and Kristina had just left, warm embraces, hugs and kisses exchanged, an eight-month pregnant Kristina too tired to stay any longer. I was just enjoying some dessert and a decaffeinated cappuccino. Dan had retired to the den to watch some game on television.

"Isn't it wonderful how this all turned out for everyone?" Barbara enthused. "Charlotte's death, I mean. She accomplished in death what she couldn't in her life — made a lot of people happy."

Surprised and not understanding what she could be thinking, I disagreed: "I'm not sure how her death actually helped very many people in the long run. William was free of Charlotte, it's true, but the scandal of her death and his love child scuttled his nomination for Treasury Secretary. His mistress couldn't withstand the glare of the spotlight focused on her and returned home to live with her disappointed, disapproving parents and give birth there. Wharton, Willis and Wilma were disinherited and are now in litigation with Jeff and Kristina to overturn Charlotte's codicil. Clifford Thurston was outed as Charlotte's lover and William fired him from Wylde Capital. He's presently the subject of a criminal investigation by reason of things discovered by Wylde Capital after his employment was terminated. Bess and Wilma broke up, their relationship irreparably damaged by Wilma's guilt-ridden reaction to Bess' unbridled glee over Charlotte's death. William has refused for now to fund Melody's art gallery or establish a medical clinic and rumor is that she may be leaving Willis for a richer guy. And Donna, Charlotte's sister, was recently institutionalized, Charlotte's death, from what I understand, being the precipitating factor. That's a lot of people that profited very little from Charlotte's death."

"Well I made it work for us," Barbara proudly exclaimed.

You can take it from there. One question led to another and soon the whole sordid story flooded out. Maybe Barbara's inherent goodness had resurfaced and her sense of guilt compelled her to confess to me, her other son. I don't know. I'm not sure. The only thing I'm sure of is how the evening ended for me, with Barbara saying: "This will be our little secret, won't it, Simon? It would destroy Jeff and Kristina if this ever came out."

What do I do? I love Jeff and Kristina, I'd never want to hurt them. They'd lose the $1 million and their baby's inheritance because of what Barbara did, not to mention Jeff only being able to see his mother as a visitor to the prison in which she'd be incarcerated for most of the rest of her life. And the hurt and shame Jeff and Kristina would feel and the ill-effect it would have on their child, to have an imprisoned, notorious murderess for a grandmother. And what would my relationship with Jeff and Kristina be, after I was the cause of Barbara's imprisonment? Hell, I love Barbara, always considered her my mother, she always treated me as her other son. Can I do this to her? To them? To myself? Reveal Barbara's secret? But can I live with the guilt of not doing it, not doing the right thing, the moral thing, the thing society demands and what Barbara, in other circumstances, would expect of me?

What to do? Maybe I'll put it all down on paper, as a work of fiction, a mystery. Then from the prospective of revisiting a finished story, ever the distant observer, decide what I should do. Better still, make it an interactive novel, where the readers vote on what they'd like the ending to be. That way the burden of decision, and guilt that will follow, will be lifted from my shoulders. What do you think I should do? I'm waiting for your vote.

EPILOGUE

People can surprise you. Even those you think you know intimately. Indeed, people often surprise themselves, sometimes to the good but more often to the bad.

Such is the case with Jeff. He overhead a conversation his mother was having asking someone about when she could "pick up the fentanyl" and suspected what Barbara might be planning to do, but did nothing to stop her and said nothing to Kristina about it. He wanted the money that Charlotte had dangled and he wasn't prepared to lose that nor endanger the health of his baby to obtain it. So he remained silent, telling no one, and let it play out, hoping for the best (whatever that meant). As it turned out, the "best" happened (except for Charlotte, of course), assuming Jeff can live with himself and his dark poisonous secret. He has a long way to go.

ABOUT THE AUTHOR

Having been a senior partner in a prominent Manhattan-based law firm, this still very busy attorney has managed to carve out time for a second successful career. His well-received first novel, *"Law Firm Down: A Story of Greed, Envy, Sloth and Ego,"* published in 2018 under the pseudonym Stephen Hollevy, was, for a period of time, an Amazon Kindle best seller e-book in its category. Now, he has written *"The Call of the Wyldes,"* a murder mystery which explores how far people might stray to protect what they have, recover what they've lost, or obtain what they want.

CPSIA information can be obtained
at www.ICGtesting.com
Printed in the USA
BVHW081346131120
593210BV00011B/57/J

9 781525 580079